SOMETHING BAD

Raising his hand to knock on the door, Ricky realized that Robin might also hear, so instead, he clutched the doorknob and slowly turned it. As the door swung silently inward, he heard the steady whirring of the ceiling fans within the room.

"Mom?" he whispered. "Dad?"

They didn't wake up, so he stepped inside, closing the door behind him.

"Mom?" he called. Then again, a little louder. "Mom?"

He approached the bed, his heart thundering against his rib cage. Although the windows were open and the cool northerly breeze had picked up, his parents' bedroom, hot and close, was foul with a heavy, hot smell that made the hairs on the back of his neck prickle up.

He stepped closer to the bed, thinking that it was strange that his parents were under their quilt on such a hot night. He reached out and tapped the quilt, about where his mother's shoulder should be.

She didn't wake up.

"Mom?" he asked, poking at the quilt a little harder.

The material felt funny, sticky-damp.

"Dad!" Leaning across her, he shook his father. "Dad!"

Suddenly he lost his tiptoed balance and fell on them, landing facedown, mouth open, on the quilt. Abruptly he became aware that the sticky dampness was everywhere, and as he breathed in its rusty metal smell, he realized it was in his mouth, and he recognized the flavor of blood. . . .

Books by Tamara Thorne

HAUNTED

MOONFALL

ETERNITY

CANDLE BAY

BAD THINGS

Published by Pinnacle Books

BAD THINGS

Tamara Thorne

PINNACLE BOOKS
Kensington Publishing Corp.
http://www.kensingtonbooks.com

PINNACLE BOOKS are published by

Kensington Publishing Corp.
850 Third Avenue
New York, NY 10022

Copyright © 1994 by Chris Curry
Previously published under the title PANIC by Pocket Books

All Kensington Titles, Imprints, and Distributed Lines are available at special quantity discounts for bulk purchases for sales promotions, premiums, fund-raising, educational or institutional use. Special book excerpts or customized printings can also be created to fit specific needs. For details, write or phone the office of the Kensington special sales manager: Kensington Publishing Corp., 850 Third Avenue, New York, NY 10022, attn: Special Sales Department, Phone: 1-800-221-2647.

Pinnacle and the P logo Reg. U.S. Pat. & TM Off.

First Printing: March 2002
10 9 8 7 6 5 4 3 2 1

Printed in the United States of America

For Kenny Curry—
the best big brother in the world

ACKNOWLEDGMENTS

First, thank you to Lawrence Morris, O.D., for sharing his knowledge and invaluable speculations on the nature of vision. Also, thank you, Kevin Shrock, M.D., for patiently answering all my bizarre medical questions.

Grateful appreciation goes to Kay McCauley and the Pimlico Agency and to my terrific editors, John Scognamiglio and Dana Isaacson.

Special thanks go to Nigel and Dave, experts on feline psychology, and to Robert, Quinn, and Doug for all that good stuff—you guys are the best!

BIG JACK

Winter cold, winter dreary
Winter leaves
No sap, no fool
Winter bones
No need to panic
Big Jack sleeps,
The little ones too.

March buds, April flowers
May blood
So green, so new
Spring veins pump
And children panic
Big Jack wakes,
The little ones too.

Summer heat, summer passion
Summer nights
So hot, so hungry
Dark desires
The children cower
Big Jack stands
The little ones too.

Autumn red, autumn brittle
Autumn cravings
So harsh, so clear
Child, run
Before he gets you
Big Jack walks,
The little ones too.

1

October 1, 1972

Wrapped in panic, smothered in fear, Ricky Piper trembled on the threshold of the shadowy hallway and steeled himself for the long journey to the living room. He would have preferred to remain with his mother and their housekeeper, Carmen, in the bright, yellow kitchen, but she'd given him permission to watch cartoons. If he didn't do it, she'd know he was afraid again. That was the last thing he wanted.

Swallowing hard, telling himself to walk slowly, he stepped onto the forest green carpeting. His resolve lasted all of two seconds before his screaming nerves made him sprint down the hall. First he passed the dark, silent dining room, then the wall of linen closets, and finally he bolted beneath the stern disapproval of a collection of Piper ancestors, framed and watching him from the corridor walls.

Ricky arrived in the front room, heart thumping, head dizzy from holding his breath. Exhaling, he wished that his mom and dad weren't so nuts about wasting electricity. Though he knew there was nothing scary *in* the house, he just couldn't stop expecting that something was going to jump out of the dark and grab him.

The air in the living room seemed thick and murky. The last dregs of afternoon sunlight seeped in between the ragged shadows cast by the towering oak outside the picture window. Not wanting to look out the window, Ricky walked backward toward the chair and reading lamp by the front door. With the sureness of long habit, he reached under the lampshade and turned the switch, holding his breath again until the friendly golden light relieved the gray gloom. Then, still without looking, he reached behind the chair and felt for the drapery cords. Finding the right one, he tugged, listening to the soothing whisper of fabric and metal until the gentle snick told him the drapes had closed on the outside world.

If it were his house, Ricky told himself as he crossed to the television cabinet and turned the set on, the curtains would stay closed *all* the time.

Felix the Cat slowly came into focus. He was using his bag of tricks to foil the Professor and Rockbottom. Ricky didn't like Felix's voice, but he sure wished he had his bag of tricks. If he did, he'd use it to get rid of the greenjacks: the little ones *and* the big one, all of them. It wasn't really the dark he was afraid of, but the jacks, who only came out at night. If he had a magic bag of tricks, he'd make it always daytime and he'd make all the grass and bushes and trees— especially the old oak—disappear too, so there would be nowhere for the greenjacks to hide. If he could do that, he wouldn't have to be scared anymore. He and his brother would be safe.

Robin, who was outside right now with Grandfather Piper, wasn't afraid of the greenjacks, but he didn't have the sight and was unaware of the danger. Ricky worried a lot about Robin because he'd just giggle when he warned him to be careful outside, even on Halloween, the worst night of the year. That was when Big Jack came out. Not only could anyone see him if he wanted them to, but he could actually snatch anybody he wanted, snatch them and take them away. But Robin wouldn't believe it. He thought Grandfather's stories were fairy tales like Hansel and Gretel or Goldilocks and the Three Bears.

Recently Robin had started teasing Ricky by making believe that he could see the jacks and even talk to them. He did all the things he knew scared Ricky, too, like climbing in the oak tree.

Because of his brother, and because he knew his parents were starting to worry about his "overactive imagination," as they called it, Ricky had started making believe too. He pretended, even to his twin, that he'd never seen a greenjack, but had been playing a game of pretend all along. It was the hardest thing he'd ever done in his entire seven years.

Like fingers, oak twigs tapped on the window glass. Shivering, Ricky hunched into a ball in the safe glow of the television set and lost himself in the cartoons.

"Richard Piper, you're going to get x-rayed to death sitting that close to that damnable machine; that is, if you don't go blind and kill all your brain cells first!"

"Grandfather!" Startled, Ricky twisted around and saw the old man, who must have come in through the kitchen door. He stood in the hall doorway, frowning disapproval. Robin, snug in the crook of his arm, grinned and extricated his abbreviated body from the old man's arms, swinging like a monkey, slipping down his grandfather's legs as if they were tree trunks. He twisted just before he reached the dark green carpet and dropped nimbly onto his hands.

"Watch this!" he commanded. He tested his balance, then began to walk on his hands, then run, toward his brother, his little legless body held straight up in the air over his head.

Reaching Ricky, he flipped himself over and came to a rest on his buttocks. "I bet you can't do that."

Ricky didn't think he could. He was almost four feet tall, a perfect boy from his head to his toes, and Robin was his identical twin except that he'd been born without legs, which made him about two feet shorter. He had a bottom and a weenie, just like Ricky, but then he just ended, in smooth curves of white skin.

"Try it!" Robin goaded.

Ricky planted his hands on the carpet and began to lower his head.

Grandfather asked, "Why is that set on, Richard?"

"Sorry," he mumbled, turning it off. His grandfather hated the television, and Ricky was just glad that the old man lived in the little cottage in the citrus orchard behind the big house. If he were here all the time, he'd never let anyone turn the TV on.

The old man's gaze was stern under his bushy white eyebrows. "Did your mother tell you you could watch that thing?"

He hesitated, knowing that if he told the truth, Grandfather would lecture his mom. "No, sir."

"You turned it on without asking permission?"

Robin grabbed his hand and squeezed it. "Yes, sir," Ricky replied, braver because of his brother's silent support.

For a moment the old man stared holes through him, and Ricky tried to shrink into the carpet, his stomach doing flip-flops as he wondered what his grandfather was going to say next.

But suddenly Grandfather Piper's face broke into a rare smile. "Well, you've got a little spunk hidden in there somewhere after all! Good for you, boy. Maybe you're finally growing some balls!"

Ricky, amazed and confused, smiled tentatively. Why would he want to grow balls? You bought them at the toy store.

Robin giggled.

"But I still don't want that cursed thing on when I'm in this house. You're seven years old, you have to exercise your brains *and* your body. Is that understood?"

"Yes, sir."

"Damn house feels like a cave," the old man said, then, to Ricky's horror, he opened the drapes. Dusk had gathered outside, and Ricky looked away quickly. "That's better," Grandfather said, looking from boy to boy with false sternness. "Do you two want to hear a story?"

"Please!" Robin cried happily.

"Please!" Ricky echoed, nearly as enthusiastic. Though the stories frightened him, he always wanted to hear them

because he'd decided that the more he knew about the greenjacks, the safer he would be.

"Alrighty, boys. I'll tell you about *my* great-grandfather.
That would be your great-great-great-grandfather, Thomas
McEnery Piper. He was blessed with the sight, as the men
of the Piper clan sometimes are . . ." Grandfather's midnight
blue eyes sparkled as he looked from boy to boy. "Or perhaps he was cursed. I don't know, because I don't have the
sight. What about you, Robin? You see the greenjacks, don't
you, boy?"

"Sure!" Robin cried. The word bubbled through his delighted laughter.

"Well, what do you say, boy? Is the sight a blessing or a
curse?"

"A blessing!"

Grandfather turned to Ricky. "And what do you say, Richard? A blessing or a curse?"

Ricky looked at his Keds and shrugged. "I dunno. I don't
see them."

Robin made a silly face. "Liar, liar, pants on fire!"

"Robin," Grandfather admonished sternly. He turned
back to Ricky, his voice getting that gentle sound that adults
often took with him, as if they were afraid he might break.
"If you could see them, Rick, what would it be?"

He looked up and stared the old man right in the eye. "A
curse, Grandfather. It would be a curse."

Grandfather Piper's eyes bored into his for a long time,
then he shook his head slowly. "I swear, boy, sometimes
you're enough to make me think there's truth in those old
stories. Sometimes I think *you* really do have the sight."

"No, sir." Ricky wanted to cry as he told the lie. "I just
pretend."

"I see." The old man paused, giving Ricky one last long
look before clearing his throat. "Well then, boys, let's get
on with it. Thomas Piper had the sight, for better or worse,
and tonight I believe I'll tell you about the first time the
greenjacks almost nabbed him. He wasn't much older than
the two of you. Have I told you boys this story before?"

"No," they lied in unison. It was Grandfather's most-told tale and Ricky's favorite.

"Come on, then, let's sit." The old man turned and walked slowly toward his favorite recliner, which sat next to the huge fireplace, directly across the room from the picture window. Robin hurried ahead, showing off his new handstand trick. When he reached the chair, he bunched his powerful biceps and propelled himself up onto the chair arm in the blink of an eye. Then, grinning at Ricky, he did his spider imitation, bugging his eyes and flexing his elbows so that he moved up and down, like a spider on its web. The sight made Ricky snicker. Robin could always crack him up.

Grandfather eased into the recliner and waited while Robin situated his small body in the crook of his arm. Then Ricky climbed onto his knee.

"Ready?" Grandfather asked.

"Ready!" the boys chorused.

"Thomas McEnery Piper lived in the family home in Glenkerrie, a village in the Scottish Highlands, west of Inverness. Just like here in Santo Verde, Glenkerrie was renowned for the way the trees and flowers and crops grew. Do you know why?"

"Greenjacks!" Robin cried.

Despite himself, Ricky glanced up at the picture window. The wind plucked one faded leaf, then another, from the old oak tree. It was still almost a month until Halloween, but most of the leaves still clung to the twigs and branches. His mom had told him yesterday that it would probably be November before the tree was only a skeleton again. He wished it were over with—a month, especially this month, took forever to go by.

"That's right, the jacks," Grandfather said. "And do you know *why* they lived there?"

"Because we did!"

"That's right, Robin. They chose that place because it was the Piper ancestral home. Greenjacks and Pipers have lived there for centuries. All over the world there are bits of land where trees and grass grow far better than they should, and these are the places of the jacks—and of people who, like some of the Pipers, see them."

Grandfather rambled on. Every story began with the same introduction, and you had to wait through it to get to the good stuff. Recently the old man had added something new that Ricky thought was really interesting: science. Grandfather said it was probably a gene that made you see the jacks and that about a fourth of all the male Pipers had that gene. When Ricky had asked his father about it, though, he'd just snorted and said that he'd believe it when he read it in *Scientific American*.

Grandfather was up to the part about greenjacks and trolls being second cousins once removed when Ricky saw a jack approach the window. At twilight it was barely visible, a small, smooth creature made of a vague glow that grew brighter as night took the sky. It reached the window, and he saw the suggestion of a gleefully cruel face peering through the glass. Ricky squirmed nervously, and Grandfather gave him a stern glance without losing the rhythm of his story.

Greenjacks, Ricky knew, were small, never more than two feet tall unless they melted together. If they did that, they lost their shifting, semihuman form, but this one looked normal, so Ricky wondered how it could be tall enough to peek in a window two and a half feet from the ground. (Ricky had measured it.) Shivering, he looked away.

"Greenjacks attach themselves to families like us because there's always a chance that they can trick someone possessing the sight into giving up his body. Sometimes a sighted man will even agree to trade bodies with one of them. The jacks' bodies aren't physical like ours are, and that means they can't taste or smell or feel anything in the material world, any more than a scientist can enter the world of the amoebae he studies under his microscope." Grandfather's smile made a million little wrinkles around his eyes. "Just like people, greenjacks always want what they don't have, and so they crave physical sensation very, very much." He paused dramatically. "They lust for it and will do anything to get it—make promises, lie, even try to scare you to death. And on Halloween . . . on Halloween they get together to make Big Jack out of tree limbs and plants. On that one night their power is so great that they can enter Big Jack and bring him to life. And that night, because Big Jack is physically real, they can use him to—" Grandpa snapped his fingers—"snatch little boys like you! Just. Like. That!"

Robin giggled again, and Ricky stole another peek at the window. A second face had appeared, human yet not, liquid and solid and air all at once, ever-changing, ever-shifting. Once, Ricky had tried to draw a picture of one. It came out looking smooth and gray-green, with huge glittery black eyes and a small mouth.

Though the drawing wasn't exactly right, the jacks sure didn't look much like trolls to Ricky. Trolls were squished and wrinkly and sort of cute. At least troll dolls were. Greenjacks *seemed* small-bodied and long-limbed, even when they weren't. Sometimes they looked more like little whirlwinds, but they always seemed old and bad and not at all cute.

One of them waved at Ricky. A glimmer of a lipless mouth twisted into a nasty smile.

Ricky . . . Ricky . . . Icky Ricky . . .

Their voices wafted in through the frames and vents of the house like a fluttering of leaves on a breeze. He heard them inside his head. *Ricky, come out and play, Icky Ricky.*

"Oouh!" Ricky jumped as something poked him in the thigh. Robin was staring at him.

Grandfather harrumphed. "Richard, what's wrong?"

He hesitated. "Robin punched me."

"Robin?"

"He wasn't listening," his brother said impishly. "I think he's looking for greenjacks."

"Well, Rick?" Grandfather asked patiently, "Do you see any?"

Before he could frame an answer, Robin said, "Ricky, I fixed it so they could see in. I pushed dirt up under the windows."

Speechless, Ricky stared at him.

Grandfather chuckled. "Very inventive of you, Robin."

"There's a whole pack of them out there!" Robin volunteered. "They're playing leapfrog."

"Good for them, but they're going to have to play by themselves," Grandfather added firmly, "if you want to hear the rest of the story. Ready to pay attention?"

"Okay." He stifled a giggle.

Satisfied, Grandfather went on, "Since it seems that you two can see the jacks"—here he gave them a wink showing that he was just playing along—"you can see for yourselves that greenjacks are very sociable creatures, and that's why they only want to be in human bodies capable of seeing and communicating with their own kind. Which is why they wanted Thomas."

Ricky . . . Icky Ricky . . . Come. out and play, hey, play . . .

Shut up! Ricky thought.

"Young Thomas knew that the little greenjacks couldn't hurt him, so he wasn't afraid, not even at night when they're most active. Early on, the little jacks tried to talk him into trading bodies with one of them. They told him he could run and play all the time and that he'd never have to do what his mother told him, or mind his manners at all, but Thomas was smart and he wouldn't do it, no matter what they offered him. When they finally stopped trying to tempt him, he was even more careful because he knew they'd try to trick him out of his body.

"And try they did. Spring and summer and fall, they tried all sorts of tricks, and one night, when he was nine years old, his vigilance slipped, and the greenjacks almost got him.

"Young Thomas was a smart boy, a brave and kind boy, but he was no more perfect than any other boy, and one afternoon, about four o'clock, he did a very foolish thing. He decided to walk along the top of a wall, even though his mother told him not to. And can you guess what happened?"

"He fell!" Robin said immediately.

Grandfather nodded. "That's right. It was a very tall wall, and he landed on his head and lost consciousness. Greenjacks can get you if you're knocked out or almost dead, of course. Unconsciousness is good because they can force you out of your body and lock you in one of theirs, but almost dead is better because you can't put up any kind of fight at all. They're in, you're out.

"Young Thomas fell on the wrong side of the wall, and when he didn't come in with the milk—did I mention he was supposed to be in the barn milking the cow, not walking on walls?—his mother and father called him and called him. When he didn't answer, they went to look for him.

"They found him just as the sun was setting. He still lay on the ground, unconscious, and though his parents couldn't see them, they knew that the greenjacks would be out. Afraid, they looked at one another, then his father picked Thomas up and carried him in, and they sat by his bed and waited to see if he would still be their son. Or if he was a changeling."

Grandfather leaned forward, frowning dramatically. "Thomas's parents prayed they weren't too late, but his father held a sword in his hand, ready to run the body through if his son had become a changeling."

"He would have killed his own son?" Robin asked, just as he always did.

"Yes, he would have. It's happened before and it will happen again," Grandfather added menacingly. "Once a jack possesses your body, nothing but a mortal wound will make it leave. Only then will it flee for its own immortal body, and only then is the poor human changeling's soul released—either to go to whatever lies on the other side, or, for the less fortunate, to return to its original body if it's not quite dead yet."

Ricky had goose bumps. The story thrilled and scared him. He could feel the greenjacks outside staring at the back of his head.

Sicky Ricky, icky Ricky, Ricky, Ricky . . .

Words were their toys, and they rhymed on and on. Ricky could hardly stand the shrill voices in his head.

"Fortunately," Grandfather continued, "when he woke

up, he was still Thomas. Do you know how his parents could tell?"

"How?" Ricky asked.

"He answered the questions his parents asked him correctly, something a jack changeling couldn't do so quickly. Also, he wasn't clumsy, like he wasn't used to his body. Finally, his eyes were still Piper eyes, midnight blue, like ours. Sometimes, not always, when a greenjack takes a human body, the irises turn darker, like the color of a greenjack's soul. Thomas remembered nothing of his accident, except for hearing the voices of the jacks as they surrounded him, and he promised never to climb the wall or do any other forbidden things again." The old man cleared his throat. "Years later, Big Jack almost got him on Halloween night, but that's another story for another night. I think it's almost dinnertime. Something smells good."

As Grandfather's voice ground to a halt, Ricky saw that the little jacks were no longer at the window. The two, and a half dozen more, were cavorting in the grass under the oak tree.

"Ricky?" Robin asked softly. "Are they there?"

Ricky looked at his brother. Sometimes, after they were in bed with the lights out, Robin would still admit to him that he maybe believed in greenjacks even though he couldn't see them. "Yeah, sure," Ricky said lightly. "They're there."

It was weird to look at his twin, to see a boy just like him except for not having the jack-seeing gene and not having a complete body. There were other differences too. Robin was brave like Thomas Piper, and Ricky was a coward.

"Ricky?" Robin said suddenly. There was no mischief in his voice, only a sort of hopefulness.

"What?"

"They're out there right now, aren't they?"

Ricky nodded.

"Grandfather?"

"Yes, Robin?" The old man smiled benignly, just as he always did after he told one of his stories.

"If I traded bodies with a greenjack, could I have legs too? Like Ricky's?"

Grandfather's eyes looked like dark pools of water as he pushed a chestnut curl from Robin's forehead. "I wish it were so, but it's not. Remember, when you dance with the devil, you become a devil yourself."

The boy nodded gravely, and Ricky could feel his brother's unhappiness and longing as if it were his own. It hurt. Robin was almost never sad. Most of the time he took pride in what he could do, and Ricky knew that was part of the reason he liked to show off so much with all his handstands and acrobatics. He could even run almost as fast on his hands as Ricky could on foot. Impulsively he leaned over and hugged his twin. "I'd share my legs with you if I could."

Robin hugged him back hard, then pulled away and gave him a small tentative smile that quickly evolved into his typical mischievous grin. "It's a good thing you can't share your legs, Ricky, 'cause you need 'em a lot worse than I do!"

"Bite me!" Ricky said, and giggled uncontrollably. Robin looked shocked, then he burst into laughter.

"Richard!" Grandfather intoned.

Ricky silenced instantly.

"Where did you learn that kind of language?"

"From you."

"Me? I don't think—"

"You said it to that Jobber's Witness yesterday when he wouldn't go away. Remember, just before you slammed the door in his—"

"Jehovah's," Grandfather interrupted. "Listen here, young man, promise me you'll forget you heard that, because if you say it around your mother, she'll fill your mouth with Ivory Soap." His sternness dissolved "And mine, too."

"I promise," Ricky said. His gaze drifted back to the window, his nervousness returning as he watched the greenjacks dance and whirl and tumble. Occasionally two or three of them would melt together to briefly form other shapes: a ghostly whirlwind of iridescence that looked sometimes like leaves, sometimes like butterflies, a small tempest of flickering greens, golds, and reds that never quite left the ground. The jacks were earth creatures, tied to the land, and they couldn't leave it except for that one night a year when they made Big Jack. Big Jack could climb trees and cross water and he could snatch people, but at least he couldn't leave nature and come indoors. The only unsafe place inside the house was the dirt-floored root cellar, and Ricky never, never ventured down there.

He shivered as several jacks suddenly merged into a tall ghostly blob that bore resemblance to Big Jack, as if they could read his mind and were performing just for him.

Ricky . . . Ricky . . . Icky Ricky, come out and play . . .

He shivered. Maybe they *could* read his thoughts. Maybe they were, right this minute.

"Look how the leaves are blowing out there," Grandfather said as he gently dislodged Ricky from his knee. He rose, carrying Robin, and walked to the window. "Quite a little tornado going under the oak. Couple of 'em."

"You see them?" Ricky asked before he realized that Grandfather was talking about the real leaves that blew around in the evening wind.

"Of course I do. My eyes are as good as ever." He shot a serious look at Ricky. "It's said that the greenjacks love to play in the falling leaves. Do you see them, Richard?"

"Uh, no." Then he saw the expectant look on his brother's face. "Oh, yeah, I see a couple now," he said, making sure he sounded like he was just playing along.

"What are the jacks doing, Ricky?" Robin asked, the longing back in his voice.

"They're dancing.

"In the leaves?"

"No, Robin," he said solemnly. "They *are* the leaves."

2

October 31, 1972

Cackling autumn leaves scuttled across the wide wooden steps of the old front porch. The night wind kissed the doorframe and whispered through the wire mesh, bringing with it the acrid spice of burning pumpkin and a last lingering trace of cold rainwater.

Ricky Piper sat in his father's easy chair and nervously rubbed his fingers over the nubby gold upholstery. It was a test of will, sitting here, but Carmen had reassured him that it would be good medicine for him to try it since there was no way the jacks could get in the house. The only thing separating the chair from the open front door was a maple end table holding a big basket of Halloween treats, candy corn and Tootsie Pops.

Ricky . . . Icky Ricky . . . Ricky . . .

No! Go away! He curled into a ball, hugging his legs within the circle of his arms, ducking his head so that his ears were muffled between his knees, so that all he could see was the vague greenish glow of the phosphorescent paint his mom had brushed on his skeleton costume.

He hated the costume because it reminded him of Big Jack.

And tonight was Big Jack's night, when anyone could see him and anyone could be snatched. Once, Ricky had asked

Grandfather how the little jacks chose which ones of them would be part of the monster, but the old man didn't know and guessed they drew straws. The rest of the little ones would be out, too, tonight, more frighteningly clear than on any other night of the year.

Last Halloween was the first time Ricky had ever seen Big Jack. He caught a glimpse of the creature from his bedroom window as it shambled around under the oak. It looked like a cross between a skeleton and a tree. He woke up Robin, but by the time his twin got to the window, Big Jack had disappeared. Later, near midnight, Ricky saw him again, this time crouched in the high branches of the oak tree right outside his bedroom window. He looked like part of the tree until he moved. Ricky screamed, but Big Jack was gone before anyone else could see him, and his parents thought he was having another nightmare about Grandfather Piper.

The old man had died last year, only two days after telling that last story about Thomas McEnery Piper. He'd had a heart attack during dinner, and an ambulance came and took him away. Ricky never saw him again, except at the funeral, where he'd looked like a big wax doll with rouge on his cheeks and powder on his face. Right after that, Ricky began having dreams in which Grandfather Piper, lying in his coffin, opened his eyes and looked at him. His eyes weren't blue anymore, but black, even the white part, all black. He'd open his mouth and say, "Icky Ricky, play with me!"

He'd had the nightmare several times before Halloween and he'd woke up screaming, so when he saw Big Jack, he let them think he'd had another dream about Grandfather. That was the smartest thing to do.

Even now, Ricky sometimes still woke screaming from the nightmares—about Big Jack, not Grandfather—and he wished his dad would cut down the oak tree. He couldn't bear to look at the leafy shadows the moonlight cast across the twin beds and the cowboy wallpaper on their bedroom walls, even though he knew there was nothing there except, perhaps, on Halloween night.

Tonight.

They were out there: in the night, in the wind.

Ricky . . . Ricky . . . Ricky . . .

But they couldn't get him, not here in the house. He knew it because Carmen had reassured him of it over and over. They couldn't even come up on the porch, she said, and he knew from his own experience that she was right about that, too. He was safe, but it didn't matter: He was still afraid.

He wished he could be more like his ancestor Thomas in Grandfather's stories. Thomas wasn't afraid; he could walk among the greenjacks at night and ignore them, not a cowardly bone in his body. He was so brave that when he was fifteen (a foolish age, Grandfather used to point out) he tried to kill Big Jack himself, but he'd failed. Grandfather would never tell them more than that, but had promised that he would when the twins were older.

Now he'd never know what had happened to Thomas. Ricky's dad had never been interested in the stories and didn't know them, so the tales had died with Grandfather Piper.

The wind sighed, exhaling smoke-scented breath through the tree limbs, mingling its song with the voices that called his name. The jack voices sounded a little like leaves rustling in a whistling wind, and when he used to make the mistake of asking if anyone else could hear them, they'd laugh and say that's what they were—leaves. Or they'd shake their heads and give one another knowing looks and say, "What an imagination you have, Ricky Piper."

When he was six and a half, he'd tried very hard to stop talking about the greenjacks, and he'd managed pretty well until Grandfather's death. Last year, because of the dream and because he'd actually seen Big Jack, he'd begun talking about them again, and hadn't stopped until he overheard his folks discussing him and saying that maybe they should have him talk to a doctor. After that, he never said another word to them or to Robin. He felt so alone that sometimes he cried, but at least he had Carmen. Though she always promised him she'd never leave, he was always afraid he'd wake up one morning and she'd be gone, especially since she'd met her boyfriend, Hector. Ricky didn't think he could stand it here without her.

He loved his parents very much, but they just didn't understand like Carmen did. His dad and mom both thought the greenjack stories were fairy tales. As for Robin, he got that wishful look on his face, like he wanted to believe, less and less frequently now.

He glanced up at the portrait of Grandfather Piper hanging on the wall behind the recliner and wished he hadn't died. Not only did he miss him, but sometimes it seemed like the old man knew he could see them.

Though Carmen didn't exactly believe, she once told him that one of her uncles back in Mexico was a *brujo* doctor and that he said he could see things, just as Ricky could. When Ricky asked her if she believed her uncle, she only said that she believed that anything was possible.

So even if she didn't quite believe, at least she never teased him or said he was too old for fairy tales. Instead, she helped him learn how to act as if he weren't afraid, and she always protected him on Halloween, either by playing along when he pretended to be sick like last year, or by taking him out before dark to trick-or-treat. Right now he could hear her and Mom talking and laughing in the kitchen while they washed the dinner dishes. Their sounds helped him have the courage to stay in the chair by the door.

More leaves, dry brown mummies, fell from the tall oak outside to tumble and dart toward the Pipers' big weird house. It was already getting dark out, and he nervously wondered how he was going to get out of trick-or-treating this year. Carmen had told him not to play sick again because everyone would be suspicious. He glanced at the bowl of treats, slowly reached for a packet of candy. It wouldn't take long to eat enough sweet candy corn to really get sick. He'd get in trouble, but it would be worth it . . .

. . . because the night was alive with burnt pumpkin and rainwater and wind.

Ricky . . . Sicky . . . Ricky . . .

"Ricky!"

He jumped as his brother's strident voice yanked him from the spell cast by the greenjacks' voices.

"Robin!" He forced himself to straighten up and make a fist. "I oughta smack you!" His brother was a ghost, his short body hidden beneath a floor-length sheet that had eye holes and a mouth hole that their mom had outlined with red paint. She'd brushed phosphorescent paint on his costume too.

Robin peered up at him and giggled. "Scared you!"

"Did not!"

"Did so. Scaredy-cat!" His gaze fell on the candy corn. "And you're stealing the trickertreats!" he whispered. "I want some too!"

Ricky tossed the packet to Robin, and he tore the cellophane and made a show of holding it to the costume's circular mouth hole and pouring it in.

"Robin Piper!" Their mother's Deep Voice, the one that meant you were in trouble, stopped him cold. "What did I tell you about taking candy?" She approached Robin and lifted the sheet from his head.

Ricky couldn't help giggling. Robin's mouth was so full that he couldn't quite close it, and you could see the orange and yellow candy corn tips poking from between his lips. His chipmunk cheeks poked out like Louie Armstrong on TV playing his trumpet. Ricky giggled harder, even though Mom threw him an angry look too.

She crossed her arms and stood glaring down at them as Robin tried in vain to start chewing. "Go in the bathroom and spit those in the trash, then brush your teeth."

Still trying to chew, Robin pivoted on his hands and went through the wood-paneled family room behind the living room, heading for the downstairs bath. A moment later, Ricky heard the toilet flush, then the water being turned on.

"Ricky?"

"What, Mom?"

"Did you give him that candy?"

He didn't answer.

"Did you?"

"He trickertreated me. I had to."

She tried to look stern, then gave up, leaning over to run her hands through his hair and kiss the top of his head. She was pretty and she had the same color hair as he and Robin. His dad called it yummy chestnut. He was always saying silly things and touching Mom's hair or kissing her neck, and she seemed to like it a lot. She had green eyes—Dad called them cat's eyes. She called Dad's eyes "mystery man blue." His parents acted weird sometimes, and even though he and Robin would roll their eyes and make disgusted noises, Ricky secretly liked it.

"Boo!" Something grabbed Ricky's ankle, and he yelped, flying out of his chair. "Robin!"

His brother laughed. "Gotcha!"

"That wasn't nice, Robin," Mom admonished.

"Sorry." He smiled sunnily at Ricky, then at Mom.

" 'Sokay," Ricky said, his heart still pounding. Robin could pad around like a cat—you never heard him come in a room unless he wanted you to. Sometimes Dad jokingly threatened to buy him tap shoes for his hands.

Mom looked from boy to boy. "What am I going to do with you two?" She bent down and slipped Robin's ghost costume back over him, then plucked a stray thread from Ricky's costume. "That's better. Where's your mask?"

"Over there." Unenthusiastically, he pointed at the plastic skeleton face he'd left on the couch.

"So are you two ready to go trick-or-treating?" she asked.

"Yeah!" Robin cried.

"Dad's not home yet," Ricky said.

"I know, sweetie. Daddy's going to be a while because he has to finish some reports for work."

The doorbell rang, the young voices behind it giggling and screeching for treats. Before Mom could answer it, Carmen bustled into the room, took care of them, and returned to the kitchen.

"Shouldn't we wait for Dad?" Ricky persisted.

She laughed. "No. Carmen will hand out the treats, and the three of us will go by ourselves."

Usually Dad handed out treats—he loved jumping out from behind the door and yelling "boo!" at the kids—and normally Mom and Carmen both went out with the twins, Mom pulling the red Radio Flyer wagon Robin rode in, and Carmen holding Ricky's hand. This sudden change of plans was too much for Ricky, and he decided it was high time to get out of trickertreating.

"I think it's gonna rain some more."

"I don't think so, Rick." She stared hard at him. "Are you still afraid, sweetie?"

Oh, yes, he was afraid. "No," he said stoutly. "I gotta go to the bathroom!"

He shot out of the chair and ran through the family room, past the bathroom, laundry room, and into the kitchen, where Carmen was drying her hands on a dish towel that had dancing spoons embroidered all over it.

"Carmen!" he whispered.

She turned, a solidly built yet beautiful woman of twenty-five, who kept her thick black hair pulled into a bun at the back of her head. "What?" she whispered back.

"You *gotta* go trickertreating with me!" he said desperately. "Please! Or tell Mom I'm sick! Tell her I have a bellyache! You gotta do something!"

"Ricky, come here." She sat down on a kitchen chair, and as he moved into her outstretched arms, she watched him with her chocolate brown eyes. "I'm not gonna tell your mama that you're sick this year. We already talked about that, remember?"

He nodded impatiently. "Please, you have to go with me. You *have* to!"

She took his shoulders and pulled him close and spoke softly into his ear. "I tried to talk your mama into staying to hand out the candy so I could go with you, but she wouldn't listen."

"You gotta make her!"

"Listen, Ricky. She wants to go because she loves you so much. And she loves Halloween—why do you think she goes to so much trouble to make those costumes for you and Robin? She can't wait to take her boys out. She told me so."

He stepped back slightly, trying to look really, really pitiful. "Please?"

Carmen took his hands. "Remember your favorite story, Ricky? About Thomas Piper?"

He nodded. "Thomas McEnery Piper. He was my great-great-great-grandfather."

"You told me Thomas was a really brave boy and that you wished you could be like him, didn't you?"

He looked down, on the verge of tears. "I guess so."

"Well, *I* know you're just as brave as Thomas. You just don't know it yet, so you need to prove it to yourself. Going out tonight will help you do that."

He shook his head. "No."

"Yes, Ricky. Have I ever lied to you?"

He shrugged. "Guess not."

"I know you sat in your papa's chair by the front door for a long time tonight. I'm proud of you. It took a lot of courage for you to do it."

"I stayed twenty minutes," he said finally. "I didn't think I could do it."

"You're a brave boy, Ricky, just like Thomas Piper. You just don't give yourself enough credit. But after tonight, you will. Just stick close to your mama and your brother, and the whole time, make believe that *you're* Thomas Piper."

Icky Ricky; come and play, Picky Ricky, hey.

"But *they're* out there." He could hear them even as he spoke.

"They can't hurt you. And they can only scare you if you let them. Ricky, you can decide not to be scared, just like Thomas." She smiled conspiratorially. "You know what'll help?"

"What?" he asked, nearly convinced.

"Be nasty. When no one's looking, stick out your tongue at them!"

He almost smiled.

"They have no right to scare you, so just tell them, real quietly, to go stick their heads in dog doodie."

He giggled. "They'd probably like to do that."

She ruffled his hair. "You."

"Carmen?"

"What?"

"What about Big Jack? He can hurt me."

She studied him a long moment. "Well, what do you do in the daytime if you see a strange man coming toward you?"

"Stay with friends or cross the street."

"Okay. Remember, you said that anyone can see him, so that means he's not gonna come after you when people are around. Just treat him like any other stranger."

"Are you sure you can't go with us?"

"Yes. And I'm also sure you'll be fine. While you're gone, I'll make sure your window's shut tight and I'll double-check the lock on the cellar door, just so you feel extra safe when you get back."

He tried not to tremble. If Carmen really believed he was as brave as Thomas Piper, then he didn't want to disappoint her. "Okay."

She gave him one more big, cushiony hug. "You're a brave young man, and I know you'll be fine. You have to tell me all about how you whispered bad names at the jacks when you saw them."

"Pottyface?" he suggested coyly.

She laughed heartily. "That's a good one. Try it, but make sure your mama doesn't hear. And Ricky?"

"Uh-huh?"

"If you get a Snickers bar, will you give me a bite?"

"Sure."

"Now, go. Your mama and brother are waiting for you."

He hesitated, trying to summon up a brave smile. At first he couldn't do it, then Carmen mouthed "pottyface" at him, and he cracked up.

"Little boys," Carmen said, smiling. "You all like the same disgusting things."

Still giggling, he returned to the living room. "Didja fall in?" Robin asked. Mom was closing the front door after handing out more candy.

"Bite me," he told his brother, as he glanced fondly at Grandfather's portrait.

"Richard, *what* did you say?" his mother asked sharply.

"I said I'm ready," he said quickly, and pulled on his mask.

She stared, not quite fooled.

"He said—" began Robin.

Oh no, he thought.

"—I'm ready," his brother finished.

"Oh," said Mom.

He looked at Robin, surprised that he'd covered for him. A second later, Robin pulled on his hand, and he squatted down.

"You owe me all your Tootsie Rolls for that!"

"One."

"Three."

"Two."

"Boys?" their mother said, raising her eyebrows.

"Two and a half," Ricky hissed.

"Deal," Robin said. "Okay, Mom, we're ready."

3

"Thank you, Ricky," Carmen said, biting into the Snickers bar he'd fished out of his bag. He'd insisted on giving her the whole thing even though it was the only one he had. "You're the nicest boy in the world."

"You're welcome," he mumbled around a sticky Yabba Dabba.

Everyone else had gone to bed, and as they sat at the kitchen table, just the two of them, Carmen watched the little boy carefully. He was so small and so afraid, and she'd felt terrible when she'd had to stay at the house instead of going with him tonight, even though she knew his mama wouldn't let him out of her sight.

"Is it good?" he asked.

"Mmmm. Very good." She resisted the urge to grab him and hug him.

Truthfully, she knew he had to go out and face his fears, to learn to be less dependent on her, but it hurt her to let him go, because he was so small and she was so afraid for him.

Ricky had been her favorite ever since she'd come to work here the week after the boys were born. Of the two, Ricky was the most fragile. He was so serious and so easily frightened that he reminded her of a wounded deer. Robin, despite his handicap, was all sunshine and smiles, and very capable of taking care of himself. The brothers were an odd pair.

She felt bad for Ricky because no one believed him when he said he saw the greenjacks, and now that he wasn't a baby anymore, she was afraid that his parents would think there was something wrong with him. His mama had been asking her recently if he'd said anything about the greenjacks, and reluctantly Carmen had lied. When she decided to talk to Ricky about it, she was surprised to find out that he already knew his parents were worried. So, even though she wasn't entirely sure it was the right thing to do, she helped him, coaching him, reminding him, trying to build his confidence.

He didn't need to be afraid of the dark, for instance—not in the house—but he was so sensitive. She thought that perhaps he really did see greenjacks since her uncle's talk of *elementales* sounded very similar. But whether he could or he couldn't wasn't the problem. His fear was, so she told him over and over that nothing could hurt him if he wasn't afraid, and tried to play on his love of the stories about Thomas Piper. She watched him now: so serious, so sad. He tried so hard. The fact that he had gone out tonight could only be a hopeful sign.

She finished the candy bar. "Thank you, Ricky. Now, tell me, how was it tonight?"

He smiled, his lip trembling almost imperceptibly. "It was okay.

"What did you see? Anything?"

He hesitated. "Greenjacks. Mostly they were all over our yard, but there were some hanging around other people's yards, too, especially on our street." He smiled, more bravely. "I did what you said. I pretended I was Thomas." The smile suddenly broadened. "Know what I did?"

"What?"

"I flipped the bird at one." He giggled.

"I told you to stick out your tongue, Ricky," she said reprovingly. Carmen missed crotchety old Grandfather Piper, but he'd sure taught those boys some bad things.

"I did that, too, but the bird was more fun. You do it like this." He made a fist and extended his third finger proudly.

She cupped the offending hand in hers. "I guess your mama didn't see you do that?"

"Uh-uh."

"Your grandfather shouldn't have taught you that."

"Is it as bad as 'bite me'?"

"Worse. It's real, real dirty. Don't do it again, okay?"

"Okay." He dug a packet of Sweetarts from his bag and ripped them open. "Want some, Carmen?"

"No thanks, Ricky."

"I miss Grandfather," he said around a mouthful of candy. "He told me about the greenjacks."

"I know." His brown hair was still pasted damply against his forehead from wearing the skeleton mask all evening, and she reached out and pushed it from his face. She wondered if Ricky would have all his problems if his grandfather had kept his creepy old stories to himself. Who could know? And whether he saw greenjacks or only thought he did, it didn't matter, because she loved him blindly and she'd do anything for him. For good or bad, nothing could ever change that. It made her heart ache just to look at him.

"Ricky?"

"Huh?" He had a Mallomar half-crammed in his mouth.

"Did you see him? Big Jack?"

"No," he said, swallowing. "I guess not."

"You guess?"

"I thought I did for a second, in a tree on Penerosa Street." He picked up a box of Good & Plenty. "But it was windy out there, so I was probably wrong."

"You're gonna be sick if you eat any more candy tonight. Have those tomorrow, okay?"

He nodded.

"Ricky?"

"Huh?"

She hesitated, then decided to say what she had to say. "Ricky, you know you don't ever have to pretend to me. If you see something, you tell me. No one else will know."

"Okay." He pushed candy off the table into his bag and stood. "Are you gonna go to bed now?"

That was his way of making sure he didn't have to go up the dark stairway by himself. "Sure," she told him, glancing at the clock. "You know what? It's past eleven. I guess Big Jack has less than an hour left to play his tricks, huh?"

He gave her a genuine smile in return. "Yeah." He fell into her arms for a hug.

They walked up the stairs together, taking care to be very quiet. She told him to make sure and brush his teeth for a whole minute, kissed him good night, then made a show of switching on the night-light in the hall between the bathroom and the twins' bedroom. She walked to her room, around the corner from the others, but stood waiting by the open door until she heard Ricky safely enter his bedroom.

4

"Robin?" Ricky whispered as he pulled the bedroom door closed behind him. The night-light was out again, and swallowing his fear, he made himself bend down and feel for the wall socket next to the door where it was plugged in. *Nothing to be afraid of in here.*

His fingers found the socket but no night-light. "Robin!" he hissed.

No reply.

Robin, who loved to tease him by taking the little light and hiding it, seemed to be fast asleep. Ricky could see him buried under the blankets on the twin bed catercornered from his, and he was too angry at his brother to be afraid. "I'm turning on the big light, you turkey fart."

He waited a second, heard no giggling from the bed across the room. If Robin were awake, he would have cracked up. Grandfather had talked about turkey farts last year at Easter after dinner and several beers with Daddy. The brothers had practically wet their pants with hysterical glee before Mom came in and let Grandfather have it for saying "fart" and Dad for letting him. Mom was really ticked.

"Turkey fart," he said again, hopefully.

Nothing.

He flipped on the light switch, but Robin didn't stir because he was completely hidden in his blankets. At least his rotten brother hadn't figured out how to get up high enough to unscrew the overhead bulb, Ricky thought as he took off his costume and pulled on his pajamas. At least he hadn't *yet*.

Holding his breath, Ricky tiptoed across the room to the window that overlooked the three-acre front yard and the oak tree. Carmen had promised to lock it, but he had to check, had to put his hand under the curtain and feel the latch, make sure it was turned. He didn't even consider looking. Last year when he looked, he'd seen Big Jack looking back at him, scratching at the glass, tap tap tapping. *Ricky come out and play* . . . He shivered as he reached behind the curtain.

His fingers found the cold metal lock. Either Carmen had forgotten or Robin was messing with him again, because it wasn't latched. Stomach churning, he frantically twisted the lock closed.

The job done, he suddenly felt proud of himself, and almost as brave as Thomas McEnery Piper, not only because he'd flipped the bird at the little jacks, and hadn't panicked when the night-light disappeared, but because he'd calmly—well, pretty calmly—locked the window.

Smiling to himself, Ricky turned right and faced the foot of his brother's bed. Robin was so balled up in covers that he couldn't even see his hair. For a moment Ricky considered yelling boo and tearing the blankets from him. Maybe he'd get a glass of water from the bathroom so he could throw it on him.

No, he decided, he'd probably just end up getting in trouble. He'd cook up a safer trick tomorrow. Briefly he glanced at the wall of closets, saw with satisfaction that they were safely closed, then returned to his own bed, which was set against the inside wall as far as possible from the window and within reach of the overhead light switch. Last January Mom and Dad had redecorated the room. They put up wallpaper covered with drawings of sheriff stars, boots, six-shooters, lariats, and cowboy hats. Then they hung pictures showing cowboys, Indians, and lots and lots of horses. Ricky loved everything about the room except for the tree outside the window and the niggling fear that there might be a secret passage hidden in the closet somewhere.

There were all kinds of stories about the house and its hidden passages. His great-great-grandfather Conlin Piper—*Thomas's son,* he realized with a little thrill—had come here from Scotland and built the first house in Santo Verde: this house. Grandfather had always laughed and said that old Conlin was too creative for his own good and that he'd built a hodgepodge of a house with a maze hidden inside it. Conlin Piper had been in the Royal Navy, and Grandfather claimed he'd found a pirate's treasure, and had built the tunnels to hide his loot safely. Dad said the story about the loot was poppycock, but that the tunnels were real, and he'd even shown them the ones behind the built-in bookshelves on either side of the fireplace downstairs. One side was fake. The bookshelf turned around to reveal a little square room in which Conlin supposedly hid a deserter during the Civil War. Behind the other, though, was a dusty staircase, so low and narrow that a grown-up would have a hard time using it. It led straight up into utter darkness.

Yawning, Ricky pulled his yellow chenille bedspread down and climbed aboard, then crawled to the end of the bed, flicked off the light, and crawled back up, pushing his bare feet quickly, safely, between the clean white sheets.

Tonight he felt so brave that he didn't pull the covers all the way over his head. He knew Big Jack was outside somewhere, but the window was locked, and before long, the clock would strike twelve and the creature would be gone for another year.

Lying there in the dark, he realized that he felt better than he ever had in his life, and it was all because he'd walked right past the greenjacks, refusing to listen when they called his name. Instead, he'd pretended to be Thomas and lifted his mask and stuck out his tongue. Later, he'd really, truly flipped the bird at one. He thought his ancestor would be proud of him tonight.

Outside, the wind picked up and oak twigs scratched at

the window. Ricky shivered with sudden alarm: What if he'd made the greenjacks angry? *They can't do anything to you!* Only Big Jack could hurt him, and he was locked out. Calm again, Ricky stretched and wiggled his toes, knowing for the first time in his life that things were going to be better now. Maybe the fear would never go away entirely, he thought sleepily, but he'd be like Thomas McEnery Piper and not be af—

"Ricky!"

His eyes jerked open.

"Ricky!" It was Robin's voice, muffled and distant.

He's still under the covers. Ricky realized that his twin was going to try to play a trick on him. Tonight it wouldn't work, he thought smugly. Not tonight.

Outside, the wind howled and distant thunder rumbled.

"Ricky!"

"What?" he whispered.

"Ricky!"

"What?" he called, a little louder.

Something tapped on the window. Suddenly he felt cold.

"Ricky!" The tapping grew insistent. "Open up!"

He slid from the bed, hesitating at the light switch, deciding to brave the dark because Robin was making so much noise that their parents might wake up. If they saw the light on under the door, he'd get in trouble for sure.

He padded to Robin's bed, paused, then poked his finger into the covers just as a brief flash of lightning lit the room. "Whatcha want, you pottyface?" He poked again, harder, and realized he felt nothing under the bedspread but a wadded-up blanket. Thunder boomed just outside. Ricky nearly jumped out of his skin. He glanced around nervously.

Tap tap tap. "Ricky!"

Just as the rain began to fall, he understood. His stinkpot brother got himself locked outside while trying to play a trick on him.

"Ricky!"

The storm noises would probably keep his parents from hearing anything, and the sudden delight he felt at having

Robin's trick backfire helped him fight down his nervousness about having to open the window again. Probably Robin was planning to scare him—he'd done it once before—by climbing out the window and pretending to be Big Jack.

The first time he'd done it, last March, Ricky'd been so terrified that he'd screamed. Mom and Dad had come running, and boy, did Robin get in trouble when they saw him sitting out there in that tree. Ricky had hidden under his covers and cried half the night, even though Robin kept trying to apologize. By the next morning, he wanted revenge, but he didn't get any because he didn't know how.

But oh boy, he sure knew how now. He'd let his twin sit out there all night. Or maybe an hour, anyway. Let him sit out there and get all wet, and then Robin would think twice before he tried to play another joke on him.

He fluffed up the lump of blankets Robin had left and returned to his bed, thinking that if his parents did come in, he'd just pretend to be asleep. Could he help it if he'd locked the window without knowing his brother was out there playing a trick on him? No, he couldn't.

He sat on the edge of his bed.

Tap tap tap. "Ricky! Ricky! Wake up, dummy!"

He swung his feet up, slipped them between the cool sheets.

"Ricky! Let me in!"

"No way," he whispered.

Then, abruptly, two words popped into his brain: *Big Jack*

"Cripes." He slipped off the bed and walked quickly across the dark, shadowy room. He'd gotten so full of himself for being brave that he didn't even think about the fact that it was Halloween night when he'd locked his brother outside. "Cripes," he whispered again. Even rat-fink Robin didn't deserve to get snatched by Big Jack. "Cripes." He pushed the curtains open.

A skeletal face leered in through the glass, a green glowing face that grinned from ear to ear. With a small yelp, he jumped back. Then he heard Robin call his name again and saw his brother's hand rap on the glass, and realized his turkey brother had tried to scare him with his own Halloween mask.

Drawing a deep breath, he undid the lock. Robin backed up a little way to a thicker part of the wobbly branch he sat on and waited while Ricky pushed open the window. Wind yanked leaves from the tree and splattered sharp raindrops against his face.

"You took my mask, you fart," Ricky whispered. "I oughta leave you out here all night."

Robin pushed the mask up on top of his head. "I thought you'd want Big Jack to trickertreat you, Ricky!"

"Shut up!" Ricky ordered, not at all amused. "Get in here."

"Why? You scared old Jack's gonna get in?" Robin grinned, full of the devil. "I'm gonna tell Mom you told me 'shut up.' "

"You just said it, too."

"Then I'm gonna tell her I saw you flip old man Clegg the bird."

"Did not."

"Did so."

"Did not."

"I saw you."

"I didn't flip off Clegg, I flipped off—"

"Who? Huh? Who?"

Ricky shrugged, not wanting to say. When Robin was in the mood to tease, anything made him worse. "Come inside. Mom 'n' Dad are gonna wake up."

"Good thing for you old man Clegg's blind as a bat or you'd be nailed already. If you give me all your Tootsie Rolls, I won't tell. You already owe me two and a half for earlier. Now I want 'em all."

Carmen always said Robin was a Tootsie Rollaholic, and Ricky guessed she was right. "I'll give you one more."

"Three."

"Two and that's fi—"

Behind Robin, near the heart of the oak, a thin branch

moved against the wind, bending itself around the trunk. Ricky felt his jaw drop open, and knew his brother said something, but didn't understand the words.

Time slowed to a crawl as he watched the branch encircling the trunk. At the end of it were five long twigs, jointed and flexing like human fingers. A second branch, identical to the first, snaked around the trunk from the other side.

A creaking sound. Wind sighed. Rain in his face. Ricky's ears filled with roaring blackness, and the same blackness appeared in spots before his eyes and filled his stomach with nausea. But he couldn't look away.

"Hey, butthead!" Robin called. "Wake up!"

Time began to flow again. "Get inside," Ricky ordered. "Now!"

"No way, José, not until you give. Three more Tootsie Rolls or I tell."

"Come in *now!*"

Alien laughter exploded inside Ricky's head, a gale of it, similar to the greenjacks' windy cackling, but deeper, more powerful, a hurricane rather than a breeze. Oblivious, Robin continued his teasing, but Ricky couldn't even hear him over the roar of Big Jack's voice.

He leaned out the window as far as he dared and extended his arms to his brother. "Come on!"

Don't be afraid of me, Ricky, I'm your friend.

Slowly, so slowly, the skeletal arms crept up around the oak, the stick fingers crunching as they gripped the bark. The thought of the creature hidden behind the trunk terrified Ricky, and he had to force himself not to turn and run.

I love you, Icky Ricky.

Then he saw it peering at him from behind the trunk. It was a skull, like a twisted burl of wood, human-sized, leering, grinning with wood-chip teeth, the eye holes so black, they seemed to suck light into them.

Icky Ricky, I want you, yes I do do do.

The laughter deafened him as the creature pulled its body higher, and higher. Ricky blinked, and in the instant his eyes were closed, Big Jack must have leapt, its sounds masked by the storm, for now it stood arrogantly on a thick limb a few feet behind Robin.

Lightning flashed. Thunder rolled.

Big Jack looked like it did last year, only clearer and closer, so close, too close. The monstrosity resembled a human skeleton, but with bones made of tortured bark and buckled wood. Naked white roots, like nerves, twisted through its limbs, and leaves and vines filled its chest, throbbing green tendrils that twined along its extremities like blood veins. One thick vine coursed up its neck, pulsing— *jugular vine,* Ricky thought, fighting the urge to laugh or scream or throw up, he didn't know which. Big Jack opened its mouth, and wet waxy leaves crept from the corners of its smile, growing perceptibly, reaching toward him.

Toward Robin.

Horrified, Ricky jerked backward. His head thunked against the sash, but he barely felt it.

Robin pointed at him and began giggling.

He forced himself to lean forward again. "Robin, you jerk, get inside!"

"Why?" Robin grabbed the limb he balanced on with both hands and pushed his body up. "Wanna see me do a handstand?"

"No!"

"What's the matter, little brother? Is bad old Big Jack out here?" His eyes twinkled. "It's not midnight yet. I guess he's around somewhere, huh?" He giggled.

"He's behind you."

Robin made a face. "Yeah, and so's the tooth fairy." He pushed up and down on his arms, doing the spider imitation.

It took all of Ricky's courage to climb onto the windowsill.

Ricky, Ricky, be my friend, you won't be afraid anymore.

Big Jack stepped closer.

Ricky balanced himself on the ledge, his outstretched fingers only inches from his brother. "Give me your hand," he said, vaguely aware that tears were running down his cheeks and into his mouth.

"Cripes, Ricky, don't cry, I was just fooling around," Robin said. "I'll come in. Jeez, I didn't mean to——"

He froze as skeletal hands clamped down on his shoulders. He turned his head and saw the woody fingers, then slowly turned back to Ricky, no fun in his eyes now, only raw, incredulous horror. A soft moan escaped his lips.

Now or never, Ricky. Will you save your big brother? Now or never, Icky Ricky!

Ricky felt the thing trying to suck his will away with its charcoal eyes.

"No!" Carefully, his gaze never leaving Big Jack, Ricky climbed back through the open window, then wriggled back out, this time on his stomach. To keep from falling, he hooked his feet on either side of the window, then, inch by inch, pulled his upper body onto the nearest branch, not stopping until his body would stretch no farther.

His brother was within reach, but he was like a statue, his hands cemented to the branch, his body still raised above it as Big Jack's viney claws dug into his shoulders.

Ricky slapped at his twin. "Robin! Give me your hand! Hurry!"

Dully, his twin looked at him, focusing only when Ricky grasped both his wrists and began yanking him forward. "Ricky—"

"Come on!"

Suddenly Robin let go. Ricky caught him and, with all his strength, began to pull him inside, realizing that his brother was paralyzed with fear. He grunted with effort, determined to win this battle with Big Jack. Robin cried out as the creature renewed its painful hold on his flesh.

Ricky struggled, gaining an inch, losing one. "I got you, I got you, I got you!" He repeated the litany as he worked, aware of Big Jack's laughter in his head and of Robin's shock-white face and fathomless eyes. "I got you!" Panting, Ricky held on. "Robin, I got you!"

Suddenly the monster released its hold. Ricky almost lost his balance as Robin fell from the limb, but he hung on to his brother's wrists, his hands slippery in the rain, gulping air, struggling to keep his feet wedged safely inside the window. After an eternity, Ricky began to pull him up, his back and arms screaming with the effort.

Robin was a foot from the window, Ricky half-inside, when Big Jack struck, sweeping across Robin, its storm of laughter echoing madly in Ricky's head. The sharp wooden hands grabbed Ricky at the elbows, pinching and holding until his fingers turned numb and started to open against his will.

Hey. Ricky, time to play!

Robin began to slip from his grasp. "No!" he cried, but his voice was lost in the howl of the storm. He watched in horror as Robin began to slip.

The wind screamed and then he saw Robin grab a branch two feet below. He hung on, then began pulling himself back up the tree.

And then Ricky couldn't see anything because Big Jack was all over him, grabbing, touching, plucking at him. Wind swirled around them, wet and rotting and green like cold swamp water. It whistled among the bony branches with a life of its own, mingling with the laughter of the thing itself.

Big Jack dragged him out of the window and into the tree. It hugged him against itself, smothering him in its green darkness, bruising him on its bark and bones. It paused for an instant, staring into Ricky's eyes until he thought he would faint. Its gaze drained him of his will while its arms crushed the life from him.

"No! Let him go!" Robin yelled from behind them.

Ricky only saw him for an instant, hanging on to the tree limb with one hand, pounding and pulling on Big Jack with the other. "Let him go!"

The thing paused, its grasp loosening slightly. Ricky drew a breath, coughing, and watched as Robin tore at Big Jack, ripping out the root nerves, yanking the blood vines. It seemed amused until the boy snapped off two of its gnarled toes. Then the swamp wind rose again, Big Jack's howl of anger within it, a part of it.

"Punch him!"

Robin's words startled him into action. Ricky fought, pulling and twisting the foliage guts, trying to break off ribs. The monster howled furiously as Robin attached himself to one of its legs and started ripping it apart.

Steeling himself, Ricky reached for Big Jack's neck and wrapped his hand around the thick, pulsing jugular vine. He pulled.

Howling, Big Jack let go for a bare instant, but that was enough. Ricky sprang back, grabbing the tree trunk and regaining his balance. Something cold splashed across his face and mouth. It tasted of plants: Big Jack's blood.

Ricky edged around the trunk as the thing reached for him, backed farther as he watched his twin do a monkey-climb right up the monster, ripping and tearing and shredding the vines as he moved. The thing put its arms around Robin as he reached its chest.

Two blocks away, the bells of Our Lady of Guadalupe began chiming the measure of prelude that would ring in the hour.

Midnight. The first bell rang.

Big Jack's almost out of time! Ricky edged forward to help his brother, who still tore at the monster's chest. "Get him, Robin!" he cried. "Hang on!"

Two chimes. With one hand, the thing shoved Robin's head into its torso, smothering the flailing boy. Its laughter blended with the rain as it extended its other hand and beckoned Ricky closer. *Come with me and I'll let your big brother live.*

Three. *I'm supposed to die! Not Robin!* Ricky stepped nearer.

"No!" Robin yelled, his voice muffled against the creature. He punched into the thing with all his might, over and over.

Four.

Green fluid still pulsed from the broken vine in Big Jack's neck, and green slime dripped from its mutilated torso, but still it held Robin. The vines growing from its mouth began to twine around his face.

Five chimes. Big Jack extended its hand again. *Come with me or he dies dies dies.*

Six. He couldn't let Robin die for him. Swallowing, Ricky reached for Big Jack's hand.

"NO!" Robin screamed as the creature's hand closed painfully on Ricky's wrist.

Seven. Big Jack paused, glanced at Robin, then stretched out its other arm, holding the boy far away from its body. Suddenly it let go, but Robin was already clinging to the arm, hanging on as Jack tried to shake him off. Face smeared with green, eyes fierce, he screamed, "No!" and refused to fall.

Ricky twisted in Big Jack's grasp, and suddenly the grip became so tight that he felt as if his bones were being crushed. He cried out, nearly fainting with the pain.

Eight. Robin swung across Big Jack's body and grabbed the arm it held Ricky with. With all his might, he began to tear at Jack's forearm, using every muscle in his hands and arms, using his teeth to bite, doing everything to make the monster let go of his brother. The monster tore at him, but he didn't seem to notice.

Nine. The wooden wrist began to crack. Robin twisted the wood fiercely, and it broke. He ripped a vine with his teeth and the hand came off, still attached to Ricky's arm.

Ricky staggered back against the tree trunk, breathing heavily, holding his wrist.

"You can't have him!" Robin screamed.

Ten.

Big Jack pulled its mangled arm back and again shoved Robin's head into the mass of oozing mashed foliage behind the ribs.

Eleven.

"Robin!" Ricky cried.

Robin's mine, little Ricky, icky little Ricky. He can't see like you can, but he's mine now. Better watch out!

Twelve. Midnight, November 1.

The leaves on the vines growing from Big Jack's mouth withered in an instant, turning brown and flying away on the breeze before the final bell finished echoing. Big Jack laughed again and let go of the oak, Robin trapped in its arms.

"No!" Ricky cried as they fell.

In the first minute of November first, Ricky stood in the branches of the old oak tree, barely aware of the rain beating monotonously against his face. He clung to the trunk and stared in shock at Big Jack's body on the ground twenty feet below. He craned his neck, trying to see Robin, but the boy was lost in the rain, buried in the dark visceral vines of Big Jack's remains.

The scene was lit by moonlight and the rainbow of Malibu lights that lined the paths crisscrossing the immense forest of a front yard, and as Ricky watched, a dozen little green-jacks gathered around the ruins of Big Jack. An instant later, a dozen more glimmering forms poured from the lifeless body of their king. A strong wind suddenly rose and the body began to break apart, the arms and hands and legs becoming nothing more than harmless twigs and branches. The roots and leafy vines crackled brown as they dried up and rode away on the wind.

Big Jack was gone for another year, and only the unmoving form of Ricky's twin lay within the circle of little jacks.

"Robin." Ricky moaned the name, and the greenjacks looked up at him briefly, then turned their attention back to Robin. They started to move around him. Ricky realized that they were fighting over his brother's body.

He realized that Robin was unconscious, not dead, just like Thomas in Grandfather's stories. That meant a greenjack could force Robin out and take his body—just as Big Jack had promised. Quickly Ricky started to climb down the tree. He had to get his twin into the house before they took him.

But the handholds ran out after a few feet, and it was too far to jump. "Robin," he whispered. The jacks barely glanced at him as he crawled back up the tree and into his window.

Once inside, he glanced briefly down and saw that the circle of jacks was moving wildly, violently, melding, coming apart, melding again. Quickly he took the back stairs past Carmen's room and down and around through the kitchen and dining room, not caring about the darkness, caring only about his brother.

Don't let them get you, Robin, don't let them get you!

He crept across the living room, avoiding the spots where the floorboards would creak. The drapes were drawn, and for once, he wished they weren't. *Don't let them get you, don't let them, don't let them.*

Quietly he reached up and pulled the wrought-iron bolt on the arched front door, then grabbed the handle and pressed the thumb latch. It clicked softly open. He waited a moment, then, slowly, silently, he pulled the heavy planked door open. His heart thumped as he got ready to run out and down the steps to the oak, to rescue Robin and carry him inside to safety.

"Hi, baby brother."

"Robin!"

Bathed in the yellow glow of the porch light, Robin waited on the welcome mat, resting on his hands, peering up at him. He was soaking wet, and a small trickle of blood oozed from a cut hidden in his hair. Otherwise he looked fine. Below, at the bottom of the wide steps, the amorphous shifting shapes of the greenjacks cavorted and tumbled in the grass. *I'm not afraid of them anymore.* The realization astounded him even more than Robin's amazing recovery. *I'm not afraid.* Suddenly he knew what it must feel like to be a grown-up. Smiling, he turned his attention back to his twin.

"Robin, you're okay! I was afraid you were—"

"Dead?"

"Knocked out. I thought you were knocked out!"

"I was."

His twin's crooked smile made the hairs on the back of Ricky's neck stand on end. Grandfather's familiar words flitted through his mind.

. . . his father held a sword in his hand, ready to run the body through if his son had become a changeling.

"Whatcha thinkin'?"

"Nothing. Are you okay?"

"Okeydokey, icky Ricky."

Stunned, he stared at his brother. Ricky *knew*, beyond all doubt, that he had never, *ever* told anyone about the name the jacks called him: It was too humiliating. His bladder let go. It didn't matter. "What?" he whispered.

"I'm okay."

"Did you hit your head?" he asked timidly, wanting to believe that he'd imagined his brother's rhyming reply.

"Just a little. Just enough." He crossed the threshold, his movements lacking their usual grace, and stared around the room as if it were something new. "Shut the door, Picky Ricky. Let's go to bed."

In shock, Ricky loitered a moment in the open doorway watching the greenjacks as they capered in the rain. One, dimmer than the others, did not jump or dance, but stood motionless under the tree, near the place where Robin had fallen. A chill raced up Ricky's spine.

Robin? he thought hard at the figure.

And he thought he heard his name, called softly, but it was lost in the leaves that chattered in the breeze.

"What's going on here?"

Ricky whirled at his father's voice and saw his parents in their robes and slippers, standing at the bottom of the living room stairs. His dad's arms were crossed, but his mother stepped forward quickly.

"You're wet. You're both wet!"

Immediately Robin began to cry. "I fell," he sobbed.

"Fell?" Mom scooped him up, mindless of his wet clothes and the leaves and dirt sticking to him. "From where? Are you all right, honey?"

He threw his arms around her neck and clung, his face buried against her shoulder, sobbing and heaving as he never had before. It was a show. Ricky cringed, wondering what would come next.

"I fell out of the tree," he wailed. "I'm sorry! I didn't mean to—"

"Rick?" His father loomed over him. "What were you boys doing?" He looked him up and down, mouth set in a grim line.

"I—I—Robin went out the window and—" He silenced, knowing he shouldn't tell the truth because they wouldn't believe him.

"It's all my fault," Robin bawled.

Amazed, Ricky stared at him.

"I was playing a trickertreat on Ricky." His voice hitched dramatically over a series of whimpers. "I . . . I wanted to scare him. I lost my balance, and Ricky tried to save me."

"There, there . . ." His mother turned slightly, and Ricky could see Robin's face over her shoulder.

His eyes were black as night, and his expression was gleeful and scary at the same time. The little-boy voice that issued from his mouth didn't match the way he looked. "Oh, Ricky, I'll always remember how you tried to save me." His hand crept into his mother's hair, bringing a lock of it to his face. He smelled it, smiling. Then, to Ricky's horror, he stuck his tongue out and licked it. The smile broadened into a jack-o'-lantern grin, and all the while, Mom kept patting his back, unaware. Dad, not noticing, crossed to the open door and closed it.

"Ricky?" His mother said. "That was very brave of you to try to help your brother, especially when he played a bad trick on you."

"I'll pay you back, I promise," Robin said. Slowly he extended his tongue and licked the satiny robe his mother wore.

"It's okay," Ricky said softly. "He bumped his head," he added. "It's bleeding."

Oh!" Mom pulled Robin away from her, as Ricky hoped she would, and examined his head. "Frank, do you think we should take him to the hospital?" She glanced at Ricky. "Go on up and get dry and go to bed, honey. Everything will be all right."

He left his parents discussing Robin's bumped head as he trudged upstairs. At the top, he found Carmen staring down at the scene below. Silently she walked with him to his bedroom, then waited outside the door until he came out in fresh pajamas.

"Are you all right?"

He nodded.

"Do you want to tell me what happened?"

"Uh-huh."

"Come on, then." She led him to her room around the corner, and they sat together on the little sofa bed she kept for when one of her sisters came to visit. "Okay, Ricky," she told him. "Tell me. It will be our secret."

He did as she asked, leaving nothing out because he knew she wouldn't just tell him he was crazy.

She asked, "So you think your brother's changed, Ricky?"

Confronted so bluntly, he had to stop and think. That was exactly what he thought. And he had proof because of the name: *Icky Ricky.*

He swallowed his pride and told her about the name.

"Maybe you said it in your sleep, Ricky." She regarded him solemnly. "Do you think you might have?"

More than anything in the world, he wanted to believe that what Carmen suggested was true. "Maybe," he said, knowing he hadn't. Suddenly he realized he'd have to go back to his room soon and see his brother. That frightened him so much that his stomach hurt.

Carmen leaned over and kissed his cheek soundly. "It's late. Let's talk about it more tomorrow. You want to sleep here tonight, Ricky?" she asked, as if she knew what he was thinking.

He nodded gratefully.

5

November 1, 1973

Legs legs legs legs legs. Balanced on his hands, he padded carefully down the staircase, his abbreviated body held up high so that it didn't thump much against the steps. *Legs legs legs legs legs.* Icky Ricky was cowering in Carmen's room, maybe sleeping, maybe not, and the parents were back in their room with the door closed.

Legs legs legs legs legs. Despite the blood in his hair, he'd convinced them he was fine, so the mother had dried him and tucked him into bed. He liked that a lot, the feel of the rough towel on his skin, the feel of her hands, the smell of her hair, her skin, the minty scent of her breath.

He snickered, remembering how upset Ricky had been when he saw him lick Mom's hair. Poor Ricky, icky Ricky, crazy, crazy, sicky Ricky.

The parents talked and talked before falling asleep, and impatiently he'd waited until they'd been silent for a long time before leaving the bedroom. It wasn't much fun being alone, but he amused himself by looking through icky Ricky's dresser and toy chest until he knew it was safe to leave.

It was just as well he'd been left alone for a while, he decided. Because of the head bump, the memories buried in his brain had been a little fuzzy at first—the memories of the house, the parents, Carmen, and especially icky Ricky, but now they were flowing into place and he knew he'd be fine, no matter who he ran into.

Legs legs legs legs legs. He hated Ricky for having the legs, but this body had some advantages. Though Robin's balance and grace were still a little messed up, they were improving rapidly and six steps from the ground floor, he let loose a whispery little laugh and flipped his body up above his head and finished his descent in handstand position. Delighted with his progress, he turned and quickly raced back up the stairs, then, still in a handstand, dashed down the hall, past his room and around the corner.

Legs legs legs legs legs. He paused a moment, waiting until he discerned the soft sawing snore coming from Carmen's room, then, arms pumping, he dashed along the long hallway that led to the back stairs. His descent was perfect this time, and he made no sounds but for the soft pad-padding of his hands against the lovely grass-colored carpet and the rhythmic murmur of his breath and his muted giggles. At last he entered the kitchen and caught the perfume of ripening pears, the tang of orange peel, and the warm smell of the bread baked earlier that day.

He crossed to the refrigerator and, balanced on one hand, used the other to open the door. He pushed it wide so that the dim light from the interior could illuminate as much of the room as possible, then he began investigating the Kelvinator's contents.

"Mmmm-mmmm-mmmm-mmmm-mmmm, what's this, what's that?" Gleefully he opened a yellow Tupperwear container, and sniffed at the gelatinous brown lumps within. "Beef, beef, beefy beef," he whispered, sticking his finger in the cold gravy. Delicately he sucked the finger clean. "Mmmm." Lifting the bowl to his face, he dipped his tongue into the gravy and lapped up a morsel of beef. He chewed slowly, savoring the meaty flavor, memorizing the rich odor of flesh laced with onions, garlic, and bay, and the feel of its greasy, grainy texture. Before replacing the lid, he used his tongue to smooth the surface of the coagulated sauce.

Licking his lips, he replaced the container precisely where he'd found it before eagerly studying other items on the lowest shelf.

"Butter, butter, mmmm-mmmm butter!" He removed the cover, then ran the flat of his tongue over the yellow surface, careful not to leave any marks. He loved butter, the slick way it felt in his mouth, so rich, so . . . There was something more, but he didn't know what to call it.

So many tastes and smells and textures to examine and sample—*Said Simple Simon to the pieman, let me taste your wares, hairs, cares, dares.* The rhyme came to him, making him feel warm and tingly inside. He had a dab of catsup, a lick of sour cream, then an egg, consumed whole, crunchy shell and all. A drink of milk threatened to overflow his mouth and belly, so he spat the rest back into the carton.

Legs legs legs legs legs. Logy and full, Robin ascended the kitchen staircase, tired, moving slowly, the bump on his head making him feel achy and irritated, not caring much if his body thumped the steps now and then. Even so, he paused in the bathroom to open the hamper and examine the dirty laundry. He withdrew a shirt and sniffed it carefully, memorizing the scent of the father's sweat, then exchanged it for a pair of feminine underwear. He studied item after item, with nose, mouth, and eyes, never tiring until he had examined every last piece of clothing. Finally he replaced everything in the hamper and returned to his bedroom. He climbed onto Ricky's empty bed, removed his pajama top and underpants, then rolled around on the sheets.

When he tired of the activity, he dressed and moved to Robin's bed by the window. With effort, he unlocked it and opened it as wide as it would go and perched on the ledge.

The rain had stopped and there was no wind. The silence choked his ears until he began grinding his teeth just to hear something. Soon he began humming to himself, wishing icky Ricky were here so he could listen to him breathe, wishing he were here so that he could have a little fun.

In the darkness he longed for a whole body, to have legs to run with and senses that could see the greenjacks and hear their songs. Most of all, he longed for revenge against Ricky, who had everything he so desired. For the new Robin Piper, the loneliness was overwhelming.

6

July 22, 1974

Tonight the refrigerator held clusters of purple Concord grapes to stuff into his mouth, and he did, cramming it so full that he could barely close his jaws over them. Next, oh joy, a covered dish of olives, black finger food, salty and iron-tasting, reminding him of blood. The olives made him crave meat, and he had to reach as high as he could to grab the white butcher paper containing a mountain of hamburger. He opened it and nibbled the raw meat delicately, savoring each taste. Then, before rewrapping it up so carefully that no one would suspect it had been touched, he ran his smoothing tongue over the rest of the mound, leaving his saliva on what his family would eat.

He never grew tired of touching other people's things, of leaving something of himself upon them, so they would unknowingly consume his bodily secretions, or wear them against their bodies. It was one of many pleasures that helped him deal with his anger at Ricky for the legs and eyes denied him.

Eating was another, but now his stomach was full, so he shut the refrigerator and padded to the kitchen door, swung onto the stool next to it, and silently undid the lock and chain, ready for another sort of indulgence.

A moment later, he was in the backyard, hidden in the

darkness of a new moon. He breathed in the night air, feeling the summer darkness surround him, the cool wind like water on his face. A hint of eucalyptus lay under the soft sweetness of the citrus trees, the gardenias and jasmine, and beneath that, a cold-water smell and the bubbling of a waterfall. He glanced at the half acre of orange and lemon trees, at the path leading toward the cottage where Grandfather Piper had lived. It had been locked and dark for nearly two years, but now that Carmen and Hector were getting married, it was being cleaned out and fixed up so that they could live in it. The parents had hired Hector full time to act as gardener and handyman.

Robin was pleased about the marriage, because that meant the bitch wouldn't be hovering around icky Ricky at night like she did now.

The cold-water smell grew stronger, and he turned toward it, smiling in the dark. "Hi, hi, hi, hi, hi," he called wishfully. The new moon held little power, and he neither expected any answers nor received them, but ever since he'd discovered that very occasionally he could hear the greenjacks' song, he was compelled to try. He treasured the times he had sensed the presence of the jacks. It was a salve for his loneliness.

Legs legs legs legs legs. Hatred for icky Ricky, with his long legs and special senses, washed over him. He'd get the cowardly little shit eventually, get him good. He could get him anytime with a pillow over the face or a conk on the head, especially after Carmen moved out, but what he really wanted was to get him on Halloween, to give him a trickertreat he'd never forget.

Robin waited until later, when they were in their beds, to tell old Icky he was going to make sure he never lived through another Halloween. Ricky didn't say anything, just jumped up and hightailed it for his precious Carmen's room.

But Robin meant what he said. This Halloween he'd do the big trickertreat, or if something went wrong, the next. He could wait a long, long time.

Sniggering, he started down the path that led from the

backyard, down through the long, narrow side yard, with its thick border of oleanders and liquid amber trees, and finally to the front corner of the house. The front was even bigger than the back, covering three acres, and so surrounded with willows, elms, pines, and filled with fruit trees, flowers, ferns, and exotic broad-leafed tropicals, that you couldn't even see the street, Via Matanza, beyond them.

The yard that icky Ricky so hated was a park crisscrossed with brick and stone paths that were constantly overgrown by the grass and bushes, no matter how often Hector pruned or mowed. To Robin the place was a paradise, the plant life an announcement that the greenjacks were present. Again he took in the scents, the blend of aromas from the plants and the trees and the koi pond, the wonderful koi pond, a hundred feet distant.

Ignoring the light-lined brick path that led to the pool, Robin moved across the yard, enjoying the thick dampness of the lawn beneath his hands. He paused, reveling in the spongy coolness, and noted how his nails dug into the moist earth, snickering when he detected the cold wriggling sliminess of a night crawler as it passed between his fingers.

Reaching the flagstones that surrounded the koi pond, he crossed them—hard, cold, interesting. The pond itself had originally been a kidney-shaped built-in swimming pool, so it was huge and deep. But many years ago, Grandfather Piper, who hated to swim, had painted it dark blue, put the rocky rustic edge on it, and built the tall stony waterfall right over the tall diving platform. And then he had filled it with fish and water lilies.

At the water's edge, Robin halted, lowering himself onto his stomach to lie between the colored lights on the cold stone so that he could stare at the water, smell it, and dangle his fingers in it to attract the fish.

"Boy kois, toy kois, fishies, fishies, fishies!" He wiggled his fingers and they came, the fishies, gold and red and bronze and black, kissing his fingers, looking for food. Finally his favorite arrived, the huge white one that everyone called the Professor. It had black circles around its eyes that looked like spectacles. He waited for it to mouth his fingers, then deftly he snatched the fish up in both hands and lifted it from the water.

"Hi, fishie, fishie!"

The koi barely wriggled in his powerful grip, and he fancied that it studied him as intently as he did it. Gently he kissed the creature, and found it cold and wet but full of life. Its odor was of algae and dark, cool water. It gasped, needing to breathe, suffocating on air, and quickly Robin ran his tongue over the creature's scaly side, tasting salt and stagnant water. " 'Bye, fish, go, fish," he whispered, and thrust it into the water, watching until the sleek white shape disappeared into the bubbles of the waterfall on the far side of the pond.

He loved the fishes. On warm nights he'd slip into the water and swim with them. The thought made him remember Ricky, locked away up in their room, and he turned and gazed up at the bedroom window. The light was out, but he thought he saw the curtain move behind the glass. Hoping he was watching, Robin waved, then pulled his T-shirt over his head and tossed it behind him. A moment later, his shorts—the mother made them for him with a little fly and no leg holes—and underpants lay beside it. He waved again, loving the way the air felt against his skin.

Ribbet. At the sound of the frog, he flipped himself silently upright. *Ribbet.* Near, he thought. *Ribbet.* Near and nearer. Another frog answered, in a deeper voice, from somewhere near the waterfall. Still another joined in and another, and soon the air was full of *ribbets* and *robbets,* croaking music high and low and in between. Pleased, he listened to the symphony, and when it was at its peak, he rose on his hands and lifted all the way to his fingers, his version of tippy-toes. Fingers aching with effort, he moved silently around the pond to the rocky waterfall, watching for a frog. Despite the Malibu lights, it was difficult to spot even one, for they sought out the shadows.

The invisible singers continued their melody as Robin settled his body next to the waterfall. He waited, listening, and while he did, he glanced up at the house and saw the bedroom light come on. Icky Ricky was up for sure. Grinning, he thought his scaredy-cat brother probably had to go pee, because he always had to turn on the light before he could even get out of bed.

Ribbet ribbet. Something moved in the darkness, and suddenly, right in front of him, he saw the dark shape of a large amphibian. It hopped even closer, and Robin grabbed it, squeezing hard to keep it from slipping out of his grasp.

The other singers fell silent.

He touched the frog. smelled it and tasted it, then spat at the bitterness. Then he worked its legs, pumping them up and down, up and down, fascinated. *Legs legs legs legs legs.* He petted it, stuck his fingers in its mouth, and looked up and smiled when he saw Ricky's silhouette in the bedroom window. Probably Ricky couldn't see him right now, but he could certainly remedy that.

Sticking the frog's legs in his mouth, ignoring the bitter, moldy flavor, he clamped his teeth down on them so that, no matter how hard it kicked, it couldn't get away. He rose on his hands, moved around to the back of the waterfall, and nimbly climbed to the top.

Settling his body on the smooth stone just above the water spout, he waved at his brother. Icky Ricky saw him, but didn't wave back. That was fine by Robin.

Legs legs legs legs legs. He took the frog from his mouth, wiping his lips and spitting, then held it up for Ricky to see, one little foot in each hand.

"Legs legs legs legs legs," he whispered, holding the frog up above his head. Slowly he began to pull the legs apart. The frog made a sound, a funny little froggy-scream. Then, after a long moment, its skin made a ripping sound and the creature came apart. Blood spattered like raindrops across Robin's face and into his open mouth. "Legs legs legs legs legs," he said, tossing the dismembered halves into the pond.

He lifted himself up on his hands. "Icky Ricky, icky Ricky, come out and play," he called, his voice melding with the waterfall and the night breeze. "Come out and swim with me." Laughing, he propelled himself over the waterfall, into the pond, surprising the fishies, and washing frog's blood from his skin. *Legs legs legs legs legs.*

7

June 1, Today

Locusts. The air hissed with their high, dry sounds, rasping, phoneline electric, screaming outside the car. Rick Piper cringed as he closed the window. He hated the locusts. He hated the desert.

Until he turned right on Vegas Boulevard and saw that the thermometer on the First Interstate Bank read 104 degrees, he wasn't even aware that his shirt was plastered to his body. *You're losing it, Piper.* Sighing, he loosened his tie, switched on the air conditioner, and let the chill air turn his sweat to ice.

Sinatra dobedobedoed at him when he turned on the radio. Wincing—a reflex born in childhood—he switched to the news. The stations rarely played any music he liked, and carrying cassettes in the car in this heat was a bad idea; they melted.

The desert, thought Rick, sucks. Clear, sunny, and hot, the weatherman was saying, yesterday, today, and tomorrow. It never changed. When he was a kid, he'd thought Southern California had no weather. Lord, had he been wrong about that.

If you don't like it, you can move. He glanced at the envelope on the seat beside him. The letter from George McCall, his attorney, had arrived two weeks ago, and he still hadn't answered it. He didn't know how. It was about Aunt Jade and her deteriorating mental state, about the house and its own state of deterioration, about sewer lines, property taxes, and a host of other aggravations related to home ownership.

The house in Santo Verde provided all the frustrations and none of the benefits, but that was his own fault. Sell it, he thought. Put crazy old Jade in a rest home with part of the proceeds. He should have done it years ago, but he just kept putting it off. He'd had title to the place since his twenty-first birthday, but he hadn't been back since he'd left for college. *Time flies.* He realized he hadn't seen it in nearly twenty years.

LOOSE SLOTS! a computerized sign blazed as he passed. Shaking his head, he thought, *You hate this place,* for maybe the hundredth time since the letter had arrived and maybe the millionth since he'd moved here in '82. *You hate the heat. Christ it's only June first and it's over one hundred.* He squinted into the sun, a headache coming on. *You hate having your kids grow up here with gambling and drinking and sex advertised on every other billboard.* Shelly's attitudes had already been affected by her surroundings, and he knew it was only a matter of time before it rubbed off on Cody, too. He could take them back to Santo Verde, enroll them in good schools, fix up the house, and live a normal life again. That was something they hadn't done since Laura was killed by a drunk driver, when Cody was barely a year old. The poor kid didn't even remember his mother.

He'd been considering a move for sometime, and now the time had come to make the decision. His contract with the local station would be up for renewal at the end of the month, and though he liked doing the show, he didn't need the work. Too, in the last few weeks, pressure from station management—a group of disturbingly sharp, closely related men who referred to themselves as "the boys"—to sign a contract that would tie him up for three years had increased to the point that he was coming home with headaches and acid stomach nearly every evening. Lately he'd been wondering if he might wake up some morning and find himself nose to nose with a horse's head.

Moving to California to take care of family matters was something "the boys" would probably understand.

Since he'd started hosting the program, a show that was similar in style to "Consumer Crusader," his syndicated newspaper column, he'd been away from home more often than not, leaving Shelly to her own questionable devices and Cody to sitters he never quite trusted. No, he didn't need the show. Besides, if he really needed the money—or the ego gratification—he'd already been approached by a Los Angeles station about doing a five-minute spot several times a week on a local morning news show. It paid almost as well as his weekly half hour, required far less work, but unfortunately would require him to get up at three in the morning Monday, Wednesday, and Friday. Still, it was his if he wanted.

All you need, Piper, is your column. Ten more newspapers had just contracted for "Crusader," and that meant he'd soon be appearing in virtually every major metropolitan area in the nation every Sunday. What more *could* he need? And if he just did the column, he'd be home a lot more, which meant he wouldn't feel so guilty all the time.

He knew the kids needed a more wholesome environment; a world-class gambling town wasn't a fit place for a teenage girl or a little boy ready for kindergarten. It wasn't a fit place for a single father, either. He shook his head. *Better be careful, Piper, or you'll talk yourself into this move.*

Joe Piscopo, bulging with obscene, oily muscles, smiled smugly down at him from a billboard by the MGM. Yeah, Rick thought, he hated it here. Except for one thing, the one reason he had moved here in the first place: It never got dark on the Strip.

He turned left on Flamingo Road, wondering if he was ever going to stop carrying around a childhood fear of the dark—the *greenjacks will get you if you don't watch out*. A simple fear of the dark ruled his life, deciding where he could or couldn't live, letting it control his every move. *Ridiculous.*

Don't think about it! Abruptly his memory tried to shut down, just as it always did when he thought too much about his past.

Not this time, he ordered himself. *Not this time, no.* He had to think about it because it was time—past time—for him to take control of his life. At. seventeen, when he first came here, his fear was ridiculous, but to continue to carry it around all these years was borderline psychotic, or something equally abnormal. "Hell," he said, and hung another left.

A moment later, Rick pulled into the garage beneath the Paradise Towers, found a space, and parked. *Home, sweet home.* He stepped out of the air-conditioned Celica and into the shadowed, cloying heat. The air smelled like stale cigarettes—not just in the garage, but everywhere in the vicinity of the Strip. That was another good reason to return to California—not that the air was more healthful, it just smelled like it was, especially in Santo Verde in the spring when the citrus orchards were in full blossom. Despite himself, he smiled as he grabbed his briefcase, locked the car, and crossed to the elevator.

The refrigerated air in the hall on the fourteenth floor outside his apartment smelled like stale cigarettes, too, and spilled booze. "Shelly?" he called as he unlocked the door. "Shelly? You here?" Sometimes the ventilation screwed up and he'd wake up in the night smelling old smoke from Dakota and Lil's apartment next door, or worse, dog-shit cigars from his other neighbor, a fat, froggy guy named Mancuso who worked weird hours and wore dark suits, even in August. "Shelly? Cody?" He tossed his briefcase on the couch.

Except for Quint, his huge orange cat, who was fast asleep in the center of the dining room table, the place was deserted. "Scat, cat!" he ordered by rote, and as usual, Quint blinked at him with utter boredom and went back to sleep. "Cheeky bastard," Rick said, completing the ritual.

He glanced at his watch. Six-ten. Shelly had promised to pick up her brother by five and bring him straight home. Irritated, he dialed the sitter's number and found out, as he expected, that Cody was still there.

The current sitter lived on the fifth floor, and precisely three minutes and forty-five seconds elapsed between the time Rick hung up the phone and when he rang the bell. Tapping his foot, checking his watch, waiting for the door to open, he realized that his darling daughter had been late coming home four nights out of five this week.

"Mr. Piper! Come in, come in!"

The door opened and Marlene Poom beamed at him through a blue tobacco haze,

"Mrs. Poom, I'm sorry about this."

She took his arm and leaned familiarly against him. "I'm just going to have to take you over my knee and give you a good spanking if you don't remember to call me Marlene," she told him, batting her eyelashes.

Now, there was a horrifying thought. "Marlene," he said quickly, "I don't know what kept Shelly. She should have been here over an hour ago."

Mrs. Poom, her big-boned face mummy brown from the desert and tautly stretched from the plastic surgeon, beamed at him and blew a smoke ring in his face. Rick was only five nine, and that gave old Marlene a good half inch on him. That was another good reason to move: Most of the women in the building were performers and stood about six foot four. Mrs. Poom claimed to be a former show girl herself—probably from around the time of the last gold rush. He tried to avoid another face full of smoke.

"Shelly's a pretty young girl, and she probably has lots and lots of boyfriends," Marlene Poom was telling him.

"That's what I'm afraid of."

"Daddy!"

"Hey, Cody!" Rick squatted, and the little boy careened into his arms. The brim of his red cowboy hat smacked into Rick's nose, bringing tears to his eyes. He stifled the urge to swear. Cody probably heard enough of that from Marlene.

Cody took his hug and pulled back, filled with dimples and glee. Except for the Piper dimples and dark blue eyes, the boy looked so much like his mother with his straight gold hair, full lower lip, and turned-up nose. Sometimes it hurt to look at him. He still missed her so much that sometimes in the middle of the night he'd wake up in a panic because he'd reach for her and she wasn't there.

Mr. Piper. I'm afraid we have some bad news . . . Your wife's been in an accident . . . A drunk driver on the wrong side of the divider . . . Sir, we think it would be best if you didn't look at the body . . . He'd never seen her again, he knew Shelly still missed her and wished Cody could have known her . . . sweet Laura. *Keep it up, Piper, and you're going to lose it in front of the dragon lady!* He cleared his throat. "I had a hard day, kid," Rick grunted. "I need another hug."

Cody obliged.

What if you take him to Santo Verde and he sees them too?

"Dad-dy!"

"Huh?" Rick plastered a smile on his face and focused on his son. *Get a grip! There's nothing to see!*

"Lookit what Marlene gave me." Cody dangled a pair of fuzzy pink dice in front of his eyes. "We went to Carnival Town today and played the racehorse game and Marlene won and she gave them to me. Wanna bet, Daddy? Double or nothing?"

Rick cringed. "Not today, buddy." Carnival Town had a kiddieland above the casino with live circus acts, which were fine, and carnival games that somehow seemed harmless at a county fair but like a gamblers' training center inside the casino. He glanced at Marlene Poom, who smiled at him as she lit a fresh cigarette off the old one. "Uh, Marlene, I'd really prefer that you don't take Cody into the casinos."

"Oh, don't be such an old poop," she scolded. "You've been there, I'm sure. It's not like we're playing poker or anything. It's very wholesome."

He snorted. "Wholesome isn't the word I would have used."

Marlene just shook her head and gave him a pitying smile. He had been to Carnival Town plenty of times during his college days, and the place was sleazy, all the more so because of the cotton-candy atmosphere it traded on. Not long ago, he'd run across a photo of himself and Craig Costello, the strangest friend he'd ever had, fondling one of the breast cream cones that adorned the walls. The gigantic plastic cones were filled with fleshy pink plastic ice cream, each scoop swirled into a half dozen voluptuously feminine mounds, every one tipped with a red nipplelike gumdrop.

"Well, Mr. Piper," Marlene commented between drags, you look pleased with yourself. Just what are you thinking about?"

"Nothing. Just a little indigestion." He scooped Cody into his arms and crossed to the door, holding his breath against another exhalation of smoke. "We'll see you Monday, Mrs. Poom."

"Marlene, honey. Marlene." She held the door. "My goodness, when you call me 'Missus' it makes me feel like I'm fifty years old!"

Since she was at least sixty, Rick thought as they headed for the elevator, she ought to be happy.

"Daddy, what are we gonna do now?"

"We're going to find your sister, and she's going to help you take a bath while I make dinner," Rick said, stepping into the elevator.

"Why do I always have to take a bath when you get home?" Cody squirmed out of his arms. "I never used to have to."

"You never used to spend all day with Mrs. Poom. Her cigarettes make you smell bad."

"And they're bad for me, too. They eat my lungs. A man on TV said so."

"I know, buddy. I know." They exited at their floor, and Rick almost asked Cody what he'd think of living in California in a real town, a real house, with real flowers and trees.

What if he sees them? He stopped the thought. Stupid childhood fantasies. *Grow up, Piper! You were a psycho child!* "Where do you think your big sister is?" he asked.

"Lemme down." The boy squirmed to the floor and ran down the hall, coming to a stop in front of their neighbors' apartment. *"Shelly!"* he screeched, and began pounding furiously on the door.

Two apartments down, Don Mancuso opened his door and glared suspiciously out at them. Rick smiled and shrugged as he hissed at Cody to be quiet. Mancuso's frog face disappeared an instant before Lil Magill opened her door.

"Cody! Cody Piper! What're y'all doin' here?" She grabbed the boy and hugged him, muffling his delighted laugh between her breasts. "And there's yore cute li'l ol' daddy! Come on in, Ricky. Bet y'all are lookin' for Shelly. Well, she's on back there." She flicked her shiny red nails vaguely toward the bedroom. Garth Brooks wailed faintly through the closed door.

"Thank God," Rick said. At least she wasn't out roaming around with that pack of overripe future beauticians she called her friends.

"Y'all want me to call her or you wanna be sociable and come in for a few?" Lil asked.

As long as they weren't fighting, Dakota and Lil's antics almost always took care of his headaches. "I'll be sociable," he told her with a grin.

"Good." Lil Magill, all six feet two inches of her, stepped back to let him enter the apartment. A Moonbeam Nights dancer, she had an Amazonian body and copper hair—its color as fake as her Georgia peach accent—piled up to add another three inches to her height. Rick enjoyed her as long as she wasn't trying to seduce him. Lil could have virtually any man she wanted, but when the mood struck—generally after a couple drinks and the Sunday afternoon airing of "Consumer Crusader"—she wanted him.

It wasn't Sunday, but she reeked of alcohol, and Rick carefully kept his gaze above her breasts as he passed her. Whenever she wanted to embarrass him, she'd point out that they were just "kissing level" to his mouth.

"Hiya, Piper!" Dakota O'Keefe, Lil's roommate and Rick's best friend, strutted out of the kitchen, dressed in an apron, bra, and Jockey shorts. He held a potato peeler in one hand, and a drink in the other. Dakota, formerly Duane, worked for the Chambre du les Femmes show, and when he had his makeup on—he specialized in Marilyn and Madonna—he was as stunning as Lil, which shot the hell out of Rick's theory that show girls were all cloned on a ranch out in the desert somewhere, probably near a nuclear testing site.

"Here's your scotch, Lil. Last call. Remember, you have to go to work." He looked Rick up and down appraisingly. "Nice suit. It's a Blass, isn't it?"

"Uh, I don't know. Could be."

"Piper, dear, you're a TV star and you look—mmmmm." Dakota smacked his lips, doing the sweet transvestite from *The Rocky Horror Picture Show.* "You look good enough to . . . You look so good in your clothes, dear, you really ought to know who you're wearing," he finished, tousling Cody's hair.

"Thanks." Rick suppressed a smile. "So is my daughter making a pest of herself?"

"Nah. She's tryin' on clothes." Lil scooped Cody into her arms. "What else you think a teenage gal's gonna do?" Cody laughed gleefully as she rubbed noses with him. "You gotta let me help her pick out some new stuff, Ricky. She's got a real nice figure, an' she oughta be showin' it off."

"Magill! For Christ's sake, a father doesn't want his daughter showing off her figure!" Dakota frowned. "Honestly, Piper, all Lil thinks about is her body!"

"And *you* don't, Dakota?" Lil laughed. " 'I do think mah breasts are bigger than yours! I got more feminine hormones than you do, Magill. And ain't mah skin so soft and purty? Bet you all wish you had skin's nice as mine.' Jumpin' Jesus,

Dakota! Except for that big old dick of yours, you ain't nothin' but the vainest—"

"Magill, don't say 'dick' in front of Cody," Dakota admonished. "It's not nice!"

Clutching the squirming boy to her bosom, Lil shook her head. "Ah won't say 'dick' if you'll quit callin' everyone by their last names. God, I hate that, don't you hate that, Ricky?" She didn't wait for a reply. "Lord, ah'm gonna be late for work." She placed Cody in Rick's arms, then turned and planted a big kiss on Dakota's lips. "See you later, sweetie. You keep your hands off Ricky, ya hear?" She snatched her bag and keys from a hook by the door and exited in a flurry of perfume and hairspray.

"I'm sorry, Rick," Dakota said, locking the door. "Lil wouldn't watch her language in front of the pope." He crossed his arms, staring at the door. "I think it's about time for her annual vacation at Betty Ford," he added, embarrassed.

"Don't worry about it." Rick felt sorry for Dakota, who spent much of his time apologizing for his roommate's frequent scenes. He glanced toward the bedroom. Country music always gave him an inexplicable urge to throw his head back and howl like a coyote. "I'd better get Shelly."

"I'm hungry," Cody said.

"Look, why don't you stay for dinner? There's plenty." He glanced toward the door. "Lil wasn't supposed to work tonight, but one of the other gals called in sick."

"I wanna stay," Cody said, wiggling from Rick's grasp. "Can we, Daddy?"

"Please," Dakota said. "You'd be doing me a favor."

"Well . . ."

Dakota smiled. "You know you can't say no to me, Piper."

Certain the invitation was sincere, Rick grinned. "Sure. What's cookin', good-lookin'?"

"Coq au vin." Dakota, queen of the double entendre, cracked no smile.

"Sounds great."

Dakota nodded. "I hope so. Piper, we need to have a chat. Cody, you want to watch TV while your daddy and I get dinner ready?"

"Yeah!"

"Okay. You can go turn it on. You know how, right?"

"Yeah!" Cody ran across the room, grabbed the remote control, and plunked himself down on the floor in front of the set. An instant later, Roadrunner and Wile E. Coyote were vying with Garth Brooks for aural dominance. Somehow, Rick thought, that seemed appropriate.

The bedroom door opened and the singer drowned the cartoons.

"Turn that down, Shelly!" Dakota immediately yelled.

The sound went down, fractionally, then Shelly strutted out of the bedroom wearing one of Lil's gowns, a strappy, spangled, peach-colored piece of spandex that revealed enough skin to keep Cher happy. She'd piled her long golden hair high on her head and sprayed it with blue glitter that matched the eye shadow coating her lids. In one hand she held a mirror so she could admire herself, and she used the other to hike up the skirt. Except for the length, the gown appeared to fit perfectly. It made her look twenty-five or maybe even thirty-five years old. Obviously, Rick thought as his stomach turned to lead, she'd stuffed the bodice. Overstuffed it.

"Lil! What do you think?" Shelly asked, undulating closer, her eyes on the mirror.

Oh, God, maybe she hadn't stuffed the bodice, Rick thought as she neared. *My daughter looks like a stripper.* The lead sank deeper.

Dakota glanced at Rick, then cleared his throat. "Lil's not here, hon."

"Doesn't this look great, Dakota?" she chirped, never looking up from the mirror. "This dress makes my boobs look absolutely like double Ds! I'm going to go to Victoria's Secret tomorrow and buy a push-up bra. Man, it'll drive Starman nuts, and I bet I could get a really *good* job in a casino."

"Oh, my God." *Did I say that?* Rick thought he might have.

"Daddy!" Shelly screamed. "How *could* you!" Crossing her arms over her breasts, she turned and ran back into the bedroom, slamming the door behind her.

"How could I what?" Rick asked slowly. He felt like he'd been punched in the gut.

"Come on in the kitchen, Dad," Dakota said, pushing him ahead. "Time to talk."

"Who's Starman?"

"The rim job she's got a crush on. Sit." Dakota pointed at the dinette set in the corner of the small, neat room. Numb, Rick did as he was told.

"I've got to get these potatoes going before my coq gets too soft," Dakota informed him in his best breathy contralto.

O'Keefe smiled, and Rick realized he was trying to lighten things up, but it wasn't going to work, because his shock was transmogrifying into anger. "Did you *see* her?" he asked, trying hard to keep his voice steady.

"I saw her. Don't get too upset about the clothes, Rick. She's just doing what comes naturally."

Not trusting himself to speak, Rick stared dully at Dakota, at the apron declaring him to be a "Hot Dish."

"She's playing dress-up, Piper. All little girls like to play dress-up." He smirked. "So do some little boys."

"She's not little. She was falling out of that dress."

"Filling up, not falling out Look, Piper, big or little, we all like to try on clothes, so quit worrying about that. You've got bigger fish to fry."

"Starman?"

"Don't let the name fool you. He's just a bellboy at Bally's. I took a look. Not a brain in his head, just a penis on legs. Wants to be a rock 'n' roll star."

"That's supposed to make me feel better?" Rick closed his eyes. "Are they having sex?"

"I don't know."

"She's only sixteen."

"Oh, grow up. And open your eyes, Piper; you're giving

me the creeps. How old were you when you had sex for the first time?"

"That's different."

"Bullshit. How old were you?"

Rick resisted the urge to close his eyes again. "Fourteen . . . But I was a boy."

"So who'd you have it with, another fourteen-year-old boy? Or the family sheep, maybe?"

"Dakota—"

"You had it with a fourteen-year-old girl, right, Piper?" He chuckled obscenely. "Or maybe a thirteen-year-old girl, you cradle robber, you."

"If you want the truth, it was a seventeen-year-old girl."

"Whoa, Ricky!" Dakota poked him in the arm. "You seduced an older woman! I'm impressed."

"Well, no . . . She, ah, seduced me."

"I'm even more impressed." Dakota put two fingers under Rick's chin and forced him to look him in the eye. "The only thing you're worried about here is that your sixteen-year-old daughter might be having sex. Why? Because you did and because you know how guys think. But there's more to your problem with Shelly, and now that you've told me about your experience with the older girl, I think you know exactly what it is."

"I don't know what the hell you're talking about, O'Keefe."

Dakota snatched his fingers back and crossed his arms, studying Rick. "Yes, you do." He tapped his foot impatiently. "Your real problem is that Shelly is a lot like that seventeen-year-old who seduced you. She knows what she wants and she takes it."

He thought about that a moment, then nodded slowly. "You're right." He felt like giving up as he spoke the words. "You're absolutely right. Dakota, I can't control her anymore. She's too young, she's going to get into trouble. I wish I understood her as well as you do."

"You have all the answers, Piper, but you're too close. You can't see them for looking."

The kitchen door flew open and Shelly, dressed in jeans and a tight yellow tank top, glared at them. "I'm going out. I have a date."

Rick started to rise. "It's a school night. You can't—"

"A study date, Dad," she said in disgust. "At the library. I'll be home around eleven."

"Shelly—"

But she was gone before he could say more.

"Rick . . ."

Rick stared at the backs of his hands, his emotions furious and futile. "There must be some way to control her."

"Don't try to control her; you'll just make it worse. Try to guide her, without her knowing it. If you try to do the old laying-down-the-law routine, she'll go dead opposite. She's strong-willed as hell. Smart, too. She's feeling her oats right now." Dakota shook his head. "That's what I wanted to talk to you about. It's not boys or clothes you have to worry about. It's Shelly herself. She's too impatient for her own good. She wants it all—money, glamour, power. And you're right. She *is* going to get into trouble. I'm afraid Lil isn't helping much, either."

"What do you mean?"

"Oh, she's been introducing her to people, trying to help her get a job."

"In a casino," Rick said darkly.

"Not exactly. Shelly can't work in a casino. She can't be on the floor where drinks are served; you know that. The FBI checks for age of majority. Lil's trying to help her get a job in a show. She believes she's doing her a big favor. I've tried to stop her, but . . ." Dakota shrugged. "Lil's pretty strong-willed herself. She means well."

"Oh, shit. The stage. This is supposed to make me feel better?"

"Hell no, Piper. I just thought you should know what's going on."

"Oh, shit," Rick repeated. "This all ties in with something I wanted to talk to you about."

"What's that?"

"I'm considering getting out of Vegas," Rick began.

Dakota raised his eyebrows. "Really? What about your show?"

"KBUK wants me to renew—an extended contract—but I've been thinking that it would be good for the kids to live in a real house in a real world. I knew Shelly had an attitude, but I didn't realize how bad it's become. Her performance tonight pretty much made my decision for me."

"You're thinking of buying a house in the 'burbs?" Dakota sounded pleased. "Make sure you get one with a pool."

"Actually, I'm thinking of moving back to Southern California. Back to Santo Verde."

"Santo who?"

"Santo Verde. It's the town where I grew up."

The greenjacks'll getcha if you don't watch out!

"Get over here and help me with the potatoes." Dakota crooked his finger at Rick, then turned and walked to the sink. "I'll peel, you slice." He handed him the knife, then tossed a peeled potato his way. "Santo Verde, huh? As a recovering Cathaholic, I find the name fascinating. I wonder which saint it refers to. The Green Saint. Saint Patrick?"

"No, it refers to . . ." Rick paused, his stomach twisting into an old, familiar knot.

"Spit it out, Piper."

Greenjacks, Big Jack, they're gonna get you!

"Something more . . . primitive."

Dakota raised his eyebrows and waited.

"My great-great-grandfather founded the town, and the name has to do with an old family legend. Santo Verde is named for a nature god that some of the Piper clan can supposedly see."

"I love it," Dakota said, starting another potato. "Are you talking about Pan?"

Rick considered. "Something similar to Pan and his satyrs, yes. The Pipers called them greenjacks."

"That's *so* romantic, Piper." Dakota paused. "Your family's from Scotland, correct?"

"Yeah."

"So why Santo Verde? Why not McPan or McJack or something?"

Rick chuckled, despite himself. "Conlin Piper used the Spanish words because he had moved to the Southwest and because he loved Mexico. He thought it was more appropriate." Rick laughed again. "Actually, 'Santo' is Italian, but he wasn't too far off."

Dakota nodded. "So what exactly is a greenjack? Does it have hooves and horns?"

This is your chance to talk about this stuff like an adult, Piper. Don't blow it! "Nothing like that," Rick said lightly. "They're more like trolls or fairies, They aren't material, except on Halloween night, when they get together and build *the* Big Jack. They build it out of twigs and branches and leaves, and Big Jack can grab you and take you away until midnight, November first." He smiled nonchalantly, hoping Dakota wouldn't notice that his hands were trembling. "At least that's how Grandfather always told the tale."

"I guess it's true what they say about you Scotsmen being mystical," Dakota told him. "That's a marvelous story. I guess Big Jack's a lot like the Green Man in England."

Rick rooked at him in surprise. "Yeah."

"I remember him, then."

"You do?" he asked, the skin on the back of his neck prickling up.

"When I was little we went to the Met in Central Park all the time, and I'd spend hours looking at those English hunt tapestries, you know? I loved them because they were puzzles. If you looked hard enough, you'd see the Green Man somewhere in the art. He was hard to spot because he always had leaves growing out of his mouth and he'd be peeking out from between the trees." Dakota laughed. "I guess it was the medieval version of *Where's Waldo?*"

Icky Ricky, come out and play, hey, play.

Rick shivered as the familiar voice played through his mind.

"Piper, what's wrong?"

"We're digging up old memories, O'Keefe. Ones I'd just as soon leave buried."

"For Christ's sake, Rick, don't tell me you were afraid of the Green Man?" Dakota looked incredulous. "He was into sex and orgies and all the finer things in life."

"I was terrified," he confessed. "I grew up on a steady diet of those stories, and the ones my grandfather told weren't about sex, they were about stealing the bodies of little boys. I took them very seriously." He tried to laugh but it was a sick sound. "I was an overly sensitive child."

Your body, Ricky, give us your body . . .

"Body theft," Dakota mused. "Every time my aunt Irene visited us—she was from Ireland—she told stories about the fairies and leprechauns. They'd take a human child and leave one of their own in its place. There was a name for it—"

"A changeling," Rick supplied, glad that Dakota knew so much. It was just too juvenile and ridiculous to explain in detail.

"Yeah, that's it," Dakota agreed. "Maybe you can answer a question for me, Piper."

"I'll try."

"What I always wondered when Irene told those stories was *why*. *Why* would these incredibly nifty beings want anything to do with humans when they were so free the way they were? That just never made any sense to me."

Rick smiled wanly. "Without physical bodies, they can't feel or taste or smell—"

"Or have orgasms?" Dakota smirked.

"Or have orgasms," Rick agreed. "They want sensation, like we have. The grass is always greener, you know?"

"Okay. Go on."

"I don't know about all the other tales, but in the Piper clan stories, anyone's body would do in a pinch, but what the greenjacks really wanted was the body of a person who had the sight. The ability to see and hear them."

"Why?"

"Grandfather claimed it was because they got very lonely if they couldn't communicate with their own kind."

"That makes sense," Dakota said. "So, Piper, did you ever see any of the little devils?"

Rick's cheeks grew hot. "I—I thought I did," he stammered. "But I had an overactive imagination when I was a kid."

"You don't sound like you're very eager to move back to the old hometown. Why not go somewhere else? Or do you have family there or something?"

"A senile aunt, but she's not the reason for going back. I own the family estate."

"Estate? You're rich? Piper, you devil, you never told me—"

"I'm not rich. The family money that my parents left for maintaining the place is about gone. It's more a matter of cutting expenses, if you want the truth. The place is an estate more because of the size of the property than because of the house. It's big, but . . ."

"So sell it."

"I've thought about it, but with the market so soft, if it sold at all, it wouldn't draw anywhere near what it's worth."

"So where's Santo Verde?" O'Keefe asked, evidently oblivious to the tremble Rick heard in his own voice.

"It's in San Bernardino County, maybe fifty or sixty miles east of Los Angeles."

"Nightlife?"

"Not that I know of."

"Sounds boring."

"It's a little bourgeois, but it's nice." He paused. "Well, the Piper house isn't bourgeois. It's decidedly weird. Conlin built what he liked, so it's sort of part Carpenter Gothic and part Spanish hacienda. It has Victorian cabinetry and Spanish wrought iron. Some of the doors are arched, some are square. There're even a couple stained-glass windows." He chuckled. "Calling it 'eclectic' wouldn't begin to describe it. Oh, yeah, it's full of secret passages."

"I *have* to see this place."

"If I pack up and go, you're more than welcome," Rick told him. "Its only about four hours from here, but it's very different. It's citrus country, nestled in right up against the mountains. In the thirties and forties a lot of the movie stars used to live out there. It's scenic. *Very* scenic." His stomach twisted as he heard himself add, "It's the greenest place you'll ever see."

"Dakota?" The door opened and Cody peered in. "Is dinner almost ready?"

"Another half hour. Why don't you take a banana and watch another cartoon show?"

"Okay." The boy reached up and took a piece of fruit, then disappeared back into the living room.

Dakota turned back to Rick. "So this house you own is the same one that you grew up in?"

"The very same."

"So how come you've never mentioned it before?"

"There are some bad memories . . ."

The greenjacks'll getcha if you don't watch out.

"How do you mean, 'bad'?"

"Oh, you know, goofy stuff mostly. Kid stuff." *Boy, does that sound stupid!* His hand trembled as he sliced a potato.

"Goofy? Kid stuff'?" Dakota stopped peeling to stare at him. "Come on, Rick. You think I can't see that this 'goofy kid stuff' is eating you up? It's why you've never gone back, isn't it?"

Rick said nothing.

"No more bullshit, Piper, dear. What's the real story?"

"There's nothing else, Dakota, really. The place is a little run-down," he added quickly. "At least that's what my lawyer says, but it's solid. It's in the best part of town, and the schools are excellent, but . . ."

Ricky, icky Ricky, Ricky, icky Ricky.

"If it's so great, then what the hell are you raising kids in this hellhole for? Gambling, drinking, drugs, hookers . . . *Mormons,* for Christ's sake . . ."

Icky Ricky, I'm gonna getcha, Icky Ricky.

"Rick! Watch out!"

Startled, Rick jumped, dropping the knife. It clattered into the sink.

"Jesus Christ, Piper! Let me see that."

Rick recoiled as Dakota's water-cold hand grabbed his left wrist.

The potatoes he'd sliced into the colander were turning red. He watched bright blood splash into the white sink as Dakota pulled Rick's arm toward him.

"You're bleeding like a sieve." O'Keefe pulled a wad of paper towels from the holder and wrapped them around Rick's fingers. "Jesus, I can't even see which finger you cut. Piper, you're as white as a baby's butt. Are you okay?"

"Not one of my smoother moves," Rick said as he took charge of his hand, pressing on the towels to stop the bleeding. It was starting to hurt.

"Are you okay?" Dakota repeated.

"Fine. Got any Band-Aids?"

"Just a sec. Let me rinse the blood off these potatoes before it soaks in or something. What Cody doesn't know won't hurt him. Keep hanging on to those towels."

Rick almost smiled. Dakota was nothing if not practical. He loosened the pressure, but the artery was still pumping. He tightened up again, feeling a little dizzy.

"You're shocky. Sit down," Dakota ordered as he left the room. A moment later, he was back with a box of adhesive bandages and a bottle of iodine.

Carefully Rick unwrapped the hand, and everything south of his abdomen tried to climb to visceral safety as the pad of his middle finger, nearly severed, started to come away with the towels. Gingerly he loosened it and let it fall back over the wound.

"You need stitches," Dakota said.

"No, I don't," Rick answered.

"If that finger was your throat, you'd be dead."

Rick snorted. "Don't be so dramatic, O'Keefe. It's not my throat."

"Well, it's gaping. What are you planning to do? Staple it shut?"

"That's a thought," he said, trying to ignore the throbbing. "But let's try a Band-Aid first."

"You need stitches. The fucking thing is positively grinning at me."

"It's cut on the bias," Rick said, keeping his voice light. "All I need to do is tape it down. It'll glue naturally." It was everything he could do to control his trembling. "The Band-Aid, please?"

"Suit yourself." Dakota shrugged and unwrapped several bandages. Wearing a disgusted expression, he handed over one, then another, his lip curling as he watched Rick tape his flesh back together.

"I can't believe you did that yourself," he said as Rick finished. "I'd pass out. Shit. You forgot the iodine. We'd better—"

"No. I don't need it. I bled out all the impurities."

"What? Have you got a death wish? If it gets infected—"

"I don't get infections," Rick said lightly. "I have the constitution of an entire bottle of antibiotics."

"Piper, you are acting extremely weird. What are you, afraid of doctors?"

Quit'cher fuckin' cryin' boy, and take your whippin' like a man! a new voice screamed in his ear. Dear God, how could he have forgotten about Uncle Howard? His head spun as he wondered what else he'd forgotten.

"Piper, you need stitches, so quit your macho man act!" Dakota stood up. "Come on. I'll get Cody and we'll run down to the emergency room—"

"Lay off, already!" Rick barked. "I cut my fucking finger, big fucking deal. I'll live."

His harsh words made Dakota flinch as if he'd been slapped. Instantly Rick felt terrible.

"Sorry," Rick muttered. "I didn't mean—"

"Mellow out, Rick," Dakota interrupted. "I've never even heard you say 'fuck' before, and now you say it twice in one breath. Just a wild guess, hon, but I'd say something's wrong."

Get out of my face! he wanted to scream. Instead, he spoke casually. "Nothing's wrong. It was just a stupid accident." God, it hurt so bad, he could hardly stop clenching his teeth to talk. The only thing worse than the pain was the humiliation.

"If I cut myself like that, I'd be squalling so bad, my face would be puffy for a week, and I'd be getting stitches and pain pills. Look at you, pretending it doesn't even hurt."

Rick said nothing. It took every ounce of control not to scream at Dakota to shut the hell up or to humiliate himself by admitting it hurt.

Crybaby, titty mouse, Ricky got a whipping! I'm gonna tell Uncle Howard, and then you'll get another! Crybaby, titty mouse.

"Rick!"

"What?"

"Here! Take these!"

Dakota stood in front of him holding aspirin tablets and a glass of water. Rick hadn't even realized he'd moved.

"Thanks."

"You're welcome." Dakota went back across the room and took a bottle of wine and two glasses from a shelf. "Merlot, Cypress. A ninety-nine. I hid it from Lil. She wouldn't appreciate it." He uncorked the bottle and poured, handed a glass to Rick.

"Thanks again."

"Welcome again. So what's eating you? When you cut yourself we were talking about Santo Verde. You said you have bad memories. They must be doozies."

If you tell, they'll take you away, away, the little men in their white coats will come and take you away, away, away.

Old memories, presumed dead, old voices, *his* voice, came alive in his head. "No, not especially, but I hadn't thought about all those stories my grandfather used to tell in years." Rick sipped the wine, then downed half the glass at once. "Going back to Santo Verde is sort of like going to the dentist to get a bad tooth pulled. You don't want to do it, so you put it off, hoping it'll get better. Maybe it seems like it does, sometimes, but it only gets worse and worse until you take care of it, once and for all. Refill, please?"

"You're intriguing the hell out of me, you mysterious

man." Dakota refilled Rick's glass, then topped off his own. He sniffed the wine. "It has a good kick, not to mention the nice bouquet. And the afterbirth is purely delightful." Suddenly he nailed Rick with a look. "So what was your grandfather, a sadist?"

Rick laughed, his stomach already warm. "No, he was great. He was sort of stuffy like the professor in 'The Paper Chase,' but he was full of the devil, too. My problem was that I was overly impressionable and ridiculously sensitive. My brother wasn't and, oh, I don't know . . ." Rick swallowed hard. *My brother.* He'd said it aloud.

"I didn't know you had a brother."

"His name was Robin." Rick had never told anyone even this much about his past, but suddenly, almost against his will, it came bubbling out. "I was an easy target for Robin. He was . . . precocious and spent a lot of time feeding my fears, telling me that the jacks would steal my body while I was asleep, things like that. He liked to tease."

"He sounds cruel."

"Little kids are always cruel." He drained another half glass in one fell swoop; then laughed uneasily. He paused while Dakota crossed the room, stirred the potatoes, then withdrew a fresh bottle of wine from the back of the cupboard and opened it. "Want to smell my cork?" he asked as he returned to the table.

Rick smiled and waited for his refill. He already felt a little smashed, a little better.

"Tell me more." Dakota's gaze was frank. "Did you hate your brother?"

"Christ, O'Keefe. What kind of question is that? How could I hate my own brother?" The wine went down like water. "I sure got pissed at him. One Halloween Robin pulled this joke on me. He made me think the greenjacks had taken him."

"How do you mean, 'taken him'?"

"He pretended to have a new personality—like a jack had possessed his body. And I, idiot that I was, believed it and thought I was next. Isn't that stupid?"

"It's not stupid," Dakota said. "Could your brother see these things?"

"No." He finished another glass and swallowed hard. "But I thought I could," he confessed. "I was the only psycho."

"Don't get maudlin on me, Piper. It's a waste of good wine. So are you still afraid? Is that why you haven't gone back?"

If you tell, they'll lock you up and throw away the key.

"Oh, maybe a little." Rick smiled to imply that he was joking. His whole body was warm now, and the finger had stopped hurting. "It's a lot more than that. My parents died, and the Wicked Witch of the West and her alcoholic husband came to take care of us. I guess I mixed the greenjack stuff into everything else that happened, and it's all left a bad taste in my mouth."

"Both your parents died?"

Rick nodded.

"An accident?"

"Shit, you're nosy, you know that?"

O'Keefe smiled smugly. "Sorry. If you don't want—"

"They were murdered."

"God, I'm sorry. I didn't realize—"

"It's okay. You couldn't know."

"What about your brother? Do you two get along now?"

"He died, too. An accident." Rick realized he'd hit another hole in his memory. "Anyway, not too long after that, I moved here and enrolled in UNLV. I've never gone back."

"I'll bet you felt guilty as hell for hating your brother, then having him die and all."

"I told you, I didn't hate him."

"Of course you did. Maybe you loved him, too, or maybe you didn't, but you *had* to hate him for scaring you. I would've hated him. It's perfectly natural."

If he hadn't been drunk, Rick would have been furious over Dakota's words, but the wine allowed him to see their truth. "Dakota, you're either horrible or wonderful, I can't decide which. How can you be so fucking blunt about things like that?"

"I almost succeeded in killing myself once. After that, it was either finish the job or face my problems head-on. I couldn't live with the lies anymore. It hurt too much." Dakota patted Rick's uninjured hand affectionately. "You're developing quite a gutter mouth, Piper. I'm proud of you. Now, tell me about your brother. I take it he was older than you?"

"No." He paused. "Well, strictly speaking, yes. By five minutes. Robin was my identical twin. Well, almost identical."

"Different personalities, obviously."

Rick nodded. "Also, Robin was handicapped. He was born without legs."

"My God, you must have been terrified before your kids were born!"

"No, it wasn't inherited. It was a fluke, a condition called Streeter's dysplasia, where part of the fetus gets cut off from—"

"That's enough," Dakota interrupted, "If you say more, I'm going to toss my cookies."

"Sorry. The point is, I think that my having legs may have made him a little antagonistic toward me." He was mortified to hear himself let loose with a stupid drunken giggle.

"Piper, dear, you have a gift for understatement. He probably *hated* your guts because you had the utter audacity to have legs." He paused. *"I* would have."

Infinitesimally, the weight in his chest lifted. "You *really* think so?"

"Shit, Piper, you think you're the only person capable of petty thoughts? Hell no. Wanting something someone else has is how wars are started. Of course he hated you. I hated my big sister because she had breasts." He ran his hand over his torso and grinned. "I'm over it now, of course, because mine are bigger than hers."

"You hated your sister because she had breasts?" Now, *this* was interesting. "Honest to God?"

"Yeah, I really did. I was horribly jealous because she had what I wanted—a female body. I didn't really understand it at the time. It took a couple years with a good therapist before I got what was going on. Piper, that's what you ought to do. See a therapist. I know a great one in California. He moved there a couple years ago. I can give you his number"

They'll lock you up and throw away the key key key.

"Thanks. I'll get the name if I think I need it."

Dakota nodded. "Do you know where Sylvan Heights is?"

Rick looked up, surprised. "Yeah. It's not far from Santo Verde, but I don't care how close this guy is, I'm not interested in—"

"No, no, no. I didn't know exactly where it was. My sister just moved there."

"The one with the breasts?"

"Watch it, Piper. She might be able to help you."

Rick made a face. "I don't need any help."

"She's an optometrist." Dakota wiped his lips and cocked his head. "I was just thinking—maybe you did see something weird when you were a kid. You ever get your eyes examined?"

"Two months ago. Healthy, normal, twenty-twenty."

"Still, if you told her about it, she might be able to tell you something."

"Dakota, if you tell her—or anybody—one word of this, I'll—"

"Your secret's safe with me. You won't have any trouble, anyway," he added. "You've found an outlet for your imagination with those crazy columns of yours. You'll be fine—I guess I was just looking for an excuse to have you and Audrey meet."

"I don't—"

"She's just your type, Piper. Divorced, barely fills an A cup, five foot three, HIV negative, and disgustingly well read." Dakota grinned. "Want her number?"

"I haven't even decided to move for sure. Don't try to fix me up yet!"

Dakota topped their glasses. "You'd like her."

Rick snorted into his wine. "Jesus, O'Keefe, brothers are supposed to beat up guys who try to screw their sisters."

"Shit, Piper, I didn't say you could screw her. You know, you're becoming positively vulgar? I said you should meet her." Dakota set his glass down and examined his lacquered red nails, a Mona Lisa of a smirk plastered on his face. "I've done that."

"Done what?"

"Punched out a guy who messed with my sister. I pack quite a powerful left hook, you know."

Rick grinned in amazement. "An obnoxious boyfriend?"

"Her husband."

"Why?"

"He beat her up, the son of a bitch." He took a deep breath, then exhaled, relaxing until the pinched look left his features. "Look, enough about that cretinous puddle of scum. I've got to whip these potatoes before they turn to mush. I'm positively starving."

"You want any help?"

"Thanks, no." Pans clattered as Dakota fussed around the stove. "You know," he called, over his shoulder, "you'll probably have trouble with Shelly about this, but it'll work out eventually."

"O'Keefe?"

"Hmmm?" he asked, stirring gravy.

"That guy, Starman, that bellboy Shelly likes? You checked him out?" he asked guiltily. He hadn't even known the guy existed.

"Took a look, asked some questions. I was afraid he might have, you know, connections . . . to certain unsavory organizations. He doesn't." Dakota glanced over his shoulder. "You're feeling like you're the world's worst father, aren't you, Piper? Well, don't. Shelly's an adolescent, which automatically means she's not going to tell you squat. Sometimes she confides in me a little."

"Why you and not me?"

"Because you're her father. Piper, plug in your brain. You were a kid once What teenager tells their parents *anything?*"

Dakota smiled and put a hand on his hip. "She talks to me because I'm sort of a big brother to her . . . and big sister."

"You're right again." Rick stared at Dakota. He wore no makeup, but his face—its features strong in a woman, delicate in a man—were disturbingly beautiful, genderless in the way of the faces of angels in some Renaissance paintings. Rick thought: *Boy, am I drunk.*

"What're you smiling about, Piper?"

"Thanks for looking out for my daughter, Dakota. You're an angel."

"Thanks. You know, Cody's going to absolutely be in heaven if you do this."

"I hope so," Rick replied, thinking about his son's Piper blue eyes.

8

June 2

Rick's stomach held an ocean of aspirin, and he was feeling a little seasick. Between his efforts to ease the dull headache, relax his tense neck muscles, and kill the throbbing pain in his hand, he'd taken too many pills. Now, lying on his back at four in the morning, watching the lights from the Strip splash their gaudy reflections against the bedroom window, aware of the warm weight of the cat, who had plastered his furry orange body against his side, Rick reached for the antacids and tumbled out the last two. The bottle had been half-full when he'd gone to bed.

Quint's tail beat angrily against his leg as he crunched the Tums—the feline considered such noises beneath contempt but the thrashing gave way to basso profundo purring as soon as he began scratching behind its ears. The cat, he reflected, had trained him well.

A car alarm began wailing somewhere below. He listened briefly to make sure it wasn't his, then turned his thoughts to the evening and wondered again if it had been worth the physical discomfort he now felt. He decided that maybe it had, in a sort of roundabout, somewhat humiliating, way.

At some point during the long, blurred postdinner conversation, Dakota had called him a control freak. Rick had laughed to hide his annoyance, but now he admitted to himself that O'Keefe was right. He'd never opened up, even as much as he did tonight—but then he'd never gotten so drunk either, not even in college. He never let himself, for fear of . . . for fear of what? Losing control, of course. Tonight's reaction to the liquor had been decidedly weird. He wasn't a teetotaler; he'd split a couple bottles of wine with friends any number of times, and usually it just relaxed him a little and made him sleepy. But tonight . . . tonight, probably because of the stress and moronic finger slicing, he'd slobbered sentimental gratitude on Dakota and, as a result, wasn't sure he'd ever be able to look him in the eye again, despite the fact that Dakota insisted he'd done nothing to be ashamed of.

Voices, a man and a woman arguing, passed by, and a moment later, a door slammed farther down the hall. It was never quiet here. Rick wondered if he could sleep in a place without voices and horns and sirens. And lights. *Grow up, Piper.*

He smiled to himself, remembering that he'd told Dakota stories about Aunt Jade's poodles. He hadn't thought of them in years—in fact, he'd forgotten about them until the moment he'd brought them up.

Remembering the dogs had been an eye-opener for him. He'd never seen the humor in them before. If most of the things he'd blocked were as stupid and innocuous as that, then the move home would be a very good thing for him as well as for his kids.

Then again, maybe Dakota was full of shit. Still, it was the first time he'd ever told anyone about his brother. Too, he was glad he'd talked about the dogs. Later, he'd even made a few jokes about Jade's bizarre sexual proclivities, and he was perversely pleased with himself for making fun of a territory so long self-forbidden. The words had tumbled out, nasty little nuances seduced by a nice red wine. And he'd loved it, absolutely loved it, and only wished he'd done it sooner. The wicked delight he had felt—and was still feeling—was as exciting as an altar boy's first forbidden peek in a *Playboy*.

All in all, he couldn't remember when he'd had a better time, throbbing hand and all.

"What a miserable little kid I was," he told the cat as he scratched behind its ears. "I never laughed." God, he'd been a serious, oversensitive little—

Gonna cut your legs off icky Ricky.

"Be quiet!" he whispered. Acid, hot and burning, seeped into his throat. The unbidden words, as always, delivered in his brother's voice, were nothing but symptoms of his own oversensitivity. He knew that most kids would have laughed off the nasty things his brother said. Most kids—like his brother, for instance—would have delighted in his grandfather's greenjack stories, but not Rick. Sometimes he hated himself for being who he'd been: a cowardly, overly imaginative child who grew up afraid of everything and haunted by untrustworthy memories. Perhaps now, things would begin to change.

For all he knew now, Robin might have been a wonderful kid. Rick's memories of his childhood were deformed, his imagination twisted. If he could imagine seeing and hearing greenjacks, for Christ's sake, certainly he could imagine things about his brother that weren't true. But why? Maybe Dakota was right. Maybe he should talk to someone.

If you tell, they'll take you away, they'll think you're crazy, crazy, crazy.

The headache beat against his skull. What did he have to tell, anyway?

Secrets.

Telling O'Keefe about Jade was a joke when compared to the *real* secrets. There were things about Robin and about Carmen—perhaps even about himself—that were too terrible to ever recall. He hoped that seeing Carmen and Hector wouldn't bring any of them back—he doubted that it would. They were purposely buried far in the past.

Secrets.

About death. About murder.

Silent tears blazed trails from the outer corners of his eyes to the pillow beneath his head. How much was real? Any of it? All of it? How much was imagination born of guilt? Maybe Dakota was right, maybe he did hate his brother, even though he had no right to. *After all,* he reminded himself, *I was born with legs.*

If you tell, if you tell, if you tell . . .

His brother's voice, always his brother's voice. He wondered if he would ever be free of it.

No, he thought, as his eyelids grew heavy. *Because it's your voice too.*

9

"Ricky? Ricky, is that really you?" said the voice on the telephone.

"Yes, it's really me." Rick stood at his bedroom window or his office window, depending on the time of day—and squinted into the afternoon glare. After a moment, he turned the wand controlling the heavy vertical blinds and watched the slats of sunlight grow narrower and narrower. "It's been a long time, Carmen." This morning he'd told the boys at KBUK he was leaving the show, and now there was no backing out. He had a stomach full of butterflies as he sat down in his chair, leaned back, and put his feet on the desktop.

"Say something so I know it's you," Carmen ordered.

"What? Why?" Her request made him nervous. When Robin was alive, there had been good reason, but now . . .

"Please."

"Is something wrong?"

"No. No. Just tell me something only you could know."

"Okay." He smiled to himself as a memory came. "You and I shaved Jade's poodle after it crapped on the couch. You told her the vet did it because it had lice."

"Ricky, it's so good to hear your voice."

"Carmen, why did we have to do that?"

She hesitated before she answered. "I'm getting to be a

superstitious old woman, Ricky. I'm scared of ghosts, that's all. Mr. McCall told me you'd be phoning. How are you?"

"I'm fine." *She's afraid I'm Robin, back from the dead,* he realized. Had she always been so superstitious? Yes, maybe she had. Perhaps this woman, the only person he trusted after his parents were killed, had unwittingly helped him become the nervous wreck he was today. "I have kids," he added.

"Kids? More than one?"

She knew about Shelly. He'd sent her a Christmas card the year his daughter was born, but he was pretty sure that was the last time he'd been in contact with her. "I have a son, too. Cody. He's five."

"How is your wife, Laura?"

"She died four years ago."

"Oh, Ricky, I'm sorry."

"Me too," he said simply. "Carmen? Did George tell you why I'm calling?"

"Yes, Ricky. You're coming home. Hector and I are so happy!"

"I'm glad," he said uncomfortably. "Uh, Carmen, what's the situation with Jade? Is she as eccentric as ever?"

"Madre de Dios, that woman. She's still crazy, and she's still got those stinking little dogs."

As her poodles had died—they seemed to meet with more accidents than anything else on earth—she had had each one stuffed. By the time Rick had left for Las Vegas, there must have been more than a dozen of them holding their various eternal positions around the house. "Does she have a living one now?" Rick asked.

"Two," Carmen said sourly.

"That's too bad," he said, thinking that Quint would have a great time terrorizing the creatures.

"You're telling me." Carmen paused. "Miz Jade's getting a little senile, too. She's supposed to keep those damn stuffed dogs in her apartment, but I keep finding them all over the house. She claims she isn't responsible." She snorted. "She's never been responsible, that one. Butter wouldn't melt in her mouth, and she's crazy as a loon."

"Apartment?" Rick asked hopefully. "Do you mean she's living in the cottage now?"

"No. We still live there. Miz Jade doesn't climb the stairs so well anymore. Remember how the downstairs is built in a circle, you know, the kitchen, dining room, living room, and then you go through the wide archway into the family room, past the bathroom and laundry room, and back into the kitchen, right by the back stairs?"

"I remember."

"Hector put folding doors on the arch between the living room and family room, and another door between the bathroom and laundry room so that your aunt has her own apartment. Remember that little room at the back of the family room?"

"Mom's sewing room?"

"Yeah. That's her bedroom."

The idea of having that woman and her dogs so close was revolting. "Carmen, how would you and Hector like to live in the main house? We can put Jade in the cottage."

"No, Ricky. She'd have a fit, and I don't think I can live in that big house. I'm sorry."

"I understand," he told her, deciding not to pursue it any further until he saw what conditions were like for himself. Chances were, he'd have the horrid old woman put in a rest home. "Carmen? Can you do me a favor?"

"You name it, Ricky."

"If I can tell you exactly when we're arriving, could you make sure Aunt Jade isn't home? Keep her away for a few hours?"

Carmen's laugh was hearty. "Sure. Are you afraid she'll scare your children?"

He smiled. Carmen always knew him so well. "Cody can probably handle her," he said, thinking of his unflinching acceptance of Mrs. Poom, "but my daughter . . . well, I want her to see the place first. She's very unhappy about leaving her friends."

"I understand. I think that's a good idea."

They talked awhile longer, making plans and arrangements. Finally Carmen announced that she would take Jade to the Melrose District in L.A., let her get her hair done, then turn her loose in the Poodle Peddler, an overpriced purveyor of useless doggie products. All he had to do was give her the high sign.

Hanging up, Rick realized his butterflies were gone and that he honestly felt good about the plans he was making. He'd thought about it for a week after the binge with Dakota, then called George McCall and told Cody and Shelly. Shelly had a temper tantrum and threatened to run away, but fortunately she ran in Dakota's direction, and he extolled the virtues of California boys, or something along those lines. At least that had turned her from teenage histrionics to accusatory glares and calm, sullen acceptance.

He'd leave the childhood fears behind and concentrate on learning to be a homeowner. His only problems would be those of the real world. He'd get a couple years worth of columns out of it, on everything from putty knives to paint to lawn sprinklers. And if Jade was too weird, he could afford to put her in a retirement home, or even rent her a small house and caretaker. He leaned back in the desk chair and put his feet up. Twining his fingers into a pillow for his head, he felt that he'd done the right thing.

He just wished the goose bumps would go away.

10

"No! I won't have it!" A queen on her throne, Jade Ewebean stomped her foot so hard that the two white poodles at her feet yelped and shook in doggy terror. "If he thinks he can just move in here like he owns the place, then he's very mistaken. This is *my* house. *I* live here!" She looked down, saw the poodles watching her, and instantly her expression metamorphosed from beetle-browed fury to sappy adoration.

She patted her lap. "Come here, my widdle wuvems. Come here, Mister Poo; you, too, Stinkums." The poodles danced on their hind legs, each pawing at one knee. "Oh, what sweet wittle poodley-pies." The dogs went nuts with joy as she scooped them into her bony lap. "Is you my babies? Is you? Oh yes, you is! Kiss mama now! Kiss mama!"

Eagerly they licked their mistress's withered, rouge-stained cheeks while Jade giggled and cooed like the nasty old lady that she was. Carmen Zapata felt the urge to puke as she watched the disgusting display.

She disliked the dogs almost as much as she despised Jade Ewebean herself. It had been bad enough back when Jade had kept only one dog, but for the last two decades, it had been double the puddles, double the crap, and double the whining and yapping. In a way, Carmen didn't blame her: The animals died so regularly that the old *puta* almost needed a spare.

Dios Mio, but she hated coming into Jade's quarters. It smelled of moldy poodle fur and old-lady sweat, and it made Carmen sick to see all those horrible dead dogs. All of them were some shade of white, ranging from ancient yellow to moth-eaten gray. One, its fur slowly tearing away in hideous clumps, reclined on top of the old Zenith TV, its glass eyes catching and reflecting the light cast by the lamp on the table by Jade's padded rocking chair. Carmen didn't remember its name any more than she remembered the names of two dozen other dead dogs that filled the apartment, but Jade knew all of them. Carmen suspected she identified them by the "lifelike" poses the taxidermist had tortured them into for all eternity. It was a sin against God.

The woman went through more poodles than ever should have been allowed into the world to begin with. They all died in strange accidents, and Carmen held the secret belief that crazy old Jade did them in when the mood struck, then forgot all about it. The last death, a little less than six months ago, nearly proved it. The dog had peed all over Jade's bedspread only hours before Carmen had opened the dryer and found its stiff, dead body, along with half a roll of fabric softener sheets.

Horrified, she'd put the carcass in a garbage bag outside the back door, intending to have Hector dispose of it, but before long she saw Jade handing it over to the kid from Seymour Taxidermy. A month later, the creature reappeared, its leg in an eternal lift. When Jade was mad at her, Carmen would find it poised over the pair of slippers she kept by the back kitchen door. Normally, though, the old woman liked to have it stand over a bowl of dusty silk philodendrons she had in her bathroom.

Tired of listening to Jade's incessant baby talk, Carmen cleared her throat. "We have to talk about Ricky and his family," she said sternly.

"It's my house." She sniffed. "Richard wasn't nice to his aunt Jade, so he can't visit. You can tell him that for me."

"Listen, Mrs. Ewebean, this isn't your house. It belongs to Ricky. He's just been kind enough to let you live here, so if you want to stay, you better treat him nice. Otherwise *he'll* send *you* away." Saying those last words felt so good that Carmen had to bite her tongue to keep from listing off all the reasons Ricky might kick her out. "Do you understand what I'm saying?"

"Ooh, Mister Poo is kissing his mommy, yes he is!" She kissed the dog back, square on the muzzle, then put her nose against the other one's face. "Stinkums, Stinkums, Stinkums, that's your name, uh-huh, yes it is. And do you know why, Stinkum-winkum, do you know why? Because you used to poot so bad when you was just a wittle bitty boy. Cute wittle puppy poots, that was you."

Carmen crossed her arms, thoroughly sick of the senile old crone. *Why don't you die? Put me out of your misery!* "Jade Ewebean!"

That got the *puta*'s attention. Her nostrils flared and her watery green eyes flashed as she glared at Carmen, her hands stiff in the poodles' fur. "How dare you talk to me in that tone of voice!"

Carmen stepped forward until she was looming over Jade, her stare so fierce that the old bitch didn't say a word. "Now, you listen good, because I'm only gonna tell you this once more. This house is Ricky's. If you're not nice to him, he'll send you away, and I'll say good riddance."

"Well, I nev—"

"Be quiet." *Madre de Dios, help me. before I strangle her with my bare hands!* "Listen. He's gonna have his two kids with him. His teenage daughter is going to be sad about leaving her friends, and his little boy is gonna feel lost in this big old house. So you're gonna be just as nice to them as you are to Ricky." She paused, savoring the bomb she was about to drop. "And you're gonna be nice to his cat, too."

Jade's nose curled as if she were smelling something bad. "Cat?" She stood, sending squealing poodles tumbling to the floor. "Cat?" Her voice rose an octave.

Carmen smiled like the Madonna herself. "A nice cat," she said serenely. "Maybe it will catch some of the mice we got running around in the walls."

"He can't bring a cat in here. Who does he think he is?" Jade sputtered with anger, little flecks of foam at the sides of her mouth.

"He's your landlord, that's who he is, and if those nasty little dogs of yours chase that cat even once, you'll be very, *very* sorry." Placing her hands on her hips, she added, "I always protected Ricky from you, and now I'm gonna protect his whole family from you. And that includes his cat."

"He can't—"

"Yes he can. He can do whatever he wants, and you better give him some respect. You remember how you treated him? Always teasing him, always making fun of him? Punishing him for being afraid? You remember that, *Tia Puta?*" Carmen felt like she might be foaming a little herself. She'd held this back for years, and now it poured out like water. "You remember how mean you were to him? Well, you better hope he's nicer to you than you were to him."

"Get out," Jade said without much fire. "Get out."

Carmen turned on her heel and walked through the archway into the living room, then pulled the triple-fold birch doors closed behind her.

She moved quickly through the dining room, pausing to flick a speck of dust from a blue vase in the center of the table. Tomorrow, before Ricky's arrival, she'd fill it with giant marigolds from the garden, his favorite flower ever since she'd explained to him that in Mexico, people believed that the flower could keep them safe on *El Día de los Muertos,* when spirits roamed the world. "Ricky." She whispered the name with fondness and dread, and wondered how he'd changed over the years.

In the kitchen, Carmen poured herself a cup of coffee and sat heavily at the kitchen table, her thoughts turning back to Jade Ewebean. It had been a month since she'd told Jade about Ricky coming home, but the old woman acted like she didn't remember. Carmen suspected that the forgetfulness was an act, an excuse to fly into a rage every time her nephew was mentioned. Jade feigned senility and helplessness whenever the mood struck, but in truth, the woman forgot nothing. That wasn't to say Jade wasn't crazy as a loon, because she was, and had been for years. Living in this house with nothing but poodles and ghosts to talk to had taken its toll.

It all served to make the woman impossible, and Carmen hoped Ricky would remove her immediately. Her and her dogs, living and dead. She hoped Jade wouldn't upset Ricky too much.

He'd always been such a timid boy, and she hoped he had found his courage in the years away from the house. On the phone he sounded like a fine, strong man, though she thought she detected a telltale trace of hesitation when he spoke of the house.

To be honest, Carmen was surprised he was coming back at all.

Something skittered in the wall, a chipmunk or perhaps a rat. The sounds always chilled her and made her think of the way Robin would race through the secret passages on his hands.

The door separating Jade's apartment from the laundry room and kitchen was ajar, and Carmen could hear her talking to herself. She did that frequently. Carmen crossed herself and whispered a spell her uncle had taught her—one that, like marigolds, protected you from the spirit world.

It wasn't regular old-lady talk, not senile ramblings, but insane babbling that was always the same. She talked to Ricky's dead twin, saying obscene things, dirty things, sometimes moaning and giggling like a schoolgirl. Sounding as if she were having sex. Hearing that over and over was what made Carmen nervous. Robin was dead, but she thought that perhaps his spirit continued to walk the halls and roam the passages within the house. *"Madre de Dios."* She crossed herself again.

11

The drive across the desert from Las Vegas, Nevada, to Santo Verde, California, had taken five stressful hours. Between Shelly's sullen silence, the cat's yowling, Cody's manic good cheer, and Rick's own doubts about the intelligence of moving back, it had, in fact, been hell on wheels. But now, as he pulled past the open iron gates and up the long, long driveway into the veritable jungle surrounding the Piper family elephant, Rick had to smile as Cody oohed and ahhed as if he'd never seen a tree before. Of course, he hadn't seen that many.

Rick noticed that the front grounds were more overgrown than ever. After parking the car next to the stone path that led to the house, he thought that he might enjoy doing some of the work himself.

"Look, Daddy!" Cody cried in his ear. "Lemon trees! Can we make lemonade?"

"Sure, we can do that." Farther up the driveway, past the garage and outbuildings, Rick saw a slice of the modest citrus grove behind the house. The trees were lushly green, some laden with lemons, most with still-greenish oranges. Rick knew the Zapata cottage was nestled within the trees, but he had little memory of the back otherwise. He'd rarely entered the grove, because the crush of trees, even in broad daylight, had frightened him.

"Can I pick some lemons?"

Rick turned to look at his son. "Later, okay?"

Cody nodded, his attention focused on unbuckling his seat belt. "Okay!" In a flash, the boy, eyes bright with excitement, was out of the car.

"What a dump," Shelly observed as she opened her door. "This place is a wreck."

"We're going to fix it up," he told her as he stood and stretched. The cat yowled from his carrier on the backseat. "All right, already." Ignoring the cat's accusing glare, Rick pulled the cage out and set it on the ground at his feet.

"This is cool!" Cody cried, and took off at a tear up the long driveway. A moment later, he was back. "I like it, Daddy! I'm gonna look at the front yard now."

"Don't go near the pond," Rick called after him. "It's dangerous."

"I won't." The boy disappeared down a shady pathway.

"It sucks," Shelly countered. "It's filthy and I want to go home. Now." She put on her little-girl face. "Please, Dad? I could go live with Dakota and Lil. I want to go home."

"We *are* home," Rick said firmly. "You'll love it. It just needs a little paint."

"Like a million gallons," she said, already reverting to her I'm-a-teenager-and-I-hate-you voice.

"Hush," Rick said softly. Shelly was wrong—it wouldn't take a million gallons; twenty or thirty would do the trick. The stucco, once a pale peach, had faded to the color of unwashed flesh, and the formerly white trim was dirty gray and peeling. He wondered if the interior was as bad. Over the years George McCall had repeatedly told him the place needed fixing up, but Rick hadn't wanted to hear it because there wasn't enough money in the estate account for renovation of the house or yard. Frankly, he'd gone out of his way to ignore this place, hiding his head in the Las Vegas sand every time the subject of the house came up.

Now he'd have to do something, and he thought it might

be fun to do some of the work himself. *My poor wallet.* Fixing up the place should raise the property value enough to make it salable if he decided he just couldn't stand living here.

The neighbors would be pleased. They probably hated the Pipers at this point. Fortunately, the house couldn't be seen from the street, but the overgrown foliage that hid it probably horrified the owners of the huge Victorians, Tudors, and haciendas that lined Via Matanza. Those houses had perfect paint and perfect yards, not a blade of grass out of place, while he had an award-winning collection of shaggy bushes and award-winning weeds.

He picked up the carrier and started toward the house, his heart thumping unreasonably hard. "Come on, Shel," he said, and reluctantly the girl dragged her feet behind him.

Wildflowers exploded in the beds lining the walkway, and the grass was very long, making Rick recall that while the neighbors had their lawns mown once a week, Piper grass demanded cutting two or three times a week. Grandfather always said it was because the greenjacks lived here.

Rick forced the thought away, his gaze falling on the koi pond a hundred feet in front of the house. It was full of dark green water, and lilies floated on its scummy surface. A memory, so vague that it consisted only of the smell of cold, swampy water and an overwhelming feeling of dread, made him stop walking. *What? What happened there?* He shivered, despite the heat, relieved that memory wouldn't come.

"Dad?" Shelly asked sullenly. "You got a problem?"

"No," he said as he realized he was standing in the shade of the old oak. The gnarled wood rose out of the ground, twisting and knotted, a trunk so thick, it would take three people to ring it with their arms. Rick had hoped that the tree wouldn't seem so huge now that he was grown, but it was even bigger than he remembered. Staring at the trunk, he recalled his old fear of the tree, recollecting the cold terror he felt whenever its upper limbs scratched against his bedroom window on the second floor. The window was dark behind the leafy branches, and he found that he felt no fear now. Pleased, he wondered if he'd feel the same way after sunset. *Yes,* he told himself forcefully, *I will.*

"Let's go inside," he said as Cody ran up. He took the key from his pocket.

"Where's that housekeeper you said we get?" Shelly asked. "Where's your aunt?"

"Carmen took Aunt Jade shopping. They won't be back for hours." *I hope.*

The black iron handrail flanking the steps leading up the wide front porch jiggled when Rick grabbed it. The art of reattaching metal to stucco, or whatever was beneath it, was a mystery to him, but he felt sure he could figure out how to do it. In all honesty, it sounded like fun. *Maybe this is what the nesting instinct feels like,* he realized with amusement.

The top step was loose, too, he noted as he stepped onto the wide wooden veranda. A moment later he noticed a frayed wire on the porch light and that the doorbell was broken. The house was definitely going to be a challenge. At least the heavy, dark door, arched and adorned with black iron fixtures that made him think of the Spanish Inquisition, appeared to have nothing wrong with it. He inserted the key and pushed the door open.

The house exhaled a pleasant, nostalgic breath of lemon wax and cinnamon potpourri, though the underlying odor—poodle—was nowhere near as pleasant.

"It's big!" Cody said, running into the middle of the room and turning in circles. "It's got stairs!"

Smiling, Rick found that the living room looked eerily as he had remembered, only older, tireder. The dark green wool carpeting had been cleaned within a thread of its life, and many of the same pictures decorated the walls, including his parents' Robert Woods prints and Jade's horrid big-eyed children and dog prints—poodles, of course—from the sixties. The portrait of Grandfather Piper that used to have the place of honor above the reclining chair had been removed, and he wondered where it was. It had been the only decent piece of art in the house. In its place was one of the hydrocephalic children with hyperthyroid eyes holding an equally deformed poodle in a beret.

From his carrier, Quint let out a bloodcurdling yowl. "You said it, cat. These pictures have got to go." In fact, it was all going to go, he decided, and if Jade didn't want to hang the big-eyed children in her room, he'd toss them in the trash. The little U-Haul trailer he'd towed behind the car contained a half dozen exquisitely framed Edward Hopper prints as well as a few carefully chosen original pieces by relative unknowns who also captured the dark Americana feel Rick had first discovered in Hopper's work. He liked the darkness at the edges, the bright, sunshiny houses with inhabitants staring uneasily off into the shadows and woods, as if they were waiting for

something

to emerge.

Piper, he told himself with a little chill, *you're twisted* But he felt so good that he didn't mind. Here he was, standing in the place he feared most in the world, and he was thinking about painting and redecorating. It made him feel like he'd broken free of a set of chains he'd worn all his life.

The van would arrive with his furniture next week—not a lot, but nice, and it would fit in here—and he could buy whatever else he needed. Happily he envisioned polished wood floors with Navaho area rugs. With paint and plaster patch, a level and a sander, he'd scour away the bad memories. He'd rip away the bad things, like the forest green carpet that reminded him of grass in shadowed woods and the heavy, dark draperies that matched. He'd get white vertical blinds, put them under light nubby drapes, lined to keep the darkness out at night. And the sun out in summer, too. *I'm not afraid!* He was very nearly giddy.

The thick swirled plaster on the living room walls was dirty and yellowed, as was every other wall in the house, he assumed. No one had painted since his parents died—and it was obvious that even Carmen's deadly bucket of TSP couldn't get rid of the years of tobacco yellow from Uncle Howard's nasty little Tiparillos.

God, I'd forgotten that. He had a sudden clear image of Uncle Howard tilted back in a white metal chair, feet up on the front porch railing, a fifth of Jack Daniel's sticking out of his crotch. *Little brown turd, don't I love you,* that's what he sang to his Tiparillo, as he sat out there getting meaner and meaner. When it got too cold, he'd come in and do the same thing in front of the TV, tilted back in the recliner. Howard would croon to himself and watch the fights, grabbing whoever walked by and demanding this, cussing that, taking an occasional punch.

He used to pretend to be asleep when Uncle Howard was drinking.

Surprisingly, he was glad to have this memory. It seemed so . . . so normal. An abusive drunken uncle made more sense than little green men flitting around in the trees.

"Dad?" Shelly asked impatiently. "Dad?"

He looked at her. "Yeah?"

"Jesus, you're always telling me that *I* space out. You—"

"Don't be rude."

She glared at him, and he had to remind himself how unhappy she must be. He said no more, but it didn't lessen his desire to lock her in the closet until she was ready to leave for college.

"What's back there?" She pointed at the wooden folding doors sealing the living room arch.

"That's where your aunt Jade lives. The rest of the house is ours." He walked over to the monstrous brick fireplace, thinking that it, like the oak tree, was as big as he remembered. "So, Shelly," he said, seeing that his daughter was peering up the stairwell, "how do you like the house?"

Shelly replied with a sullen glare, but Cody came running out of the dining room, calling, "It's great!" He crossed to the fireplace, tried to look up the chimney, then moved to one of the built-in bookcases beside it and counted the shelves, patting all the ones he could reach. Rick hoped he didn't accidentally find the secret latch that would open it, and resolved to fill both cases with books as soon as possible.

Shelly snapped her gum. "This place is boring," she said, popping her gum. "It's totally dead."

Silently Rick counted to ten. "Give it a chance, Shel."

"I hate it here." *Snap. Snap.*

I will not blow up I will not blow up I will not blow up. "Please, Shelly," he said, trying to sound patient and understanding. "Give it a chance." *She's just left all her friends behind in Vegas,* he told himself again. Friends like Starman the Bellboy and Lil and that girl gang she ran with. Okay, not a gang exactly, but he didn't like the way they all wore at least two pierced earrings in each ear. Several had nose piercings, too. It wasn't natural. At least he'd removed his daughter before she'd put extra holes in her lobes. Probably. Casually he tried to catch a glimpse of her ears.

"What?" she whined, catching his gaze.

"Nothing." Her ears were hidden in her hair. Probably just as well, he decided. What he didn't know wouldn't hurt him.

"Where's my bedroom?" Cody asked.

"Shall we go upstairs and pick one out?"

"Yeah!"

"I'm choosing mine first," Shelly announced. "I'm older."

"Shelly," he said evenly. "I thought you might like the big bedroom in front."

The room he and Robin had shared was the second largest in the house, and in deference to his old fears, he decided that, for his own piece of mind, it would be best not to put a male Piper in that room. For Shelly, however, it would be perfect. "It's nice and airy," he told her. "You'll like it."

"Is it the biggest bedroom?"

"Except for the master suite, and I'm taking that," he said firmly.

"I don't want it if it's got stupid paint."

"You can choose your own paint, dear heart," he said, knowing he'd live to regret his words. No doubt she'd choose black.

She nodded. "Show me."

Rick walked up the stairs, Cody dancing ahead, Shelly dragging behind. With every step he saw new projects, from replacing the worn carpeting to replacing a missing bracket on the dark mahogany handrail. At the top of the stairs, he set the carrier down and opened its door. Tentatively Quint peered out, took a step, two, sniffing, then all at once, took off down the hall.

"Dad?"

"What, Shelly?"

"Which way is the room?"

"It's right there," he said, leading her to the first door on the right.

She pushed it open and walked in. Then he heard her moan. "Gawd, this is *gross.*"

"Of course it's gross," he said, irritated.

"What?" she whined.

"Nothing." He entered the room, not remembering the cowboy wallpaper until he saw it. He'd loved it, but it explained Shelly's reaction to the room.

"It's just the same as it was when I was little," he said softly. "But we'll take care of that, pronto, Shelly. First project, I promise."

She didn't answer, and he just stood there, staring, and feeling far less fear than he'd expected. He remembered being terrified here, between Robin's tricks and the greenjack stories, but now it was just a room that he'd shared with his brother until Carmen and Hector moved into the cottage and he inherited her room. He'd rarely entered this room after he was nine or ten years old.

"Daddy!"

He turned to see Cody behind him, grinning like he'd won the lottery. "What, Cody?"

"Please, I want the cowboy room! I love it! Please!"

Damn. "Cody, we'll put new wallpaper—with cowboys or spacemen or dinosaurs, anything you want—in any other room. I think your sister needs this great big room. She has so many clothes that she'll want that whole wall of closets."

"He can have it," Shelly mumbled as she turned and left the room.

Thanks a lot. "Cody? Wouldn't you rather have new wallpaper? This is kind of dirty and old. Look, there's a rip in it."

The rip—a gouge, really—was right over his old bed. Sudden images assaulted his brain, visions of Robin sitting on his chest in the dark, grinning and giggling and stabbing a butcher knife at the wall above his head.

Are you scared, icky Ricky? Gonna wet your pants, little brother?

No, Rick told himself, *this is just another example of your oversensitivity.* Robin had been teasing him with a toy knife, a rubber dagger, and he'd twisted the memory into something that had never happened.

Then how did it gouge the wallpaper?

"I don't care about an old rip. I want this room. I like it. I really, really, *really* like it." Cody showed his dimples.

"But . . . why? I'll get you new wallpaper."

"I like it because you had it when you were little. Please, Daddy?"

He was about to arbitrarily say no, but common sense made him hesitate. What could it hurt? Even if the knife had been real—and of course it wasn't—what did it matter now? Robin was gone and the past was . . . the past. Cody knew nothing of Rick's twin or of the greenjack stories. "Sure," he said, finally. "I guess you can have this room if you really want it."

His newfound nonchalance deserted him as he spoke the words, and the hairs on the back of his neck stood on end. *Grow up, Piper!*

"The rooms all suck."

"Shelly, you're back."

"I guess I'll take the one at the end of the hall. The one with the bathroom."

"Sorry, kid. That's the master suite. It's mine."

"You said I had first choice."

"I also said the master is mine."

"I'm the girl, I should get the bathroom."

He grinned at her. "But I'm the grown-up."

If looks could kill. "That's not fair."

"Fairness has nothing to do with it, darling. This is a family, not a democracy."

"But I should get the bathroom. I'm the girl—"

"And when you're the girl—woman—paying the bills, you'll get to claim the room with the bath."

She set her lips in a thin line. "Maybe I'll run away."

One. Two. He wouldn't lose his temper. *Three. Four.* Maybe he would. *Five. Six.* Running away was a new threat. *Seven. Eight.* Maybe he should just give her the suite. *Nine.* Maybe he should send her to a nunnery. Or a military school. *Ten.*

"You may choose from any of the other bedrooms on this floor," he said, surprised and pleased at the firm finality in his voice.

She tried to make him spontaneously combust with her eyes. "Then I'll take the yellow one. The one as far away from you as possible."

"That's fine, Shelly. As I said, you can choose your paint." He smiled pleasantly. "Anything but black."

She moaned and rolled her eyes, then flounced out after he complimented her, quite sincerely, on her uncanny imitation of Lurch on *The Addams Family.*

A moment later, Rick realized that she'd chosen Carmen's old room, the one that would allow her the most freedom. Its door was around the corner from the main hallway, and the kitchen staircase was immediately accessible. He almost went after her, suspecting that her prime motivation in making the choice was the ease with which she could sneak out of the house. *Don't accuse her unjustly,* he told himself, knowing that, not only would he feel terrible for misjudging her, but that he didn't want to plant the idea in her head if she hadn't thought of it herself.

"I'm starved!" Cody yanked Rick's hand insistently. "I wanna eat."

"Well, then, we'd better feed you." Rick checked his

watch. It was almost two in the afternoon, and he wondered how the kid had held out so long. Excitement, maybe.

Although Shelly had her license, he had never let her drive the Celica in Vegas. He made a few brownie points with her now by asking her to drive into town and pick up lunch. It was miraculous how her sullenness let up as he dangled the keys over her hand.

12

McDonald's had never smelled so good. When Shelly returned a half hour later bearing burgers, fries, and chocolate shakes, Rick was pleased to see that his daughter was actually working at maintaining her sour attitude. He detected a trace of enthusiasm lurking behind her studiously indifferent stare and Walkmanned ears.

They ate in the kitchen, which still had the yellow spoon-and-fork wallpaper Rick had helped his mom put up at age five or six. The 1950s round-shouldered refrigerator, gingerbread trim above the window over the sink, and yellow and white counter tile gave the room a kitschy look, as if it had been done over by a nostalgia nut. Rick liked it very much, but he always had: It reminded him of his mother.

The cat, lured downstairs by the perfume of Big Macs, made its grand entrance shortly after they opened the sacks. After taking his due, a quarter of a patty and a piece of bun, the cat stalked back into the dining room.

" 'Scuse me a minute." Rick shoved the last of his sandwich in his mouth and followed Quint, somewhat concerned about hidden poodles and open windows. There didn't seem to be any, but when the animal came to the closed doors to Jade's quarters, it sniffed, put its ears back, and growled, then assumed the imbecilic openmouthed, cross-eyed position of felines who didn't like the smell of something. Obviously Quint didn't like poodles.

Rick chuckled, until the cat suddenly turned around and sprayed the entry doors with everything he had, not once, but twice.

"Quint!" Rick scolded. The cat's acknowledgment was a scathing glance, then it flicked its tail, cat for *fuck you,* and marched back upstairs.

Rick looked around for something he could use to wipe up the urine, secretly pleased with the cat's editorial comment. Locating a box of Kleenex on a lamp table, he took a handful and wiped up the mess. Rising, he looked around to make sure the kids weren't watching, then tried the center latch on Jade's doors. It was locked from the inside, which was just as well: A herd of dead poodles lurked within, and he didn't want his son discovering them by himself.

"Dad?"

At Shelly's voice, he whirled guiltily.

"Yes, sweetheart?" He hid the wadded Kleenex in his hand, feeling like he'd been caught doing something wrong.

"Can I take the car again? I'd like to drive by the high school." She gave him a killer smile.

"Well," Rick began as Cody bounded by on the way back up to his new room, "I don't know . . ."

"I won't be too long, I promise, and I'll be really, really careful."

"I guess it would be okay," he said finally. He knew her charm tactics were purely false, a manipulation she knew would work, but as he handed her the keys, he told himself that the sooner she got to know her new home, the sooner her pleasantness wouldn't be an act.

"Thanks, Daddy!"

He watched her drive off, then headed back up the stairs, deciding it was time to investigate the so-in-demand master suite. He paused to check on Cody, who was happily counting sheriff's badges on the wallpaper, then continued on to the suite.

They died in there . . .

He swallowed hard, staring at the closed double doors. Why did he want this room, with its horrible memories,

memories he'd never been able to block, no matter how hard he tried?

Perhaps it was a knee-jerk thing: This was the grown-ups' room, after all. Or maybe it was the fact that there were good memories associated with it too. That was it. He smiled with the realization that Cody wanted his old bedroom, dingy cowboy wallpaper and all, for the same reason he wanted this one: because it was his parents' room.

He felt like he was six years old again as he opened the doors. The room was nearly as large as he remembered, with shining hardwood floors beneath scattered braid rugs, and aging white curtains over the windows. The double bed was the same one his parents had slept in.

The murder bed.

He shut off the thought. It was the same 1940s waterfall headboard, but a different mattress, not his parents' mattress. This mattress had a history he didn't want to think about for various tawdry reasons, the primary one being that it had been Jade and Howard Ewebean's conjugal bed for many a year, and the secondary being the occasional, unthinkable visitors Jade had invited into it.

Robin's riding the range tonight, Ricky, boy, hi ho, Silver! You don't know what you're missing!

He wouldn't have believed it if he hadn't seen it.

Disgusted, he studied the yellow hobnailed bedspread. It belonged to the Ewebeans. *The stories it could tell.* His parents had a handmade quilt, with a white background emblazoned with a blue and green wedding ring pattern, It had been stained and sodden with blood the night he found them.

At least you don't believe in ghosts, Piper. Purposefully he crossed the room, flopped down on the bed, and found the mattress to be an unendurable landscape of hills and valleys. Too small, too. He was used to his king-sized water bed, warm in winter, cool in summer, and only fifty percent waveless because he'd decided a little sloshing would keep him young. He stared at the ceiling and decided that the minute the furniture arrived, he'd get rid of the dark forties stuff and install his smooth bleached oak furnishings, his spread and curtains. It had all been dearly acquired on Gallery Road in Santa Fe, southwestern as all get-out and perfect for this house, primarily because it would help exorcise the memories of his parents' murder.

"Merowlll." Quint thunked his feline bulk onto the bed and nonchalantly padded onto Rick's stomach, centering himself. The cat hooked Rick into his stern orange-eyed gaze, and began kneading some serious bread in the breastbone region.

He scratched Quint behind the ears. He had the right idea, and Rick decided to take a lesson from the animal and make this house his own. He'd put his mark on it just as surely as Quint had on Jade's doors, though, he amended, with perhaps a tad more savoir faire.

He smiled, comfortable for the first time since they'd arrived. Gently Rick pulled the fuzzy paws forward, and the cat settled down, eyes dosing, purr rumbling. A nightly ritual done in daylight, he thought as his eyelids drooped, a good omen or not?

13

"Oow! Jesus! Get off me!" Rick's eyes flew open to see the cat, ears back, tail huge, clinging like Velcro to his chest. Its claws sank deeper into his chest as Rick tried to pull it free.

"Damn it, Quint! Get off me!" He shoved the cat, and this time the claws ripped free, taking skin and cloth with them. "Damn! Jesus Christ!" Quint hissed and sprang away. A moment later, low growling commenced beneath the bed.

Rubbing his chest, Rick sat up and looked around the shadowed room, disoriented, his brain muddled with sleep. "Be quiet!" he whispered, but Quint ignored him, and continued to growl steadily. Rick's mind started clicking things into place, and suddenly registered alarm. The last time Quint had acted like that was when a burglar had broken into the apartment. Swinging his feet off the bed, he thought *Robin!*

Rationality took over an instant later, and disgusted with his first reaction, he crossed the room and switched on the light. His watch read five o'clock—he'd been asleep for more than two hours. Where was Cody? Shelly? His car? He hadn't meant to leave them alone.

The cat's growl suddenly swelled, almost covering the sound of a door opening downstairs, and volleys of high-pitched yipping heralding the arrival of Aunt Jade and her poodles. "Lord, give me strength," he whispered as Quint

swatted the heel of his shoe from beneath the bed. The ca
was going completely out of its mind now, making high-
pitched growling-yowling-chewing noises full of evil intent
"Come on, kitty," he coaxed. "Calm down. They're jus
dogs. They're no match for you."

Quint, always a smart cat, *huffed* a couple times, ther
quieted.

"Cody!" Carmen's contralto overrode the yapping. "Hi
Cody!" As Rick straightened his clothes and combed hi
hair, he heard his son say something, though Rick couldn'
make out the words. An instant later, hands clapped, once
twice, and Carmen snapped a command in Spanish that Rick
recognized from his childhood. She'd told Jade it mean
"Hush, love pups," but the true translation was something
like "Shut up, you stinking little turds!"

Next he recognized Jade's gratingly nasal voice complain-
ing about something. Knowing Jade, it concerned the pres
ence of a child in her house.

My house, Rick corrected. *And the old bitch is razzin*
my son. That, he decided, as he closed his bedroom doo
and headed for the stairs, wouldn't happen more than once
Jade had been the evil stepmother incarnate and had mad
his childhood miserable. Not Robin's, just his. Robin ha
entertained her. "You bitch," he muttered, reaching th
stairs. The fear she had instilled in him as a child had turne
to hatred about the time puberty hit. And that was goo
because if he'd had anything more to be afraid of, he woul
have lost his mind.

"Ricky?" Carmen called as the poodles renewed thei
yapping. Steeling himself, he reached the bottom of th
stairs. *Here we go,* he thought, stepping into the living room
Show time.

"Daddy!" Cody, safe in Carmen's arms, giggled happil
"Lookit! Those are the doggy rats you told me about in th
car, huh, Daddy?"

Carmen grinned as she approached him. Transferrin
Cody to her ample hip, she hugged Rick with her free arm

then soundly kissed his cheek. "You're so handsome, Ricky. So handsome."

He felt himself blush. For a moment he couldn't hug her back because there was something, some little thing on the edge of his memory, something about Carmen Zapata that worried him, though what it was, he didn't know. More subconscious hooey, he decided, and forced himself to return the hug.

"You haven't changed a bit," he told her as he began to relax. He'd forgotten that being hugged by Carmen was one of the better things in life. He'd forgotten how comfortable she was, how warm and safe she felt. Even now that he was taller than she, he still felt engulfed by her. Suddenly he felt good about being here because she was exactly what Cody needed.

"You're a good boy, Ricky, to say I haven't changed. But I'm an old lady, fifty-five."

"That's not so old."

"You can see the gray hairs and the crow's-feet and you still say that." She beamed at him. "Thank you."

Carmen in a blue flannel nightgown, the rotting green odor of the koi pond clinging to her. It's our secret, Ricky.

He pulled away.

"What's wrong?"

"Daddy's funny," Cody said.

A throat was cleared. Dogs whined, and a grown man winced at the noise, which sounded like sandpaper on dry snot.

"Aunt Jade," he said smoothly, "I hope you're well."

"Doggy rats," she intoned. "Explain doggy rats."

She stood by the sofa, her dogs' red leashes wrapped around her. All he could see of them were their snarling, cowardly muzzles poking out from behind her legs. Jade herself had changed little, except that the tall, heavy-boned woman was thinner and slightly stooped now.

As always, she wore too much makeup. Her foundation had sweated into the loose wrinkles on her face, emphasizing the clownish circles of rouge ornamenting her prominent

cheekbones. Worse, mold blue eyeshadow covered her eyelids from the clumps of mascara on her eyelashes all the
way up to her plucked-out and painted-on eyebrows. A single wart with two wiry black hairs grew on the side of her
nose.

The woman, Rick thought, was a witch, and her expensive
but out-of-date—and season—clothing only emphasized the
effect. She wore a long black batwing jacket and matching
straight skirt that ended, regrettably, above her bony knees,
and her red scoop-necked blouse showed off her crepey
cleavage to great disadvantage.

The only change was her hair. Formerly mouse brown, it
was now jet black and swept up in some sort of beehive
throwback. More than anything, Jade Ewebean looked like
Cruella DeVille with a hangover.

"I'm waiting for an answer, Richard," Jade said.

Do you have any idea how much I despise you? The
woman had made his life hell, though he had to admit that
she'd had one positive influence on his childhood. If she
hadn't made him quite so miserable, he might not have
graduated high school early and had an extra year away from
her.

*If you hadn't been such a wimp, Piper, you might have
gotten away even sooner.* His feelings ranged from disgust
to amusement when he thought of how he'd removed himself
from his impossible home life. He got straight A's, then ran
away to college. It never occurred to him to do what kids
did in books and movies. He could have run away and joined
the army or even gone hog-wild and run off with the circus.

The circus. The carnival.

Delia.

The name brought a physical jolt. *Delia.* Oh, God. Delia.
She'd been with the traveling carnival that arrived in Santo
Verde each July. He'd met her on the Fourth of July only a
few days before his parents died. How could he forget about
Delia? She was the first girl he'd ever kissed, the first he
had loved.

"Ricky? Ricky?" Carmen shook his elbow. "Is something wrong?"

"No. It's just strange to be back here."

"Yeah," Carmen said, pointedly glaring at Jade. "Some things never change."

Jade stared down her nose at Rick. "I'm waiting for your explanation."

I don't have to answer her, Rick thought. *I can tell her to go to hell.* He opened his mouth, then closed it again. *I'm an adult. I should be civil.*

Luckily, Carmen spoke for him. "You leave him alone. This is his house and he's the boss now."

Jade harrumphed, but something in her posture changed. Obviously she was aware of the truth in Carmen's words.

"Richard," Jade sniffed, doing a turnaround reminiscent of Shelly's teenage manipulations, "this woman doesn't know her place. I worked my fingers to the bone taking care of you, and what do I get in return? A rude maid that I can't fire."

Thank God. "If you'll recall," Rick replied calmly, "my parents stipulated in their will that the Zapatas would stay on as caretakers as long as they wanted." If it hadn't been for Carmen, he never would have survived long enough to leave Santo Verde. The Zapatas were free to leave, of course, but the Ewebeans had been forbidden to fire them.

Jade strode toward Rick, bringing the poodles and an almost visible cloud of perfume with her, Rick tried not to recoil as she laid a spotted hand on his wrist. As tall as he, she looked him straight in the eye. "*You* can fire her, Richard. I did everything for you; I think you should do this one thing for me. Fire her. Get me a nice maid, one who shows me some respect." Her grip tightened.

"No." He'd never directly crossed Jade and her horrible temper before, and he found it felt very good.

Her nails dug painfully into his flesh. "You *must.*"

"I won't fire her, Aunt Jade."

"I insist."

"No," he repeated. "But maybe . . ."

"What?" The claws loosened slightly.

"Maybe you would prefer to live in a nice retirement home?"

The hand flew from his wrist and slapped his face, hard. "How dare you, you—" She drew her hand back to strike again. Rick caught it and held on, which wasn't easy. The woman was surprisingly strong. Somewhere in the background he heard Carmen first call on the Mother of God, then cut loose with a stream of Spanish invective centered around the word *puta.*

"Don't do that again, Jade," he said with deadly calm.

"Boy, is Daddy p.o.'d," Cody told Carmen. "He only talks real quiet like that when he's p.o.'d."

One of the poodles yipped, then attacked his leg, not biting, he realized, but wrapping its paws around him and rubbing. *Just like his mama,* he thought as he kicked it away without taking his eyes off Jade. "Listen carefully, Aunt Jade. If you ever do that again, I will send you and your dogs away. Behave yourself, and you may stay in your apartment. Do you understand?"

Immediately she switched back to simper mode. "Oh, Richard, I'm just an old lady. Sometimes I just blither on, you know. You'll forgive me, won't you, dear? My, my, you're so handsome. You look so like your brother, but you have a kinder face. A younger face, more boyish."

Carmen had warned him that Jade was losing her mind. God, she gave him the creeps talking as if Robin were still alive. He let go of her hand. She didn't move away, but stood her ground, keeping that brown-nosed smile painted on her face. The old bat, he believed, was possessed more of cunning than senility. He cleared his throat. "Abide by my rules, you can stay. Upset my family and you go. Another thing. Keep your dogs in your apartment. I don't want my cat upset either."

"A cat?" Her lip curled. "You have a cat?"

"Yes."

"She knows that already, Ricky," Carmen hissed.

"I hate cats."

"I hate poodles."

"Cats live outside."

"This one's a house cat. He never goes outside."

"Where are you going to keep him, then? In your boy's room?"

"The cat gets the run of the house, except for your apartment."

"But I was here first," she said in a victimized voice.

"No, *I* was," Rick said firmly. "I just left for a while. *I* own the house, not you."

"My poor little puppies are used to their freedom."

"Don't let her fool you, Ricky," Carmen said. "I never let those dogs loose in the house. They pee everywhere."

Rick took sudden perverse pleasure in knowing the poodles would be blamed for Quint's misbehavior.

Cody squirmed out of Carmen's arms and squatted to peer at the animals. "What're their names?"

Jade said nothing, so Carmen leaned down and whispered something in the boy's ear. He giggled with delight.

"She told him something dirty," Jade sniffed. "Do you want a dirty woman like that around your boy?"

"Yes." Rick found Carmen's occasional earthy language delightfully creative, and she saved any true obscenities she deemed necessary for her native tongue. The Spanish epithets for the Ewebeans had helped get him through his childhood. They thought the words and phrases were respectful; they were anything but. *Tia Puta,* as far as Jade knew, meant "Aunt Beautiful."

"Carmen says the dogs' names are Mister Poo and Stinkums," Cody announced. His giggling reached hysterical proportions.

"You can't touch my babies," Jade said haughtily.

"We wouldn't dream of touching them, Aunt Jade." Rick said demurely. Outside, he saw Shelly pulling into the driveway.

"See that you don't." Jade turned, almost tripping on her dogs, inserted a key in the lock on the folding doors, and slipped through, revealing none of the interior. Rick heard the lock click on the inside.

"Good riddance," Carmen muttered. She opened the front door just before Shelly knocked, and smiled at the girl. "You must be Shelly. I'm Carmen."

"Hi," Shelly said as she walked in. At least she'd used a pleasant tone of voice.

"You just missed the doggy rats," Cody told her. "They smell yucky." He giggled, then added, "So does Aunt Jade."

Shelly sniffed the air, her nose curling. "Opium," she said. "A whole case of it."

Cody considered this a long moment. "She should just say no."

"Dad?" Shelly asked, her tone perceptively sweeter. "There's a mall here. Why didn't you tell me?"

"It's news to me, sweetheart."

"Can I have some money? I could get some clothes for school."

"I suppose," Rick said, digging out his wallet. He found two twenties and handed them to her. "Receipts, change. I want to see what you bought."

"Be back by seven," Carmen added. "For dinner."

Shelly nodded at Carmen, then turned back to Rick and batted her eyelashes at him. "That's not much money. Could I have your MasterCard, Daddy?"

Borrowing his car, being promised a car of her own— something he'd agreed to consider during the endless drive across the desert—and borrowing his plastic, all in one day? *She's going to milk me for all the guilt and presents she can because of this move.* He knew he had to stop it now. This wasn't going to be much fun.

"Can I, Daddy?"

"No, Shelly."

Her face clouded. "That's not fair!"

He plucked the twenties from her hand.

"Daddy!" she cried, shocked.

"What's not fair? That you can't use my money, my car, and my credit rating anytime you want?" He paused. "Listen, Shel, if you want money from me, then you're going to have to work for it."

"Doing what?" Sarcasm edged her voice.

The snotty tone made him want to slap her, but he knew bemusement was the best revenge. "How about gardening? You could help Hector," he suggested with a smile. He glanced at Carmen, not wanting her to think he was insulting her husband. "This place is too much for just one man during the summer."

"It's usually not so bad," Carmen said quickly. "Hector's been in bed with a virus all week."

"Gardening." Shelly looked like he'd told her to scrub the house down with a toothbrush. "You're kidding, right?"

"No, I'm not. Look, hon, I know you don't want to garden, but I have to pay an extra gardener. Hector needs the help. I'm going to have to hire other people to fix things up around here, and it's going to take a lot of money. So why don't you look for a job so that you'll have all the spending money you need? Maybe check McDonald's or the A & W or—" he paused, trying to get her interest up "—maybe at one of the clothing stores you like. Then you could afford all the clothes you want, and you wouldn't have to fight with me about it."

"In Vegas one of my friends worked at The Gap," she said thoughtfully. "She had an employee discount." She gave him one more daddy-dearest look. "Okay, I'll look for a job at the mall. Can I have the money back, please, Daddy? I need to dress nice to get a job."

He handed the twenties back. "It may take a little while before you find work," he cautioned, but she just kissed his cheek and raced out and climbed in his car—without asking. Shaking his head, he watched her drive off.

Carmen was smiling at him "Kids."

"You said it."

"Daddy?"

"What, Cody?"

"Can we go exploring?"

Ah, an easy one. "Sure we can."

Carmen pulled a ring of keys out of her pocket. "I got these made for you. They've all got ID tags, so you go look around while I see how Hector's doing."

"Thanks, Carmen. I'd like to say hi."

"In a day or two, okay? I'm afraid he still might be contagious."

"Sure. Give him my best."

14

His father's workshop looked the same as it had the last time Rick had seen it, so many years before.

"Wow!" Cody stared at the huge room, then trotted around, heedless of the fine layer of dirt that coated everything in the room. In the boy's wake, dust motes danced up into the light.

Rick sneezed.

"Is this a barn?" Cody asked, turning a circle in the center of the room.

"No. It's a workshop. A *big* workshop."

The huge, high-ceilinged room was light and airy, because of its white paint and the high windows and skylights built into it. "Conlin Piper had this built so he'd have a place to build his sloop," Rick explained.

"What's a sloop?"

"A big sailing boat. After he built it, he used this to store the boat in the wintertime."

"Where'd the boat go?"

"It and Conlin were lost in an accident on Lake Arrowhead many years ago."

"Oh. What's that?" Cody pointed at a covered vehicle in the far corner of the room.

"I don't know. Let's look." He crossed to the shrouded form and lifted the edge of the tarp. Something scuttled beneath the canvas.

"Christ!" he cried, dropping the cloth and leaping back.

Cody giggled. "You're funny, Daddy."

Immediately he felt foolish. "I think we have rats," he told his son. "Move back a little. We'd better set some traps before we do any more exploring."

"But what's under there? I want to see."

"You can see it later. It's your aunt Jade's old car."

Cody nodded, satisfied. "What's that?" He pointed at the ceiling this time.

Rick looked at the equipment hanging from the huge center beam. "It's a winch." He remembered sitting on the workbench and watching his dad hoist an engine out of an aging Ford. "My dad used it to pull engines out of cars."

"Why'd he do that?"

"He liked to build new cars out of old ones. I hoped the Monster was under the tarp, but your aunt must have sold it."

When I get through with this car, Ricky, his father would tell him, *I'll keep it for you until you're old enough to drive.* Rick smiled sadly. Dad was killed before the car could be completed.

"What's the Monster?"

"He named the car for Frankenstein's monster because they were both built out of old parts."

Cody laughed, delighted.

His dad had worked on the hotrod through most of Rick's life. Remembering all the hours he'd spent out there with his dad, talking, laughing, working, planning, made him realize that he'd forgotten many of the good things from his childhood, not just the bad.

Tears sprang in his eyes, and he roughly wiped them away. Relieved that Cody hadn't noticed, he crossed to the workbench. A small hand-lettered sign hanging above the counter read, IF IT WORKS, TAKE IT APART AND SEE WHY. Rick smiled, blinking back more tears. His father always joked that it was the Piper family motto.

God, he missed his father.

"Daddy?"

His own son took his hand and tugged. "What's wrong, Daddy? Are you crying?"

"No, no. Just got some dust in my eyes. What do you say we see what's in these drawers?"

They opened drawer after drawer, and Rick was glad to find that evidently only the hotrod had been removed. The metalworking tools were all there: the acetylene torches, the cutting tools and hammers. Two welding masks filled one drawer. They'd called them Martian masks, he and his dad. None of it had been touched since the last time he'd used them, a few months before leaving home.

Three tall cabinets stood at the end of the long work-bench. Rick opened the first one and let the good memories stored within flow over him, He'd spent a lot of time out here helping his dad—the workshop had been a place where he didn't have to contend with his brother, and that made it all the better. As time passed, he'd even found a hobby of his own, one that pleased his father, who wasn't at all concerned that Rick wasn't especially interested in building cars. Instead, he built metal models, which were a lot better than the plastic Revels of the Mummy and Dracula, because he built them from scratch, with only his dad, and later, Carmen, lending an occasional hand.

Gently he lifted a foot-tall brass and copper piece out of the cabinet. He'd built it several years after his parents died.

It was a skeleton, begun as an *El Día de los Muertos* figure meant to be a Halloween gift for Carmen. Originally it held a guitar he'd snipped and torched from distressed metal and wore a sombrero, but those accessories were stored in the back of the cabinet because he'd transformed it into a sculpture of Big Jack, giving it a spray of little copper leaves to hold and filling its rib cage, with more. As proud as he was of it, he couldn't bear to look at the piece, and hence, he'd never given it to Carmen.

"Wow! What's that?"

"It's sort of a Halloween ornament," Rick said, handing the figure to Cody. "In Mexico they make all sorts of skeleton decorations for the Day of the Dead." Involuntarily he shivered, but forced himself to go on. "Usually they're made out of papier-mâché, but I made this one out of metal."

Cody turned it in his small hands. *"You* made this?"

He couldn't help being pleased as hell. "Yes. When I was twelve or thirteen. Do you like it?"

"It's cool!"

"Would you like to have it?"

"Yeah!" He turned it in his hands. "What's he holding?"

"Leaves. They aren't too good, are they?"

Cody shrugged. "Why's he got leaves?"

No jack stories, Rick thought. "The Mexican figures usually hold something representing a person's profession or hobby. A doctor might have a stethoscope or hypodermic, a singer might carry a guitar—"

"This one's a gardener, right?"

"Right."

Cody continued to turn the figure in his hands, and his happy expression filled Rick with more pleasure than he'd felt in a long time. Smiling to himself, he looked back in the cabinets, saw his other, lesser efforts, and remembered how much he'd enjoyed working with his hands. *Maybe I'll take this up again,* he thought. *Maybe Cody would like to learn how.*

A sculpture hidden behind some copper squares caught his eye, and he lifted it gingerly from the shelf. It was a small, angular horse, the last thing he'd worked on before he'd left home. He turned it in his hands, thinking the workmanship wasn't too shabby. The horse and its saddle were complete, but he'd never even started the horse's rider, Don Quixote. *Knight of La Mancha,* he thought fondly. *Slayer of windmills.* His hero.

Pretty weird hero, Piper. But there was something grand about the character, something he had always admired and identified with. *You identified with the quixotism, Piper, because you were as nuts as the don was.*

Fondly he turned the figure in his hands, thinking that

he'd like to do this again someday. He envisioned a life-size Don Quixote mounted near the koi pond, his tribute to Cervantes and Daumier, and craziness. *What the hell. I think I'll do it.* It would be a talisman to keep his own imaginary demons at bay.

"Daddy!"

Rick whirled to see Cody backing slowly away from the shrouded car. He took three quick steps forward and snagged his son up, scratching his wrist on the skeleton the boy clutched to his chest.

"What's wrong, Cody?"

"There's somebody in there."

Rick could feel Cody's heartbeat hammering against his hand. He tried to sound calm. "Why do you think someone's in there?"

"I looked. I looked under the sheet, and somebody looked back."

"From where? The car?"

"Uh-huh." Cody buried his head against Rick's shoulder.

"Cody, listen to me. You didn't see anyone. You just imagined you did."

Ricky, you didn't see anything. You imagined it. How many times had he heard that himself? And now he was saying it to his own son.

"I saw it."

"I'm going to set you down and we'll both look, okay?"

"No."

Relieved, Rick patted his son's back, keeping his eye on the car. "Listen, Cody, I'm sure there's something under there, but it's just a rat. A big old rat. That's probably what you saw, that or your own reflection in the glass."

"Uh-uh. No way."

"If you're sure, then I *have* to look, Cody."

The boy backed into the workshop's doorway. "Okay. Look."

Heart pounding, Rick flung the tarp back. But there was nothing in the car but mounds of antique trash and stuffing from the seats. He took a deep breath. "It's rats, Cody.

They're nesting in the upholstery. He dropped the tarp back over the Rambler. "Let's go in now, son. Tomorrow we'll buy some traps."

15

Shelly returned from the mall with a poet shirt, a pair of Guess jeans, and eighty-five cents in change, knowing her dad was going to be pissed. He was totally hung up on value-shopping, as he called it, which meant he thought she should buy last season's clothes for next season, or worse—for the following year. Christ, he could be a pain in the ass.

She locked the car and knocked on the front door, and Carmen, who seemed okay but kind of nosy, let her in. As she carried her bags up to her room, she thought that at least Dad probably wouldn't make her take the clothes back—he'd say she should, but he was a softie, and she'd get off with the same old lecture, which was an annoying but small price to pay. She removed the tags from the clothes before putting them away, just in case.

Dad wasn't that bad overall, she guessed. He was just really, *really* ignorant. He'd always tell her he'd get smarter when she was twenty-five or so, and she knew that was supposed to be a joke, but it really pissed her off. The man could be so self-righteous.

Closing the closet, she crossed to the north window and opened it, breathing in the cool, citrus-scented breeze. Below, she could see the shingled roof of Carmen's little house rising up in the middle of the citrus orchard. It'd be great having all that fresh-squeezed available anytime she wanted it. Except for squeezing it, of course—but maybe Carmen would do that.

In a way, she realized, she was glad they moved here, because her father probably wouldn't be on TV anymore. Almost all her friends—her *girl*friends—went nuts over him, always wanting to come over and stuff. They'd act stupid and flirt when he was around, and when he wasn't, they'd tell her how lucky she was, how cute he was, blah, blah, blah. That bimbo Sally Dugan, who was a grade behind her, for Christ's sake, even had the audacity to ask if she thought her dad would go out with her. Shelly wanted to freak, but instead she told Jill to go ahead and ask, because if there was one good thing about her father, it was his frigging code of honor. That's what he called it.

The good part was that she knew he'd never screw around with her girlfriends, even if he found a whole pile of them in his bed. The bad part was that he quizzed her dates to hell and back and he didn't approve of half of them. He'd let her go out, but he didn't approve. To his credit, he'd only forbidden her to date two guys. The first was Sterno Stevens, who rode a hawg—and she was sort of glad Dad had interfered since Sterno was trying to talk her into getting his name tattooed on her butt. The other was Starman Henessey. That happened only a few weeks ago, and she'd almost run away over it. Dad would shit a brick if he knew that Starman himself had talked her out of it.

She turned to the west window and pushed it open. There wasn't much to see, just a flagstone path leading toward the front yard and the little roof over the kitchen door below. And a lot of green. Grass, pine trees, honeysuckle, junk like that. Sighing, she flopped on the queen-sized bed. Dad sure made life hell when he didn't like her dates. That's why she'd tried to keep Starman from him—he was twenty-two and definitely off limits, if Daddy had his way.

She sat up and looked around the room. Something was missing. A television set.

There was one downstairs in the living room, and she decided it was time to get acquainted with it. She rose and left the room, going around the corner to the main staircase since she didn't want to go through the kitchen and have to bullshit with Carmen.

Entering the living room, she quietly approached the TV.

"Girl, what's your name?"

Shelly jumped about out of her skin, then whirled to see a gross old lady sitting in the easy chair, a pair of whining poodles in her lap. Jade.

"I gotta go," Shelly said.

"No, girl. Sit down. What's your name?"

"Shelly."

And hell began. She sat there and listened to the old battle-ax yammer on and on and wished she hadn't come back to the house so soon. She even started to wish she'd taken the Celica back over the Cajon Pass, and had just kept driving until she was back in Las Vegas.

Jade was telling her all about her poodles, but Shelly was thinking about the day. She'd checked out the town, and decided it wasn't as nerdy as she'd feared. The mall was small, but it contained all the right stores: The Gap, The Express, and Nordstrom's. And on the outskirts of town there was a real prize, the A & W root beer stand her dad had mentioned. The parking lot had been filled with mini trucks, four-by-fours, Trans Ams, and restored classics, the kind of cars acquired by rich teenagers—the kind she wanted to be friends with. Her spirit had soared as she pulled Dad's flashy little Celica into the lot. Inside, she found extremely cute guys behind the counter, who, it turned out, would also be seniors at Santo Verde High. One of them introduced her to some of the other kids in the restaurant, and by the time she finally left, she felt like she'd already made some friends.

Now here she was, back home, ready to forgive her father, at least as long as he didn't bitch too much about the new clothes. But he was nowhere to be seen. Instead, she was trapped by Jade, who was every bit as horrible as her dad had said. And more.

"What kind of name is 'Shelly'?" The old Ewebean fixed her beady little eyes on her. "What's it short for?"

Shelly resisted the urge to shrink back in the ratty gold easy chair. She glanced out the living room window, but no one was coming to save her. "It's not short for anything. It's my name."

Jade sniffed, and the smelly poodles at her feet both looked at her. "Poor excuse for a name. It's not surprising, I suppose, considering your father."

"What do you mean by that?"

"Richard was always a . . . a weak child. He had no backbone. He was afraid of his own shadow. A weak man chooses a weak name." The old bat shook her head.

She'd never thought about her name much, but now she felt like defending it—and her father—but she couldn't make herself meet that steely-eyed gaze. She looked at her knees instead. "My father," she said softly, "isn't afraid of anything."

"Shelly, you're back early."

She looked up to see her dad standing in the dining room doorway, along with Cody. His dark hair was windblown, and his normally pale skin was flushed with color. He looked like he'd been running. Her brother's eyes were bright as he trotted across the room and thrust something copper-colored at her.

"Look, Shel, look what Daddy gave me. He made it when he was a kid."

Normally she would have said something obnoxious, but she was so glad to see them, she took the thing and turned it in her hands. "Cool," she told Cody. "What is it?"

"It's a Mexican Halloween skeleton."

"For *El Día de los Muertos,* "Dad explained, as if that was supposed to mean something to her.

Jade snorted. "Useless junk."

"I like it," Shelly said, looking up at her father. "I didn't know you were an artist, Dad." She threw Jade a fuck-you glance.

He looked amazed, then smiled and shrugged. "It could be better. Did you have a nice afternoon?"

She nodded. "I put in job apps at The Limited and Miller's Outpost. I met some kids at the A & W, too."

He smiled. "That's where I used to hang out. Everybody showed off their cars there."

"They still do, Daddy. All the kids had cars, nice cars. Do you think . . . I mean, the high school is so far away . . ."

"We'll find you a car, hon."

Shelly hardly believed her ears. She'd wormed a promise to think about it out of him while they were driving here, but this was a voluntary statement: It meant a whole lot more. She handed the metal skeleton back to Cody, then grabbed her father and hugged him. "Thank you, Daddy."

He beamed at her. "A girl's gotta have wheels, right?"

"Right," she said, vaguely aware of Jade's disgruntled snort. "Can I have a VW Bug?"

"Maybe. If we can find a good used one."

"What kinda car did you have, Daddy?" Cody asked.

"I didn't have a car," he said, staring in Jade's direction.

"Why not?" Shelly asked in amazement. "Your family was loaded."

"He didn't need a car," Jade intoned. "And, Richard, *she* doesn't need one either." She pronounced the last word "eyether," which further irritated Shelly.

"I'll be the judge of that, Jade."

The old lady stood, her poodles tumbling forgotten to the carpet. "Why don't you be a man for once, Richard? Don't buy the girl's affections. Be a man. Your brother, he's a man."

Shelly saw her father's face go dead white, his lips thin to a grim line. "Robin died before he became a man, Jade," he said.

"You're wrong, Richard."

"Shelly," her dad said, in his scary calm voice, "have you seen Carmen?"

"No."

"She's in her house," Jade said, settling back in her chair. "Feeding her husband. Come on, Mister Poo," she said, her voice turning to a sugared coo as she patted her lap. "Come kiss Mama, Stinkums."

The poodles jumped onto her lap and began licking her ugly red cheeks.

"Cody," Rick said, "go on up to your room and get ready for bed." Shelly thought he sounded really weird.

"But I didn't have dinner yet."

"Then go up to your room and get ready for dinner," he said in the quiet voice that meant trouble. "Now."

Shelly nudged her brother, and he took off; he recognized the voice, too. The poodles yapped madly as he tore up the stairs.

"Shelly," he said, ignoring Jade, "would you go out back and ask Carmen if she's cooking tonight? Tell her it's fine if she doesn't want to. We'll go out."

"She already said she's cook—" She paused, realizing he was trying to get rid of her. "But I'll go make sure," she finished quickly.

"Thanks, hon."

She entered the hall, then moved into the shadows to listen.

"Jade," her father said a moment later. "As I told you before, if you want to remain here, you will not question how I handle my children, nor will you insult any of us. But there's one more condition I forgot to mention earlier. You won't mention my brother again, in front of me or my children."

"Too bad you're not more like your brother, Richard."

"He's dead, Jade, so don't talk about him like he isn't. He's been dead for a long time.

"Only to you. But you wanted him dead, Richard. You were so jealous of him, so jealous of your poor little brother."

Confused, Shelly listened closely. She knew her father had a brother—a twin, not a "little" brother—and that he'd died a long time ago, but that was all she knew. Dad didn't like to talk about him.

"The subject is closed," her dad said.

Jade just giggled like an over-aged schoolgirl. "How I love him, his attentiveness, his charm. He's afraid of nothing.

He's not like you at all, Richard. And you, you had the legs. What a waste. He should have had legs, and you should have been the freak."

It was everything Shelly could do to not burst back in and ask what they were talking about.

"Be quiet, Jade."

"You had legs, but you were so jealous of him," Jade continued. "He tells me, you know. Him with his poor little body." Her voice became dreamy. "Such nice, strong arms. And so much fun. His eyes glint with fun. He's not a poop, like you. He knows how to live. How to love a woman. He's a *real* man."

"You whore," he said in that same deadly quiet voice. "You slept with your own nephew, you filthy, fucking whore."

Shelly, shocked, stepped backward and bumped into a dining chair. It crashed.

"Shelly!" Her father's voice was serious and stern.

"Yes, Daddy?" she peeped, scared to death. He never, never used words like that.

"Come here, please."

She did, wondering what he was going to do. He sounded crazy-calm, like he did when he'd told her Mom had died.

She almost flinched when he put his hand on her shoulder. Behind her, she could feel Jade's eyes boring into her back. "Shelly, did you eavesdrop just now?"

"Yes."

"I'm glad."

"You're glad?"

"Because I have to tell you some things, and I've been putting it off. Now I have to tell you. Please go check with Carmen, then meet me upstairs, in the study."

"Study?"

"The room with all the bookshelves."

"Oh, yeah, right."

This time she didn't wait to hear more.

16

"So, Shel, to sum it up, I had a crummy childhood. I was a chicken, and my brother was a bully. We were a charming pair. There were a lot of hard feelings. Things we didn't work out before he died." Rick hesitated, then added, "Things we probably wouldn't have worked out anyway—and that's why I've never told you much about my brother. There's nothing very good to tell."

Shelly nodded thoughtfully, and Rick had a glimpse of what she'd look like as an adult.

"Dad? Can I ask a question?"

"Sure."

She hesitated. "It's really gross."

He could guess what was coming, and controlled the urge to say no. "Ask away."

"Did your brother *really* sleep with Aunt Jade?"

Yep, that was the question. Although he was glad he'd told her the basics, he would have just as soon skipped this part. "You shouldn't eavesdrop."

"I'm sorry."

"Don't do it again."

"I promise. So is it true?" she persisted, too eagerly.

Well, he told himself as he looked into his daughter's sharp green eyes, *the truth will out.* "Yes," he said simply. "It's true."

"How do you know?"

"I saw them."

"That *is* disgusting." She made a face. "How *could* he? I mean, besides it being incest and all, how could he lay— sleep with that old bat?"

Gonna make more little Piper boys. You can fuck her, too, icky Ricky.

"Dad? Are you okay?"

Rick rubbed his temples, a futile effort to exorcise his brother's voice.

My voice?

"Da-ad!"

"I'm sorry." He smiled. "It's hell getting old. What were you saying?"

"Why would your brother go to bed with that shriveled-up old bat? Was he crazy?"

"I think maybe he was so angry about his deformity that it made him a little crazy. It made him hate me, too. Here I was exactly like him but complete—I had legs. No wonder he spent most of his time torturing me. It was very important to him to prove himself worthy physically. He always wanted to race down the stairs—he could go faster on his hands than I could on foot. And he thought of himself as a—" Rick floundered for a word other than *cocksman*— "a lady's man," he finished lamely.

"It sounds like your brother was a certified jockstrap."

Rick laughed. "I think you're right."

"Dad? Did your parents know he was mean to you?"

"I think they might have suspected," he replied as old pain welled up.

"You didn't tell on him?"

Shifting uncomfortably, he glanced at his watch. "Shelly, it's getting late, and I really need to catch a shower before dinner."

She studied him a moment, then rose. "Okay. Thanks for telling me that stuff, Dad. It sure is weird."

"Yeah, I know. I'll see you downstairs."

She left, and a few moments later, he stood in his dressing room and pulled a change of clothes from his knapsack. His gaze fell on the corner where he'd hidden the night he and Robin overheard their parents discussing them. He shivered as he turned to look at the low cabinet that contained the passage door they had entered through. Though he hadn't blocked this memory, he had filed it very deeply.

A moment later, he stood under the hot water, letting it beat down on him, washing away the grime, but not the memory of the night he spent in his parents' dressing room. Brought to the surface by an innocent question from his daughter, it refused to sink again.

June 7, 1975

"Come on, baby brother. We're going to have some fun." Before he opened his eyes, Ricky felt Robin's eyes boring into his flesh and smelled his Tootsie Roll–scented breath. There was no reason to pretend to be asleep: Robin would only get rougher and rougher until he could force him to reply.

"What time is it?" Ricky murmured, trying to sound unafraid.

"It's almost ten, icky Ricky, almost ten, and we're going for a run."

Ricky opened his eyes as Robin yanked him upright. "I'm sleepy."

"Come on, come on! Get in the closet, sleepy Ricky."

"Okay." Rubbing his eyes, adrenaline waking him up, Ricky crossed the room, Robin cavorting around him, herding him. He climbed into the closet, and Robin hand-flipped in after him, then pushed the hidden lever to open the passage.

There was no point in refusing to go with him any more than there was a reason to ask him where they were going, so Ricky crawled into the darkness after his brother. As they passed the staircase that led down into the bookcase opening in the living room, Ricky heard the television set: His parents were still up.

That meant they wouldn't be going down to the kitchen. That was one of Robin's favorite things to do, ever since Halloween almost three years ago. Ricky had seen him leave on his midnight excursions any number of times. Usually he disappeared into their closet and took the passage down to the bookcase door, sometimes he took the stairs, front or back, and other times he went right out the window and down the tree.

Several times Rick had been forced to go with him. To make him go, Robin threatened to do all sorts of horrible things to him, including throwing him out the window and being smothered in Saran Wrap.

Robin often spent half the night roaming the house. He liked to start in the kitchen, first going through the refrigerator and tasting almost everything in it. Ricky had seen him spit in the milk, and once, he peed a little in a fresh pitcher of lemonade. The next day, watching Mom and Dad drink it, Ricky was almost sick, but Robin had reminded him that they were already pretty sure Ricky was crazy and would think it was his idea.

But the worst was the night that Robin had held him down and forced gobs of raw hamburger into his mouth. He'd thrown up bloody red meat into the toilet, and it looked and smelled like guts. He could barely think about it, even now.

"Come on," Robin whispered. He led him away from the comforting sounds below and into a dark, claustrophobic crawl space. Ricky was entirely lost, but Robin moved quickly and easily through the dark, almost as if he possessed a sixth sense that let him see in the dark. *He's a greenjack* Ricky reminded himself. *He probably* can *see in the dark.*

They descended no stairs tonight, just crawled through the passages hidden on the second floor. "Here we are, sleepy Ricky," Robin said at last. "You go first."

Knowing that argument was useless, he slipped past his brother and found himself in a small cabinet, empty except for a couple pairs of Mom's shoes.

Robin made him climb out. They were in their parents'

bedroom—their dressing room, to be exact. "Hide there," Robin ordered, pointing at a dark corner behind a rack of coats. He did as he was told, then Robin cozied in next to him. "Now we wait," he said. "And if you make a noise, I'll tell them *you* made *me* do this."

Soon their parents arrived. Ricky cringed into the darkness upon seeing their feet, seeing them slip their shoes off. He looked away when Mom's hand appeared, rolling down a stocking, but Robin craned his head, wanting to see more.

A minute later, the feet disappeared into the bathroom, and as soon as the shower came on, Robin said, "They're gonna do it tonight."

"Do what?"

"It, stupid. They always do it Friday night."

"Do what?" Ricky's insides were crawling.

"Sex, asshole, sex. They'll turn on the radio and then they'll do it."

Ricky and Billy Galani had been walking home from school last spring when they saw a little dog and a big dog stuck together on old man Clegg's lawn. When Billy finally stopping laughing, he told Ricky they were having sex. That was pretty much all he knew about sex except for the kissing and hugging stuff, which he thought might almost be sex.

As soon as Mom and Dad were in bed, Robin moved to the very edge of the dressing room so that he could see them. Ricky stayed where he was, a horrible sick feeling in the pit of his stomach.

"Shall I turn on the music, Grace?"

Their father's voice was easy to hear and understand.

"In a minute. I don't think I'll be able to relax until we make a decision about sending Robin away to school."

Ricky saw his brother's back stiffen.

"I know, Gracie. We have to make a decision."

"There's something I haven't brought up that might be important to our decision" She hesitated. "It's about Ricky."

They're going to send me to the funny farm instead! His heart in his throat, legs cramping, Ricky almost lost his balance.

"What about Rick?"

"I think he's afraid of his brother. I know that sounds silly, but . . ."

Robin's head swiveled, and his hateful gaze fell on him. Ricky shrank farther into the corner.

"I don't think it's silly," Dad said. "I've noticed it too. It's just that the boy's afraid of so many things."

"I know. Frank, do you think that Robin's scaring him on purpose?"

"Well . . . I never mentioned this before, you know, boys will be boys, but Robin does have a mean streak in him."

"What do you mean?" Mom asked.

"I caught him with a nest of baby birds. They didn't even have feathers yet. He was—" Dad's voice cracked. "He was doing things to them."

"What things?"

"You don't want to know."

"Tell me."

"He was tearing them apart with his bare hands. Tearing the wings off."

Mom made a shivery noise. "All the more reason to send him to the special school. He needs counseling for his handicap."

"Yes, I agree." Dad was quiet a moment. "About Rick. You know, he's always been terrified by those greenjack stories Pop used to tell. I wonder if Robin repeats them."

"To scare him?" Mom asked.

"Yes."

"But why would he want to scare his own brother?" she asked.

"For the same reason he maimed the birds," Dad explained. "He has no legs—so he cripples the birds. With his brother, it's jealousy. Poor Robin. He looks at Rick and sees a perfect mirror image—except that it's more perfect than he is."

I want your legs legs legs, Icky Ricky, and your eyes, too, boo hoo! His brother's voice in his head was so real that

Ricky jumped before he realized Robin wasn't really speaking.

In fact, his twin was paying no attention to him now. Robin splayed his hands on the carpet and began pushing himself up and down in the slow, controlled way that always meant he was angry. Ricky didn't dare move, even when a charley horse knotted one of his calf muscles.

"Robin's always so concerned about Ricky," Mom said. "You know that Ricky's been asking to move into Carmen's room after the wedding?"

"Yes."

"Well, Robin came to me and cried, saying he didn't want to sleep alone."

"Now, *that's* interesting." Dad's voice got a little louder. "He came to me, too, but he didn't cry. He said that he didn't think Ricky should move because he shouldn't be alone when he has nightmares. Grace, I think Robin told us each what we wanted to hear. Robin's the one who doesn't want him to move. Robin also told me that Ricky sleepwalks. Is that true?"

"I've never seen him sleepwalk," Mom replied. "I think that's an out-and-out lie."

"Let's tell Rick tomorrow that we're going to let him move. It won't hurt anything, and it might help."

"What about the boarding school?"

Dad cleared his throat. "It's a good school, expensive, but within our means. I'll call them tomorrow and get Robin's registration going."

Robin settled down onto his body and made fists with his hands. Sparks seemed to fly from his eyes when he turned a slow, deliberate stare on Ricky.

"Good," Mom said. "You know, Frank, I hate to admit it, but sometimes I'm even a little afraid of Robin. He's always so sunny and happy, but sometimes there's something so cold in his eyes."

"I guess we should have had this talk a couple years ago," Frank said. "I should have seen it sooner. When Rick's with me out in the workshop, Robin's never around, and Rick is so . . . so *normal*. When he's not afraid, I think he's far more normal than his brother."

Robin silently slapped a fist into his open palm.

"Then separating them is the right thing. It's settled." Dad's voice dropped a little. "A little night music, my dear?"

"I'm ready."

Ricky heard a click, then the radio came on, filling the air with classical music.

Even after the soft moans and whispers began, Ricky didn't dare move. He couldn't even feel his legs anymore. Robin remained by the doorway, never glancing at Ricky, his attention utterly on their parents' activities. His face was hard-set in an ugly, frightening scowl.

Time passed. Soon Ricky's mind' felt as numb as his legs. Despite his fear of his brother, he was nodding off when a hand touched his shoulder.

"Shhh!" Robin hissed in his face.

The music was off and Dad's soft, steady snore filled the room. Dazed, Ricky looked around, his eyes coming to rest on his brother's, a foot from his face. The look in them brought him to full terrified alertness.

"Into the cabinet, icky Ricky," Robin whispered.

Carefully he tried to move, but his legs were rubbery. An instant later, the pins and needles started, and Ricky groaned.

"What's wrong?"

"My legs are asleep."

Robin started to laugh. He covered his mouth with his hands and shook with glee, little raspy sounds escaping. Finally he stopped and grabbed Ricky by his pajama collar. "They think they're gonna send me away, icky Ricky, and it's all your fault! You know what that means?" he whispered hoarsely.

Ricky stared dumbly at him.

"You know what that means?"

He shook his head no.

Robin pulled him forward until they were nose to nose. His breath stank. "It means you're dead. I'm gonna getcha, icky Ricky, and I'm gonna getcha soon. Way before school starts. Not even gonna wait for Halloween. Crazy hazy Ricky, numb and dumb. I'm gonna kill you. Nighty-night."

He let go of Ricky, then slipped silently into the cabinet and was gone.

Rick turned off the shower and stepped out, pulling the towel roughly over his body. He'd spent the rest of the night hiding in the dressing room. His fear of Robin, and what revenge he might take, overrode the joy he had felt over his parents' words.

He pulled on his fresh clothes and drew the comb through his hair. It was a wonder, he knew, that he had survived.

"Dad!" Cody called from the hall. "Carmen says come and eat!"

He smiled at the sound of his own son's voice. "Coming, kiddo!"

17

It was nearly midnight, and Rick lay on his bed, exhausted, yet unable to sleep in this roomful of memories. He was also concerned about the cat, who was acting decidedly strange. Not only had Quint refused to leave the room again after the one foray downstairs, but he hadn't even left his hiding place under the bed when Rick had come back upstairs. Silently he cursed Jade's poodles.

On his way down to dinner, he worried a little about dealing with open drapes and windows because he just didn't have enough energy to deal with his neurosis or psychosis or whatever the hell 'osis he had. But he needn't have worried: All the drapes were closed. Silently he had blessed Carmen, who had remembered. He blessed her again at dinner as her cooking rekindled his appetite: He'd forgotten that Carmen was a killer cook.

The only negative thing at the dinner table had been Jade. Evidently she'd used up her day's supply of nastiness, as well as any brain cells that were still functioning properly, and this combination put her in a bizarrely jovial mood that was harder for Rick to tolerate than her previous nastiness and hostility.

He was almost certain she'd forgotten his warnings about mentioning Robin, because she brought him up about every five minutes, usually to remark obscenely on his prowess as a lover. Shelly seemed to find it disgusting yet funny, and

Cody was too busy building things out of his mashed potatoes to pay the least attention.

Rick, however, hated every last minute and was grateful that Carmen hustled her back to her quarters as soon as they were done eating.

Then, after she showed Shelly and Cody how to operate the TV set in the living room, the housekeeper had turned her attention on him.

"Come on, Ricky, you help me clean up and I'll give you a treat." She nodded her head toward the kitchen, and he followed her, happily remembering all the other times she'd said that, then shared a private stash of cookies or cupcakes with him.

They did the dishes by hand, she washing, he drying, and when they were done, she brought out the treat: a fifth of Sauza Gold and two shot glasses. She brought them to the kitchen table and poured two shots.

"This isn't what I expected." He grinned and tossed back a shot.

She matched him. "Yeah, you thought I was gonna give you a Snickers bar, right?"

"That's right," he said with total honesty. "So how do you stand doing dishes by hand?"

"There aren't that many dishes, Ricky. Besides, I've always done them this way. I don't know what I'm missing." She patted his hand.

"Dishwashers are a necessity of life. Mine broke down once and I couldn't get it fixed for a week. After three days, we were out of dishes. We had to buy paper plates and cups and plastic forks."

She laughed. "You're supposed to wash the dishes every day, buster."

"Well, I tried. I put them in the sink with hot water and soap, then I went to write my column. By the time I was done, the water was too disgusting to put my hands in."

Carmen snorted. "So what'd you do? Hire somebody to do it?"

"Well, yeah. Shelly said she'd do it for twenty dollars, so—"

"Twenty dollars? Ricky, you must have money growing out your butt!"

"No, but it seemed reasonable. It was such a disgusting job and all."

"Boy, that girl sure knows how to work her daddy!"

"Yeah, I know. Anyway, tomorrow we'll order a dishwasher."

"I'm not gonna argue with you!" She poured another round. "One more to help us sleep. I read your column every week, Ricky. It's good. You're pretty funny, you know that?"

"Thanks. I enjoy it."

They talked for a few more minutes, she bringing him up-to-date on the repair of the house, Hector, and the neighbors, he telling her about his life in Las Vegas.

"Carmen? Does Jade always talk about Robin so much?"

She studied her hands. "Tonight was worse, but she's never stopped talking about him. The dirty old woman."

"Do you think she's dangerous? To the kids?"

Carmen considered. "Only her mouth."

"Good." Rick twined his fingers behind his head and stretched against them. "I'm bushed. Shall we call it a night?"

"In a minute. Ricky, I want to ask you something."

The tone of her voice gave him a chill. He said nothing.

"Did you see them?"

"Them?" he asked, knowing very well what she meant.

"Them. Don't play with me."

"That was a long time ago. I was a scary little kid. My imagination—"

"Have you looked?"

"No. There's no need."

"Madre de Dios, you're telling me you don't believe in them anymore, but you won't look out the window? I think you're lying to yourself."

"Would I come back if I believed in them?" He held the shot glass with both hands to hide their trembling.

She stared holes through him. "No, I guess you wouldn't. I'll tell you what I think, Ricky. I think you better take a look, just to make sure."

"And what if I see them, then what do I do? Check myself into an asylum?"

"Quit feeling sorry for yourself. You just go look out the window and you'll be free of them, once and for all."

"Maybe."

"Does Cody know the stories?"

"No."

"Good. You make sure and have him look out the window tomorrow night, and make sure you're with him, whether you saw them or not. He's young enough, he'll tell you if he sees something. If he does, I think you better go back to the desert."

"You really believe—"

"I just believe anything is possible." She stood up. "Come on. You gotta look."

"Carmen—"

"We're gonna get it over with. Come on."

She took his trembling hand in her firm, dry one, making him feel seven years old again. Meekly he let her lead him into the living room. Cody and Shelly were sprawled in front of the TV, Cody fast asleep. Carmen let go of his hand, stepped forward, and scooped Cody into her arms. "Okay, Shelly, time for bed."

"What? It's too early!"

"I know. But your dad and I want to talk."

"Dad, can't you talk in the kitchen?"

"There's a little TV on the dresser in my room," Rick told her. "You can take it in your room for now."

"Little?" she asked doubtfully.

"Shel, Carmen and I want to watch something on PBS."

"What?" she whined.

"An opera," he said.

"Yeah," Carmen lied. "When your dad was little, we always watched the opera."

Shelly rolled her eyes. "You're kidding."

Rick put his arm over Carmen's shoulders. *"Rigoletto.* Hey, I have an idea, Shelly. Why don't you watch it with us? You're old enough to enjoy—"

"No, thanks." Shelly stood. "I'll take him," she said, lifting Cody from Carmen's arms. She started up the stairs.

"Night, Shel."

"Night."

Carmen crossed to the set and turned it off, then flicked off the light switch. "You can see better if it's dark. You ready?"

"Sure," he said dully. Outside, a summer breeze had come up, and he told himself he didn't hear his name within it.

He controlled the old panic quite well as he waited for her to return to him. Suddenly his hand was in hers again and she was leading him forward, toward the window. "Don't trip," she said as he raked his shin on the end table by the easy chair. She led him to the center of the picture window. "Stay there."

He closed his eyes and waited, listening to the drapes open, listening just as he had so many times so many years ago. He swallowed, feeling as if he were in front of a firing squad.

Her hand returned, and he could feel her standing next to him. "Ricky, look now."

He couldn't open his eyes. The wind called.

"Ricky?" She waited.

"I can't."

Both her hands enveloped his. "Yes, you can. You have to."

"No." His voice broke.

"Ricky, they can't get you in here."

You jerk, he thought fiercely. *You asshole, you moron. You're making a fool of yourself. Again.* He was afraid he was going to cry.

Carmen's voice was soft and gentle. "Remember Thomas, Ricky? Remember him?"

Thomas McEnery Piper. He remembered his first hero, the one preceding Don Quixote. Slowly, he opened his eyes.

They were out there in the night, dancing beneath the oak, their voices riding the wind. In the night. In the wind.

Ricky . . . Ricky . . . Ricky . . .

"No," he whispered.

"You see them?" Carmen asked.

He pulled away from her. "No. Good night, Carmen."

Barely controlling his panic, he took the stairs as sedately as he could, then, out of sight, he trotted to his room. The door had no lock, so he shoved a chair under it, then threw himself down on the bed and stared at the ceiling, his eyes wet.

Since then, he'd gotten up to check on Cody, and found him peacefully asleep in the bed nearest the door. The curtains weren't closed, but that was fine because he could see that the window was locked tight. Shelly, too, was fine, asleep on the bed, the TV still playing. He'd turned it off and returned to bed.

That was an hour ago. He stared at the ceiling a moment longer, then rose and walked into the dressing room.

After that night, when they'd heard their parents talking about sending Robin away, Ricky's spirits had briefly soared, but Robin took his revenge so quickly and gleefully that his life grew instantly worse.

Before June 7, the night of the eavesdropping incident, sleeping in the same room with Robin had been a trial that he could stand because he knew he could go to Carmen's room if it got too bad. But on the night of June 8, he nearly didn't make it.

June 8, 1975

Ricky had almost asked to sleep in Carmen's room, but he didn't want to do it in front of his parents—he worried that they might ask him why—and he couldn't get her alone. Finally he'd gone to bed, and was so tired that when he saw that Robin appeared to be asleep already, he didn't even wonder if he was playing possum or not. He didn't have the energy to wonder. Sometime later, he awoke.

Eyes in the dark.

Ricky felt them staring at him, watching him, and he pulled the covers around his body, over his head, and waited, almost suffocating in the close crush of blankets, feeling the eyes boring into him, feeling his own hot breath push the sheet in, out, in, out, like a doctor's mask on TV. His fear receded slightly as he made believe he was Hawkeye Pierce performing open-heart surgery and everyone was cheering and applauding, especially his parents and even his brother. Then, finally, the inevitable song began.

"Ricky, icky Ricky, I see you-ooo."

"Stop it," Ricky whispered into the sheet.

"Stop it, drop it, says icky Ricky." There was a thump as Robin dropped to the floor. "Whatcha scared of, sicky icky?"

"Nothing!" Ricky pulled the covers from his face and gulped the fresh, cold air. "I'm not scared of nothing!" But it took every ounce of courage not to hide his head again.

"Nothin'?" came his brother's voice, closer now. "Not afraid of nothin'? Liar, liar, pants on fire. Icky Ricky, you're afraid of me! Me! Me!"

Panicked, Ricky reached for the bedside lamp and turned the switch. Nothing happened. He tried again.

"Maybe it got unplugged, picky Ricky. Why don'tcha come down here and look?"

Ricky bit his lip to keep from crying. "Stop it!" he pleaded.

Robin didn't answer. Instead, Ricky heard his brother's hand-slaps as he crossed back to his own bed, the creak of the handgrip attached to the headboard, the protest of bed-springs as he swung energetically back onto his bed.

Burrowing into his covers, Ricky relaxed slightly. Usually Robin's teasing only lasted a few minutes, and though he still imagined he could feel his brother's eyes on him, he closed his own, hoping the worst was over, letting drowsiness overtake him slowly, peacefully . . .

"It's kinda hot in here."

Startled, heart pounding, Ricky awoke, knowing time had passed, but not how much. The bed frame creaked, and he saw Robin's silhouette across the room. He was perched on the end of his bed, next to the window.

"Don'tcha think it's kinda hot in here?" As he repeated the words, he turned the latch. Thin moonlight slashed the room as the white curtains fluttered with the incoming breath of night air.

Ricky . . . Ricky . . . Ricky came the voices on the wind.

"Ricky, Ricky, Ricky," sang Robin.

Ricky pulled the covers back over his head.

"Icky Ricky, Icky Ricky, come out and play." Robin bounced up and down on the bed, babbling softly.

"Close the window," Ricky begged.

"It's only open a little," Robin said innocently.

"Please." Ricky choked on the sudden flood of tears. For a short time, he'd lost his fear of the greenjacks, but under Robin's constant threats to throw him out the window, the fear had returned.

"Crybaby, titty mouse."

Suddenly Robin swung off his bed, and almost instantly was on top of Ricky. He yanked the covers once, twice, and Ricky lost his grip.

"Hi, hi, hi, icky Ricky!" Robin's strong hands clamped on Ricky's throat and started to press.

"It was kinda fun fuckin' with you, baby brother." He seemed oblivious to Ricky's thrashing. "But we're not gonna play anymore." He laughed through his teeth, hissing like a snake. "I'm not gonna kill you, icky Ricky, don't worry, I'd never kill you. I'm just gonna take you outside."

Ricky coughed, his vision blurring. He stopped fighting, unable to think.

A second later, Robin's hands loosened, and Ricky gulped air as his twin grabbed him around the waist and yanked him off the bed. They rolled in twisted somersaults across the floor, Robin propelling, Ricky unable to fight, barely able to breathe. By the other bed, Robin let go and climbed up on his bed. Before Ricky could drag himself away, Robin reached down and grabbed him under the armpit and hauled him onto the bed as if he weighed nothing.

Ricky . . . Ricky . . . Ricky . . .

"No!" Ricky choked on the word. "No!" He kicked, but Robin only laughed and pulled him up against the open window. He pinned his arms with one hand and clamped the other over his mouth.

"Shhhhhh! You're so stupid, icky Ricky. You're such a scaredy-cat. You don't know anything!" As he spoke, Ricky cringed, hearing adult fury hiding behind his brother's falsely cheerful tones. "Be quiet and listen, Ricky Piper, Ricky Diaper. You don't know what you're missing. If you go outside with me tonight, you get to live forever. You don't have to go to bed or eat your vegetables. You can do anything you want and never get punished. You get to play all the time!" He grinned. "Would you like that, little brother?" The hand was lifted from his mouth. "Would you?"

"No!" Ricky whispered.

A string of drool dripped onto his cheek. "Aw, come on, icky Ricky. If you don't go with me, I'll tell the folks all about how you don't think I'm your brother, and then they'll know you're the crazy one and they'll have the men in the white coats come and take you away, away." Robin's teeth glinted in the streak of moonlight. "Hee hee, ha ha, ho ho!" He paused. "They already decided you're crazy anyway. They changed their minds again. I heard them talking again this morning. They're going to send *you* away, not me."

"You lie." Ricky hissed.

"I heard them. They don't like you anymore, Icky Ricky; they've decided to send you away and keep me here. So why don't you go with me outside instead? It'll be a lot more fun, it really will. And you get to see your real brother. He misses you, Ricky. He misses you a lot."

"No!" Ricky whispered. "You killed him. You took his

body away, and nobody knows he's alive. He can't talk to anybody."

"No, no! That's not true!" Robin sounded happy and sincere now. "He has lots of new friends. Friends you can have too. Friends you can share. All we did was trade bodies for a while, just like trading marbles or baseball cards. I'm letting him use my body while I use his. He has legs now, Ricky. He's happy because I gave him my legs."

"You want *my* legs!"

"Shhhhh! You don't want Mommy and Daddy to hear you, do you? If they hear you saying crazy things again, you'll be sorry!"

"You just want my legs!" Ricky repeated, but more softly.

"Not true, baby brother. I want your eyes, too." Robin pushed him up against the windowsill. "I only want you to share, Ricky. Is that a bad thing? To share with friends? Robin's sharing and he's happy. He has legs. But he misses you. He wants you to come out and play."

"You lie," Ricky whispered again.

Robin's expression changed, hardened into a scowling mask, the eyes glittering like black onyx. Strange eyes, animal eyes, not his brother's eyes. Ricky moaned as Robin twisted one hand into his hair and pulled.

"If you won't go with me willingly, then I guess it's time to play, little brother," he whispered. He grabbed Ricky under his arms and lifted him up into the window. "We're gonna go down there, and I'm gonna choke you just a little more, and then you get to see your brother again."

Ricky . . . Ricky . . . Ricky . . .

Gathering all his will, Ricky kicked Robin as hard as he could. His brother fell back on the bed, clutching his stomach.

"You little shit!" he hissed. "You little shit!"

Ricky started screaming, his voice loud and raspy, not stopping as he hopped down from the window and ran across the room.

"You stupid little shit!"

As he was about to open the door, he heard his parents'

door open and close, his mother's hurried footsteps, his father's slower, heavier ones just after. He sighed, and sat on the edge of his bed. He might as well let them think he had a nightmare, because even though they might be on his side now—he wasn't entirely sure—they'd never believe that Robin tried to kill him.

As the doorknob began to turn, Robin grinned and propelled himself across the room and onto Ricky's bed. Then his twin's arms were around him again, so tight he could hardly breathe. "You little shit," he whispered again, and began rocking him back and forth in his arms, a pretend soothing for the grown-ups to see.

Light bloomed overhead and then his mother was at his bedside, his father standing behind. He could see Carmen waiting behind them in the doorway.

"Another bad dream, Ricky?" his mother asked, her gentle embrace removing him from Robin's rough one.

She smelled good, like Breck shampoo and Ivory soap, and Ricky nodded, burrowing into her shoulder, putting his arms around her neck, letting himself cry just a little.

"Do you remember the dream, Rick?" his father asked softly.

"I forget," he muttered, clinging to his mother.

"He just screamed," Robin said. "He screamed and I woke up."

"It was good that you tried to make your brother feel better," Dad said hesitantly.

"Yes," agreed Mom, though she glanced oddly at Dad as she said it. She stroked Ricky's hair and rocked him.

"Is there anything you need to tell us, Rick?" Dad asked.

He was tempted to tell until he saw Robin's threatening glare. "No."

Dad stared at him a moment, then nodded,

"Frank, would you mind shutting that window?" Mom asked as she continued to hold Ricky.

He saw a look pass between his parents, then Dad said, "Robin, I thought you learned your lesson about that window when you were seven." He closed the window and turned the latch.

"I was hot," Robin said softly. "I'm sorry, but I wasn't playing. I think maybe I have a fever."

Mom let go of Ricky and felt his twin's forehead. "Well, you're a little warm, I guess."

Dad picked Robin up and carried him back to his bed. "No more open windows, son," he said, tucking him in while Robin smiled angelically. "You get some sleep now."

"Thank you, Daddy."

Dad returned to Ricky. "What about you, Rick? Do you think you can go back to sleep now?"

"Can I sleep in Carmen's room?" he asked.

Mom and Dad exchanged glances. "Sure, honey," Mom said. She kissed his forehead, then stood. Ricky ran past her, out of the room, and took Carmen's hand.

"See you later, Ricky," Robin called.

In the hall, Mom kissed him again, then a concerned look crossed her face. "Look at those dark circles. A little guy like you shouldn't have such big circles under his eyes."

"I'm okay," Ricky said.

"He just needs sleep, Miz Piper, and I'll make sure he gets it." Carmen smiled. "I don't allow bad dreams in my room, so you don't have to worry about him anymore."

He stayed with Carmen that night, and all the nights thereafter, until, on June 25, she and Hector were married, and he inherited her room with the nailed-shut passage in the closet and the lock on the door.

Suddenly the cat jumped on the bed, startling him from his reverie. "Well, it's about time," he said as Quint planted himself on Rick's chest and began to knead with his claws, eyes half-closed, purr rumbling, looking completely happy and moronic. Absently Rick petted the animal. He'd acquired Quint four years ago, a few days after Laura was killed. He'd had to be strong for Shelly and Cody, but he had no one to lean on himself, and the lonely nights were especially bad. Over and over again, he'd wake up sobbing and reaching for his wife, and he didn't know how he could go on without losing his mind. Then Dakota O'Keefe, a new neighbor he barely knew at that time, knocked on the door and showed him a tiny orange kitten, no more than a month old. Dakota had found it abandoned in the alley behind the theater where he was working. It needed to be fed with an eyedropper every hour, he'd explained, and he couldn't do it because he had to work, and his roommate was allergic to cats. He begged Rick, who worked at home, to watch it for a day or two while he tried to find it a good home.

Reluctantly, still in a depressive haze, Rick took the kitten. Within an hour it had burrowed into his shirt and fallen asleep against his heart, remaining there while Rick worked on his column. That night he put it to bed on a finger towel in a shoe box lid that he placed on the nightstand. When the dream about Laura's death came, he woke up sobbing, and found the kitten snuggled up between his shoulder and neck, watching him, purring as hard as it could, and gently batting at the tears as they ran down his cheek. They'd been together ever since. The cat knew his moods and had proven itself to be a great listener. Rick could tell it anything.

He scratched behind Quint's ears. "I thought I saw the greenjacks," he told it. "You know what that means?"

Quint purred louder and settled down, watching Rick through slitted eyes.

"It means I'm nuts," he told the animal. "Completely, utterly bonkers."

The cat purred.

"Ready for the rubber room," he added, almost asleep.

Ricky . . . Ricky . . . Ricky . . .

Fear exploded within his gut, and the cat exploded on top of it, digging in its claws and hissing, before racing for its spot under the bed, where it started growling with a vengeance.

"Shit!" Had he dreamed the voices or not? he wondered. Either way, he'd scared the piss out of the cat.

"Shit!" he repeated. He got out of bed and knelt on the floor, pulling the bottom of the bedspread up. "Hey, cat, come on out. It's okay."

Quint stared at him, unblinking. The growling ceased.

Icky Ricky, icky Ricky, come out and play.

The cat hissed, the sound turning into a high-pitched yowl. Ears flat back, Quint swatted at Rick's face.

"Christ!" He pulled back just in time. "What the hell's the matter with you?" The feline moved farther under the bed, growling.

Hey, icky Ricky, come and play, hey . . .

The cat growled again.

The voices, Rick thought. *He hears them, too.*

Hey, Ricky, come and play . . .

Softer now, fading into the night. They never called for long, he remembered. Never for long.

18

"Daddy!"

Cody's call brought Rick instantly to consciousness, his stomach lurching behind somewhere, his brain dizzy, disoriented, and alarmed. The cat sprang off the bed, growling.

"Daddy!"

"I'm coming!" He staggered to the bedroom door and fumbled with the lock. "What's up?" Seeing that his son was fully dressed, he glanced at his wristwatch, was appalled to see it was past ten A.M.

His son stood a few feet back from the door, staring at something on the floor. "Lookit."

He followed Cody's gaze down to the stuffed poodle standing just outside his door. It was bluish white and wore a purple rhinestone collar, its hind leg was held lifted, ready to urinate. Rick pulled his bare foot back without thinking.

"You're funny, Daddy!" Cody giggled, squatting to study the animal.

"Did you put this here?" This was the dog that Carmen had talked about, the one she found dead in the dryer only six months ago.

"Nah. It smells yucky." Gingerly Cody patted its head. "But it wasn't here when I went downstairs before."

"When was that?"

"I dunno. It was light out, though. Carmen said I was an early bird and wanted to know if I eat worms." He giggled. "I said no, so she made me breakfast. She *cooked*, Daddy. Pancakes, just like at McDonald's, only better."

"Well, Cody was Aunt Jade up?"

He made a face. "I didn't see her."

"Where's your sister?"

Cody shrugged. "Can I go now?"

"Where are you going?"

"Carmen's gonna let me pull weeds!"

Rick had to smile. "How fun."

"Yeah!" Cody's voice betrayed complete sincerity.

"Don't go near the pond."

"I know. Carmen said." He turned and skipped back toward the stairs.

With a last withering glance at the petrified peeing poodle, Rick shut his bedroom door.

Fifteen minutes later, feeling considerably more human, he reopened it, snagged the poodle by its raised leg, and walked toward the back stairs. Pausing, he knocked on Shelly's door, but there was no reply, so he headed on downstairs, the poodle held distastefully out and away from his body like a lethally loaded diaper.

Carmen's arms were in dish suds up to the elbows. "Sleep okay?" she asked without turning around.

"Like the dead."

"Sometimes the dead don't sleep so good."

He'd never known how to react to Carmen's dire pronouncements, so he did what he'd always done and ignored it. The cheerful morning light that streamed in through the windows made her superstitions seem especially silly. "Jade paid me a visit sometime this morning," he said.

"Oh?" Drying her hands, she turned to face him, her eyebrows rising as she saw the dead dog. *"Madre Dios."*

"I found it outside my door." While he was dressing, it had occurred to him that maybe Jade had picked up the odor of cat piss and was getting even, but he decided not to mention this possibility to Carmen.

"That filthy old *puta*." Carmen took the dog from Rick. "Excuse me a minute." She stomped through the laundry room and pounded on the locked hall door, the back entrance to Jade's apartment.

Rick couldn't quite make out what they were saying, but Jade sounded haughty, and Carmen, heated. A moment later she returned without the dog. "She says she didn't do it. You want some breakfast?"

"No, thanks. Well, who did it, if she didn't?"

Carmen crossed herself. "She did it. *Mentirosa*. She does it all the time."

"*Menti . . . ?*"

"She's a liar, Rick. She lies."

"Has this happened before?"

"Sure. Every time I find that dog standing over my slipper, she says she didn't do it. You should have a good breakfast."

"I can't eat in the morning. Who does she say takes them?"

"She takes them, Ricky. I told you."

"Are you sure?"

"Ricky, I don't even want to say it." Carmen crossed her arms and nodded. "Crazy old *puta*. She's lost her marbles. Like I told you last night, she talks about him all the time. He makes love to her, he sneaks food from the fridge, he steals her dogs. She does whatever she wants, then blames him. Can you believe it, the stories she tells? She's loco, that one."

"Are you sure she's not dangerous, Carmen? Really sure?"

"I wish I could say no so you'd have an excuse to send her away, but she's harmless, except for the sex talk. And she'll get into your refrigerator and get her germs in your food—you should get a lock for it or she'll get her germs in everything. You should lock your bedroom, too. Sometimes she goes upstairs, you know." Carmen paused. "It's not good for you to skip breakfast, Ricky."

"I always skip breakfast, so you don't need to remind me anymore," he said with a smile.

"Okay, okay," she said quickly. "Tell me about last night, when we looked out the window. Did you see th—"

"Excuse me," he interrupted, having no intention of talking about last night either. "Do we have a Sears catalog around here somewhere? We should pick out a dishwasher."

"They don't have the catalog anymore. But there's a store in Montclair and another one in San Bernardino. Take your pick." She blew air noisily out her nostrils. "But first we need to talk about the greenjacks."

"I'd better go now," Rick said quickly. "I have to get back and get to work. I'm way behind on my columns."

She shook her head, "poor, little Ricky" written all over her face. "Whatever you say."

"Are there any features you especially want on the washer?"

"I really don't need it, Ricky." Her tone betrayed her continuing irritation with him.

"Well, I do," he said lightly. "What am I supposed to do on your day off? The three of us will use up every dish in the house in twelve hours, we always do. And if you're gone for more than a day, well . . . I have to have a dishwasher."

She started to protest.

He held his finger to his lips. "Shhh. It's for me, okay? I'm buying. But you can use it if you want."

"You want some lunch?" she asked, glancing at the kitchen clock. "It's almost lunchtime."

"No, thanks." The clock was a circa *1965* plastic plate, olive with copper hands and numerals, uglier than sin. As soon as his stuff arrived, he'd replace it with his own kitchen timepiece, a reproduction of a vintage yellow and white rhinestoned Felix the Cat clock with the ticking tail and shifting eyes.

Rick smiled, suddenly understanding her. She'd spent her whole life watching out for him, and now he was back and her instincts were up and saluting. "Carmen, I ate so much last night that I won't eat again for a week. Stop worrying about me. I'm going to go out for a while. Is it okay if I leave Cody with you?"

"Of course it is! You know Shelly took your car, right?" She saw the look on his face. "She said you knew."

"She lied," he said, suddenly tired. "Do you know where she went?"

"She said she was going to the mall to put in job applications at some more stores."

"Well, don't let her take my car again without double-checking."

"I'm sorry, Ricky. I didn't realize—"

"It's not your fault, Carmen. I should be apologizing to you. I can't believe how badly she's behaving."

"No, she's just being her age." Carmen smiled wryly. "Of course, she's doing it in spades."

"She's very difficult for me to control."

"We'll turn her around. Kids that age, you give 'em a little bite of cake, they'll take the whole thing." She shook her head. "A lot of little kids are cruel. A lot of big kids are selfish."

"Cody's not cruel."

"Neither were you, and he's a lot like you, just happier. More outgoing. But he hasn't started school yet either. He'll have to learn to be a little mean so he can take care of himself." She paused, considering. "You never liked school very much, did you?"

"No," he admitted. "But it wasn't that bad. I knew how to stay away from the bullies." *And everybody else,* he thought.

"Cody will have it easier because he doesn't have the pain you had."

Rick's throat tightened up. "Carmen—"

"We have to talk, Ricky. We both have things we need to say to each other." Her voice was fierce with emotIon. "You know? You remember?"

Carmen kneeling by the koi pond, pushing her hands into the cold corrupt water, so green, so alive . . . Our secret, Ricky, our secret . . .

Roughly he shook his head. "No. I don't remember."

She studied him a moment, then drew a key from her pocket. "Here, you can use Hector's truck. He's better today, but he's not going anywhere."

"Thanks." He accepted the keys and opened the back door, then turned and looked at Carmen once more. "I'm sorry," he told her quietly. "Sometime we'll talk."

"Okay."

19

Having picked out a dishwasher and arranged for delivery, Rick left Sears, stopped at the market for Pepsi and rattraps, and returned to the house shortly after one. Pulling into the driveway, he was annoyed to see that Shelly was still gone, but he hid his irritation as Cody raced to greet him.

"Daddy!"

Rick swept the mud-caked child into the air, eliciting a volley of delighted giggles. "You making mud pies, Cody?" He set the boy down.

"Hector and I are pulling weeds!"

"How you doing, Rick?" Hector asked as he approached.

"Fine." Shaking hands, Rick thought that the small, lean man hadn't changed except for the salt and pepper at his temples and in his mustache. "Should you be working today? Carmen said you were pretty sick."

"I'm fine. I just had a little flu bug, but you know Carmen. She'll try to make you stay in bed if you've got a hangnail."

Rick agreed, then asked Hector if he thought the koi pond could be turned back into a swimming pool. They discussed the possibilities for a few minutes until Cody insisted he and Hector had to get back to work.

Indoors, Rick let Carmen feed him lunch, and was relieved when she didn't try to bring up the past. In fact, except for Shelly's stunt, everything was going very, very well. Before going upstairs to work, Rick and Carmen divided up the rattraps, and he didn't protest when she said she'd do the house and the root cellar. He took his out and placed them in the garage and toolshed, then finally entered the workshop.

He didn't lift the tarp off the car this time, but toed a couple bait boxes in underneath it, and placed the rest in the base cabinets.

Time to get to work, Piper. He had a column due in two days, and he couldn't be late with it. Normally he kept the syndicate supplied with at least six weeks worth of columns, but he'd gotten lax lately. They had nothing in reserve, so he not only needed to get this one done, he needed to write several more, pronto.

I'll go up in a minute. He'd been thinking about building a big Don Quixote off and on ever since he'd found the unfinished sculpture yesterday, and he was dying to see what he'd need in the way of supplies. He would allow himself that, he decided, before he went in and got to work.

He began pulling equipment and metal from drawers and cabinets, setting it out on the counters, taking stock, and making plans in his head. At one point he nearly went inside to find a notebook so that he could write down the particulars of his project, but remembering that before he'd worked with no plans, only sight and intuition, he squelched the urge. He would design the don by the seat of his pants.

Minutes turned into hours, but Rick, feeling at peace and happier than he'd been in years, had no notion of time until the workshop door opened. "Dad?" Shelly asked. "Carmen told me you needed to talk to me?"

Reality came crashing rudely back.

"Shelly, you took my car without permission," he said as he set down a box of flaring tools.

She looked at the ground. "I thought you wouldn't mind."

"Why would you think such a thing?" His stomach started twisting up. Shelly could frustrate him like no other.

"Well . . . you let me take it yesterday."

"You asked permission yesterday."

"I didn't want to wake you up, and it was for a good reason: I put in job applications all over town and—"

"Damn it, Shelly! You know perfectly well that you have no excuse for what you did. It was wrong. Why can't you admit it?" Crossing his arms, he took two long strides toward her.

"I thought—"

"You didn't think, Shelly, you just assumed you'd pull another one over on dear old Dad. You've taken advantage of me for the last time."

"Daddy, I didn't mean to—"

"I knew it would be hard on you leaving your friends back in Vegas, and I've tried to be extra nice to you. But instead of appreciating that I let you use my car yesterday, you decide that gives you carte blanche to take it whenever you please."

"If you'd buy me a car, it wouldn't be a problem anymore."

One. Two. She's your daughter, you can't kill her. *Three. Four. Five.* Maybe you could ship her off to a nunnery. *Six. Seven.* The pressure in his ears and the black spots in front of his eyes started to diminish. *Eight. Nine.* Carmen would help him with her from now on. *Ten.*

"Shelly," he began calmly. "Let's talk about what you've asked for in just the last two or three days."

She rolled her eyes and started to back out the doorway.

"Don't move," he ordered.

"Da-ad . . ."

"And don't whine. Now, if I remember correctly the day before we left Vegas, you said you needed a NordicTrack—"

"Well, I do."

"Shhh. The same day you said your ears stick out too far, and you'd like to have cosmetic surgery to pin them back."

"They do! They're horrible."

"You have very nice ears, as I recall. Of course, I haven't seen them in years because they're hidden under your hair." He smiled sweetly. "But if you keep interrupting me, I'll be glad to pin them back for you."

She glared, but said nothing.

"In the car coming here, you asked for blue contact lenses. But your eyes are twenty-twenty."

"My eyes are drab."

He shook his head, almost amused. "Your eyes are the same green as your mother's were, and hers were beautiful."

Shelly didn't respond, just stared at something on the floor.

"You also asked for a car, cable television, your own phone line, and a television for your room. First, how do you propose I pay for all these things?"

"You should take that spot on the morning news like you were talking about?" she asked meekly.

Lord, why did I tell her about that? "If I did take it—and frankly, getting up at three in the morning three days a week doesn't appeal to me—I would use that money to fix up the house.

"Listen, Shelly, I'm not saying you can't have those things you want. I'm saying you're going to have to pay for them yourself."

"You said you'd buy me a car!"

"Unless things change around here, that won't be happening."

"Can I use yours?"

"Nope. You blew that today."

"Then how am I supposed to get a job if I don't have a car?"

"Ride your bike." As he spoke the words, he realized the movers hadn't arrived yet. He glanced at his watch, saw that it was nearly six, and figured they'd pull in tomorrow.

"I hate you!" Shelly cried. "You're mean and I hate you and you're horrible and disgusting!" Her shot taken, she turned and flounced out of the workshop, slamming the door behind her.

Rick shook his head, knowing she'd calm down soon enough, then put his tools away and went in to clean up for dinner.

20

Dinner was a Carmen Zapata specialty: pork loin, slow-roasted until it fell apart under a fork, black beans, sliced radishes and tomatoes, guacamole, sour cream, fresh salsa, and warm flour tortillas to wrap it all up in as one saw fit. Food of the gods. Rick now sat in the lumpy old recliner and stared at the television without digesting what he saw because all the blood in his brain had gone south to help digest the obscene amount of food he had consumed. He felt logy and content.

He'd insisted that Carmen and Hector join them tonight, and they'd had a wonderful time, especially since Shelly and Jade, the current malcontents, had refused to join them for dinner. Jade wanted to watch television in her room, so Carmen had taken her a tray, and Shelly pretended to be too infuriated to eat. That didn't bother Rick at all, because when he'd checked his car to make sure it was locked—it wasn't—he'd cleaned out a pizza box, McDonald's wrappers, and three large soda cups.

Carmen and Hector had gone home nearly an hour ago, and now he and Cody had the place to themselves.

His son was sprawled on the floor in front of the television, his head propped up in his hands. They'd flipped a coin for the early evening reruns: heads, *Murphy Brown*, tails, *Married with Children*. Cody, with tails, had won. As he watched, Kelly Bundy miscalculated and walked into a wall.

Rick stifled his laugh, because, while he didn't believe in censorship, he wasn't sure he should let his son know he was amused by dumb-blond antics.

His gaze drifted to the draped picture window, and almost instantly, he heard their voices.

Ricky . . . Ricky . . . Ricky . . .

Shivering, suddenly wide-awake, he wondered if he'd always heard the voices only when he thought of them. It certainly seemed so now. Back when he was a kid, he'd thought about them all the time, so he had no way of knowing, did he?

He'd been a regular little obsessive back then.

Carmen's admonition to find out if Cody could see them had haunted him since last night. *Now,* he decided, *it's time to find out.* Steeling himself, he tilted the lumpy old chair upright and rose, stretching, fighting down the anxiety that was already threatening to turn his knees to rubber. *Thomas Piper,* he reminded himself, *wouldn't be afraid.* His hands trembled. He felt like a child.

Remember the Halloween when you stuck out your tongue and flipped the bird to the jacks? Remember how brave you were . . . for a few hours, until Robin climbed out in the tree and you saw—

"Bull," he said aloud.

"What, Daddy?"

An ad was on, and Cody was staring at him.

"Nothing."

"You wanna have some ice cream? Carmen said we can make sundaes. There's Redi-Whip and cherries and chocolate sauce."

"Not now, sport. Maybe later."

"But—"

"We just had dinner. I'll pop if I eat anything else."

"I'm starved," Cody whined, but the ads were over and his interest was back on the set.

"Later." As he spoke, Rick crossed to the window and, without pausing to reconsider, pulled the drapery cord.

The greenjacks were out there, faint in the summer dusk,

a dozen of them, maybe twice that, it was always hard to tell. The evening wind was up, and they moved through the blowing grass and tumbling leaves, dancing and cavorting among them, human yet not human, possessing faces yet featureless. As he watched, they became aware of him, turning, coming closer. Watching him.

The panic started low in his abdomen, spread heavily into his legs and arms, making his brain dull and frantic at the same time. *Pretend you're Thomas.* Carmen's words echoed in his head, and he did what she'd said, though he felt like a fool.

Several came closer, melding together to form long-limbed wraithlike figures tall enough to peer in the window. He barely retained control of his bladder, but then he thought: *I'm Thomas. I'm not afraid.*

The old trick helped. For the first time in his life, he remained calm enough to examine them, to really see how they resembled liquid mercury, unable to retain form when they melded together, but were merely long-limbed and ghostly. *I'm not afraid,* he thought again. And he began to believe it. He tried to think of them as fog shifting in the wind.

Ricky, icky Ricky, sicky Ricky, Ricky, Ricky, Ricky.

The voices stirred his fear, and he tried not to hear them. Most of the greenjacks remained back beneath the oak so that they could see and be seen, though the formless wraiths stayed at the window, sometimes showing a suggestion of hollow eyes or a mouth, though never for long.

On his seventh Halloween, he'd gone out among these creatures and found that he was able to live through the fear. To transcend it. Then the few hours of freedom were cut short later that night when Robin climbed out the window and . . .

What? Rick wasn't sure. Robin had changed, he knew that, but was it because he'd grown sour over his handicap, or had Rick, always so guilty over his normalcy, merely read more into his brother's teasing than he should have? The notion that Robin had switched bodies with a greenjack seemed ludicrous to Rick now.

It had to be nonsense. But here he was, a grown, hopefully rational adult, and he was looking at greenjacks and listening to their rhyming catcalls. He smiled sadly. *I'm nuts,* he thought, *that's it. But at least I'm not afraid, thanks to my patron saint, Thomas.*

Slowly he raised his right hand to the window, made a fist, and extended his middle finger. It felt as good as it had when he was seven. He lifted his other hand, fisted, extended that finger, too, mouthing the words "screw you."

There was a reaction of sorts: The voices dimmed slightly—probably in amazement, he thought wryly—and their movements slowed down. The wraiths at the window seemed less stable than before. Experimentally he wiggled the fingers, pistoned his hands up and down half an inch.

"Daddy!" Cody's arrival at his side was so loud and unexpected that Rick froze where he was.

"Daddy! You're making a flip-off!"

"No I'm not." His hands slowly obeyed his order to unclench.

Cody giggled. "Who you flipping off, Daddy?"

"No one, Cody. I was doing, ah, isometrics."

"What's that?"

"Exercises."

"Well, it looked like flip-off, Daddy. Do you know flip-off?"

"Yes, I do. But who taught you, young man?"

"Lil." He giggled and slapped his hands over his mouth, then spoke between his fingers. "She showed me how, but she said I couldn't tell you. You won't tell on me, will you, Daddy?"

"No. As long as you don't do it anymore." *That bitch.* Of course, he himself had learned it from his grandfather, but the knowledge had come vicariously. That was . . . normal, but for Magill to purposefully teach a child . . . *that bitch.*

He stared at the jacks. As darkness grew, their activity, if it had indeed slowed, now increased again. They reminded him of ants, so ceaseless were their movements.

Rick's heart lurched as he saw one, especially dim, just becoming visible as the night grew darker, standing by itself under the oak. Its very stillness made it noticeable.

It reminded him of the one he'd seen the night Robin changed.

Bullshit, he told himself. *Don't even think it.* But he couldn't help himself, and his next thought was strong and hard and directed: *Robin.*

The greenjack looked and raised one arm—Cody yanked on his shirt cuff. "Whatcha looking at, Daddy?"

Jesus, he'd forgotten about his own kid. Glancing down, he saw Cody staring up at him, a quizzical look on his face. Rick swallowed. "What do you think I'm looking at?"

Cody pressed up against the glass. "Cool!"

Oh, no. "What's cool?"

"The wind. It's blowing good!"

Thank you, God.

"Daddy, let's go outside and smell the wind!"

"No, Cody, I don't—"

"Please, Daddy, please!"

"It's dark out."

"Not very. Come on, just for a minute. Please?"

He tried to spot the dim greenjack, but it was nowhere to be seen. "I don't know."

"Please?"

What could it hurt? He'd been among them before, hadn't he? Suddenly it seemed like a good idea, a final step to cure him of his fear. "Okay, but just for a minute."

"Yay!" Cody took his hand and dragged him to the front door, waiting impatiently while he undid the bolt. Slowly the door creaked open, and they stepped out on the wide front porch.

The jacks saw them.

"This is fun!"

Rick swallowed his fear as the greenjacks gathered at the base of the steps. Suddenly Cody let go of his hand and raced down the stairs. Rick cringed as the creatures, giggling and singing, surrounded his son.

"Come on, Daddy!"

"Coming." *Dear God, what am I doing?* He took one step, two, finally all six of them. Then he was standing on the stone walk at the base of the stairs, and the little jacks lined the border.

Cody, on his knees in the grass, windmilled his arms and giggled.

Rick could feel the jacks, like cool breezes, touching his legs. *I'm Thomas,* he told himself again, feeling foolish as hell. *I'm Thomas and I'm not afraid.* Heartened, he stepped off the path and sat down on a wrought-iron bench in the grass near the oak.

They gathered around him and they felt very cold, chilling his legs. Gingerly he reached out. A jack flickered through his hand, a cold, slimy feel. It returned, impaling, itself upon him. Repulsed, Rick drew back.

"Cody, let's go in now."

"Just a second, Daddy."

Rick stood, his legs swathed in repulsive greenjacks. A deep chill enveloped him. "Let's go, sport," he managed as he looked around, hoping to see the solitary jack again. He saw nothing, and the voices were growing louder. Too loud.

"Now, Cody."

"Just another minute."

"Well, I'm going to go make myself a sundae. If you want one too—"

Cody was past him, up the steps in a flash. Rick followed quickly. Before he closed the door, he took one last look, and for a moment he thought he spotted the solitary figure, but in an instant it was caught in the midst of the others, lost to his eye, but not to his mind.

21

The phone woke him at eleven-thirty.

"So how's it going out there in the butt end of California?"

Rick chuckled. "I miss having you around, O'Keefe."

"You just miss my gutter mouth." He paused. "You're lonely. Want my sister's phone number?"

"Stop trying to fix me up, Dakota. Listen, I'm building Don Quixote for the garden. Wait'll you see it. When do you think you'll have a chance to visit? You've got a standing invitation, you know."

"Wait a minute. You've lost it, right? You're on drugs? The old twat with the poodles raped you? What the hell does 'I'm building Don Quixote in my garden' mean?"

"*For* my garden. It's metal sculpture. I used to do it when I was a kid."

"Piper, I'm impressed. You're a Renaissance man, and here I thought you only excelled at writing cleverly snide comments about trucks, and bras, and cake mix. Guess I'll have to get a look at this. Does he have a big, hard lance?"

Rick laughed. "He will. The biggest one you ever laid your eyes on, O'Keefe."

"I'll visit soon." Dakota spoke in his sultriest voice. "Can't pass up the world's biggest lance, right?" He chuckled. "But what will your neighbors say?"

" 'How'd that guy get such a big, buxom blonde to pay attention to him?' is what they'll say."

"And I'll just smile and tell 'em that you can lick your own forehead. You'll never be lonely again."

"Bite me," Rick said, and instantly regretted the words because Dakota said he'd be glad to.

"So, Piper," he said after a few more minutes of banter and innuendo, "Have you see any of those jack-off things you were telling me about?"

"Greenjacks, not jack-offs." Rick paused. "But I like your term better. Wait a minute, Christ, I told you about those, didn't I?"

"That and more, Piper, dear. You're such an easy drunk, you *had* to tell me. You were *compelled*. But you didn't answer my question. Have you seen any jack-offs?"

He almost lied, then thought: What the hell? "Yeah, Dakota, I saw some. Isn't that a kick?"

Dakota didn't tease. "Does Cody see them?"

"No, it's just me. Nobody else is crazy. Same old story." He tried not to sound bitter.

"You're not crazy, you're just feeling sorry for yourself. Knock it off." Dakota didn't say anything else for a moment. Then: "What about that fat-bottomed cat of yours? Has he seen anything?"

"No, he just hates the poodles. And I don't blame him.

"Have you held Quint up to the window and shown the things to him?"

"No." Rick hesitated. "He did act odd last night at the same time as I imagined I heard the jacks. But I think it was coincidence."

"Maybe, maybe not. Look, cats are always staring at things normal people . . . Sorry Rick, you know what I mean—"

"Yeah, yeah, go on."

"Well, cats see things people don't. They stare at things in corners, and sometimes their fur stands on end."

"That's called a pylo-erection, O'Keefe," Rick said lightly. "Just thought you'd like to know."

"I know that. We always had cats. I know all about them." Dakota gave a small, throaty laugh. "I knew what I was doing when I went to the pound and chose Quint."

"You said you found him—"

"Well, I saved him from the gas chamber. He needed you, Piper, but I think you needed him more."

"I don't know what to say."

"Say thanks."

"Thanks," Rick repeated. "Really, thanks."

"You're welcome. Now, seriously, first chance you get, have the cat check out the jack-offs. See what he does."

"I hate to say it, but that's a good idea, O'Keefe."

"Of course it is, sweet thing. Call me back soon and tell me what happens."

22

After hanging up on Dakota, Rick went to check on his son one last time and was surprised to hear him giggling. He paused outside Cody's bedroom and waited a moment.

"Cody Thomas Piper," his son said softly. More giggling. "I wanna be a cowboy." Muffled giggles laddered the scale and down again. "Five."

"Cody?" Alarmed, Rick rapped on the door twice before opening it. In the shadows, he could just see his son's form in the bed nearest the window.

"Hi, Daddy!"

Rick flipped the overhead light on, making Cody squint and rub his eyes. "That's too bright!"

"So what's going on, sport?" Trying to appear casual and easygoing, he crossed to the bed and sat down next to his son. The frame creaked, a familiar sound.

"Nothin'."

"Who were you talking to?"

"My friend."

"Where is he?"

"You can't see him."

"Can *you* see him?" Rick asked, alarm returning.

Cody just giggled. "Of course not! You're silly, Daddy. He's invisible."

Rick felt better. Shelly had invented an invisible playmate

that lasted her entire seventh summer. This sort of thing, he could deal with. "What's your friend's name?"

"Bob," Cody told him solemnly. "His name's Bob."

Shelly's friend had been named Joyce. *What normal names children give the invisible,* he thought with amusement.

"Well, Cody, I heard you laughing in here. What were you guys talking about?"

"Bob wanted to know my biology."

"Your biology?"

"About me."

"Biography."

"Uh-huh. I told him about me and about you, too. That you're a big TV star."

"Was a little star," Rick corrected. "But thanks. It's kind of neat to have your own kid brag about you."

"Are you gonna be on TV again?" he asked hopefully.

"Maybe after a while." He might have to take the job if he was going to do all the renovations on the house that he planned. "It's getting late, sport."

"But Bob wants to talk some more."

"Not tonight." Rick raised his voice slightly. "Cody's going to sleep now, Bob. You can talk to him again tomorrow, okay?" He waited a moment, his ear cocked. "Bob said good night."

"No he didn't," Cody replied.

"He didn't? Well, what was that he said then?"

"Nothin'. He didn't say nothing."

"Anything," Rick automatically corrected. "Well, maybe he can't hear grown-ups. You tell him."

The boy was a born giggler, but once he got it out of his system, he looked around the room and announced, "Daddy says I gotta go to sleep now, but we can talk tomorrow. Okay? Bob? Okay?" Cody looked at Rick. "He won't answer me."

"Well, he probably went to sleep." He leaned down and kissed his son's forehead. "You too." He rose and walked to the door. "Good night, Cody."

"Night."

Rick flipped off the switch, adding, "Good night Bob," as he pulled the door closed. He smiled to himself.

Cody's giggle broke the silence.

"Cody?" he called sternly.

"Bob says good night," Cody called.

"Go to sleep, kiddo," he admonished. Shaking his head, he returned to his own bed. His son hadn't seen the greenjacks, but he turned right around and invented an invisible friend. He wondered if Cody would imagine greenjacks if he knew the stories.

As Rick lay down and switched off his lamp, he wondered if he himself would think he saw them if he hadn't been told the stories. He honestly didn't know.

23

July 16

Despite, or perhaps because of, all the memories he'd allowed himself yesterday, Rick slept like a baby until he awoke at eight Wednesday morning. Relaxing, staring at the ceiling, enjoying the morning sun, petting his cat, and feeling serene and calm, he was at peace for about three minutes.

"Shit." The serenity was swallowed by a rush of stomach acid that came with the sudden realization that he had a column due day after tomorrow and he hadn't even given it a moment's thought. "Shit." He didn't know what the hell he'd write about since he'd misplaced his notes on athletic shoes during the move.

He dragged his unwilling body out of bed and rubbed the small of his back. Among other things, he expected the furniture movers to show up today, and Lord, would that be a blessing for his abused spine.

In the shower, he stood under the water and let it play over his face and shoulders. "Massage," he said, not minding the water spraying into his mouth, only wishing he could adjust it to pound the tension out of his shoulders and neck. "I need a shower massager." He smiled: He'd buy several and write about those. He could test them this afternoon after working up a sweat moving a little furniture with the van guys, or after horsing around with his sculpture, and write his column tonight. It would be easy and fun, as columns allowing vague sexual innuendo and double entendre always were, the paper would spring for the shower gadgets, and he'd have an afternoon of—he groaned, but thought it anyway—good clean fun.

When he exited the shower with its puny little sprayer, he heard Shelly outside his door, calling his name in a dull, whiny voice.

"What, dear?" She hated to be called "dear," and he hated to be whined at. Synchronicity, he decided, pulling his jeans on.

"Can I take the car today?"

"No."

"Why not?" Hormonal teenage whining, four-star quality this time.

"Number one, it's my car. Number two, I told you yesterday that it's off limits."

"That's not a good reason."

"I can't think of a better one," he called smugly.

"Daa-ad, I need it. I *have* to go back to the mall."

"You've spent two days there already."

"I was doing job interviews."

"All day?"

"Daa-ad!"

He pulled on loafers, smirking because she was getting ticked, taking untold pleasure in applying karmic torture. "Have you actually applied anywhere, Shel?" he called. "Give me the truth, I can take it."

"Yes! Everywhere! And I'm supposed to be back at Nigel's Beauty Supply at eleven for an interview with the manager. I think she might hire me."

"That's great. You can walk."

"Daa-ad! My hair'll get all screwed up."

"Messed up. I'll drop you off, and you can walk home when you're done."

She mumbled something unintelligible but unmistakably rude, so he cheerfully informed her that if the movers showed up soon, she could take her bike. She mumbled something else, then begged him for a ride at ten-thirty. He made her wait a moment, then told her he'd do it. She left after that, doing sort of a combination drag-stomp to show him he wasn't being a good, cooperative father.

The jeans were okay for another day, but the socks were the last pair, and the dressing room was practically bare. He needed to do laundry. The meager supply of shirts he had brought in the car had dwindled to one slightly used blue-stripe button-down and a gaudy blue and black rayon shirt with distant Hawaiian bloodlines. He chose the Hawaiian, and as he slipped it on, his gaze dropped to the three twenty-four-inch base cabinets built into the wall.

Tense with memories, he hooked a finger around the door handles of the one he thought hid the secret passage. He pulled it open and peered inside, jumping when Quint, afflicted with terminal curiosity, rubbed up alongside him.

The empty cabinet had two wooden shelf supports attached halfway up. The shelf itself lay in the bottom of the cabinet, making him suspect that no one had used it in many years. Then he realized that the Ewebeans probably just threw their belongings inside without ever worrying about refinements.

He reached up on the inside back and felt for the lever, found it easily, and pushed it. Silently, surprisingly, the hidden panel in the back of the cabinet slid open, revealing the utter blackness beyond.

Involuntarily he shivered as cool air wafted over his face. Something scuttled somewhere in the passage, something small and blessedly distant. *More rats,* Rick thought, *more D-Con.* Quint hissed, then stepped tentatively toward the darkness.

"Uh-uh, no way, cat. You're not going in there." He pushed the animal away and released the lever to close the panel, then rose and crossed to the bedroom dresser, where he'd left the Pavilions bag containing the D-Con. After grabbing a few traps, he retrieved his little high-beam flashlight from his duffel bag and returned to the cabinet.

The cat watched balefully as Rick kneeled down and

opened the cabinet. After he readied the bait traps, he pushed the lever again and watched the panel reopen. He flicked on the flashlight.

If Robin hadn't eavesdropped that night, would they still be alive?

Rarely had he let himself consider that possibility, but the police had never caught the murderer. Robin did have his reasons: School was going to start in a week, and he'd be sent away. After his attempt to get Rick out the window failed, he might have been desperate enough . . .

Nonsense. You saw him that night in a clean yellow-striped nightshirt. Besides, as strong as he was, Robin hadn't even been able to force him out the window.

Quit driving yourself crazy, Piper! Set the damn traps and close this thing before the damn cat climbs in!

He shined the light into the opening and gasped when he saw the knife.

It lay just inside the passage, and seeing its long, thin blade filled his guts with ice. Carefully he picked it up by the end of the handle and brought it out where he could examine it more carefully. It was a filleting knife, its twelve-inch blade coated with dust, its cork-covered handle speckled with blackish stains. *Blood.*

The murder weapon.

Suddenly nauseous, Rick threw the knife back in the passage. He let the panel close, barely recognizing the strangled whimper he heard as his own. He slammed the cabinet door shut, then rose, frantically searching the bedroom, then the bathroom, for something he could use to secure the cabinet doors. Frustrated, he ended up standing in middle of the dressing room, telling himself he didn't need to secure anything. That's when he noticed the wire hangers hanging right in front of him. He snagged one and unkinked it, then quickly ran the wire through the cabinet handles and twisted it tight, so that nothing could get in.

Or out.

He sat back, breathing hard, still queasy, and feeling very

childish and ashamed. Quint, who cared only about his stomach, circled around him, yowling.

"I put that wire there to keep you out of the cabinet," he told the cat. Instantly he felt better, because he could tell anyone who wondered, including himself, that the cat was the reason. The wire would do until he could disable the panel. He grinned. The cat would be his excuse to nail up every panel in the house.

He busied himself, trying to forget about the knife in the passage. After feeding the cat, he called to verify that the movers would arrive, then gathered his laundry and carried it downstairs, only to find Carmen tossing Cody's clothes in the washing machine. Silently she took his clothes from him, looked them over, then threw them in with Cody's things.

"I can do our laundry, Carmen."

"Hey, don't worry about it. I get paid for this, remember?" She eyed him. "What's on your mind?"

"I need a hammer and some nails."

She raised her eyebrows but didn't ask questions, just directed him to the toolbox on one of the laundry room shelves. He took a handful of tenpenny nails and a claw hammer. "I'll bring this back later."

"Hold on, Ricky. You're gonna let me feed you breakfast today."

"Well, coffee, maybe."

She made him eat toast, too, then they lingered over second cups while he told her about the movers and jotted down what he wanted them to put where, and whether to leave, store, or get rid of various pieces of furniture already in the house. When he told her, with great delight, to take down all the hyperthyroid paintings and return them to Jade, Carmen nodded approvingly.

"But the most important thing is to make sure all the furniture in my room is taken out and the new stuff put in. If I have to spend another night without my water bed, my back's going to be ruined for good."

"A water bed." Carmen made a funny face, "I didn't know you were such a playboy, Ricky."

"I got it for my back, not for . . . that."

"I'm teasing you, Ricky." She laughed. "You're so serious. How do you write those funny columns?"

Embarrassed, he shrugged.

"You ready, Dad?" Shelly swept into the room on the heels of her words. "We have to go! I can't be late."

He glanced at his watch. She was right. "Okay." He glanced at the hammer and nails on the table. "I'll get those later, Carmen. Is Cody around? I can take him with me—"

"He went to Home Depot a while ago with Hector. They're buying weed killer and things. That boy of yours just loves working in the yard."

Rick found that mildly amusing. "I hope he's not driving Hector nuts."

"No, he loves the company."

"Let's *go*, Dad!"

24

Armed with half a dozen decadent handheld shower massagers, Rick returned a couple hours later to find a moving van blocking the driveway, several roomfuls of ratty furniture stacked by the garage for the Salvation Army to take, and four burly guys with terminal butt-crack dragging his own furniture into the house, none too carefully. Carmen, hands on her hips, seemed to be in her element as she ordered them around.

"Need help?" he asked her.

"No, I'm fine," She lowered her voice. "Morons, they're morons. They bang up everything."

"That's what they're paid to do," he said lightly. He didn't want to think about it.

Rolling her eyes, she looked heavenward. "They did the three bedrooms first. Cody's in his room putting away his things."

"So my bed's up there?"

"Yeah, but I think they broke it. It's in a bunch of pieces."

"It's supposed to be," he said, then realized she was teasing him again. "If you don't need me, I'm going to go put it together."

"You should make them do it."

He shook his head. "Like you said, morons. It only takes a few minutes if you know what you're doing." He paused. "Oh, Christ, the cat. I left the cat up there."

"I know, don't worry. I put him in my house."

"You're an angel."

"I know," she said, and blessed him with a smile.

"Call me if you need me."

"Sure, Ricky."

Upstairs, he found Cody having a great time unpacking and generally making a mess. Watching him, Rick thought that it would be a good idea to nail the closet panel shut right away, not only to keep Quint out, but because if Cody discovered it and went inside, he could be bitten by a rat. Since he didn't know about the passages, he was unlikely to find it, but Rick decided he'd get to it, along with all the other panels in the house, within the next few days. The old beds and dressers were gone, replaced by his son's roomful of high-impact white furniture, and topped off by his race-car bed. The room looked a million times better.

He left the boy shoving Legos in one of the drawers beneath the closet and walked down the hall to his room.

"What a relief," he said, looking in. Despite the stacks of packing boxes, the master suite looked bigger than ever with his smooth bleached-oak furniture in place of the heavy, dark stuff. He set to work on the bed and, an hour later, had the mattress filling with the help of a garden hose he'd borrowed from the toolshed. Meanwhile, Rick attached a shower head, assured Carmen he was almost done using up all the hot water, and put away some of his clothes.

Twenty minutes later, the bed was filled. He coiled the hoses and headed downstairs, thinking that since he couldn't test the shower massage until the water heater refilled, he'd kill an hour by starting work on the frame for his metal sculpture. That was, if Carmen didn't need him.

A moment later, as Carmen shooed him out the front door, Shelly returned to announce she'd gotten a job at Nigel's Beauty Supply and that she could get makeup really cheap. Her sullenness had evaporated completely, and when she whirled and kissed him on the cheek, he was filled with desire to buy her a car, cable, a phone, and whatever else she wanted. He refrained from saying so, and as he walked to the workshop, he contented himself by hoping that having a job would teach her some respect—if not for him, then for his wallet.

25

Two hours later, he pushed the welder's mask back and surveyed his work. It didn't look like much, but it was big. He grinned. The base and half the horse's frame were complete. It was merely a stick figure, a simple skeleton upon which he'd build. Tomorrow, after the column was safely sent off, he'd finish the knight's form, and after that, he'd start the real work: the painstaking heating, bending, and cutting of the metal he would weld together to eventually create his horse and rider.

Now, however, the dinner hour was closing in, and he needed to take a shower or three very badly. Grabbing his shirt from the stool where he'd left it, he thought about putting it on, then used it to wipe his brow instead. He paused, looking at the frame. "What the hell," he said, and pulled the mask back over his face, deciding to allow himself just a minute more to complete a couple little finishing touches before cleaning up for the night.

"Hi!"

Startled, he turned, taking the acetylene torch with him, accidentally pointing it toward the friendly feminine voice.

She stood about ten feet away and was in the process of stepping farther back, her eyes on the flame.

Flustered, he shut off the torch's valve. "Sorry," he said, putting the tool down. "I didn't mean to— You startled me."

"I didn't mean to startle you," she said, retracing her steps. "Your housekeeper said I'd find you here."

Three feet from him, she halted. Rick stared dumbly, aware that she was the least Vegas-like female he'd seen for some time. She was no more than five three, with slender bones and small breasts. She wore a scoop-necked white tank top, tucked in to her jeans, and her mane of gold-red hair floated around her shoulders. *This woman is my type,* he thought, remembering Dakota's efforts to fix him up. He'd have to explain that to O'Keefe sometime.

"I'm Audrey," she said, extending her hand and smiling.

"Rick—" He snatched his hand back before it reached her, shoved the mask up, reextended his arm. "I'm Rick Piper. I'm afraid you have the advantage . . ."

"Oh." She looked flustered this time. "You didn't know I was coming?"

"No," he said sheepishly. "I don't even know who you are." *But I'd like to find out.*

"My brother was supposed to phone you to let you know I'd be bringing this by." She pulled an Express Mail envelope from her shoulder bag and handed it to him.

"Your brother?"

"Duane."

"Duane?" he asked, puzzled.

"Oh." Her smile lit up the room. "You probably call him Dakota."

Before he could react, she was talking again, words spilling out in a nervous rush. "He said it came for you Monday and that it was vital you got it, but he didn't have your address, so he sent it overnight to me and asked me to bring it over and make sure I gave it to you myself." She smiled. "I just live over the hill in the Heights."

"You're Dakota's sister?" he asked in amazement. He owed Dakota an apology. O'Keefe did know his type.

Audrey smiled. "He described you to me, but you don't look quite like I expected."

In response, Rick set the letter down and pulled the welder's mask from his head and placed it on the workbench.

He looked down, saw the dirt and dust caked on his chest, hands, and arms, the stains on the jeans, and wondered what his face looked like. He grabbed his shirt and wiped his forehead. "I'm a mess, aren't I?"

She laughed, just a throaty little chuckle, and he liked it very much. He thanked God for California girls. The Beach Boys were right.

"Duane talks about you sometimes," she said. "He always says he wishes your, ah, sexual persuasion was, well, different." She blushed.

"I'm glad it's not," he heard himself say. In Las Vegas, sex was a buy-and-sell commodity, and Rick hadn't responded mentally or physically to a woman in a long, long time. Now his brain was alert, and there was an embarrassing twitch in his shorts. "Dakota's a very good friend."

She nodded. "He's a good guy." She continued to study him. "You're not small at all."

Before it dawned on him that she was talking about his height, he'd grabbed his shirt and draped it over his arm so it would conceal any embarrassing bulges in his jeans. "Small?" he asked, his voice cracking. He felt as if he were fourteen again, very embarrassed and very friendly.

"He said you were short. I thought you'd be five two or something."

"Five nine without shoes."

She grinned. "That's tall. Men taller than that give me a stiff neck." Suddenly she blushed. "I—I'm sorry, I don't know what gets into me sometimes. I didn't mean that the way it sounded . . . I mean . . ." She regained her composure with visible effort. "Aren't you going to open that?"

"Huh? Oh, yeah. I guess I should." He snagged the envelope, fumbled, finally ripped it open. Inside was a folded piece of paper. A single sentence, in Dakota's flamboyant hand, occupied the entire page: "I told you you'd like my sister." He stared at it. Stared some more.

"Is something wrong?"

"No. I, uh, hell. Here." He thrust the note at her.

Audrey stared at the note, then blushed to the roots of

her hair. "That rotten brother of mine," she began. "I was so nervous coming here because he kept calling me and telling me that . . . that . . . Christ. This is ridiculous." She took a deep breath. "I think Duane's playing matchmaker."

Rick nodded. "Dakota told me you were my type. I didn't believe him."

"He told me the same thing about you. I didn't believe him either."

"Want to have dinner with me?" he asked solemnly.

"Yes," she replied, her voice controlled and dignified.

"Want me to shower first?" he inquired even more gravely.

"That would be *very* nice." A giggle got loose, and she clapped her hand over her mouth. "I'm sorry," she said a second later. "This is all so weird."

"It is," he agreed, putting away his tools.

"So what is that?"

"It's a metal sculpture for my garden. With any luck, it'll look a little like Don Quixote." He closed the last cabinet. "Did your brother happen to mention I have children?"

"Yes. Why?"

"Just checking. You can see the house while I clean up. I have to take a shower," he added unnecessarily. Then he blurted, "I have to take several."

She laughed. "What?"

On the way into the house, he explained, then left her with Carmen and Cody while he went upstairs.

Half an hour later, Audrey drove them to Briarwood, an English pub with sawdust on the floor and a piano player who wore a garter on his sleeve and played Joplin at the correct tempo, something that constituted heaven as far as Rick was concerned. Sitting there drinking pints of Ballards while they waited for their food, he felt as if he were renewing an old friendship, not on a first, blind date that had been engineered with absolutely no subtlety whatsoever.

"I've never been here before," Rick said.

"Do you like it?"

"Love it." The piano player launched into "The Pineapple Rag." "This is my favorite kind of music."

"Really?" Audrey studied him. "You're not just saying that, are you? Duane didn't tell you?"

"Tell me what?"

"That I'm nuts for this stuff."

"Rags?"

She nodded. "Rags, jazz, pretty much anything written between *1895* and *1925*."

Dream woman. "No, he didn't tell me anything except that you were just my type."

She smiled. "Sometimes my little brother's pretty smart."

"So," Rick said, studying her clear green eyes, "I hear you're an optometrist."

"And you're a journalist. I've been reading 'Consumer Crusader' for years. Duane said you did a TV show in Vegas." She waited as the matronly waitress set platters of fish and chips in front of them.

"You folks care for malt vinegar or lemon?"

"Lemon," Rick and Audrey said in unison. *This is too good to be true,* he thought. *Way too good.* Something had to go wrong soon.

"Lots of lemon, tons," Audrey called after the server. "So are you going to do a new show?"

"Not unless I need the money."

"Are you a writer first and consumer advocate second, or the other way around?" She paused, a piece of fish raised to her lips. "I'm sorry. I'm asking too many questions."

"No, it's fine. I like both, but I guess I lean toward the consumer side. My first year in college, I discovered all those books on subliminal advertising, and it kind of bloomed from there." He smiled.

They talked through dinner about things he couldn't recall later. The time flew by, the ale loosened them up. "So what has your brother told you about me?" he asked over coffee.

"Not a lot. He told me who you were, which was a kick

since I always read your column, and I think I already told you that. He described you as 'regrettably straight,' that you had two kids and wanted to get your daughter away from Vegas."

"Did he tell you why?"

"Oh, boy, did he." She sipped her coffee. "That came out the other night after he had another fight with Lil. He said she's encouraging your daughter—"

"Shelly."

"Thanks, encouraging Shelly to become a show girl." She shook her head. "I wish Duane would kick Lil out, once and for all. She treats him like dirt, but the poor guy never could resist a stray."

Hearing that gave Rick pause.

"Is something wrong?"

"I might be one of his strays."

She reached across the table and squeezed his hand. "No. Lil was a prostitute. Couldn't get a job. He helped her clean up her act." She smiled. "As far as you're concerned, Duane's a wee bit star-struck."

Rick squeezed her hand back, and neither let go. "You're not," he said coyly.

She laughed, a delightfully musical sound. Her hand was on top of his, and she slowly moved her finger over his palm. It drove him nuts. "I guess not," she agreed.

"Are you sure Dakota didn't say anything about me?" he asked.

"Like what?"

"Well, did he say anything about my eyes, for instance?"

She cocked her head. "Your eyes? No, I don't think so. Why?"

"Oh, I don't know," he said casually. "I just wondered if he'd said anything else. I used eyes as an example . . . a paean to your profession."

"He didn't say a word, Rick, but he should have. You've got the most incredible dark blue irises. Are they contacts?"

"Nope. They're characteristic of the Piper clan."

"Well, they're gorgeous." She finished off her coffee. "What'dya say we blow this Popsicle stand?"

"What do you have in mind?"

"How about a yogurt stand? There's one just down the street. We can walk."

A few minutes later, they were strolling along the Via Pecado, downtown Santo Verde's picturesque main street. White firefly lights twinkled in the limbs of the small trees lining the sidewalks, and warm yellow glowed from the storefronts of the restaurants and businesses still open. They bought chocolate cones at the yogurt stand and continued to stroll. Rick had never willingly walked in town after dark before, but wasn't too surprised to find that on these civilized streets, there were no greenjacks to torment him.

She'll drop you like a hot coal once you tell her you see little green men, so you'd better not talk about eyes anymore, Piper, not if you want to see her again.

"Is your last name O'Keefe? Dakota mentioned that you used to be married."

"See? He *did* tell you something about me. Yes, it's O'Keefe. I was young and stupid when I got married. It didn't last long, and I threw the name out with the husband." Sidelong, she looked at him. "Did Duane tell you why we broke up?"

He almost said no, then decided bluntness had worked fine so far. "Yes, he did. Dakota was bragging about his left hook, and I asked him who he hooked. He told me." He waited, but she said nothing. "He said the man abused you."

"That's a nice way of putting it. He broke my jaw once. My wrist, too. He was a drunk. Lil's a drunk, too. I wish Duane would learn from my mistakes. He sure lectured me about Ron, so you'd think he'd learn."

"How long did you stay with him?"

"Too long. Five years. Let's sit." She indicated a white bench outside Much Ado About Books, a venerable bookstore where Rick had bought all his Batman comics way back when. "I don't know how much longer I would have stayed if Duane hadn't grown up and caught him shoving me around."

"He abused you the whole time?"

She nodded, gave him a half smile. "Hard to believe I'd stick around?"

"Actually, it is. You seem very sure of yourself."

"After I left, I lived with Duane for a while. He was pretty screwed up himself; he hadn't discovered his true calling yet. I also went to a shrink, who told me I had to stop feeling like I deserved to be treated like dirt. Ron always told me I deserved what he dished out, and I took it for truth. My therapist said it was because I had one of those deadly cold daddies who was into bare-butt spanking. She also thought he'd abused me, but I don't recall. Those are such in things right now, blaming everything on your parents and being sexually abused. I'd prefer to think I got screwed up all on my own."

"Adults do screw up their kids, though," Rick ventured.

"Sure, of course. But I learned that instead of blaming your problems on other people, you look at them as your responsibility. To overcome them is your challenge. It's the only way to grow. At least the only way I could. Your yogurt's melting."

Rick looked down and saw that his hand was shrouded in melting chocolate. Absently he wiped it off, then tossed the remains of the cone and the napkin in the trash can across the sidewalk.

"Good shot."

"Go on" he said. "Please."

"I'm not boring you?"

"No! The opposite." The things she'd said made him want to tell her about Robin; he was bursting to spill his guts. But he didn't dare. "You were saying?"

She smiled uncertainly. "Oh, well, I just decided to take responsibility for my own self-destructive tendencies, and I overcame them." She smiled. "For the most part, anyway. In the process, I went back and got my O.D., took some assertiveness training, and tried to get it together."

"From the looks of things, you've more than succeeded."

She blushed. "Thanks. It's taken ten years and lots of hard work to get where I am now. I opened my own office last year." Her nose crinkled as she grinned. "I'm pretty proud of that."

"You should be."

"My mother used to call me 'Little Audrey,' like in the comics?" She made a face. "And my dad called me his calico kitten."

"That's nice," Rick said, confused.

"Yes, but I took it to mean I was powerless."

"I had a cute little marmalade kitten," Rick said. "He grew into a big bruiser who takes crap from no one." He smiled. "Especially me." He took her hand, and she immediately twined her fingers among his.

"I like your attitude, Rick." She turned on the bench to face him. "So what about you? Any brothers or sisters?"

"A brother," he said, "Deceased."

He used discretion as he talked, describing his twin's handicap, touching on the greenjacks, mentioning that he was a gullible kid who believed the stories and, hence, was teased by his embittered brother. When he got to the part about his parents' murder, he only said that it happened. "I was afflicted with Ewebeans after that," he finished.

She chuckled. "That sounds like a horrible disease."

"It was. Is. You didn't see her, but Aunt Jade still lives in the house. She keeps poodles, and when they die, she gets them stuffed."

"So how'd you turn out so normal?" she asked.

He laughed, long and genuinely. "Boy, have I got you fooled."

"Well, then, I guess I'll just have to work on figuring you out. You look tired, Rick."

He glanced at his watch. It was already past ten. "I don't want to go home yet," he said conspiratorially. "Do you?"

"No. There's a jazz club a couple miles from here down on the boulevard. They serve gourmet coffee. I'm not up to any more drinking," she said apologetically.

"Me either. But jazz sounds fine."

On the way to the car he stopped to call home. Carmen answered, said everything was fine, did he have his key, and have fun. He'd had one phone call, a person, sex unknown, named after a state, who wanted Rick to call back.

They stayed out till midnight, talking like old friends. Then Audrey declared morning would come too soon and she drove him back to his house, pulling all the way up the long driveway and turning the car around in the wide parking area in front of the garage.

The lawn was crawling with greenjacks, and Rick's stomach twisted so hard, he thought he was going to vomit, even though he still sat in the passenger seat. *You have to walk through them. Do you want this woman to think you're nuts? Remember, they can't hurt you.*

"Rick, what's wrong?"

"Nothing," he told her. "I, ah, just realized I have work tonight. I need to take five more showers and write my column before noon tomorrow."

"Poor guy," she said from the driver's seat. "It's a dirty job you have to do."

They laughed, then slowly, slowly, leaned together, eyes locked, lips trembling. Anticipation wove through his body, made it tingle deep in his abdomen and long into his limbs. Hour-long seconds passed, deliciously, then their lips met and it was a first kiss, chaste, gentle, and warm. Exciting.

After, they pulled back enough to gaze at each other. Audrey's nostrils were flared and her pupils were so big, they looked perfectly black.

Rick took this as a good omen. "Can I see you again?"

"I was afraid you'd never ask," Audrey murmured.

They agreed on dinner and a movie for Friday night, then Rick reluctantly got out of the car. She waved and drove away.

Icky Ricky, dicky Ricky, Ricky, Ricky, play today!

Thomas, Thomas, Thomas, he thought back. *Thomas, Thomas, Audrey, Thomas.* By the time one more Audrey slipped between the Thomases, he was at the door without breaking into a run.

Shelly was in the living room watching an ancient Godzilla movie. "Hot date, Dad?"

She was still in a good mood. "Dakota's sister, Audrey. Dakota sent her to see how we're doing. She's pretty nice."

"Yeah, I bet!" Shelly teased him for another minute, then brought him up-to-date on her new job, which she'd begin tomorrow, the brands of makeup they carried, and all sorts of other things he didn't actually care about, but loved because it meant he was back in communication with his daughter. He listened attentively, noting that not once did she demand any material gifts. Tomorrow, he decided, he'd call the cable company. One could only do without *Southpark* for so long.

Within a half hour she wound down, and together they closed up the house and went upstairs. Still energized from his time with Audrey, Rick managed to install two of the shower heads, one in each upstairs bath, and test them. Stretching luxuriously in his bed, enjoying the warmth and the way it felt against his neck and back, he thought that in the morning he'd switch them for the others, and test those before doing the column. "Life is good," he told the ceiling.

Beside him, Quint flattened himself out to soak up every square inch of warmth his body would allow. The cat always seemed to know exactly where the warm spots were, and it occurred to Rick that he'd read somewhere that they could see infrared-heat waves. *Cats can see things we can't.* That's what Dakota had said when he urged Rick to see if Quint could see the jacks. He couldn't get to sleep because he had Audrey O'Keefe on the brain. Part of it was delightful, part of it wasn't. If they continued to hit it off, what would she say if he told her about the jacks? That would be the end of it: Nobody wanted to date a psycho.

"Okay, cat, let's take a walk." He rose, slipped a robe on over his shorts and T-shirt, then scooped up the cat, holding it against his chest so it was looking over his shoulder.

The house waited silently as he walked quietly down the

front stairs, then tiptoed across the living room, praying that Jade's poodles wouldn't hear him. Without pausing to think twice, he slipped between the draperies and the picture window.

They were out there in the grass beneath the oak, doing their endless dances. Slowly they became aware of him and turned to watch him as he watched them, a few moving closer to the window.

Behind him, muffled noises from Jade's room startled him. He listened a moment, and realized that the old lady was talking in her sleep, giggling and moaning, sounding like she was—*how disgusting*—making love. The cat growled low in its throat, prompting Rick to scratch its ears to calm it. He waited, but Jade continued to make her obscene sounds. *To hell with her.*

Icky Ricky, come play, hey, Ricky.

The cat didn't react this time, but its ears were aggressively forward, its attention focused on Jade's folding doors.

Several greenjacks melted together and oozed up, wraith like, just outside the window. "Okay, kitty," Rick whispered as he turned the cat toward the window. "Look at this."

Two seconds passed before the cat reacted, then Quint's muscles tensed, its claws sinking into Rick's arm. Ears back, the cat growled, not low and menacing this time, but the high-pitched panicked sound of a frightened animal. The wraith shifted toward the left, and the cat's head moved with it.

Suddenly the cat hissed and tore Rick's flesh, frantic to get away. "Jesus," he whispered as he clamped one hand on the front paws, and trapped the back under his arm. He was barely able to keep from yelling as the feline's hind legs kicked his side through the thick robe.

"Shhh!" He slipped out of the drapes and moved to the stairs and up, the sounds of Jade's now loud moaning mixing with the cat's whining snarl.

Finally he entered his room, shutting and locking the door before letting the cat free. Quint hissed again, then disappeared beneath the headboard of the bed.

26

Rick finished his column with an hour to spare, which was fortunate since he hadn't had time to hook up his fax, so at eleven-fifteen he drove downtown and had it sent from a stationery store.

After that, not quite ready to return to the house, he cruised through Santo Verde. The older business and residential areas had changed very little, retaining their old-fashioned, moderately well-to-do charm, but the outskirts of town had grown tremendously between the new housing tracts, condos, and businesses. As he passed the mall, he stifled the urge to stop in and see how Shelly was doing—she'd hate that. When she'd come to the study this morning to tell him good-bye—she'd conned Hector into giving her a lift—she'd still been in her newfound good mood, and he hoped it was going to last. If it did, he decided to buy her an inexpensive new car for her birthday next month.

As he drove away from the new area and back toward the house, he turned off on Cuerpo Podre and took the long, winding avenue until he arrived at the tall wrought-iron arches of Santo Verde Cemetery. He paused, then turned in, deciding to pay a visit to his parents' graves.

The cemetery, which occupied a series of small rolling hills, looked much as he remembered it, filled with oaks and pines and oleander hedges, very green, very peaceful. At least in the daylight hours. *I'll bet this place is infested with greenjacks at night.* He smiled grimly. Since the cat's reaction last night, he couldn't help thinking that maybe he really was seeing something, and had decided that after he got to know Audrey better, maybe he would ask her about variations in people's vision. Very subtly, of course.

He pulled over and parked the car, then plodded up a steep pathway. Soon he reached the oldest section of the grounds, The Garden of Souls, a place rife with looming crosses and pensive angels. Here and there stood ornate family mausoleums dating back to the early nineteenth century. They constituted California's version of ancient history.

Rick wandered among the monuments, reading the names and dates, noting signs of earthquake damage, perversely wondering how far down the ground squirrels burrowed.

Strolling down the other side of the hill, he entered The Eternal Playland, one of the children's burial areas. Some of the graves here were new, and one even had a Lucite covering that protected a color portrait of the dead child's smiling face. Chilled, he averted his eyes and continued quickly along the narrow path until he reached The Forest Eternal, an older area containing the Piper plots.

Despite his other fears, Rick had always enjoyed coming here, even as a child. He'd favored it over the regular park because everyone here was . . . quiet. He smiled to himself. And though he himself had no intention of ending up here—cleansing flames and a brisk ocean breeze were his preferences—he especially liked this area because of the decidedly nonreligious monument central to the family domain. Like the angels and cherubs and obelisks elsewhere in the park, it was a marble sculpture, but this, chiseled by an Italian artist friend of Conlin's, was a Scottish piper, complete with bagpipes and kilt. As a child, Rick came here often to sit at its feet. Sometimes he talked to it, pretending it was his ancestor Thomas. Who knew? Maybe it was. He found he'd still like to think so.

He stood before the piper and studied the strong taciturn

features shadowed under its tam. It stared back, bearing little resemblance to any of his relatives, living or dead. He stuck his hands in his pockets. "How's it hangin', Thomas?" Belatedly he looked around to make sure no one heard him, and was relieved to see that only the ghosts, if any were around, might have heard. Secure in his isolation, he approached his brother's grave. "Robin Emeric Piper," he read aloud. "Born 1965. Died 1981. Beloved nephew."

Aunt Jade, of course, had chosen the epitaph. "Beloved nephew" was putting things mildly.

Looking at the grave had little effect on Rick. He didn't miss his brother, hadn't shed a tear when he'd died. He was numb, unfeeling, where Robin was concerned. Beneath the numbness there was something else, something he didn't like to think about.

Dakota's voice intruded: *Of course you hated him.*

Maybe . . . *Was he really as cruel as I remember?* he wondered. Certainly he liked to tease, but Rick had been so . . . so touchy. So oversensitive.

Slowly he moved to the Celtic cross ten feet behind Robin's marker. PIPER was chiseled into the cross arm, and at its base were the words TOGETHER IN LIFE AND IN HEAVEN. Below the cross, to either side, were two flat bronze markers, one for Franklin Richard Piper, 1940–1975, the other for Grace Dorian Piper, 1946–1975.

As Rick knelt in the grass between the markers, hot tears sprang to his eyes. Flowers, he thought, he should have brought flowers.

September 1, 1975

They died during the dog days, on a night so hot and humid that the water coolers did nothing but release warm steam through the ceiling vents. They were off now, and the night was quiet except for the soft whirring of the ceiling fan.

Since moving into Carmen's old room in July, Ricky, no

longer having to contend with his brother's tricks, or oak limbs tapping on the window glass, slept better than he ever had before.

But tonight sleep would not come, and unaccountably nervous, he'd gotten out of bed to check the twist-lock on the doorknob half a dozen times. Now, at five past midnight, he lay on top of the damp sheets and listened to the heavy silence, while sweat trickled off his forehead. His head felt thick with the heat, and able to stand it no longer, he rose and went to the window overlooking the backyard, his fear of the night and the greenjacks now secondary to the stifling misery of the room. Turning the latch, he pushed the window open wide.

The cooling breeze fluttered the curtains around his face, evaporating perspiration from his forehead, from the lids of his closed eyes.

At that moment he realized that he hadn't heard the greenjacks calling him tonight. Even with the window open they remained silent.

He opened his eyes and peered out, but saw only the dim yellow glow of Carmen's porch light within the dark orchard.

No greenjacks.

No crickets.

Wind ruffled through his hair like familiar fingers, and despite the heat, goose bumps prickled across his neck.

The wind died.

Time ended.

Something was going to happen.

The night waited, the wind, the boy.

He crossed to his desk and sat in the chair. He folded his hands on the blotter. And waited.

Somewhere, a board creaked, once, twice. It might be his brother wandering through the secret passages, spying on others while they slept. Or perhaps it was only the house settling in the heat of the night, its timbers like heavy, swollen limbs.

He sat, listening, unmoving, staring at the Felix the Cat clock above his desk, glancing at the Batman calendar hanging beside it, considering minutes, days, and hours, thinking about how slow time passed when something was about to happen.

At 1:15 he heard new noises downstairs, faint sounds muted by the thick walls of the house and his own closed door. He sat up straighter and listened carefully. *Robin's in the kitchen.* He imagined his twin basking in the cool breath of the open refrigerator, balancing on one hand so that he could reach up and take the milk carton from the top shelf, then settling down on his legless body to take a drink, swirl it around in his mouth, and spit it back in. He would carefully close the carton and replace it before committing his other mischiefs, which might be running his tongue over the butter, or chewing small wads of raw hamburger before working the fouled pieces back into the main lump of meat.

At 1:35 there was silence once again.

An instant passed and it was 1:51. Ricky wondered what Robin was doing now, whether he had returned to his room or was still roaming the house . . . If Robin didn't want you to hear him, you didn't hear him.

The clock over the desk said 2:15, and it was just as hot and sticky as it had been at midnight, and Ricky, still wide-awake, continued his vigil. To pass the time, he thought about his brother, and how he would be sent away to a special boarding school in a week's time. Ricky could hardly wait, and each time Robin teased him now, he reveled in the knowledge that soon he would have far less to fear. That knowledge had carried him through the endless hot days and nights of July and August.

Three o'clock in the morning. Even though his brother was still here, Ricky knew, he had already begun to relax, to feel safer within these walls. But not tonight. Instead, the tension, the anticipation he felt, had wound tighter and tighter, and before long, he knew he would snap.

At 3:15 he heard something that sounded like a human whimper, followed by a thump.

He waited, unthinking, unfeeling. Numb.

At 3:20 the house sighed and settled as the night exhaled its first cool breeze into the room.

Ricky remained at his desk, back straight, hands neatly folded, a schoolboy ready for his lessons.

At 4:30 in the morning, the first glimmering of dawn shone in the east window next to the desk.

And broke the spell.

Woodenly he rose and walked slowly to the door. His stomach had tied itself in knots because it knew the waiting was over. He put his ear to the door, listened, heard nothing, then lay down on the floor and peered through the narrow space between door and carpet. The hallway was deserted.

Standing, he unlocked the door and slowly opened it.

The house lay still in the predawn shadows as he ventured into the hall.

Turning the corner, he cautiously approached Robin's room, and was relieved to see that no light shone from beneath his door. Ricky tiptoed past, then continued down the corridor until he arrived at his parents' room.

His brain, dazed and paralyzed by something unidentifiable for these last few hours, suddenly came to life. Why was he here? Why was he about to disturb his parents so early in the morning? He found he didn't know, but to do so was an imperative he could not ignore.

Raising his hand to knock on the door, he realized that Robin might also hear, so instead, he clutched the doorknob and slowly turned it. As the door swung silently inward, he heard the steady whirring of the ceiling fans within the room.

"Mom?" he whispered. "Dad?"

They didn't wake up, so he stepped inside, then, still fearing that Robin would hear, closed the door behind him.

"Mom?" he called. Then again, a little louder. "Mom?"

In the bathroom, a faucet dripped.

He approached the bed, his heart thundering against his rib cage. Although the windows were open and the cool northerly breeze had picked up, his parents' bedroom, hot and close, was foul with a heavy, hot smell that made the hairs on the back of his neck prickle up.

He stepped closer to the bed, thinking that it was strange that Mom and Dad were under their quilt on such a hot night. Shrugging to himself—grown-ups did all sorts of weird things he didn't understand—he reached out and tapped the quilt, about where his mother's shoulder should be.

She didn't wake up.

"Mom?" he asked, poking at the quilt a little harder.

The material felt funny, sticky-damp. "Mom!" He practically yelled it, fear curling through his bowels.

"Dad!" Leaning across her, he shook his father. "Dad!"

Suddenly he lost his tiptoed balance and fell on them, landing facedown, mouth open, on the quilt. Abruptly he became aware that the sticky dampness was everywhere, and as he breathed in its rusty metal smell, he realized it was in his mouth and he recognized the flavor of blood from a hundred cuts he'd licked, from a bloody nose last year, from . . .

"Dad! Mom!" Falling backward, he screamed their names. "Wake up!" he cried as he backed toward the wall. He gulped for air. "Please wake up!" Frantically he felt for the light switch, smearing his hands over the wall. "Wake up," he pleaded once more as his hand hit the switch.

Light bloomed overhead.

For a moment he couldn't comprehend what he was seeing. The white homemade quilt with its blue and green wedding ring patterns had turned red. His mother's eyes were open, her mouth, too, and briefly he thought she was about to speak to him. Then he realized that her head was tilted back at an unnatural angle.

He moaned. Her head was almost off her body, there was red meat in her neck, and white bones, gleaming. Beside her, his father . . . His father was the same. Ears ringing, Ricky sank to the floor, blackness invading his vision.

Ricky's stomach moved, roiling, and as he vomited, he saw their blood all over his clothes, his hands, and knew he had their blood in his mouth. He vomited again.

He tried to stand up, couldn't. *Have to get out of here!*
Have to! Now! Grabbing the doorknob, he pulled himself
up, refusing to look at the bed, refusing to think. As he tried
to open the door with his slippery, sticky fingers, he heard
himself crying but thought it was someone else. Finally he
got the door open and slammed his body out into the hall.

"Ricky!" Robin was watching him from the threshold of
his room. "Hi, icky Ricky! Wanna play?"

Ricky stared at him without comprehension.

Robin grinned.

I'm gonna getcha, icky Ricky, I'm gonna getcha good!

Ricky ran, racing down the stairs, tripping and rolling
down the last ten, not even aware that he'd broken his arm
as he regained his feet, only aware that Robin might be following him as he started running for the kitchen.

The glass in the back door was shattered, the screen torn,
and the door stood wide open. As he raced into the backyard,
into the orchard, he heard Robin call his name, heard his
hand-slaps, but he kept running, running, running, until he
reached Carmen's doorstep.

As he pounded on the door, he glanced back. No one was
there.

Between the grave markers, Rick Piper wept silently. He
wept for himself and for his parents.

He wept for what might have been.

The days after the murder had been a blur. He spent the
first two in the hospital, and there had been so many questions, so many policemen, so many nightmares. Eventually
the police announced that the house had been broken into,
nothing stolen, except for a stainless filleting knife from the
kitchen that never reappeared. It was presumed to be the
murder weapon. Though a few suspects were questioned, no
arrests were ever made.

And Robin didn't go away after all.

That was a long time ago. Wiping his eyes, he stood and

brushed grass from his pants. *A very long time.* He moved away, only to stop once more at Robin's grave. "You couldn't get me, so you killed them instead, didn't you?" He kicked a small stone, and it hit Robin's marker with a thunk. "I hated you. I still hate you."

Admitting it made him feel better. The only thing he still couldn't reconcile was the childish notion that his brother had exchanged bodies with a greenjack, when logic dictated that the handicapped boy had gone mad.

He stared at the grave and tried to understand his brother. *It must have been hard to be handicapped,* he told himself. *It must have been awful to look at me every day and wonder why you were the one without legs. No wonder you hated me.*

And no wonder I hated you. "You told me I was crazy," he whispered bitterly. "You told me they were going to send me away. You threatened me and called me names. You told me you were going to kill me. And you *tried.* Goddamn you, you *tried.*" Unthinking, he kicked the headstone. It hurt like hell and increased his fury. "Goddamn you, you even said it was my fault they died! Fuck you!" He raised his voice, not caring if anyone heard. "Fuck you! Fuck you!"

The tears came back, hot and furious, tears of anger and hate and frustration. He dropped to the ground, exorcising twenty-six years of anger and hurt.

Finally the tears dried, and then, guiltily, he realized why he had never declared his hate and anger toward Robin before. *He saved my life that Halloween night when we were seven. He let Big Jack take him instead of me.*

"Oh, God," he moaned, falling to his knees, knowing he himself was mad. "Oh, God."

Finally, slowly, he regained control of himself. *Can't think about this.* Rising, he knew he still couldn't handle the memories, the confusion that went with them. He washed his face at a water fountain and went back to the old Garden of Souls section to lose himself in other people's history.

27

"This house is riddled with secret passages," Rick told Audrey as they sat at the kitchen table after their date Friday night. "The blueprints disappeared way before my time, so I don't even know how many tunnels there are." He sipped his coffee. "This morning we had that installed—" he pointed at the new dishwasher "—and the workmen broke into a passage we didn't even know existed."

"Really? In the kitchen?" Audrey said over her coffee cup. "Maybe your great-grandfather liked to sneak midnight snacks without his wife catching him."

Eat it up! Robin whispers, shoving raw hamburger down his throat. Eat it up!

"You look like you've seen a ghost, Rick. Are you all right?"

"Fine." He didn't think the raw-meat story would be appropriate. "My brother traveled the tunnels all the time," he added lamely.

"You didn't?"

"No. I've been in them, but not willingly. When I was very young, my grandfather took me through a few of the main ones, which was okay, but later, Robin knew how to force me to go with him."

"Most little boys would love secret tunnels in the walls."

She paused, studying him. "I take it your brother made that miserable, too?"

"Yes, that and the fact that I was ridiculously afraid of the dark." He set his cup down. "I still don't like it. Grandpa Piper's stories about the greenjacks had more effect on me than they should have."

"Greenjacks," she repeated. "You mentioned them before. What are they, anyway?"

Over fresh cups of coffee, he told her Grandfather's stories, surprised and rather pleased to find he still knew them word for word. "Pretty silly stuff to be afraid of, huh?"

"No, it's not silly at all. Fairy tales are the worst! I was scared silly by Hansel and Gretel." She pushed red hair away from her face and lowered her voice conspiratorially. "When I was about five, my favorite uncle, Craig, told me the story. I was okay at first, just really impressed, you know? But then, every time he'd come over, he'd say, 'Let's see if your fingernails are clean.'

"The first time, I didn't know what was going on. I held out my hands, and he examined my fingers very closely, very seriously. Uncle Craig was a big, tall man with lots of black hair, one long eyebrow, and a very deep voice, so when he looked at me from underneath his brow and intoned, 'Well, those nails are pretty dirty. I guess we won't have you for dinner . . . this week!' I was sure he meant it." She looked at Rick. "So can you guess what I did after that?"

Rick shook his head. "What?"

"Every Sunday, before Uncle Craig came over, I'd go out in the backyard and frantically scrape my nails in the dirt until they were caked! I was scared to death of the man, scared to death. And he never even knew it."

"How old were you when you lost your fear?"

"I didn't. Uncle Craig got killed when I was seven." She smiled thinly. "It was tragic, really. He worked for CalTrans. They were paving part of I-10, and he had a freak accident with a steam roller."

Rick decided not to smile.

"The last time I dug in the yard was right before we went to the funeral." She stifled a giggle. "You know, just in case. At the service, I was sitting next to my mother, and I remember hearing her make this little 'tsk tsk' sound, you know? I tried to keep my hands hidden for the rest of the day." She sipped her coffee. "About a month later I overheard her telling my dad how much my hygiene had improved lately."

"Thank you," Rick said.

"For what?"

"That story."

"Oh?" She raised her eyebrows quizzically.

"I've never thought about other people's reactions to fairy tales before." He shook his head, amazed. "Never. I can't believe how shortsighted I've been. I mean, I knew I overreacted because I judged my reaction against my brother's opposite one. It's never occurred to me that anyone else would take a story as seriously as I did."

"Well, I sure did. Lots of people do. That's a pretty insulated view you had there, Piper."

"I never talked to anybody about it. Robin constantly told me I was crazy and if I told about any of it—fear of the greenjacks, fear of my brother—the grown-ups would find out I was nuts and send me to an asylum."

"What a cruel little monster he was! You must have hated him."

"When Dakota said that, I denied it. Now I know it's true." He shook his head. "It just never occurred to me that anyone else might be frightened."

"Well, plenty are. We all talked about it when we were kids." She paused. "By 'we,' I mean girls. I think there's a difference between the sexes. It was okay for us to be afraid and to talk about it, even to enjoy it." She smiled. "Every time we had a sleep-over, we had a seance and ended up screaming ourselves silly. But little boys have to pretend to be brave. And males don't seem to talk to each other about serious stuff. It's 'Hey, Bud, pass me a cold one,' or 'Yo, Jo, lookit da tail on that chick.' "

Rick laughed. "There's a lot of that. But look at Cody. He's not into impressing anyone with his testosterone yet, but he seems to have no fear of the dark, or anything else in particular. Driving here from Vegas, he wanted to stop up at Madland, you know that old West movie place up on I-15 by Madelyn?"

"Out of Barstow?"

"Yeah." He paused. "There were ads along the road for the Haunted Mine Ride for a hundred miles before we passed the place, and I was starting to wish I could chloroform the kid." He pitched his voice up an octave. " 'Daddy, I wanna go in the haunted mine! I wanna see ghosts! Are there zombie miners there?' " He laughed.

"Are you still afraid of things like that?" she asked softly.

"Yes." He'd never admitted it before, but it seemed fine to tell. "I did not want to go in there. Fortunately, we were on a schedule. But it made me feel funny knowing that if there had been time, I would have found a way out of it."

"Do things that jump out at you really bother you, like the ghouls in the Haunted Mansion at Disneyland?"

"God, I've never been in there. I'm afraid of making an ass out of myself, squealing or something. I'm a roller coaster man myself," he added in the deep, stupid voice he equated with rednecks.

She smiled briefly. "You didn't answer my question. Is it the dark or things jumping out at you that you can't handle?"

"Let's put it this way: My brother thought the height of amusement was jumping out of dark corners and yelling boo. He didn't do it too often," he added, studying his hands. "He always waited until some time had passed and my guard went down, then 'boo!' and he'd laugh and laugh. It made me jumpy. I ended up with nerves of cellophane."

"You learned to always be on your guard. It must have done wonders for your self-confidence, too," she added dryly.

"Oh yes, wonders." He drained his cup. "More?"

"Sure."

He took their cups to the counter and poured more from

the Mr. Coffee. "The last thing I meant to do is whine about my past," he said, sitting back down.

"Lord, you're hard on yourself, Rick!" She paused. "Can I ask you a question?"

"Sure."

"It's a weird one."

He laughed. "Go ahead."

"Those greenjacks. Did you think you could see them, like the boy in the stories?"

Rick slopped his coffee. "What?"

"You did, didn't you?" she pressed. "It's no big deal. Lots of people think they see things. Not just kids. Every other person in Ireland would probably say they've seen a leprechaun or fairy at one time or another." She smiled. "Nowadays people see little gray aliens, but it's all the same thing. I think."

"Yeah, I used to think I saw them. I thought—still think—I probably just wasn't too well adjusted."

"Well, you had a sadistic brother, and a lot of these things are tied up with abuse. A person can't stand thinking that someone who supposedly loves them is hurting them, so they invent something else to take the blame. From what I've read, it happens a lot."

"That makes a lot of sense." He paused. "And it probably applies to me. No wonder your brother was always telling me to see a shrink," he added casually. "Listen, Audrey. Can I ask you a weird question too?"

"Fair's fair."

"Well, in your practice, have you ever run in to anyone who can see things other people can't? Like infrared rays, for instance?"

"That used to happen to cataract patients, but that's not what you mean, is it?"

"No, I mean naturally. Like cats see infrared."

She considered. "It's possible, but it would probably be impossible to detect during an eye exam unless it was a person with an ocular deformity. James Thurber had that problem. The brain fills in what the eye doesn't pick up."

She smiled. "But he put it to good use—he put the things he saw into his cartoons."

"What about someone with twenty-twenty vision? Could they see something?"

"Rick? Do you still see them?"

"No, no, no, of course not," he replied hastily, then started to skate. "I have a cousin back in Scotland who says he's seen them all his life. He's intelligent, has a good job, and seems perfectly sane. But he sees them. I've just always wondered if maybe he really does."

"What does he say they look like? Are they solid?"

"No, not at all." He described them briefly, leaving out all mention of Big Jack.

"Something like that sounds like it's in the realm of light waves, so it's possible." Audrey studied him a long time. "Let me do a little research."

"If it's any trouble . . ."

"None at all. It's fascinating. I saw a UFO once, but when I made the mistake of reporting it, the authorities told me I was seeing things." She gave him a wry smile. "But I know what I saw—I just learned not to tell anyone about it."

"I believe you," Rick said sincerely.

"I thought you might," she replied, giving him a look that made him certain she knew there was no cousin in Scotland.

"Let's talk about something else," he suggested quickly.

"Okay. The other night you promised to tell me about your old girlfriends."

"I did?"

"Uh-huh. So who was your first?"

He hesitated only briefly. "Her name was Delia."

"And how old were you?"

"Ten."

She smiled. "Tell me all about it"

"It's pretty weird."

"All the better."

He smiled and sat back in his chair. "Her full name was Delia Minuet, and I met her at the carnival on Independence Day Weekend in 1975."

July 4, 1975

The Masello Brothers Carnival and Sideshow arrived in Santo Verde just in time for the July Fourth weekend of Ricky's tenth year. According to his dad, the carnival had come to town at this time every year for as far back as he—and even Grandfather Piper—could remember, but this was Ricky's first visit.

Last year they'd been on vacation at the Grand Canyon, and before that, other vacations, chicken pox, and the mumps had made them miss it.

Now Ricky, standing next to Mom on the warm, clear morning, could hardly wait as they stood in line for tickets. The red and gold banner, the colorful pendants waving across the whole front, the smells of popcorn and cotton candy on the warm breeze, and most of all, the rides. Behind the buildings and tents, he could see the top of the Ferris wheel and the dinosaur back of the Wild Mouse, not to mention whirling umbrella chairs and the occasional lift of an octopus arm.

"Lift me higher, Dad! I wanna see!" Robin, already riding high in their father's arms, almost managed to pull himself onto his head before their dad boosted him onto his shoulder.

Inside, it was even better. Ricky played ring toss and won a rubber snake, rode the roller coaster with Dad, then consumed a cone of sticky pink cotton candy and two snow cones.

Only two things marred the first couple of hours. One was when he and Daddy and Robin rode the Ferris wheel together, and Robin, seated between them, whispered to Ricky that he was going to push him off the swinging bench when they reached the top.

That wasn't too bad because he knew his brother wouldn't do it, not with Dad around. It was the horror ride that was the really bad thing.

From the moment he laid eyes on Train to Terror, Robin

wanted to ride the little cars into the horrors hidden in the darkness beyond. And he wanted his brother to ride with him. Just the two of them, he kept insisting, It would be fun.

Ricky equally did *not* want to ride, not at all, but especially not with Robin. His lower lip kept trembling and he was afraid he was going to start crying any second now. Just looking at the ride scared him so badly that he could hardly think. He didn't want anyone to know how afraid he was, because at every opportunity Robin reminded him that if they knew, their parents would think he was crazy and send him away. And even though he'd actually heard Mom and Dad say they thought Robin was scaring him and that they were going to send him away to school soon, Ricky realized he wouldn't quite believe it until it happened.

"Come on," Robin goaded. "Ride with me, Ricky."

Ricky shook his head no, and his father squatted down and looked him in the eye. "It's just a ride. You love roller coasters, right?"

"Well, yeah."

"This is just a different kind of ride. It's fun. And it's safer than a roller coaster any day." Daddy patted his shoulder. "You know your brother can't go on all the rides you can go on, and he'd really like you to go on this one. I think that's nice, and I think it would be nice if you did, don't you?"

It wasn't nice. He wanted to get him on the ride, then scare him or push him out of the car or Ricky didn't know what. Something awful.

"Why don't we all go on the ride?" His mother stepped forward and put her hand on Ricky's shoulder. "This ride scares me, so maybe Ricky can ride with me and you can ride with Robin?"

Robin looked mad, but Daddy nodded. "That sounds like a good plan, don't you think, Rob?"

"Okay." He smiled so wide that it looked like his face would split in half. "But maybe you should ride with Mommy if she's scared. Then I can still ride with Ricky. That'd be *really* fun. Huh, Ricky?"

But his mother was already leading Ricky toward the ride. "Maybe next time, dear," she told his twin. She and Dad exchanged glances.

"Rick's riding with your mother, Robin," Dad said firmly.

Trembling, Ricky allowed Mom to lead him into the next car. It looked like an insect, shiny black with blood-red trim. Just before the screaming darkness swallowed the car, he glanced back. Daddy and Robin were right behind them. Robin grinned at him and slowly drew his finger across his throat.

Quickly Ricky faced forward, and Mom put her arm around him and pulled him close. He muffled his eyes and ears against her body, stuffing his fingers in his ears and squeezing his eyes shut for good measure.

And he endured. After an eternity, she gently pulled his fingers from one ear and told him it was almost over. As they emerged into light, she assured him he didn't look like he'd been afraid at all and told him she was glad he let her hang on to him.

Ricky knew that wasn't how it worked and he knew she knew, but in that moment he loved her so much, it hurt, because she let him keep his dignity.

A little later, they had lunch (corn dogs dipped in French's mustard, and Cokes with tons of crushed ice—the best junk food on earth), then went to a magic show where a man with a curly mustache sawed a lady in half. Ricky hated it, but didn't know why. After that, they saw a show in the big top with clowns in a car and a trapeze act that looked like fun.

When they exited the big top, Ricky spotted a long tent painted with a series of wonderfully weird pictures. A man at the ticket booth was talking about the pictures on a loud speaker, and Ricky halted, mesmerized by the voice and the pictures. There was one of a cow with part of a second little cow growing out of its side standing by a goat with four eyes, two on each side of its face. Other pictures showed two babies joined at the chest, Siamese twins, he realized; a cocker spaniel with a horn growing out of its forehead; and a man with pins stuck in his skin. The last painting was of a family that didn't look quite right, and the banner over it said THE SMALL FAMILY! LIVE! DIRECT FROM THE CAVERNS OF CONNEMARA.

"Can we go in there?" he asked his parents.

His father looked at Robin, then Mom. "I don't think that's such a good idea, Rick."

"I want to go in too," Robin said.

Their parents looked at each other for a long time, and finally Dad nodded. "Okay, just for a few minutes, though." As he bought the tickets, he said, "It's all fake."

There were all sorts of things in jars, some so goopy you couldn't tell what they were. Maybe some were fake, like the cow—you could see the stitches—and the four-eyed dog didn't look real either. But the Siamese twins, Ricky was sure, had been alive at one time. They floated in formaldehyde in a huge jar, and you could even see the fine hair coating their bodies. They were face-to-face, eyes closed, arms around each other in an eternal embrace. Awestruck, saddened and fascinated, Ricky stood there until a tap on his shoulder made him look up. Robin had craned over to whisper, "Someday I'm gonna put you in a jar, just like that."

Ricky ignored him, his attention already caught by a sign directing them toward the Small Family—SEE THEM IN A REPLICA OF THEIR OWN HOME! LIVE! the sign said. He walked down the short corridor and came into a little room with a stage that looked like a cave—a funny, brightly painted maw with shamrocks and curly-looking kids' furniture. Folding chairs were set up on the floor below the stage.

"Audience," he heard a man's voice call from behind the stage. "Somebody get out there."

Embarrassed, Ricky turned to leave—his family hadn't followed him in yet—then a kid's voice said, "Hi."

He turned back and saw a little girl who was very short and had kind of a large head and long arms. Her long brown hair was tied back with a blue ribbon, and she had big blue eyes. When she smiled, she had dimples.

"We'll have a show in ten minutes," she said.

"What's your name?" he asked, walking closer.

"Delia Small." She giggled. "Mr. Masello, the owner, he said we have to be the Small family. Get it? Small?"

"Uh-uh."

"We're dwarves, you know." And she whistled a few bars of "Hi ho, Hi ho." "Dwarves. Freaks."

Ricky was shocked. "That's a bad word."

"What is?"

"Freaks. My parents said so. Doesn't it make you mad when you get called that?"

"No."

"What's your real last name?"

"Minuet. Like a song. I think that's a much better last name than Small, but Papa says Mr. Masello knows what's best."

"I like your name," Ricky said.

"What's *your* name?"

"Ricky Piper."

"Hi, Ricky."

"Hi, Delia."

They looked at each other and giggled. Then he whispered, "My brother's a freak, but no one's supposed to call him that."

"Is he a midget?" she asked.

"No. He's got no legs."

"He's a half boy?" she asked excitedly.

"Huh?"

"A living torso, but with arms. He has arms?"

"Sure. He walks on his hands."

"Mr. Masello would kill to get a half boy."

"I don't think he's for sale," Ricky said, then paused. Then he grinned. "But I wish he was!"

They giggled. "Is he rotten?" Delia asked conspiratorially.

"He tries to kill me." He said it like a joke.

"That's pretty rotten," she said, and Ricky Piper decided he was in love.

"There you are!" Ricky's mom walked up. "Don't wander off like that. I was worried about you." She turned and called, "He's in here, Frank."

"This is Delia," Ricky said.

"Hello, Delia," Mom said.

"Hi, I gotta go get ready for our show. You'll stay, won't you?"

"Can we, Mom?"

"Sure."

Delia disappeared behind the set just as Rick's dad came in, Robin in his arms. Other people soon followed, and in a few minutes the chairs were filled. Delia, her parents, and little brother came out and did a skit about mining gold in Ireland. It was silly. At the end, when they took their bows, Delia grinned at him and waved. Next to him Robin leaned over and said, "Your girlfriend's funny-looking," and without a second thought, Ricky punched him in the stomach.

"Richard Piper!" his mother said. "What on earth?"

Robin was staring at him with a funny look on his face, sort of a cross between amusement and fury.

"He said something bad about Delia."

"Well," said his father, "we expect you not to solve your problems with your fists, Rick. Apologize to your brother."

"I'm sorry," he said, and it was easy because he felt suddenly brave and knew he wasn't sorry at all.

"That's okay, Ricky," Robin said like some Goody Two-shoes kid off a TV show. "I had it coming."

How could he compete with that?

They stood to leave, and as they filed out, he heard his dad tell his mom that it was nice to see he had backbone. He smiled to himself, still shocked that he'd pounded Robin.

Outside the tent, a tall, dark-haired man stopped them, saying to his father, "Hello, sir, did you enjoy the show?"

Frank Piper nodded.

"I'm John Masello. My brother Vince and I own the carnival." He looked at Robin. "And what's your name, young man?"

"Robin," he said brightly.

"I bet you can do some pretty neat tricks, huh?"

"Sure."

"What is it that you want, Mr. Masello?" Dad asked. He sounded angry.

"I noticed that this young man is special and I was wondering if, since you were at the freak show, you might be interested in giving him a better life."

"What are you talking about?" That came from his mother, and she didn't sound happy either. Delia chose that moment to come out of the tent. She stood next to Ricky and listened intently.

"People with deformities often like to be with their own kind," Masello said. "This boy could make huge sums of money and have many, many friends who would never judge him by his looks." The circus man pulled two cigars from his pocket and offered one to Rick's dad, who shook his head. "Forgive me for being forward," Masello continued, "but would you be interested in letting Robin here travel with our show?"

"I told you he'd do anything for a half boy," Delia whispered to Ricky. "Those cigars are imported from Cuba!"

Ricky stifled a giggle.

"His contract would be very lucrative," Masello went on. "He'd make enough for his handsome brother here to go to college, and he could keep the whole family in—"

Say yes, say yes, say yes. Ricky prayed.

"No," Dad said with stern finality. "We're not interested."

"Let me give you my card—"

"No, that won't be necessary." He turned to his family. "We're going home."

"Ricky," Delia said. "Can you come back? Tonight, maybe?"

Go outside at night? For an instant he almost said yes, but common sense set in.

"No, but I live just two blocks from here. Could you sneak over to my house?"

"Ricky, come on," called Mom.

"Just a second."

"What's your address?"

"It's 667 Via Matanza. That's—"

"I'll find it. Can you meet me outside?"

"You don't have to sneak. My mom won't mind. How early can you come?"

"Six-thirty?"

"Come to the door at six-thirty. She'll invite you to dinner."

"Really?"

"She invites everybody to dinner."

"That sounds great." She paused. "Will your brother be there?"

"Yeah. Why?"

"What's wrong with him?"

"He was born that way."

"No, not that. He's . . . I don't know, creepy. No offense," she added quickly.

"No offense. I think he's creepy too. You're the first person besides me to ever say that, though," he told her with delight. Maybe Delia would be able to see the greenjacks, too. But even if she couldn't, he could hardly wait to talk to her some more.

"See you tonight," she said.

"See you."

"How about some fresh coffee?" Rick asked, bringing the pot to the table.

"Thanks." Audrey pushed her cup toward him. "What a romantic story."

Rick shrugged.

"But I won't let you leave me in suspense. Did your mother invite Delia to dinner?"

"Yes. We had a great time, too. It was the first time I ever felt like I had a real friend my age—you know, the kind who understands things about you that would make other people think you're crazy."

"I know," she said softly.

"Anyway, my parents got a kick out of her—Delia was very mature for her age, very feisty—and I wished with all my heart that I could have her for a sister instead of Robin for a brother."

Audrey smiled. "I thought you said she was your first love."

"She was. We saw each other every day until the carnival left town, and my mother told her to come back the next year. But Mom and Dad died two months later."

"So you never got to see her again?"

He gave her a ghost of a smile. "I saw her. We just sneaked around after that first year."

"Why did you have to sneak?"

"My brother mostly. Plus Aunt Jade and Uncle Howard would have made fun of her."

She cocked her head. "A while ago you said Delia asked you what was wrong with your brother. What did she mean by that?"

He chose his next words carefully "He hated her from the moment they met. He even called her 'Troll' to her face. She stayed away from him, but it wasn't because of the name-calling—she could handle that. It was because she didn't trust him. I think she must have sensed his meanness." He gazed at Audrey, wanting to tell her the whole story, but afraid to.

"Delia had been raised in such a different way than most people," he ventured. "She really didn't notice physical things: They didn't mean much to her. So I think that because she didn't spend time feeling sorry for Robin or cutting him slack because he had no legs, she could sense his cruelty very easily. She hated his eyes," he allowed himself to tell Audrey.

"If you were identical twins, weren't they just like yours?"

"They were darker than mine, almost black," Rick explained. "Delia said that when she looked into his eyes, she could see he didn't have a human soul."

Audrey's green eyes had grown large. "That's a pretty strong statement for a little kid."

"Well, frankly, I didn't think he had a human soul either." The words were out of his mouth before he could stop himself.

"Rick, really?"

He nodded, his guts tying themselves in knots. How was he going to tell her more without sounding crazy?

"Why?"

"Because Robin told me so, and I believed him." He shook his head. "I always believed everything he said, and he claimed he was a little jack who'd possessed my brother's body, and that my real brother was outside with the jacks . . ."

"Don't stop now!" She gestured impatiently.

"Well, when we were seven, Robin pulled a Halloween joke on me that backfired. He took a skeleton mask and climbed out our window into the oak in the front yard to scare me. He wanted me to think he was Big Jack." Rick clutched the coffee cup to keep his hands from shaking. "To make a long story short, he fell out of the tree and hit his head. After that, he started claiming—but only to me—that he was a changeling or whatever you want to call it. He said what he really wanted was my body since I could see—" *Oh, shit,* he thought, *Oh shit, oh shit, oh shit.*

Icky Ricky, sicky Ricky, dicky Ricky.

For the first time tonight, he heard them. Had they been calling all along or had his guard just gone down? Or maybe he just thought he heard them. *I hear voices,* he thought. *Oh joy That probably means I'm certifiable. Just what Audrey wants.*

Audrey shook her head. "Children are incredibly cruel. You must have been terrified."

He took a deep breath, grateful that she'd said nothing about his slip. "I was incredibly gullible. I believed it all."

She reached across the table and took his hand. "Do you still?"

"No. Robin's personality changed when he fell on his head, so I assume he sustained some kind of brain damage."

She nodded. "Probably. But you still see the greenjacks, don't you." It was a statement, not a question, but her hand stayed firmly on his.

"N-No," he replied, flustered. "Like I said, I had a deadly imagination."

"The other night you told me you didn't want to judge yourself by your brother anymore. You're doing it."

"I don't understand," he said dully.

"You saw them, your brother didn't. I bet there are more kids who think they see things than ones who don't. I mean"—she grinned at him—"didn't you ever have an invisible friend?"

"Shelly did," he answered with relief. "And Cody's just acquired one." He smiled. "His name is Bob. Bob the invisible friend."

Their laughter broke the tension.

"My invisible friend's name was Miranda," Audrey said, "because that's what I wanted my name to be. The cutest girl in school was named Miranda."

"Cody doesn't know any Bobs," Rick said thoughtfully.

"Maybe he got it off TV. Bob Newhart, maybe?"

"I'll bet you're right." Rick stroked one of her fingers. "So you think lots of kids see things that aren't there?" he asked, trying to sound very casual.

"I *always* see prowlers if I let myself," Audrey confessed. "In shadows at night, my robe hanging on a hook by the door becomes a living, breathing intruder. It moves. My eyes see it. God, I hate sleeping alone."

He didn't say a word, just sat there and watched the color come up from under her collar, flushing her skin redder and redder until she looked sunburned.

"I wasn't coming on," she sputtered.

He squeezed her hand. "Too bad." Seeing the look on her face, he quickly added, "Since Laura died, I've been out half a dozen times, blind dates mostly, nothing serious. Not like . . . What I mean is, I haven't done this in a long time, Audrey."

"Me either." She squeezed back.

"Okay if I'm blunt?"

"You'd better be." She smiled softly.

"I'm in no hurry and I'm not going to rush you. In fact, I want to go slow." The truth was, *want* had nothing to do with it; he *needed* to go slow.

"An-ti-ci-pa-tion," Audrey sang softly.

"Yes, anticipation's good," he agreed.

They sat in silence a long moment. "Rick, you see green-jacks—saw greenjacks." She stared into her coffee cup. "I've seen a ghost. Have you?"

He thought about it. He'd been so hung up on his own brand of critter that he'd never thought about hauntings. "Um, no, I don't think so," he said finally. "You saw one, huh?"

Silently she got up and brought the coffeepot back to the table. Her hand shook as she poured. "Yes," she said at last. She overfilled his cup, slopping coffee onto the table. "Oh, sorry. She reached for a napkin, but he beat her to it.

"Relax." He blotted the spill. "Tell me about the ghost."

"I've never told anyone before."

"I won't tease you," he promised solemnly. "I'll believe you."

"I know. That's why I'm telling you, but, Rick . . ." She swallowed. "When I'd been married about a year, my mother died. She hated Ron and she'd begged me not to marry him, but I did anyway." She shook her head. "We fought and fought and ended up not speaking.

"The night she died, Ron had come home drunk." She looked down. "He beat me up. It was ten past midnight—I kept looking at the clock. Ron was snoring on the couch. I was in bed, and I hurt so much, I couldn't sleep. He'd punched me in the ribs several times," she added, her mortification obvious, "and I realize now I had some broken ribs. It even hurt to breathe.

"I hadn't spoken to Mother in nearly a year, and I was thinking about her, about how right she'd been about Ron. I was only nineteen, still so young and stubborn that I couldn't make myself call her and tell her so, but I sure thought about it. I wanted to go home, but my pride wouldn't let me.

"Suddenly I smelled her perfume—she always wore White Shoulders—and I opened my eyes. She was standing by the bed, plain as day. Just standing there looking down at me." Sudden tears welled and ran down her cheeks.

"God, I'm sorry," she said, picking up a napkin and dabbing at her eyes.

"It's okay."

She nodded. "She was dressed in a powder blue suit I'd never seen before, and she was a little plumper than I remembered. I remember what I said. I asked her a question. I asked, 'Are you going to take me home now?' She didn't say anything, she just smiled and held out her hands.

"I took them." Her own hands trembled as she spoke, and he took them in his, held them still. "Rick, her hands were as warm and solid as yours are now.

"I sat up in bed and put my arms out, and she sat next to me and pushed my hair out of my eyes like she always used to do. We stared at each other and I said, 'I love you, Mother,' and she said it back, but, Rick, I was looking right at her. I heard her, but her lips didn't move."

The hairs on the back of his neck rose.

"She held me," Audrey said softly, wonderingly, "and told me she loved me over and over.

"The next thing I knew, I woke up. The phone was ringing. It was my father, calling from the hospital. His voice was shaking. It was almost two in the morning. He said Mother had a stroke and she'd died at ten after twelve. There was nothing the doctors could do."

Silent tears ran down her cheeks, but now she smiled through them. "My mother came to tell me good-bye. I know it."

"That's beautiful," Rick said softly.

"Yes."

Close to tears, he wanted to confess, once and for all, that he still saw them. But he couldn't

28

"Dad!"

Jolted by the scream and the sudden pain Rick's fingers caused as they dug into her arms, Audrey pulled out of the good-night embrace.

"Rick?" He stood there, eyes glassy, chestnut hair mussed from her fingers, the color draining from his uncomprehending face. He didn't seem to see her. "Rick!"

"Dad!"

Slowly his head turned toward the staircase, and then the lost look left his features and everything clicked into place. "It's Shelly!" He turned and ran up the stairs, Audrey close behind.

"Dad!"

The cry was loud as they rounded the upstairs corner.

"Shelly!" Rick slammed against her door, then grabbed the knob and turned it, practically falling into the room as the door swung open. "Shelly!"

"My God!" Audrey whispered as she entered behind him. Shelly sat in the middle of her bed, clutching her covers protectively around her neck. Her nightstand light cast a yellow glow over the room and the things it held.

On the bed, on the dresser and chest and desk, were toy dogs. All of them were pointed at Shelly as if watching her, and they were all in different positions, everything from begging to lifting a leg to urinate. For a moment Audrey couldn't comprehend what she was seeing, then she remembered Aunt Jade and realized these were the deceased poodles Rick had mentioned. At the time, it was funny; they'd laughed over the story. Now it was horrifying.

"Daddy," Shelly whimpered. Her eyes were huge, her dark blond hair tangled around her face so that she looked like a little girl.

Rick swept a poodle off the bed with the back of his hand, then he had his arms around his daughter, rocking and consoling her, whispering, "It's all right, it's okay," over and over again. Shelly's shoulders shook with quiet sobs.

In a few minutes, the girl regained control, She looked up, directly into Audrey's eyes, and suddenly she felt like an intruder. "I'm sorry, I shouldn't be here. I'll go."

Shelly didn't react for a moment, then she mumbled, "No, it's okay." Then she made a face. "Man, what a feeb I am," she added shakily.

"No, you're not, Shel."

"You won't tell anybody that I screamed and stuff, will you, Daddy?"

"Of course not."

Audrey jumped as something grabbed her legs from behind.

"Cool!" Cody pushed around her and into the room. "Lookit the doggy rats! One, two, three," he counted, "four, five, six dead doggy rats. Cool!" He looked at his sister. "Did you steal 'em from Aunt Jade?" he asked, wonder and awe in his voice.

"Of course not, butthead," Shelly sneered. "And who told you, you can come in my room?"

"You screamed, huh?"

"Up yours!"

"Shelly's a screamer," Cody sang. "Shelly's a screamer!"

"Cody, be quiet," Rick ordered sternly. "Do you know anything about these?" He gestured around the room at the dogs.

Cody shook his head. "Uh-uh, no way. I bet Bob put 'em here."

Cody did it, Audrey thought.

"Cody," Rick said, "come clean." Obviously he, too, subscribed to the theory that a kid blaming an invisible friend was guilty without trial.

But the boy didn't giggle or look away from his father's eyes. "No, Daddy, I didn't do it."

"Shelly? What happened? Do you remember anything?"

"I woke up. I heard a noise and I woke up. I felt like somebody was watching me, and I wasn't sure if it was from a dream or not, so I turned on the light." She glared at Cody. "I'm gonna get you, you little turd."

"Shelly, no." Rick stood up. "I don't think your brother did it. I think your aunt did it." He glanced at Audrey as he added, "She's a few bricks short of a load."

Audrey nodded. Right before Shelly screamed, while they were in the front foyer indulging in a little lightweight necking, weird sounds had come from the old lady's room, moaning and whispering. Rick looked embarrassed and explained that she did that almost every night.

"Come on, Cody," Audrey said. "I'll see you to your room.'

Rick was gathering poodles and dropping them in an empty packing box still in the room, his face distorted by an expression of utter disgust. He looked up. "Thanks. I'll be there in a minute."

Cody took her hand and practically dragged her out of the room and around the corner to his room. "Come on! You gotta see my wallpaper! My dad had it too. It's the same paper, I'm keeping it."

He talked a mile a minute as he took her around his room, showing her his treasures, which seemed to involve Legos and plastic dinosaurs more than anything else. "And you know what? There's secret tunnels in the house."

"There are?" Rick had mentioned that he'd kept that information from his son. "Who told you?"

"Bob. He's my friend. He talks to me at night. Someday he's gonna show me the tunnels."

"Come on, you get in bed now."

"Okay." He dimpled up at her and jumped into his red race-car bed by the window.

A tree limb just outside scratched the screen lightly. *That's the tree Rick hated.*

"Kiss me g'night."

She smiled and did as he ordered. "Good night, Cody."

"Is your brother a boy or a girl?" he asked abruptly.

"A boy," she said immediately.

"How come he has boobies?"

Boobies? "Well, um, why don't you ask Duane about it when he visits? Or ask your father."

"Who's Duane?"

"Dakota. His real name's Duane. Dakota's his stage name."

Cody lay down. "Okay, g'night," he said.

As she left the room, Rick approached, carrying the box of dogs. He looked upset. "I told Shelly to make sure she locks her door from now on." He paused, grimacing. "I'm sorry. I'm really sorry about this."

"Don't be silly," she told him as they started down the stairs. "It's not your fault. By the way, Cody knows there are passages in the house."

Rick stopped in his tracks. "He does?"

"He says Bob told him."

Understanding dawned on his face. "Jade probably told him." He adjusted the box in his arms, his upper lip curling with distaste. "I'll just have to make sure everything's sealed up." He put the box of poodles on the floor at his feet. "I can't keep her in control. She must have gone up the front stairs while we were in the kitchen and put these things in there to scare Shelly." His face clouded.

"But Shelly said a noise woke her up, so it must have happened just before we got there."

He smiled grimly. "I have an answer for that, too. She went up the back stairs while we were out here."

"But we heard her making noises."

"Only for a few minutes when we first came out. We

were out here for"—he consulted his watch—"almost half an hour."

"Time flies when you're having fun," she said, smiling a little.

"Yes, it does." He reached for her, and she started to snake her arms around his waist. Then, from Jade's room came a moan, followed closely by Jade's clear, loud voice crying, "Fuck me!"

Shocked, Audrey looked at Rick. He looked back.

"Fuck me." Louder, more demanding. The words were followed by a series of obscene grunts and groans.

Rick turned beet red, and she was pretty sure she'd done the same.

"Fuck me!"

"Rick? Maybe she has, uh, marital aids? She's not all that old, is she?"

"Early sixties. Carmen told me she takes hormones."

"Fuck me!"

Audrey snickered. "Better tell the doctor to cut her dosage!"

Rick started laughing, pulling her close and burying his head on her shoulder to muffle the sound. She felt hilarity rising from a tickle in her abdomen, up, up, into her throat, and it exploded from her mouth, gales of it. She clung to Rick, trying to keep quiet, but he was shaking with stifled laughter also.

"What a night," Rick whispered, his words hiccuping over the laughter. "Fine Italian cuisine, slapstick movies, coffee and ghost stories, and"—he swept one arm grandly toward Jade's room—"and, the *pièce de résistance,* stuffed dogs and sex-crazed old ladies."

He laughed again, too abruptly to be able to muffle the noise. Audrey would have doubled up if she didn't have him to cling to.

The noises from Jade's room stopped abruptly.

"Oops," Audrey managed. "She heard us."

"Yeah."

"Or she shorted out her vibrator," she couldn't help adding.

Rick snickered again, and they silenced as they caught each other's gaze. Another good-night kiss was coming up quick.

Before their lips met, Audrey heard a key click in a nearby lock. She and Rick pulled apart, and as she watched the handle on the louvered door start to descend, her legs turned to jelly.

Rick simply picked up the box of dogs. Four stiff pink legs poked out of the top. She couldn't help herself; another hysterical giggle escaped.

The door opened and she beheld Jade Ewebean for the first time. She gasped, then clamped her hand over her mouth to trap the laughter that wanted to escape.

Jade's black hair floated in a tangled mess around a face coated with red lipstick, thick eyeliner, red circles of rouge, and sparkly white powder that had creased into her wrinkles so that they looked like scars. Mascara had smeared beneath her eyes. She looked like Bette Davis in *Whatever Happened to Baby Jane?* The face made Audrey want to scream. It belonged in a house of horrors.

But the tall, bony body made her want to laugh. The woman wore a peignoir set of red polyester and black lace. *Thank God she put on the robe,* Audrey thought, barely controlling herself. It was as sheer as the gown, but the double layer faded her body from what would have been horrific pornography to moderately disgusting translucence.

Rick had moved toward his aunt, and Audrey remained in the shadow of the staircase. The old bat didn't see her, but her reaction to Ricky was amazing.

"Richard," she crooned. "My sweet little Ricky. You've come to see your auntie, haven't you?"

"Jade—" he began. Immediately she cut him off.

"You're so like your brother, Richard, but you still look like a little boy." She unbuttoned her robe and let it fall open.

I'm in a Felini film. Audrey moved slightly so she could see around Rick. *Oh, my God!* she thought, shocked.

Jade's robe dropped to the floor, leaving her saggy body backlit by the lamplight from her room. The gown was short, and even in the dim light, Audrey could see the blue veins knotting her legs. Her gaze traveled upward and stopped. Jade had huge breasts, trussed into the gown's flimsy black lace bra. She squinted, not believing her eyes. A Fredrick's gown, she thought, seeing that the nipples thrust bare from the lace. They, too, were big and damp and lumpy, like two wads of red bubble gum. They looked rouged.

Jade kneaded one in her gnarled hand. "Come to your aunt Jade, Richard. Let's give you a kiss."

Rick's back had stiffened the moment she'd entered the room, and he hadn't moved since. Now he spoke, so low Audrey could barely hear.

"Don't do that."

"Why? Are you a bad boy? Got a stiffie for your dear old aunt?"

"You make me sick." The words dripped cold fury. "There are children in this house, Jade."

"I don't see any children now, Richard. Come here." She stepped nearer.

"What you do in the privacy of your room is your business, but don't bring it out here," he said icily. "If you do this again, I won't even send you to a rest home. I'll have you committed. Stay away."

She made an obscenely childish face. "You're no fun. You never were. You'd be so nice if you were like your brother."

"My brother is dead!" He nearly yelled the words, then was silent a moment, regaining control, Audrey realized. "Get out of my way, Jade."

"What?"

He stepped toward her. "Get out of my way. These belong to you. They belong in your room. I'm going to put them there, and they're going to stay there. If they don't, I don't care about the cost, you're out of here. You scared Shelly half to death." As he spoke he pushed past her, shoving her out of the way with the box. He disappeared into the room, and Audrey heard thumping as he dumped the dogs on the floor. "Don't upset Shelly or Cody again," he warned, reappearing in the doorway.

At that moment she spotted Audrey. Jade's painted face was almost comic as it raced through a series of reactions. Then she laughed. It was a horrible sound, like fingernails raking a blackboard. "I see why you don't want your auntie, Richard. You fucked that flat-chested little whore instead." She sniffed. "You have shitty taste, nephew. Shitty." She spat in Audrey's direction. "Whore."

Rick's face had hardened into a stony scowl. He took a step toward Jade, his hands coming up. She couldn't see his face. If she could, Audrey thought she'd run. The open boyishness that so attracted Audrey to Rick had disappeared entirely, replaced by anger so potent that it seemed to come off him in waves. "Rick," she said tentatively. "Rick, it's okay."

He ignored her, hands level with Jade's neck, eyes glittering and furiously intent. Another step and he'd be on her.

"Rick!" Audrey cried. "Stop it!"

For an instant he focused on her. But then his hands closed on Jade's shoulders—not her neck, Audrey saw with relief. His fingers made white marks on the skin below her collarbone, and he forced her to turn around.

Audrey ran forward, reliving her own old fears. "Don't hit her!" she cried. "Rick! Don't—"

He turned the woman around and slowly forced her up against the wall. "I won't hit her," he said without taking his eyes from Jade's face. He kept her shoulders trapped against the wall. "She used to hit me all the time, Audrey. I didn't tell you about that. She used to take a belt to me. Once, she whipped me until my pants were shredded. I had to stay out of school for a week. She thought it was funny. Didn't you, Jade? You thought it was funny."

"Richard, don't be so mean." Jade's voice quavered. "You're hurting my shoulders."

"Rick," Audrey began, then stopped. There was nothing she could say.

"Richard, please!"

"Daddy?"

Audrey looked up, saw Cody rubbing his eyes at the top of the stairs.

"Go back to bed, Cody," Rick called, his voice only slightly strained. "Everything's okay."

"Okay."

Audrey was amazed that the boy obediently did as Rick asked.

Rick drew a deep breath and released it with a shudder, then let go of Jade. He bent and picked up the red robe and threw it at her. "Cover yourself up and never leave your room dressed like this again. My children and my friends do not need to see you like this. Neither do I."

"You'll never measure up to your brother, you little prick!" Jade spat at him as she flounced past, pulling the door closed behind her.

"My brother's dead," he said quietly as Jade's lock clicked home.

"Rick?"

He turned and looked at her, his face open again, boyish, but heartbreakingly sad. "Audrey? I'm sorry. I'm really sorry. I'll understand if you don't . . . I lost control."

She went to him and took his hand. "You didn't lose control."

"Yes, I did."

"No. I lived with a man who had no control, and because of that, I thought for a second that you were going to hit her. I'm sorry. If I hadn't been hit, I wouldn't have thought it."

"I wanted to hit her. I wanted to kill her."

Slowly she pulled him forward and put her arms around his waist. "I wanted to kill her, too, Rick." She smiled up at him. "Anyone in their right mind would want to kill her."

"Does this mean you'll see me again?" She felt his body

relax against her slightly. His voice trembled with caged emotions. She wished he would cry, but knew he wouldn't.

"Yes, I want to see you again. I mean, it can't get crazier than this, can it?"

He studied her a long time before answering. "Yes, it can."

Something in his voice, a finality, a surety, troubled her, but she looked into his eyes and said, "We'll just take it one day at a time, okay?"

"Okay."

They kissed chastely, and he saw her to the door. She thought it was odd that he didn't accompany her down the walk to her car, but then, he'd been through so much.

On the drive home, she wondered about him, thinking that there was more under the surface than she'd realized. At first she thought he was a sweet, sincere guy, sort of shy, very intelligent, and stamped with her brother's seal of approval, which was damn hard to come by. There was a darkness lying just below the surface, though, and she didn't know if it was something that could be exorcised or not. She also thought the cousin in Scotland didn't exist.

29

"Quint?" Rick called as he locked his bedroom door behind him. "Quint? Where are you, cat?" He waited a moment. "Here, kitty, kitty. Time to eat."

The cat wasn't answering. *Christ,* he thought, *on top of everything else, this is all I need.* "Quint?" He walked into the dressing room, automatically looking at the cabinet, relieved to see the hanger holding it shut. He scanned the floor and the shelves above the clothes racks. "Quint?"

The cat wasn't in the bathroom either. "Here, kitty, kitty."

Then he heard a hiss behind him and returned to the bedroom. "Quint?"

A low growl emanated from behind the headboard. Grabbing his flashlight from the nightstand, he got down on his hands and knees. "Quint?"

The cat was crouched at the halfway point in the eight-inch-wide space between the bed and the wall. Its ears were back and its eyes reflected green in the flashlight's beam. It growled menacingly.

"What's wrong, cat?"

Quint's only answer was another hiss.

"Okay, have it your way." Rick rose and went into the bathroom, poured fresh Iams in the dish and replaced the stale water. Usually Quint would come running when he heard the crunchies tumbling, but not tonight. *Why?*

A scrabbling sound in the wall gave him the answer. Rats.

Quint wouldn't know a rodent if it bit him on the ass. Maybe he'd seen one, smelled one, something. After all, Rick hadn't checked for entries into the room other than the passage. He squatted down in front of the bathroom vanity and opened the door, inspecting the openings the plumbing traveled through, and saw a small opening between the pipe and the cabinet. He reached up and retrieved his flashlight from the counter, shined it on the cabinet floor, behind the rolls of toilet tissue.

A mouse turd, just one, lay in the back of the cabinet. "Uh-huh, I see," Rick said, rising. "Ouch!" he cried, banging the back of his head on the counter. "Shit!" He rubbed the sore spot as he returned to the bedroom, got a bait trap, and placed it in the cabinet. "Here you go, you little son of a bitch!" He rose, successfully this time, and brushed his teeth, then stripped to his shorts. He'd had enough showers for one day.

After he climbed into bed, the cat joined him almost instantly, plastering his body against Rick's side, draping his head and arms over his shoulder. "You're a big baby, you know that? Big cat like you, afraid of a little bitty mouse."

The cat stared at him, unperturbed.

Usually Rick read himself to sleep, but tonight he snapped off the lamp and lay in the dark, absently stroking Quint's fur. "It wasn't a good day for me either, fur-ball."

The cat purred.

He didn't know what to do about Jade. She'd frightened Shelly, called Audrey names, and caused him to stop thinking and almost do violence. My god, he thought, if he hadn't been brought to his senses when he heard Audrey's anguished "Don't hit her!" he actually might have done it.

What if she parades around like that in front of Cody? The thought filled him with dread. Maybe he could rent her an apartment. She didn't really need a retirement home. She wasn't so old and feeble that she needed one. Or crazy enough to be locked away. And unless he buckled under and took the TV job, he couldn't afford it, so his threats were somewhat empty. *Rent her an apartment,* he advised himself, *and get her out of the house.* But even if he was only putting out another thousand or so a month for her upkeep, he'd still have to take the TV job, that or give up good restaurants, the theater, the symphony, and the occasional rock concert. There were other expenses to consider. Now that he had the room, he wanted to buy a real piano so that the kids—and he himself—could learn to play. His primary computer was getting old and crotchety, and he wanted a laptop so that he could work in bed, too. The kids needed things, the house, too, all items that he could eventually afford without going into debt if he just left Jade where she was.

Put her out on Sunset Boulevard and let her hook her room and board. He smiled devilishly. *You don't owe her a place to live.*

That was the ultimate truth. The Ewebeans had been their guardians, if you could use that word without laughing, after their parents died, but from the first, they did it only for themselves. The Ewebeans were just like the innkeeper and his wife in *Les Misérables.* He remembered clearly the day they showed up, a few weeks after their parents' death.

October 1, 1975

The arrival of Jade and Howard Ewebean from Larkin Hill, a little nest of inbreeding located in the northernmost reaches of California, did not fill Ricky with joy. These, his only living relatives, were people who rightfully belonged only in small, backward towns in the middle of nowhere. Here in Santo Verde, they qualified as the cream of the crap, as his father used to say. As they pulled up the drive, Ricky, watching with Carmen, had the sinking feeling that the Beverly Hillbillies were moving in.

He'd heard his parents talk about the Ewebeans, but he'd never seen them before. They were the only relatives left. His dad had sometimes joked that gypsies must have left his sister, Jade, on his parents' stoop one night, because she didn't look or act like any of the other Pipers. Grandfather had studiously pretended she didn't exist.

Seeing her for the first time, Ricky thought that, except for the way her breasts were trying to pop the buttons of her faded plaid dress, she looked a lot like the woman in the painting called *American Gothic*. And Howard looked just like the man, skinny and bald and sour. All he needed was a pitchfork. Ricky stifled a giggle.

"Come on, Ricky," Carmen said, touching his elbow. "We better be polite."

Heart sinking, he watched them climb out of a dirty, smoke-belching pink and gray Rambler. Aunt Jade turned briskly toward the open car door. "Come here, Buffems," she called in a cloying, nasal voice. "Come here, Buffem-wuffems."

He heard yipping, and a second later, he saw a dog leap from the car. It was a poodle, small and white, with a poofy, goofy haircut and a green plaid collar studded with rhinestones. Its high-pitched frantic whining turned briefly into a growl as it saw him, then Jade called it again, and it threw itself into her arms. It was the most loathsome creature he'd ever seen.

Then a girl slithered out of the car, and he forgot about the dog. Ricky knew she had to be his cousin, Evangeline. She was about three years older than him, and the look in her pale muddy eyes, combined with the smile she bestowed on him when she noticed him staring at her, said she'd instantly pegged him as kibble for the horrible poodle. His blood ran cold.

"Oooh, wittle Buffems," Aunt Jade cooed into a fuzzy pink ear. "Is you my wittle baby? Is you?"

Buffems licked her face, waggling its tail like a golfball on a stick. Suddenly he saw its weenie stick out and rub against Jade Ewebean. He slapped his hand over his mouth a second too late to keep the giggle inside, and the sound of it hung in the air like a big red arrow, pointing directly at him.

Aunt Jade looked at him. Uncle Howard looked at him. Evangeline looked at him. Even the poodle looked at him.

"You," Howard Ewebean grunted. "Which one are you?" Ricky stared dumbly at him.

"You deaf, boy?" Aunt Jade asked. "Answer your uncle." The poodle growled, its gums obscenely pink.

"I, I—"

"This is Ricky," Carmen said, putting her hands protectively on his shoulders. He leaned gratefully against her.

"What's the matter with him?" Howard demanded. "He a mute?"

"No," Carmen said. Ricky could tell she was angry and trying to hide it. "He can talk, but he's just lost his parents, so he doesn't feel much like it, you know?"

Jade drew herself up to her full, considerable, height and threw her shoulders back. "You're the maid?"

"Housekeeper," Carmen replied with dignity.

"Well, you ain't going to be the maid long if you mouth off to me again."

"Miz Ewebean." Carmen spoke calmly. "Did you and Mr. Ewebean read all the legal papers?"

"Course we did," Howard grunted.

"Then you know you can't fire me. It's in the papers. My husband and I take good care of the boys and the house. We see nothing bad happens to any of them. The Pipers, they knew that and they put it in their papers. If you did read them, you know that too."

Howard grunted and blew his nose into a wrinkled handkerchief.

"We'll see," sniffed Jade. "We'll just see how much you'll care about those boys when you don't get your paycheck."

"The lawyer's office sends my money, and since you say you read the papers, you know that, too, so don't pretend to be stupid, Miz Ewebean. And don't pretend I am either. That way we'll get along a lot better."

"Look, Mama." Evangeline's voice was high and whiny, and she never took her eyes off him as she spoke. "Look at the boy. He's staring at Buffems like he never seen a dog before."

"You never seen a dog, boy?" Aunt Jade asked.

"Madre de Dios," Carmen said quietly to Ricky. One of her hands left his shoulder, and Ricky knew she was crossing herself.

"Speak up, boy," Howard grumbled.

"I—I've never seen such a fu—funny-looking one." A small hysterical giggle escaped, and he felt his face flush.

"It's a sin against God," Carmen hissed.

"I thought they had money," Jade said to Howard.

"They do," Howard said. " 'cause we got it too, long as we take care of their brats."

Jade nodded knowingly. "Pity. I guess having money don't mean having fashion sense. You're a stutterer, boy?" she asked.

Ricky shook his head no.

"Where's the freak?" Evangeline Ewebean asked loudly.

"You got him locked up somewhere?" Howard chimed in.

Carmen's hand tightened on Ricky's shoulder. "We don't call him words like that. His name is Robin."

"Yeehaw!"

As if in answer, Robin's joyful cry pierced the air. Ricky and the others turned toward the house, and Ricky watched the leaves in the oak tree move as Robin, invisible, climbed down from the bedroom window. Suddenly he dropped from the lowest branch to the ground. He landed on his hands, elbows flexing, and then he ran forward, hands hidden in the overgrown grass.

"Oooh, look at it!" squealed Evangeline.

The poodle let loose a hysterical volley of yaps and strained to get free of Jade's arms.

"Stop it, Buffems," she ordered. "Will you look at that thing move?" she asked.

"Hauls ass," Howard allowed.

Robin arrived at the walkway leading to the driveway, and the slap-slap of his hands hitting the bricks seemed very loud to Ricky. The Ewebeans just stood there and stared, Jade clutching Buffems against her breasts, until Robin arrived next to his brother. Ricky moved closer to Carmen.

"Hello, Aunt Jade. Hello, Uncle Howard." He paused, looking Evangeline up and down. "Hello, Evangeline."

She giggled.

"I'll be goddamned, if that ain't the goddamnedest thing I ever saw." Howard slowly shook his head. "Belongs in a circus. What'd you say his name was?" he said to Carmen.

"Robin," she said.

"Robin? Hell!" cried Howard. "He don't look like a robin. He looks like a lump to me. He oughta be called Lumpkin, 'cause robins got wings."

"He's gonna grow up and be third base," Evangeline supplied.

The poodle, still yipping, suddenly squirmed free of Jade's grasp. Instantly it turned to face Robin, its legs stiff, its lip curled. *Eat him,* Ricky wished, then closed off the thought.

"Lumpkin," said Robin merrily. "Lumpkin, Lumpkin, Lumpkin!" With that, he flipped into a handstand and ran, head down, across the yard, climbing the oak tree like a monkey.

"Don't that beat all?" Howard said, chuckling and sending his boozy breath in Ricky's direction. "That thing's gonna be a hoot."

"Give Ricky a nickname too," Robin yelled from the tree.

Howard snorted, but before he could open his mouth, Robin screamed, "He's icky Ricky! Icky Ricky! Call him Icky Ricky!"

The Ewebeans looked at Ricky and laughed.

Things deteriorated after that. Rick stared at the ceiling. Howard was a mean drunk, Jade was his match, and their daughter didn't fall far from the tree. Evangeline, at thirteen, was well into puberty and intent on torturing every male she came into contact with.

Rick yawned. The first few years were bad, but he still had his locking bedroom and Carmen. When he wasn't in school, he lived by spending countless hours at Carmen and Hector's or, if he couldn't, remaining locked alone in his room, reading, writing, thinking. The Ewebeans didn't miss him, the Ewebeans didn't care. At night, when he'd wake up screaming because he'd dreamed again about finding his dead parents, they ignored him or hollered at him to shut the fuck up.

Two years later, when he and Robin entered early adolescence, things became far, far worse.

A silent tear ran from his eye. Quint moved one paw up and touched it, just as he had when he was a kitten.

Rick stared at the ceiling. *I don't owe Jade Ewebean a thing,* Rick thought drowsily. *Not a damn thing. She owes me.*

30

After a month of work, Don Quixote still didn't look much like a knight errant, but his noble steed had taken on a distinctly horsey cast. Rick stood back and surveyed his work with satisfaction. The legs and tail were completed, and if not perfect, they at least had the long-limbed wraithiness that he so admired.

Scratching his chin thoughtfully, Rick studied the belly of the beast. He wasn't sure how to handle the penis, and as a result, he'd spent the morning perusing equine genitalia in his Metropolitan Museum of Art book. Eventually he decided that his horse must indeed have one, but wasn't sure of the logistics—macho or subtle was the problem now. After a final moment's thought, he chose subtle; nothing flashy, a simple Daumieresque pointy suggestion of stallionhood.

He used his discarded shirt to wipe the sweat from his forehead, then pulled the mask back down and went to work on the underside of the horse. After a few moments, he was snickering to himself, feeling juvenile, and wishing Dakota were here to crack a few of his off-color Mr. Ed jokes.

He'd heard from Dakota regularly. O'Keefe had made a point to phone him—as well as Audrey—every Sunday to get the lowdown on their latest date. Each week he also asked if he'd told Audrey that he could actually see the "jack-offs," as he called them. Rick would say no, he hadn't, and don't you tell her, either. Since the night he'd told her the tall one about the cousin in Scotland, he'd religiously sidestepped the topic every time it started to come up, and Audrey was kind enough to let him. He would have liked to know if she really had done any research, but it was easier to avoid the whole thing.

Still and all, things were going very well. Over the last few weeks he and his family had settled into a pleasant routine. Though Rick still avoided going out at night as much as he could, he found that his rather Pavlovian response to the phrase "I'm Thomas" helped him see the greenjacks as something more closely related to annoyance than crippling fear. It concerned him far more that he saw them at all, though the cat's reaction had made him suspect that he wasn't completely mad. That knowledge diminished his fears more than anything else, and perhaps that was why he'd originally told Audrey as much as he had.

As for Shelly, she spent most of her time at her job in the mall and the rest of it with new friends, other high school kids, none of whom, as far as Rick could tell, wanted to be exotic dancers or rock stars.

There'd been no serious trouble between father and daughter since she'd been working, and Rick had quickly rewarded her, and himself, with cable and paid half the fees to have her own phone line installed. So far, she'd asked for nothing else and had even talked about saving for a car. Impressed, Rick had started to secretly scan the used-car ads with the intention of giving her the surprise of her life for her seventeenth birthday at the end of the month.

Cody, meanwhile, had turned down Rick's offer of metal sculpting lessons in favor of studying under Hector Zapata's green thumb. Rick wanted to feel hurt, but gardening was so much safer than what he proposed that, in truth, he was more than a little relieved that Cody was occupied with vegetables, flowers, slugs, and snails, not to mention the coveted twice-weekly rides with Hector on the sit-down mower. Bob the Invisible One was still his best friend, but

Rick figured that once school started and Cody made some real flesh-and-blood friends, old Bob would be history.

Cody also adored Carmen, and she was as good with him as she had been with Rick. Her protective streak still ran deep, which made life much easier for him.

She and Rick got along fine now that she had ceased mentioning the need for the two of them to talk. As much as he loved her, he couldn't help being uneasy around her. He felt like she knew something he didn't, and suspected that it had to do with the fleeting visions of her in the blue nightgown, smelling of cold, still water, that had haunted him since his arrival. He couldn't shake it, but he couldn't place it either—not that he wanted to. He only wanted it to go away, and had come to suspect that the vision had something to do with whatever it was she'd wanted to talk to him about since his return. The past, he told himself frequently, was the past.

That old blast from the past, Aunt Jade, had behaved herself amazingly well since that one awful night. He'd barely seen her, and no more poodles had made unwanted appearances. He'd never gotten her to admit that she'd told Cody about the passages, but he was certain she had: She wouldn't look him in the eye when she denied it.

Rick had briefly feared that all was lost with Audrey after Jade's obscene demonstration and his angry reaction, but that wasn't the case, and their relationship continued, tentative and slow, but very enjoyable. Delicious, in fact.

He was falling in love, he knew that, and he didn't try to fight it. If they were to continue, he supposed he would eventually have to tell her the truth about the greenjacks. He couldn't lie to her forever. In the back of his mind, he had a partial plan that had something to do with waiting until Halloween and making sure she saw Big Jack—assuming, of course, the creature actually existed. So many of Rick's memories were elusive or nonsensical that he sometimes wondered if they were all false versions of what had really happened.

And that possibility was too upsetting to dwell on. He'd

decided the only healthy thing to do was to stop thinking about the past and concentrate on today: the challenges of home ownership, career, and family.

The only real problems he had were with the house and his own indulgences. He intended to begin renovations, but there was no time between his column and his sculpting. When he began the Quixote project, it was supposed to be something he did once or twice a week, a hobby, nothing more. But he'd become obsessed with it to the point that he'd apologized to Carmen for his laziness. Carmen, bless her soul, had responded that he actually *was* working on the house, because the sculpture would be a decoration for the garden. Thin as it was, he appreciated the excuse and used it whenever he felt guilty.

As he welded another seam together, he reminded himself that there were some things that needed to be done soon, excuse or no excuse. Although he'd driven two nails into the hidden passage in Cody's room, he hadn't sealed any of the others yet because he was still putting fresh bait inside them: It took a long time to do in twenty years' worth of rodents.

Even out here, there were still rodents. Frequently he heard their scrabbling around the ancient Rambler in the corner. He'd replenished the bait several times, but they kept coming.

"Ricky?" Carmen stuck her head in the open doorway. "You want some lunch?"

He turned off the torch and removed his heavy gloves and welding mask, which took the temperature in the work-room down about a million degrees. "Lunch?" His damp hair clung to his forehead, and he pushed it back with his fingers.

"I'm making chili dogs." She smiled. "Cody says they're your favorite."

"He does, huh? You never made hot dogs for me!"

"They had pork guts and hooves in them back then. I didn't want to poison you. I got chicken dogs."

"Beaks and claws!"

"Ricky!' She feigned anger.

"Sorry. Sure, I'd love one. Do I have time for a shower?"

"If you hurry!" With that, Carmen turned and walked quickly away.

A few moments later, Rick ascended the stairs, humming contentedly to himself until he saw that the door to his room was ajar. He knew he'd latched it—he always did.

Entering, he saw with relief that everything appeared normal and decided that Carmen must have come in to take his laundry basket and had forgotten to close the door.

"Quint?"

No answer. Shit.

By now he knew to check under the headboard for the cat. Sure enough, he was there, ears and whiskers flat back, unwilling to come out. The feline had uncharacteristically sulked virtually all the days they'd been here, acting frightened and nervous, and exhibiting none of his usual cocksure arrogance. Now he growled in a high-pitched tone that spoke of fear, not aggression.

"Quint?" he called, feeling on the nightstand for his flashlight. "Quint?" His hands closed on it and he brought it down, flicking it on and shining the beam on the cat.

The animal was soaking wet.

"What'd you do, cat?" he asked, chuckling.

The cat growled.

"I'll bet you saw a mouse and ran so fast, you tipped over your water bowl. Is that it, fur-ball?"

The cat was not amused.

Poor idiotic cat. Smiling to himself, he left Quint where he was, walked into the dressing room, and stripped, dropping his dirty clothes on the floor. He'd have to remember to put them in the hamper before Carmen saw them.

He entered the bathroom, surprised to see Quint's water bowl pristinely full, the floor around it dry. "Where the hell did the water come from, Quint?" he called as he opened the shower door.

"My God." He staggered backward, not comprehending what he saw hanging low in the shower. "My God." His bare buttocks hit the countertop and he stood there, blood pounding in his head, making him dizzy. He stared. "My God."

It was a poodle, soaking wet and limp, its white fur matted, its pinkish flesh showing between the clumps of fur. The shower massager's hose was knotted around its neck.

"Jade, you crazy bitch," he whispered as his heart slowed down. "Great, just great." She'd hung one of her damned stuffed dogs in his shower and probably ruined the hose to boot. *At least I have a couple spares under the sink.*

He put his hands around the animal.

The dog was soft and warm.

He snatched his hand back, moaning softly at the sight of the creature's black bulging eyes, thickened tongue, a little trickle of blood from one nostril.

Frantically he washed his hands, pushed the shower door closed with his toe, then pulled his dirty jeans back on.

The cat was her real target, he thought wildly. Jade had tried to kill his cat.

Slamming his door behind him, he flew down the front staircase to Jade's door. He yanked on the handle. Locked. "Jade! Open up!" he yelled. "Now! Unlock this goddamned door!" Inside, a dog yipped wildly.

Carmen raced into the room, Cody and Hector behind her. "Ricky! What's wrong?" she cried. "What is it?"

"She—she—"

Cody was clinging to Carmen's skirt, peering at him with wide eyes.

"Cody, it's okay, go to your room," he said as calmly as he could. The little boy stuck his thumb in his mouth and started toward the stairs. "No, wait!" God knew what else might be up there. "Don't go up there."

Out of the corner of his eye, he saw Carmen cross herself. "Cody," she said, "why don't you and Hector take your lunch over to our house. Your papa and I gotta, we gotta . . ." She faltered, looking at Rick.

"Plumbing problem," he said lamely.

"We gotta fix the plumbing, then we'll come over, too."

"Why you mad at Aunt Jade, Daddy?"

"Uh, I'm not mad." He could barely control his breathing. "We'll be over in a little while."

Jade's heavy footsteps could be heard approaching. "Hector," Carmen ordered, "Take him."

"Come on, Cody." Hector scooped the boy into his arms. "We've got Pepsi in our fridge," he said, leaving the room. "You want a Pepsi?"

"What happened?" Carmen whispered as Jade started to turn her lock.

"She hung one of her poodles in my shower," Rick whispered. "She knotted the sprayer cord around its neck. I think she tried to kill my cat."

Carmen stared at him, then hissed, "Shhhh!" as the door opened.

"What's going on here?" Jade's black hair was wild above a long green terry robe. She wore no makeup, and looked faded and dry and old. One poodle bared its teeth and growling from behind her calves.

"How dare y—" Ricky began.

Carmen grabbed the bare skin just above the back of his pants and pinched. He silenced.

"Well, what is it?" Jade asked huffily.

"Miz Jade." Carmen put her hands on her hips. "What were you doing just now?"

"Taking a nap," she huffed. "What the hell does it look like?"

"I thought maybe you were taking a shower."

She showed no real reaction to Carmen's words. "Why would I shower in the middle of the day? We were having our nap, weren't we, Mister Poo?"

"Where's Stinkums?" Rick asked calmly.

Jade looked flustered. "Stinkums? Come here, Stinkums."

She turned and disappeared into her rooms.

Rick started to follow, but Carmen grabbed him by the belt loop. "Don't tell her," she ordered.

"Why not? She knows. She did it."

"She wouldn't kill her own dog."

"Before you said—"

"Forget what I said!" Carmen snapped, her eyes fierce.

"Carmen, she's nuts. She tried to kill my cat."

"You told me that already, but I didn't see any scratches on her."

"She's probably wearing that robe to hide them."

"No. The cat would have scratched her hands."

He could hear Jade moving around in her room, calling Stinkums in a quavering voice. "Look, Carmen, she's the only one who could have done it."

"Don't say anything to her. Not yet."

"Stinkums?" Jade's voice was tinged with hysteria now. "Stinkums?"

"You do what I say, Ricky. Promise."

She smells of the pond, of cold water, rich with life and death . . . The front of her nightgown is sopping wet. "Our secret," she says. "It's our secret, Ricky. Forever."

"I promise."

Jade ran back into the living room. "Stinkums is gone! My little Stinkums!"

"We'll find your dog," Carmen said gently. "You go finish your nap. Ricky and I will find him."

Jade stared at them.

"Go on. He's around here somewhere. The bitches are in heat outside. I'll have Hector look out there."

Jade stared at them suspiciously, and Rick could barely contain himself. He trembled with an almost overwhelming urge to do violence to the woman until, staring at him in alarm, she slowly retreated into her room and shut the doors.

"Stinkums?" he heard the old bitch call as she turned her lock. "Stinkums?"

"Come on," Carmen ordered. He followed her into the kitchen, where she collected a garbage bag and a butcher knife. "Let's go," she commanded as she started up the back stairs. Silently he followed her, wondering what the knife was for.

At his room, she opened the door and went in. He followed, feeling impotently angry and afraid as she marched into the bathroom. He stopped to check behind the bed to make sure the cat was all right.

"Ricky, can you come in here?" she called.

Reluctantly he entered the bathroom and saw that she'd used the knife to cut the hose. The dog lay on the counter, and his stomach lurched as he watched her wiggle its head, then pry its mouth open and peer inside. *"Madre de Dios, I don't know how she told those dogs apart,"* she said, still prodding the animal. "It hasn't been dead long."

"No."

"It's neck's broken. Must've snapped when it was hanged. Ricky, hold that bag open for me, please."

Jade's screams began as Carmen dropped the dog, shower head and all, into the bag. Startled, Rick dropped the bag, and it thumped sickeningly to the floor.

"Stinkums! What have you done with Stinkums?" She hobbled forward, and Rick could see that the stairs had taken their toll. As she passed the bed, Quint's horrifying yowl rent the air, followed by violent hissing.

Jade shoved past Rick, bending with surprising agility and grabbing the bag, muttering the animal's name over and over and over. She pulled the poodle from the black plastic and held it to her chest, kissing its dead muzzle, cuddling it, stroking it, talking to it.

Rick felt sick.

Jade rose on creaking legs, looked Ricky straight in the eye, and slapped him as hard as she could. "You're evil!" she cried. "You killed my dog! You killed my Stinkums!" She reached out to slap him again, but this time he caught her wrist. He wanted to twist it, to break it.

"I didn't kill your damn dog, Jade" He was shocked by the controlled icy coldness in his voice. He saw Carmen staring at him in surprise. "You tried to kill my cat," he continued, his voice growing chillier. "He got away, so you did this." He gestured sharply at the animal in her arms.

"No I didn't! You killed my Stinkums!"

"Maybe Robin did it," he heard himself say in a nasty,

sarcastic tone. "You blame everything else on him. Why not this too? Maybe Robin did it, Jade."

"Ricky," Carmen began.

"She's like a spoiled little kid," Rick continued. "She does whatever she wants, then blames my brother."

Carmen crossed herself.

Jade squeezed the poodle harder, and something disgusting leaked from its rear end. "I have to call Mr. Whalen," she announced, storming from the room.

"The taxidermist," Carmen said dully. She opened the vanity, removed a sponge and cleanser, and one of the extra shower massagers. "Here." She handed the head to Rick. "You fix this while I clean up."

Silently he did as she asked. Carmen handled problems with action; it didn't matter what the action was, but she believed you had to do something—vacuum, tie knots in string, scrub down the kitchen—it didn't matter what.

"Excuse me," he said, reaching past her for a wrench he'd left in the medicine cabinet.

Carmen watched him, amused. "You never did learn how to put away your toys, did you, Ricky?"

Her words eased the tension between them, and they quickly finished their work.

"Now," she announced, "I'm gonna call Hector." She went to Rick's bedside phone and dialed, spoke rapidly in Spanish, then turned to Rick. "Okay, let's get your cat's stuff. His box and his toys. Throw away the food—Hector's taking Cody to the store to buy more."

"What? Why?"

"Your cat's gonna live with us for a while. At night you can bring him back to sleep with you, but then you bring him right back."

"I don't see why—"

"He'll be alive, Ricky."

"Okay, but I'll feed him here—"

"No. You got too much rat poison around. It'd be easy to poison his food. I'll feed him. Just change the water every time you bring him back."

A chill traveled down Rick's back. Carmen's seriousness scared the hell out of him.

Five minutes and several painful scratches later, Quint was secure in his arms, and he and Carmen walked out back and into her cozy little house. Hector and Cody were gone. She shut the door. "He'll be fine. Let him go, he likes it here. We won't let him out."

He took off Quint's leash and collar and was amazed to see the cat immediately start acting like his old self, moving through the house, rubbing, examining, stopping just short of marking his territory, thank God.

"He won't explore the main house," Rick said. "Maybe it's too big."

"He doesn't like it. He knows. Cats know things, Rick. So do dogs." She snorted. "You can't tell it with those inbred rats of Jade's, but a real dog, he knows, just like cats."

"Knows what?"

"In a minute. Sit down." She pointed at a rocking chair nearby and disappeared into the yellow and white kitchen. "Good," she said. "They brought all the food over. I'm gonna heat it up for us."

Rick loved the Zapatas' two-bedroom, one bath cottage. It was a square little Spanish-style bungalow built with arched doorways and ceiling fans like the main house, but much more comfortable and cozy. It had rusty brown carpet, much newer than the stuff in the main house, and the pale eggshell walls served as a background for an assortment of weavings and hangings. Across from the fireplace, an organ took up a short wall, a beautifully bright Mexican blanket hanging behind it to muffle the sound. Ricky had considered the bungalow a haven when he was a child, and he realized now that his feelings hadn't changed.

"Okay, come and eat."

He entered the kitchen and took a seat across from Carmen at the little pine table. They made small talk while they ate. When they were done, Carmen scraped the leftover chili into a bowl and gave it to Quint.

Rick shook his head watching the cat make happy growl

sounds as he devoured the food. "That's the first time he's been really interested in food since we moved."

"It's that house, Ricky. He doesn't like that house." She went to a cupboard next to the refrigerator and withdrew a bottle of tequila and two shot glasses, brought them to the table, then fetched a small plate, a knife, a tub of margarita salt, and a whole lime and brought them also.

"It's kind of early for a drink, isn't it?" Rick asked, thoroughly enjoying the scent of lime zest as she cut into the fruit.

"Yeah, it's early, but we're gonna do it anyway," she told him. "You're never gonna calm down otherwise, and it's time for us to have our talk. I think this is the only way you're gonna sit still for it."

She held him with her eyes, and he found himself nodding agreement. "What about Cody?"

"You should've let me teach you Spanish, Ricky. I told Hector to buy cat food and then take him to the movies. We have all afternoon."

"Swell," he muttered as she poured the shots. "Just great." He should have known Carmen would get her way in the end.

31

The ritual of lime, tequila, and salt was one Carmen found comforting. It was something to do, something to occupy a worried mind, and to return serenity to an anxious one. She hoped it would work on Ricky, because the things she needed to talk to him about, to force him to remember, certainly weren't going to calm him down.

She licked a spot on her hand and shook salt on it, then waited while Ricky copied her. Solemnly they swallowed their shots, then bit into the lime wedges.

"I'm worried about you," she began. "You're wound up tight, like a watch that's gonna break."

He shrugged, and she couldn't help but smile: It was the same gesture that he'd often made as a child.

"I'm okay."

"You will be." She poured two more shots. "Let's do it again."

"I don't want to get sloshed."

"You're not gonna get sloshed, Ricky. You're just gonna relax a little. Drink."

"Yes, boss."

They performed the ritual again. "You gotta calm down, Ricky, or you're gonna do something you shouldn't."

"What do you mean?" he asked defensively.

"You let the old *puta* get under your skin. If you're not gonna send her away, then you better ignore her. You're so

angry right now that I think you're gonna explode soon."
As she spoke, she poured two more. She figured it would
take at least four shots to get him loose enough to really
talk to him.

This time he downed the liquor without protest. "I'm
fine, Carmen, I told you."

"Stop it!" she snapped. "Stop lying to me. Stop lying to
yourself. You lie all the time. You see those little jacks, but
you won't admit it. You'd rather think you're crazy than to
admit you see them, wouldn't you?"

He said nothing.

"Answer me, Ricky."

He slammed the glass down on the table. "What the hell
am I supposed to think, Carmen? Nobody else sees them.
What the fuck am I supposed to think?"

"Watch your mouth. You're a fool. You gotta just accept
that you've been gifted with the sight."

"It's not a gift. It's a curse."

He was hiding so much from himself. "Robin used to tell
you everyone would think you were crazy if you told on
him or if you told other people about the greenjacks."

"How . . . how'd you know?" Obviously he was shocked.
"I didn't tell you . . ."

"No. I heard him threaten you. You were so embarrassed
that I didn't say anything to you. He knew your soft spot. I
thought you'd grow out of it, but all you did was learn to
hide it. You still don't trust yourself at all." *And maybe you
shouldn't,* she thought, watching him. She loved him as if
he were her own, but . . .

His dark blue eyes had glazed over. "So you got me drunk
to tell me I need to trust myself?"

"No. I got you drunk so you wouldn't think I was crazy
when I tell you what I'm gonna tell you." She had the sinking feeling he wouldn't believe anything she said, but she
had to try.

"What do you have to tell me?" He sounded like he was
waiting for his death sentence.

"Ricky, things have been happening in that house ever since you left."

"What do you mean?"

"Jade didn't kill her poodle. She wouldn't do that."

"So who did?" he asked skeptically. "Why did you tell me she put that other dog in the dryer?"

"Because I thought it might stop when you moved in. Sometimes these things work that way. You just never know."

"What would stop?"

"The spirit."

"What?"

"That house is haunted."

"Yeah, right. So a ghost tried to kill my cat but missed and got the poodle instead," he said caustically. "Who's the ghost? My dead brother?"

"Yes."

"And this ghost could pick up a dog, break its neck, and tie a knot around its neck, all after hosing it down so it was nice and wet."

"It could make someone else do it," Carmen said.

"Possession?"

"Probably. I think it's sort of a . . ." She searched in vain for a word. "An *espectro ruidoso*. You know, a noisy ghost."

"A poltergeist?"

"That's it."

"It's really hard to buy, Carmen. Sorry."

"Look at your cat, how he acts here and there."

Ricky said nothing for a long while. When he finally spoke, it was in a soft, beaten voice. "He sees the greenjacks, Carmen."

"What?"

"The cat can see them."

"Good. Then he sees the ghost, too. But why do you believe him, but not yourself?"

Slowly Rick smiled. "I guess I have to. He's not going to try to spare my feelings, is he."

The last comment was a statement, not a question, and Carmen breathed a sigh of relief. Maybe he'd come around.

Then he said, "So who's being possessed, Carmen? Me?"

She swore at him, a long stream of Spanish invective that made him flinch, even though she knew he couldn't understand a word. This wasn't going the way she wanted. *"Madre de Dios,* Ricky," she said after a moment. "You gotta stop feeling sorry for yourself. I told you, things have been going on since you went away. For instance, do you know how many dogs have died in the last fifteen or twenty years?"

"A lot."

"More than what you think. There were some that couldn't be stuffed."

"What happened to them?"

"What didn't?" Carmen threw her hands up. "Want one more?"

"Yeah."

She poured. "One got ground up in the mulching machine. Another was roasted in the oven. A few years ago, one got in one of the passages. *Madre de Dios,* the smell. Rats ate most of it before we found it. Another was run through with knitting needles."

"Good God. How?"

"You name it. Some are honest accidents, I think—chewing electrical cords, choking on toys, and Hector certainly tried to avoid the one that ran under the lawn mower . . ." She grimaced. "But the things like today, that's mostly what happens. Things that can't be accidents."

"Carmen, from what you're telling me, Jade is certifiable."

"She can hardly get up a flight of stairs when she's herself, Ricky. How do you explain the dog we found stuck on the weather vane?"

Ricky's eyes widened. "Well, I guess if I can buy greenjacks, I can buy a ghost." He looked longingly at the empty shot glass, but made no move. "I still think Jade's doing most of this herself—and poltergeists are supposed to be directed by people." He made a silly-looking smile. "I read a book once."

"You're plastered, Ricky," Carmen said, feeling pretty plastered herself. At least the tension had dissipated.

"Carmen, did you know Jade makes sounds at night like she's making love with someone?"

"Puta." Carmen shook her head. "I gotta apologize—I never go over there at night. I knew she used to, but I was hoping she didn't anymore. She's so old."

"That's silly."

"It's unholy." Carmen crossed herself. "Ricky, I think she's having sex with your brother's ghost, that's what I think." She crossed herself.

He looked unconvinced, and at first she was surprised, then she figured it made sense. If he claimed to see green-jacks, but didn't even believe himself, why would he believe her?

"Carmen?"

"What?" She smiled and squeezed his hand again. He was guileless now, once again the little boy she would have given her life for. "What, Ricky?"

"There are things I can't remember."

"Like what?"

"There was something about a baby."

Madre de Dios, she thought, *here it is.* "Yes?"

He raised his eyebrows, then took his hands back and pushed his dark hair away from his face. "There was a baby that died." He paused a long moment. "Evangeline had a baby, didn't she?"

He's starting to remember. Carmen tried to hide her nervousness. *Let him get it on his own,* she prayed. She didn't want to tell him. "No," she said finally. "She was good at getting pregnant, though."

"Oh, God." He looked at Carmen with heavy eyes. "I'd forgotten. You called her 'Our Lady of the Abortion Clinic.' "

"By the time that girl was fifteen, she must've been to the women's clinic half a dozen times to get rid of her mistakes. But she never had a baby," Carmen said harshly. "Remember? She ran off with a Hell's Angel or something, when she was about sixteen."

Rick nodded. "I drank too much."

"Me too. I'll make coffee." She stood and set to work, wondering if he would remember any more on his own.

"Did you know that Robin wanted to get Evangeline pregnant?" Ricky asked. "Jade, too."

She spooned ground beans into the coffeemaker. Good, he was still thinking. "Why?"

"He wanted to make sons who had the sight. For the jacks," Rick shook his head. "He wanted me to. . . . do it too. I guess he thought I'd be more likely to produce children with the gene."

"The gene," she repeated. *Keep him thinking about children.* The coffee burbled as she set two cobalt-blue mugs on the table, then brought the pot over and poured. "You must've been very worried that Cody might have the gene."

"I was, but there was no need." He sipped his coffee. "When he was born I talked Laura into letting his middle name be Thomas. At the time, I didn't know why that meant so much to me. I didn't remember until I came back." He smiled. "Cody's nothing like I was. He's fearless. And he doesn't see things."

"The name fits." She smiled gently. "He's a lot like you, Ricky. Just remember, he didn't have a mean brother teasing him all the time." In truth the boy reminded her very much of Robin when he was very young, before his happy, mischief-making personality soured and turned mean. She watched Ricky, thinking how frightening it was to see Robin's chill anger on his face when he'd confronted Jade. "Ricky," she began slowly. "Speaking of Cody, are you going to take him away Halloween night?"

"I hadn't thought about it." He paused. "I want to be here . . . I want to see Big Jack." He stared into his coffee. "That is, if I didn't imagine him."

"You think you might have?" she asked hopefully.

"I . . . no. I mean, I remember seeing him. But maybe I made it all up because I felt guilty when Robin fell out of the tree. Carmen, I think about it a lot. He *did* change after that."

"Yes, he did," she agreed solemnly.

"Well, he got hit on the head. Maybe he sustained some brain damage."

"Could be."

"I always felt sort of responsible—"

"You shouldn't. You didn't make him climb out there."

"I know I didn't. But I shut the window, then took my sweet time opening it again."

"Ricky, you thought Big Jack was out there."

He made a disgusted sound. "Yeah. And then, when Robin lost his balance and fell while climbing back in, I made up this whole scenario about how Big Jack was trying to get me, and he sacrificed himself for me."

"You could be right," Carmen said soothingly. "But what about the greenjacks? You still see those, and you said your cat sees them."

"There might be a logical explanation." There was hope in his eyes as he spoke. "You know that Audrey's an eye doctor?"

"Yes."

"Well, I told her about a fictitious cousin of mine who sees them, and she said it's possible for eyes to work differently, even that it could be a genetic thing. She said she'd research it."

"Has she found out anything yet?" Carmen asked, pleased that he'd looked for help, even in such a roundabout way.

"I haven't let her talk about it. I—"

"You need to."

"I know."

"What about Big Jack?" Carmen continued. "You're saying that though you see the little ones, you don't believe in him?"

"Yeah." He paused, studying his fingernails. "Maybe I don't. It seemed so real. Emotionally I believe, but intellectually I don't buy it. That's why I want to be here. If it does exist, I want Audrey to see it."

"Maybe you should let Hector and me take Cody up to Madelyn. My sister's having a Halloween party for her grandkids." Despite her love for Ricky, she didn't want his son to be with him. *If Ricky thinks he sees Big Jack, who knows what will happen?* She had to make him remember about the baby, for Cody's sake.

"We'll see, Carmen. I think I'd feel better keeping him with me. We'll see."

They started on their second cups, Ricky silent and thoughtful. Finally he looked up. "You know when I asked you about Evangeline having a baby?"

"Yes?" She could see him struggling to hide from the memory, and decided to prompt him a little. "Maybe you were thinking of Jade's baby."

Ricky's hand shook, slopping coffee over the rim. "Jade." He shook his head. "There's something about Jade's baby, and you said it was our secret. You had on a blue nightgown and it was wet and it smelled liked the koi pond." He shook his head. "You said it was our secret, but I can't remember—"

Carmen realized she was trembling, too. "His name was Paulie," she said, trying to hide her dread. "You loved him very much. Do you remember that?"

32

Waves of blood thundered inside Rick's skull as he stood, deafened and trembling. He tried to see past the black splotches swimming across his vision as he fought down rising nausea and staggered into the bathroom. He fell to his knees and hugged the toilet bowl.

The baby drowned in the koi pond.

He tried to save it and almost drowned too. Carmen was—Carmen was what?

It's our secret, Ricky.

Rick rose slowly, his head aching, his mind clearer, and turned on the cold water, running it into his mouth and over his face.

The laughter began deep in his abdomen, as undeniable and unstoppable as the sickness had been. It burst into his chest, and he grabbed at his throat to stop it, but then it was bubbling out his lips, in fits and snorts, then full-fledged hysterical belly laughs that made him double over.

He tried to stop, but he couldn't. Tears sprang from his eyes, and he made high falsetto noises as he gasped for breath between the giggles that felt so full of hilarity, yet were utterly devoid of it. He felt Carmen take his elbow, and he let her guide him into the living room, sit him on the couch. He laughed as she brought over a box of Kleenex, he laughed as she sat down beside him and said his name once, twice, three times, commanding him to snap out of it.

He couldn't. His sides hurt, but the laughter continued like a roller coaster, up and down, rising to the brink of madness, plunging down into an abyss of despair, but it was all laughter.

If you don't laugh, you cry.

That's what his dad always said. *Words to live by, Rick.* Thinking it now made him laugh all the harder. *If you don't laugh, you cry. If you don't la—*

Carmen slapped him, hard. He put his hand to his stinging cheek and stared at her, hurt. He felt real tears welling up in his eyes, and fiercely he thought, *If you don't laugh, you cry.* The hilarity came back enough to make him laugh slightly.

"Don't do it, Ricky. Don't laugh anymore," Carmen said. "Cry or scream or yell, but don't laugh. You scare me." She reached out to pat his knee as she had a thousand times in the past, but this time he flinched back, not wanting her to touch him. He looked at her and saw that her eyes were solemn and sad.

"I apologize," he said carefully, "for losing control." If it hadn't been for the chili dogs and tequila shooters, he didn't think he would have reacted so badly.

"It was a very bad thing, about the baby."

It's our secret, Ricky. We must take it to our graves.

October 31, 1980

The first time Ricky had seen Robin doing it with Evangeline was a summer day about a year after the Ewebeans had moved in. The twins were only eleven, and Rick didn't even quite know what he was seeing.

Everyone else was gone, and Ricky had ventured down the back stairs to find something to eat. He'd poured a bowl of Cheerios and was about to get the milk out of the fridge when he heard Evangeline giggle and start moaning. There were grunting sounds, too, coming from the family room. He tiptoed through the laundry room, past the bath and

downstairs bedroom, as the noises became louder. At the
edge of the family room, he stopped and peered around the
corner. Evangeline was lying on the old tweed couch that
used to be in the living room, her short skirt hiked up above
her bare hips. Robin was on top of her, grasping her thighs
and thrusting in and out, his body swaying back and forth.
Shocked, Ricky stood there and watched until Robin sensed
his presence and looked up. All he did was grin.

Not long after that, he walked in on Robin and Aunt Jade
doing the same thing in the library upstairs. No one saw him
that time.

Before long, Robin started telling him how much fun it
was to screw the women, actually encouraging him to do it,
too. Ricky was horrified.

Now that he was nearly fifteen and had had his first en-
counter with Cindy McGuire, a seventeen-year-old cheerleader who seduced him one night and with whom he knew
he would be in love forever, he wasn't so much horrified by
his relatives' behavior as he was disgusted.

Even before Evangeline ran away, most of Robin's atten-
tions went to Jade, who was, Ricky realized, a total nympho.
In the last year, Ricky had grown six inches, his voice had
stopped breaking, and lots of girls called him, either to see
if he'd do homework with them or just to talk. Sometimes
he'd go to matinees with one, though he still avoided going
out at night. He smiled. Cindy said he had great dimples.

The downside was that Jade had tried to seduce him too.
No, he corrected, not seduce. Fuck. That's what she did, she
and Robin, they fucked. It was filthy, disgusting, and nasty.
Sometimes when he passed by Jade, she'd pinch his butt or
make a remark about how nice his pants fit. She made him
want to puke.

Jade and Robin were not careful about where they did it,
and it amazed Rick that Howard had never caught on. But
then his uncle was so far gone into his bottle of Jack Daniel's
most of the time that he wouldn't notice anything.

Rick had heard his aunt and uncle arguing about sex too.
Jade would yell at Howard that he couldn't get it up because

he was drunk, and he'd yell at her that she was a dried-up old cunt. Rick thought they both made valid points. Jade no longer looked like the woman in *American Gothic,* but had taken to coating her long, horsey face with vast amounts of makeup, ratting her dyed brown hair into a big bubble-shaped helmet, and wearing clothes meant for teenage girls. She had the body for it, but not the face. She also had pictures of the Beatles all over the house, especially Paul McCartney. It was completely creepy.

Evangeline had been gone for less than a week when Jade announced she was pregnant. She and Howard got into a screaming match that night after he asked whose it was. "It's yours, of course," she'd maintained, and Ricky couldn't hear exactly what he said, but it had something to do with his preferring a maggoty whore over his wife. After that comment, there was a loud crash. The next day, Howard had a shiner.

Now Paul George Ewebean, a handsome little boy with the midnight blue eyes of the Piper clan, was almost two years old. Jade paid no attention to the child, leaving his care to Carmen. Almost immediately after he was born, Carmen began taking Paulie to her house at night, which made Rick, who found he really liked the child, rest easier.

As much as he could, Rick spent time with Paulie, too, reading him stories out of his old Little Golden Books that Carmen had retrieved from an attic trunk, putting him in a stroller and taking him for walks around town, and even telling him the greenjack stories.

All the while, he wondered if the baby could see them.

He and Carmen tried to keep Robin away from the baby, although sometimes, when Howard wasn't around, Jade would commandeer the child and hand him to Robin straight out, giggling and sniffing and saying, "That's your dada, that's why you're so handsome, not like your ugly pretend dada." Robin would throw the baby up in the air and catch him again. If he tried to take Paul outside, Rick always followed.

Last July Rick became fairly certain that Paul had the

sight. While he and the boy were watching TV one evening—no one else was home—he opened the drapes in the living room. Greenjacks were everywhere, their movement constant and energetic. As always, he looked briefly for the quiet, still one he'd occasionally spotted over the years, but it was nowhere to be seen.

"Here goes," he whispered, turning Paul so that he could see out the window. Immediately the baby cooed and gurgled and began to laugh, his little arms going out, reaching for the glass.

"See them, Paulie?" Rick asked, trying to remain calm. "Do you see the jacks?"

Paulie laughed until several of the creatures merged just outside the window. Then he drew back and sobbed, hiding his face on Rick's shoulder.

"It's okay, Paulie," he murmured, shutting the drapes. "They can't have you. I'm going to tell you a story about your ancestor, Thomas McEnery Piper, and how they almost got him." He rubbed his nose on Paul's, making him giggle happily. "But they didn't. And they won't get you either. I'll make sure."

From that moment on, Rick knew that he had to protect this child, and in many ways, that was the best summer of Rick's life. Having someone else to worry about helped make him strong, gave him purpose. He told Carmen that he'd like to have the toddler move into his room with him, and Carmen soon agreed. Rick became more watchful than ever.

Then, on Halloween night 1980, when Paulie was almost two years old, everything changed.

Since the night Big Jack had claimed Robin, Rick had been very careful not to be alone on the thirty-first. He usually spent the time until midnight, when the physical danger was over, with Carmen or at a friend's. He preferred Carmen because he never had to drum up an excuse to not go out. That other Halloween, over seven years ago, seemed like a vivid dream now, but it still worried him, especially because of Paulie.

This year, as usual, Jade and Howard had gone to the Dew Drop Inn, a sleazy roadhouse just outside of town on Cub Road. The Dew Drop was having a party featuring bobbing for apples (in beer) and a "naughty" costume–cum–wet–T-shirt contest that promised a grand prize of a ten-dollar gift certificate to Frederick's of Hollywood. Since the Dew Drop was where Howard spent a good deal of time with rednecked buddies, he was happy to go drink while Jade flaunted her boobs in competition for the fancy underwear.

Rick watched them leave that night. Howard wore what he always wore: rump-sprung jeans and a short-sleeved plaid shirt. Jade had a butt-length red T-shirt on that she'd drawn a Star Trek insignia on, black panties, no bra, fishnet nylons, old Beatles boots, and Spock ears. She'd put her hair up and drawn her pale eyebrows into Vulcanian shape. Rick had to laugh: With her long-jawed face and squinty eyes, she looked like Mr. Spock in drag, rather than the Vulcan's main squeeze.

Carmen and Hector came over as soon as the Ewebeans left, and Robin was off with some sleazy kids from school traveling around the neighborhood even though they were too old to trick-or-treat. Robin had invited Rick along, goadingly informing him he had to bring his own eggs and toilet paper. As always, Rick declined.

The Zapatas, Rick, and Paulie had dinner, then passed out candy until nine P.M. After that, they turned out the porch light, turned on the TV, and dug into the huge pumpkin pie Carmen had made.

At ten, Hector kissed his wife and went home to bed. Full of pie and candy, Paulie had curled up in the old recliner in the corner. Carmen and Rick sat on the couch nearby and watched television, both glancing often at the baby, both mindful of noises from outside and in, watching for Robin, for Big Jack too.

They were keeping Halloween vigil, as they had for seven years. Before, it was to protect Rick, and now it was to protect the baby, too. Carmen would remain here until after midnight—when Big Jack's power dissipated—then Rick would take Paulie upstairs to his room and lock them in. Paulie slept on the sofa bed, just as Rick had, years before.

But that would come later. Now the fireplace crackled warm, comfortable heat into the living room. Rick's eyes grew heavy and his head would start to droop and he'd jerk awake. He kicked his shoes off and stretched his toes toward the fire. Beside him, Carmen had drifted off and was snoring softly. He wouldn't wake Carmen, he decided; it was less than an hour until midnight, and he could stay awake until then easily. Yawning, he turned his attention back to the Creature Features Halloween marathon. They were showing *The Creature from the Black Lagoon,* which he'd seen about a trillion times. He rubbed his eyes. You'd think they could show something newer tonight of all nights. He yawned again. Something in color.

RICKY! Ricky Ricky Icky Ricky Ricky!

Ricky bolted upright, disoriented and frightened. Beside him, Carmen continued to sleep.

"Ricky!"

Faintly he heard Robin calling him from somewhere outside.

He sat up and glanced at the recliner. The baby wasn't there.

Icky Ricky, come and play, hey, come and play, Ricky, Ricky, Ricky!

Rising, he ignored the little jacks' taunts. "Paul?" he whispered. "Paulie?"

He automatically glanced at the grandfather clock across the room. Quarter to twelve. He'd been asleep for, God, at least half an hour, maybe more. The baby could be anywhere. He turned to wake Carmen, then stopped as he heard the voices.

Out here, icky Ricky, we have your boy toy, boy toy, boy toy!

Ricky didn't like to talk to Carmen about the greenjacks anymore. He didn't want to be a coward.

"Ricky!" came Robin's faraway cry. "Hurry! Ricky! Help!"

He noticed that the front door didn't look right: The heavy black bolt had been pulled back.

With a last glance at Carmen, he raced to the door, determined that for once, he was going to be brave.

"Ricky!" Robin called.

Rick walked out into the night.

Play hey, play, hey, Ricky Ricky Ricky Ricky.

"Shut up," he whispered.

"Ricky!"

The Malibu lights, the filthy few that still worked, cast little light, but as Ricky squinted in the direction of the voice, they served to backlight Robin's legless long-armed form as he waved from near the now-putrefied koi pond. The rocky waterfall bubbled behind him. Glancing around, Rick saw no sign of Big Jack.

"God," Ricky whispered, seeing Paulie's silhouette rise from a squat beside him. The baby waved, and Rick heard his delighted giggle. "No," he whispered.

He started running across the lawn, not even noticing the greenjacks.

Instantly Robin grabbed the little boy and hoisted him above his head like a rag doll. "Come and get him, Icky Ricky!" he screeched.

Paul's gleeful shriek turned into a cry of terror as Robin threw him into the middle of the dank pond.

"No!" he screamed, running faster, his bare feet squishing through the wet grass, his legs feeling the chill caresses as he raced through masses of gibbering jacks.

Icky Ricky, icky Ricky, icky Ricky.

At the edge of the pond, Rick stopped.

"He's drowning!" Robin called from across the fetid water. "He's drowning! Save him!"

A few bubbles rose near a cluster of water lilies in the center of the pond. Rick glared at Robin. His brother could swim; he'd seen him down here frolicking in the water on any number of summer nights. If he wanted to, he could rescue the baby. But why would he want to? He threw him in. The baby was bait, Rick realized as he pulled off his sweater and moved to the water's edge. What Robin wanted most was Rick.

The pond smelled richly of cold water and wet, rotting plants.

The water lilies tugged at his clothes as he swam past them, and then he felt the underwater plants and grasses waving all around him. Rick searched frantically, unable to see anything but small glimmers of moonlight between the lilies, fighting panic each time the water grasses coiled around his ankles like cold, slimy fingers.

He came up for air, then scissored back down. Again.

The third time, at the deepest part of the pool, he blundered blindly into Paulie. Swiftly, he seized the limp body and turned to push himself up from the bottom.

Something wrapped around his ankle, began pulling him back. Wildly Rick twisted to get free, but something sharp twisted around his other ankle now. He strained forward, suddenly felt the slimy plaster pool wall against his arms. Peering up, he could see vague moonlight—he wasn't under the lilies. Frantically he pushed Paul's body upward, up toward the light, blindly shoving him onto the pavement.

He grabbed at the wall with his hands, wishing the rock sides extended farther down to give him purchase.

His lungs felt full of fire, and his legs seemed encased in barbed wire, and suddenly something dragged him across to the other side of the pool. His lungs started to give out as blackness edged Rick's consciousness.

No! Don't let him win!

Water exploded into his throat, choking him, and he began to struggle, fiercely kicking at the bonds restraining him. He grabbed at the side of the pool. Whatever had him—

Big Jack, you know it's Big Jack, he can go anywhere out of doors, of course he can go in the water, there are plants down here, too.

—gave slightly, coming up with him. His head cleared the water, and he coughed, gasping for breath, as water cascaded over his skull. He was beneath the waterfall. He grabbed at the rocks, clung to them, pulling upward, straining, straining harder.

It was so hard, so hard. He coughed again, wanting to rest, wanting to just give up.

You won't just die, they'll steal your body! He'll win!

At that moment he was yanked under again, and he could feel the bonelike hands and arms clearly now, embracing him, squeezing him. His own arms were still free, trying to grasp at the rocky outcroppings. *You still have a chance.*

His toes connected with the side of the pool. Using every ounce of strength in his possession, he bent his knees and shoved off the side.

This time, *it* came up with him, breaking through a net of lilies and grasses. Rick clutched at the sharp rocks on the side of the waterfall, higher now, gaining ground.

Gasping, he spit out fetid water. And came face-to-face with Big Jack himself.

The creature was as he remembered. The jungly green smell, so like the odor of the pond, the pitch black eyes that bored into his, the pulsing, twisted vines, the lacework of thin white roots, all parodies of human physiology. He saw it all in a millisecond, the bark-chip teeth, the mouth opening with the obscene vines spewing forth, twining around his throat, pulling and twisting like tentacles.

"No!" he screamed. Letting go of the rocks, he used his hands to tear brutally at the Green Man, wrenching the throbbing jugular vine until it broke, spewing chlorophyll in his face. He yanked the mouth vines from the creature. They came away dripping green, attached to a kinked jigsaw of white roots.

Big Jack faltered, and Rick tore his feet free, pulled his body up into a ball, then kicked straight out, his feet smashing into the green growing out of the thing. Jack's arm-hold loosened, and Rick flipped his legs backward to hit the poolside, then kicked, shoving off and up, flying out of the water, tearing the skin off his feet and hands and arms and legs, banging his cheek into a rock, moving, crawling, staggering, until he was free of the thing.

He crawled onto the pavement, tearing a final vine away from his ankle, crawling toward Paulie's still body. He reached the boy and began artificial respiration, just as he'd been taught in school.

"Icky Ricky, you're so brave." Robin sidled over to him, moving sideways like a crab. "But you're too late. Your precious little baby was under there way too long. He'll come back to life, all right, but he'll be one of us." Robin cackled insanely, staring at something behind Rick.

Rick chanced a quick look back, saw Big Jack lumber out of the water. When it straightened, it stood at least eight feet tall. Paulie coughed. *He's alive!*

Robin's cold hand grasped his arm so hard, he couldn't pull free. "Two for the price of one," his twin whispered in his ear. "That's what I was hoping for. Two for one."

Swaying, scarecrowlike, Big Jack stepped toward them. Robin giggled madly and let go of Rick's arm, backing away from the creature. "Well, little hero, guess it's not quite midnight. Maybe I'll have your body tonight yet. Maybe I'll have your *eyes!*"

"Fuck you," Rick whispered back.

Robin laughed and did a handstand, then, body raised overhead, he fled across the grass and disappeared into the house.

Big Jack stepped closer, vines dripping and snapping in the night wind. Ricky backed up, away from Paulie, thinking he had a better chance of saving both of them if he led the monster on a chase.

Icky Ricky, we've got you now! came Big Jack's powerful voice.

"You have squat!" Rick yelled. "You want me, you have to catch me first!" He leaped sideways and started zigzagging across the lawn, and the church bells began to chime the midnight hour.

It chased him, fueled by long-standing greed and desire. Rick ran, feinting this way and that. Big Jack barely inches from him. Suddenly, on the eighth ring, Rick lost his balance, landing hard and skidding across the dew-damp grass. Big Jack's twig fingers encircled his neck, choking him.

The eleventh bell sounded, and Ricky barely heard it over the ringing in his ears. He couldn't breathe.

The final bell chimed. Slowly Big Jack began to disintegrate, twig fingers dropping off, leaves drying up and scattering. The arms and legs fell into a pile of kindling around him, and then he was surrounded by a tumble of luminescent little jacks as they gave up their Big Jack for the year and swarmed over Rick, screaming and taunting and laughing.

He ignored them to run to Paulie. He fell to his knees and helped the coughing toddler sit up, thunking his hand against his back to help clear his lungs.

"Are you okay, Paulie?" he whispered. "It's all over now."

Paulie coughed violently, then whispered, " 'Kay." It was the best thing he'd ever said.

For just an instant, Rick let himself collapse on the lawn, let himself feel his muscles quiver, became aware of his cuts and bruises, his exhaustion.

Ten feet away, the little jacks watched. He closed his eyes and then opened them again as he felt a cool, feathery touch on his arm. Quickly he looked sideways, saw the faint outline of a single little jack beside him. It touched him again.

Ricky . . .

The voice was so soft, he could barely hear it. The strident jumble of voices from the other jacks assaulted his mind, but he concentrated on this one.

This voice, soft and gentle in his head, was a shimmer on the wind, a solitary sound separate from the others. He knew the inflections of this voice. They were his own.

"Robin?" he whispered. "Robin?"

Ricky . . .

The voice seemed anxious, mournful.

Too late . . .

"What?" he cried desperately.

Changed, he's changed . . .

"No!"

There was no reply, only another sad caress.

Ricky . . .

The sound of his name in his brother's voice made hot tears stream from his eyes.

Remember Thomas . . .

A small voice, faintly riding the wind.

Rick's head ached. "That's all I can remember."

"There's more, Ricky," Carmen said, her eyes boring into his.

The tone of her voice alarmed him. "He died," he said, his eyes burning. God, he'd loved that little kid, and he'd tried to save him, redemption for losing Robin, but that, too, had failed. If he'd only awakened Carmen. "I remember the funeral . . ."

"Ricky, you said he coughed."

"Yes. He did."

"Then why did he die?"

Helplessly, gut twisting, he looked at her. "I don't know! You came out and called the ambulance." *The blue nightgown!* "You were wearing the blue nightgown and you picked him up."

She nodded. "Yes."

Suddenly he heard a key in the lock and then Hector's cheerful voice called out, "Anybody home?"

Rick stood and went to the sink to wash his face. An instant later, Cody was hugging his waist, and grateful to be released from Carmen's prison, he picked up his son. "Your sister's working late tonight. How about you and I getting a pizza?" he asked with false cheerfulness. "Just us guys?"

"Yeah!"

"See you later," he called to the Zapatas as he escaped the cottage.

"What'd you and Carmen do, Daddy? Why's Quint at their house? What kind of pizza do you want?"

He welcomed Cody's endless questions because answering them let him forget about the one Carmen had asked. How *had* Paulie died?

33

Even native Californians seemed amazed when September turned into the hottest month of the year, but it invariably happened, and was invariably forgotten the following September, when the weathermen and everyone else expressed dismay over the extended dog days of summer.

And so, on the first day of kindergarten, when Cody insisted upon wearing his new fall clothes, Rick hadn't tried too hard to talk him out of it. Taking him to school, Rick was mildly embarrassed until he saw that most of the other kids wore sweaters or jackets even though, at eight in the morning, it was eighty-five degrees, on its way to the hundred mark. Fortunately, his teacher, Miss Cantrell, had instantly charmed the children into shedding a few layers, and since then, everything with Cody had been peaches and cream. The boy had it bad for Miss Cantrell. Lacking apples, he took her a barely ripe orange from the orchard every day.

He'd made some friends besides Bob the Invisible, too, which pleased Rick since Bob had remained fairly important instead of becoming more invisible, as he had expected. But now Bob ranked behind Craig, Matt, and Doug as Cody's priorities. And way behind marrying Miss Cantrell.

Shelly had settled in as well. Late in August, Rick presented her with a little red Bug with only thirty thousand on the speedometer. She hadn't said a word about it not being the coveted PT Cruiser, but instead, became invaluable to Rick and Carmen because she wanted to run everyone's errands for them.

Now that school had started, her life revolved around that and her job. She tried out for and made the cheerleading team—something so incredibly wholesome when compared to her previous goals that Rick still could barely believe it. And even though her phone rang so constantly that Rick bought her an answering machine as a back-to-school present, she was doing reasonably well in school.

For over a month now, Rick had tried not to be alone with Carmen. He hated the dark, serious way she would watch him when she thought he wasn't looking, and though he knew it had something to do with his memory lapse concerning the death of Paulie Ewebean, he'd decided once more that the past was the past and that he would dwell in the present.

Now, in mid-October, the heat had finally ended, and the occasional warmth of a Santa Ana wind had become a pleasant experience instead of a hellish one. As Rick lifted the welding mask from his face and stood back to study his statue, he told himself that life was turning out pretty damned good.

From the tip of Don Quixote's lance, ten feet in the air, down to Rosiante's hooves, his masterpiece was virtually complete. *Semimasterpiece,* he corrected, smiling to himself. Maybe it wasn't great art, but like life, it was pretty damn good.

Except for writing his weekly column, Rick had done nothing but indulge himself in this sculpture, and he'd assuaged his continuing guilt about letting the house go so long by having Hector buy interior paint for the entire house. They'd work on it this winter.

The rat problem seemed to have died down somewhat now, but he still hadn't sealed the rest of the passages, and since Quint had made it obvious that he much preferred to spend his days at the Zapatas' and only come back at night to sleep with Rick, he really saw no need.

Rick lowered the mask and fired up the torch, fixed a small curl on Don Quixote's breastplate.

"That's better," He set the mask aside and put down the torch. He had a lot to do before Audrey arrived.

She'd been wonderful to him, only mentioning in passing that if he wanted the information on vision, she had it. Thus far, he hadn't asked—he'd learned to ignore the greenjacks over the last few months. But he was going to ask her soon, because he needed to be honest with her if their relationship was going to proceed to a more serious level. As it was now, every time it started to, he'd find an excuse to hold off because he didn't want to start something under false circumstances. Fear of rejection, he knew, held him back, even though Audrey seemed more open to the idea of greenjacks than anyone else—even Carmen, who, he'd finally realized, had protected and loved him *despite* his stories about the jacks.

Scratching sounds, faint and annoying, came from the vicinity of the old Rambler. The vermin living in the car were either very smart or very resistant. He'd have to put out yet more bait for these guys.

But not now, he thought as he checked his watch. It was nearly two o'clock already. The piano movers would show up at two-thirty and have Don Quixote moved out to the oval of cement he'd had poured behind the koi pond before Audrey arrived around four o'clock. He smiled to himself. He'd planned on putting the knight out there as a talisman long before he remembered Paulie's drowning. It seemed more fitting than ever, he thought as he locked up and went inside to grab a quick shower.

34

"Hi, sorry I'm late!" Audrey entered the Piper house and sidled away from Rick, so that he couldn't see the package she held behind her back.

"That's okay, I'm running late, too." Rick gestured at his untied tie. "Whatcha got behind your back?" he asked, approaching her.

She smiled. "You'll see soon enough."

"How long are you going to keep me in suspense, evil woman?"

He was like a little boy, practically bouncing with curiosity. She adored that side of him. "I'm going to keep you in suspense as long as I can," she said mischievously.

"Animal, vegetable, or mineral?" he persisted.

"I'll never tell." She grinned at him. Ever since she'd discovered how much Rick loved surprises, she'd been bringing him odd little goodies wrapped up tight as drums so he'd have to really work at them to get them open.

What it was made no difference. He just seemed so pleased and amazed that someone had thought about him—it must have to do with being raised by Ewebeans, she thought wryly—that she loved watching him. Last week she'd given him a pair of little windup sneakers, and they'd walked them back and forth across the table at Scomillo's any number of times before a tall, thin waiter curled his lip and looked disgusted. They'd snickered over that the rest of the evening. The week before, it was a bag of watermelon candy; the week before, a Koosh ball. She had a feeling that a stick of gum would please him as much as tickets to the theater. Well, almost as much.

Watching him watch her as he knotted his tie, she wondered if tonight would be the night; they'd been seeing each other all summer, and nothing but necking had happened yet. When he'd said he wanted to take it slow, she'd been happy, glad to know he wasn't after her for a quick slam bam. But now, even allowing for her ever-present impatience, things seemed to be at a standstill.

Here was a man who was sweet and sensitive, intelligent, and just mysterious enough to drive her crazy. Here was a man with the self-control of a monk. Every time they held each other and kissed good night, it became very obvious he wanted her as much as she wanted him. Last week they went dancing, slow dancing, and his desire was so evident that it took every ounce of self-control she possessed not to let fly with a crude remark to the effect of a hard man was good to find. She didn't know whether he'd take the remark as invitation or insult. He had such strange reactions to things sometimes, and she didn't want to risk the relationship.

Plainly Rick Piper had a lot more willpower than she did. And that just served to intrigue her all the more.

"What are you thinking about, Audrey? You have a funny look on your face." Straightening his tie, he approached her, his smile dimpling the cheeks of that boyish face, the skin around his eyes crinkling just right.

Heat squirmed low in her belly and she blushed. "Here," she said, bringing the gift out from behind her back rather than answering his question. "I was late because I had such a hard time wrapping this."

His eyes lit up. "What is it?" He held his hands out, and she placed the long, thin package in them.

"That's for me to know and you to find out," she told him.

"Let's sit down." He led her to the couch, laid the long

package on the coffee table, and began working on unwrapping it. She'd smothered it in tape and ribbons to prolong the pleasure of watching him as long as possible.

Suddenly she was a little nervous. This was a serious gift, the first one that cost her more—a lot more—than five bucks. It was a sword, an indoor reminder of Rick's sculpture.

She'd purchased it on a whim. While browsing in one of the antique stores on Euclid a few days ago, she'd spotted it in one of the cases. Polished and in perfect condition, it was a beautiful cavalry-style saber with a slightly curved blade and an ornate bronze hilt. The shopkeeper had told her it was of British design, an officer's weapon, most likely used during Wellington's Peninsular campaign against Napoleon near the end of the eighteenth century. Judging by the price, it had probably been used by the general himself. After drawing and quartering her wallet to acquire the weapon, she hoped he'd like it. Her anxiety built as she wondered if he'd like it or if he'd think it was presumptuous of her to give him something so expensive.

"I . . . I can take it back if you don't like it. It might not be right . . ."

He grinned at her, his long-fingered hands dancing among the bows, dutifully untying them instead of cutting because he knew she liked to watch.

"You love torturing me, don't you?" he asked, trying to undo a particularly stubborn piece of ribbon.

She just smiled. Tonight they were going into Los Angeles to see *Les Misérables,* which had just reopened at the Chandler Pavilion. Both had seen it before, but they wanted to see it together. He'd surprised her with the tickets last week; the best seats in the house, he'd told her, obtained by pulling what he called "reporter" strings. So tonight it would be dinner, a play too romantic and schmaltzy for anyone to resist, then home—hers or his, she didn't know or care which—to share the bottle of champagne she'd stashed in a cooler in her car. After that, she intended to try to get him to unwrap *her.* Her patience had run out.

That was the other reason she arrived late; it had taken her forever to get dressed. She'd left the office early and gone to Victoria's Secret, where she invested in a form-fitting beige teddy loaded with tiny silk buttons and matching panties that had multiple ribbon closures. She also bought a garter belt for the first time in her life, specifically because of the snappy things you had to undo to get the nylons off. Her outerwear included hook-laced high-heeled boots, a midcalf black linen skirt which buttoned up the front, and a white high-collared silk blouse with more than thirty miniature button loops for him to undo—and that wasn't even counting the cuff buttons. Finally, she'd pulled her red hair up in a sweep of loose curls, then instead of securing it with a couple of clips, she'd used two dozen bobby pins.

She wanted to be unwrapped in the worst way.

"Audrey?" He was smiling at her. "Earth to Audrey."

"Hmmm?"

"What's on your mind?"

"I'll tell you later."

"I'm ready to open this." He was down to the wrapping paper, all the ribbons piled on the floor next to him.

"Rick, is it hot in here?"

"No," he said, his impatience showing as he plucked' at the paper. "But you look feverish. Are you up for tonight?"

"Oh yes." She smiled. *I hope you are too.*

"Tissue paper," Rick said dryly. "I should have known." He began turning the package over and over until, at last, he uncovered the shining steel blade. "Audrey," he whispered, lifting it away from the wrappings, "it's beautiful." He took hold of the saber's hilt, hefted it, then stood and tried it out, cutting delicate figure eights in the air.

"It's in honor of your sculpture's completion. You're almost done, right?"

"It's beautiful," he told her as he made like a Musketeer. "Wonderful, marvelous. Lord, Audrey, it's incredible! I'll hang it over the fireplace. Thank you."

"You're welcome." She glanced at the clock. "We should get going."

He leaned down and kissed her, then took her hand as she got to her feet. "Thank you so much!" he repeated, his eyes dancing with delight. "For now, I'm going to put this in my room and lock the door." He made a face. "Can you imagine what would happen if Jade got her grubby mitts on it?"

With that, he raced up the stairs. A moment later, he was back. "Before we leave, I have to show you something. It'll just take a minute. Close your eyes," he ordered.

"Rick?"

"Come on, do it. It's my turn to surprise you."

"Okay," she laughed, and shut her eyes.

He led her out the front door, and she waited while he shut and locked it. Then he put one hand around her waist and the other on her elbow and guided her down the front steps.

"Watch out, the grass is wet," he warned. "We're heading toward the old pond. It's pumping out right now, so it kind of stinks. Did I tell you it used to be a swimming pool?"

"No." She laughed. Rarely was he so maniacally happy.

"It was. Hector and I are going to muck it out next week, then the replasterers will come and everything will be refitted, and before you know it, voilà, a swimming pool."

"What will the koi think of that?"

"They've been gone for years," he said, a touch of sadness in his voice. "Ewebean disease, I guess." His voice lightened. "There used to be colored Malibu lights out here. Ultra sixties. My dad installed them. Watch out, the ground dips here. Okay, step up." Her feet encountered a hard smooth surface, and they stopped walking. "Open your eyes."

She did. They stood before the murky, reeking pond. Directly across from them, Don Quixote sat majestically upon his bony steed. "Wow," she murmured. The piece was beautiful and a little frightening at the same time.

"Once Hector installs the new lights," he said, "we'll be able to see his silhouette from the house all the time," he told her proudly. "I'm thinking of changing the landscaping a little so he can be seen from the street too."

"It's wonderful, Rick," she said sincerely.

"Thanks." He looked around, his expression changing slightly, a trace of nervousness showing through his good humor. *Does he see them?* She wondered. *Does he think he sees them?* He hadn't brought up the greenjacks in months and wouldn't even let her talk about the research she'd done—but she was pretty sure he hadn't stopped thinking about them.

"It's getting dark," he. said, his voice suddenly nervous. "We'd better get going now. We're only going to have time for fast food as it is."

She almost tripped trying to keep up with him. He acted like devils were after him, but she said nothing. His strangeness was part of his charm.

35

They ended up at Rick's because Shelly was spending the night at a girlfriend's and he didn't want to make Carmen watch Cody any longer than necessary. That was fine by Audrey. Her apartment was little and cramped, and the people downstairs cooked fish or liver virtually every night, an unromantic aroma at best. She was also convinced the couple across the hall from her both suffered from Tourette's syndrome.

When they came in the house, Carmen eyed the champagne bottle Audrey held, then asked him if he wanted his cat back tonight. He hemmed and hawed for a moment, then Carmen told him that Quint was welcome to stay at her place. He nodded and mumbled something about having to work late anyway.

Audrey was pretty sure Rick blushed when he said it, and hoped work wasn't really what was on his mind. Going to the ladies' room at intermission and maneuvering through all the buttons and bows had been a Herculean task, and she was more intent then ever on making it pay off.

"I'll get the glasses," he said after Carmen left. "You want to watch a movie or something?"

"Sure." *Something sexy.*

"I have lots of tapes. Why don't you pick something out?" He turned to go into the kitchen.

"Rick? Where are the tapes?"

He made a face. "That would help, wouldn't it? I had them there"—he pointed at the bare bookcase to the left of the fireplace—"but that didn't work out." He crooked his finger, and she crossed the room. In a low voice he said, "Jade got into them." He pulled his keys out of his pocket and selected one. "They're in my room," he said. "Do you remember where it is?"

She nodded. She'd seen his room the first time she'd come over, when he'd given her a grand tour of the house.

"They're in my dressing room in a cabinet right beneath my jackets. It's the cabinet without the hanger through the handles."

"Why is that?"

"The cat. He loves to open doors, and there's a passage behind the one with the hanger. I'm afraid he might accidentally push the latch and end up"—he pitched his voice to sound like Peter Lorre—"lost in the bowels of the mansion."

"Gotcha. I'll find it." She smiled at him. "Do you have any apples?"

"Red Delicious, fresh from Oak Glen. You want some with your champagne?"

"Yes. We'll be totally decadent, yet fat-free. Be right back."

After she let herself into his room, she was surprised to see the wire lying on the floor between the two cabinets. Quint's work, she thought, kneeling. She opened the wrong door first, found it empty except for a box of D-Con. Curiously she looked for the interior latch Rick had talked about, but gave up quickly. There were better things to do: champagne to drink, apples to eat, a man to seduce.

She quickly restrung the wire through the cabinet's handles, then opened the other cabinet and, moments later, was overjoyed to find a copy of *Time After Time,* a romantic fantasy filmed in the seventies. The fact that he owned it spoke volumes about the man. As she rose, she glanced around the room, having a brief but uncomfortable feeling that something was watching her. She saw nothing. *Don't be silly. You'll get as nervous as Rick is, and then won't you be the pair!* Reentering the bedroom, she saw a twenty-five-inch TV set and VCR across from the bed. Should she suggest they watch it up here? *No, too forward.*

She walked back down the stairs. The movie concerned Jack the Ripper stealing H. G. Wells's time machine to escape to modern times, and the timid inventor's resulting chase and romance. When Wells fell in love in the movie, the woman who wanted him had to do all the work. She smiled to herself. Old H. G. was a lot like Rick Piper: too shy and retiring for his own good.

But there were good things about that. No doubt because of the sadistic asshole she'd been married to, Audrey was instantly turned off by men who approached her first, no matter how gently; she needed to do the pursuing in order to feel safe. Hence, the attraction to *Time After Time*. Hence the attraction to Rick Piper.

"Find something good?" he asked as he entered the living room and placed a large tray on the coffee table.

"Yes. You're a romantic, aren't you, Piper?" She held up the box for him to see. "No sense denying it. You've been caught."

"Guilty," he said sheepishly. "Have you seen it before?"

"Yes. I never get tired of it." She smiled coyly, thinking that the movie would be great inspiration. She slipped it into the machine.

"Bring the remote," he said, sitting down. He patted the cushion next to him. "And come sit with me."

"Pretty classy, huh?" he asked as she sat. The champagne rested in a silver ice bucket, and four shiny-wet apples were piled in a crystal bowl. Two linen napkins and two champagne flutes also sat on the teak tray.

"Not bad for a Vegas guy," she said.

"Are you implying you expected plastic glasses?" He grinned at her and began to remove the foil from the bottle, Suddenly Jade's obscene moaning began.

"Christ," Rick said. "Jesus Christ. Not now."

She almost suggested they go to her place, then remembered Cody.

"Fuck me!" Jade cried. High-pitched lusty "Oh, oh, ohhs," followed.

Audrey stifled a giggle.

"That's it," Rick said, showing no signs of amusement. "I'm going to tell her to knock it off."

Audrey put her hand on Rick's wrist. "If you do, she'll just cause a scene." She paused. "There's a VCR in your room."

He considered. "There's nowhere to sit, though," he said slowly.

"Fuck me, fuck me, fuck meeee!"

Rick grimaced, obviously interpreting his aunt's behavior as a reflection upon himself.

Audrey snickered. "We can sit on your bed. I mean, that is why you've got that entertainment center on the wall across from the bed. To watch TV, right? You must love movies, with all the equipment you've got."

"Yes, well, that unit used to be in my living room back in Vegas. I put it up there instead of down here because I was afraid I'd spend a lot of my time up there, staying away from Jade." He looked pained. "Besides making those . . . noises, she also goes through other people's belongings and takes whatever she wants—or mangles them, one or the other. She did that with the tapes when I had them down here. Never admitted it, of course." He made a face. "She got sticky stuff all over them. It was disgusting. She must've been eating Twinkies or something."

Audrey smiled demurely. "Are you sure it wasn't Cody's doing?"

"No, he makes little bitty fingerprints. Lord." He rolled his eyes as Jade's lewd noises reached another crescendo.

"At least she's multiorgasmic," Audrey teased lightly. She had to get him out of here before he lost his good mood. "So what do you say? Shall we take this tray and the movie and watch upstairs?"

"You don't feel awkward?" he asked.

"No. Has anyone ever told you you're terribly old-fashioned? Especially for a guy whose best friend is a she-male."

"Your brother's very moral." Rick sniffed dramatically, and placed everything back on the tray. "In his own way."

"I'm teasing you, Rick." She crossed to the TV and ejected the tape.

"I know," he said, gathering everything together on the tray. "I guess I am old-fashioned." They started up the stairs. "Seeing the things my brother did with her"—he nodded back in Jade's direction—"and her daughter, maybe had an effect. They did things animals wouldn't do." Outside his door, he hesitated. "You're sure you're okay with this? I could get some chairs from the kitchen."

"I'm fine with it." She paused. "Are you?"

"I just don't want you to think I'm trying to take advantage."

She laughed; she couldn't help it. "I don't think that at all," she said with utmost sincerity.

"I need to know you, and you need to know me," he added, setting the champagne on the nightstand. "We need to talk more."

"I agree." She put the tape in the machine and brought the remote to the bed. "If there's anything I haven't told you about myself yet, I will when I think of it. I'm out of deep dark secrets, so I hope you feel like you know me. Mind if I take my shoes off?"

"Please." He looked flustered. "I'm only taking the spread off because I paid so much for it—not because I'm trying to—"

"I know," Audrey said quickly. "And I don't blame you, it's gorgeous. In fact, if you don't mind, I'd just as soon we move the blankets, too, and sit on the sheets. They're more comfortable."

He looked at her for an instant. "No problem."

After he was done, she sat on the edge of the high bed and swung her legs up, grateful her skirt was full enough to let her sit cross-legged, a nice innocent position that wouldn't make him so nervous. "So, Rick, do you have any deep dark secrets you haven't told me?" she asked lightly as she hit the remote and started the movie.

He handed her an apple. "Yes."

She studied him a long moment. "Well, you can tell me when and if you want to. I'll take you at face value."

It was his turn to stare at her. "What if you got involved with me and then found out I'm a raving maniac?"

"I'm a big girl, Piper. I'll take my chances. Besides, there's nothing more boring than a really normal person," she added. "Pour the champagne," she ordered as the movie's theme swelled.

They nibbled apples and sipped champagne. About the time Wells got his first kiss, Audrey stretched her legs out in front of her and used a couple pillows to prop herself up against the high headboard. Rick did the same, letting himself move closer to her in the process.

"Is there any champagne left?" she asked a while later.

"Mmm." He poured the last two glassfuls. "To us," he said as they clinked glasses. "You really don't care if I'm a raving maniac?"

"Not in the least." She moved closer to the center of the bed. He. did, too, until their legs barely touched. It excited her beyond reason. "You look a little loopy, Rick," she said.

"I'm easy," he said, draining the glass.

"You're anything but easy." She felt tipsy herself.

Quizzically, he looked at her. He took her glass and set it on the nightstand, then took her hand. "This is a great movie." On the screen, Mary Steenburgen had Malcolm McDowall in a clinch.

"It is," she agreed. "So, Rick, do you think women should be that aggressive?"

"The right woman . . ." He got off the bed. "Excuse me a moment." He went into the bathroom, shut the door. She heard water running, then he was back. She smiled when he went to the bedroom door and turned the lock.

He saw her smile and, blushing mumbled something

about not wanting Cody to get the wrong idea. She agreed gently.

She waited for him to climb back on the bed, then pointed at Steenburgen on the screen. "No matter how hard I try, I just can't be that aggressive. You know, to just grab a guy and not let go."

He didn't answer except for a coy smile. He took her hand again.

"Rick?"

"Hmmm?"

"You know what I am good at, though?"

"What?"

"I'm really good at wrapping up presents."

He turned slightly to face her better. "What do you mean?"

"Well," she said, trying to stay calm and cool, "I have another present for you."

"Audrey, you shouldn't give me all these presents."

"I wouldn't if I didn't want to. But this one's special. It's a present for me, too. And I *really* want to give this to you. *Really.*"

"What is it?" He grinned broadly.

"You'll have to find it and unwrap it to see."

Rolling his eyes, he said, "Here we go again. Well, where is it? Are you going to give me a clue?"

"Well, okay. There are a hundred and twenty-two closures on this gift. You have to undo all of them. It's big, weighs better than a hundred pounds."

"Good Lord, Audrey, where is it, in your car? You shouldn't be spending money on me—"

"Hush. Here's another clue." She pulled a single bobby pin from her hair. "Now there are a hundred and twenty-one closures left."

Understanding crossed his features so suddenly and completely that, in the heartbeat that he stared at her, mouth slightly open, she thought: *I've blown it.*

"I just love surprises," he said as he sat up and stared down at her. He touched her hair, her cheek, bent over her and gently kissed her lips. "And I never get tired of unwrapping things." His hand stole up to her hair and removed another pin. "A hundred and twenty. This is going to take a while," he told her. "All night, probably."

"That was the plan," she whispered.

"One hundred nineteen."

36

In the dream, he was making love to Audrey. He lay over her, his head between her breasts. Her skin, milky white but for a light sprinkling of freckles on her arms and legs and across the tops of her breasts where the sun had kissed her, smelled deliciously of female musk.

"Rick," Audrey moaned as he kissed one breast. "Rick," she cried again as he trailed his lips across to the other.

She called his name over and over again as he slowly traced his tongue down the slope of her breast. He moved his mouth down her body, losing himself in her salty-warm taste, in the silky smoothness of her skin, in the rich scent that he'd been addicted to since the first time he'd caught it. He swirled his tongue down and down, past her navel, into the patch of soft reddish hair, pausing to listen as she called his name again, wanting to drive her as mad as she drove him. Her body arched against him, her fingernails digging into his flesh. "Rick, now! Rick!"

"Rick!" Her voice in his ear, urgent, needing him, bruising his biceps with her fingers.

He groaned, reaching for her, wanting her.

"Rick! Wake up!"

"Audrey?" His voice cracked, not wanting to work. He was not below her, but facing her, on his side. She was pressed up against him, her mouth near his ear. His erection was pressed against her thigh. *Oh God, was I humping her like one of Jade's poodles?* Instantly he went soft.

She didn't seem to notice. "Rick! Wake up, please!"

His brain kicked in, discerned the urgency in her voice. "What?"

"Someone's in here. I heard noises."

"I locked the door," he murmured, not wanting to get up.

"I didn't imagine it."

That got his attention. "Of course not. I'm sorry—I was sleeping like the dead."

"I'll say," she whispered. "You're *sure* you locked the door?"

"Positive." He rubbed his eyes. That helped a little. "What did you hear?"

"I thought I heard something moving around. It sounded like it was in the dressing room."

Suddenly goose bumps rose on his arms and neck. "I'll check it out," he said, hoping his voice sounded firm and strong. He sat up and swung out of bed and, not bothering with a robe, crossed to the light switch by the door and flipped it on. He tried the knob.

"Still locked," he said to Audrey, who sat up watching him. Her smile and the locked door made his nervousness go away. "And I've got the only keys."

"Maybe I *was* dreaming," she said without conviction.

"Maybe. I know I was." He smiled, looking at her breasts, thinking about what he was doing in the dream.

She grinned broadly. "You're a friendly fellow."

Looking down, he blushed.

"And you have a gorgeous ass," Audrey snickered. "No wonder Duane wanted you."

He just stood there, dumb and excited.

"And it looks like you're up for seconds," Audrey observed coyly.

Nodding, he took one step toward the bed, then stopped cold.

"Did you hear it?" Audrey's expression had transformed from desire into worry.

He nodded. "I think there are still some rats living in the passages." He stepped toward the dressing room.

"That's probably what I heard," she told him. "A rat. I saw the bait in the cabinet."

"With the tapes?" He glanced back at her.

"No, the empty one. I forgot to tell you. The wire was on the floor when I came up before. I replaced it."

"It was off?" Adrenaline pumped into his bloodstream.

"I'm sure it's nothing," she said quickly. "The doors weren't open or anything. I assumed Quint had played with it and pulled it off."

Snagging up his flashlight, he turned on the dressing room light, crossed to the bathroom, and flicked that light on as well. A little surge of superstitious fear made him check the shower stall, but it was devoid of poodles or other vermin.

Audrey padded into the dressing room as he reentered from the bathroom. "Find anything?"

"Well, the bathroom's safe."

"Good. I have to pee." She held out her finger. "And I brought my traveling toothbrush. Can I use your toothpaste?"

"Be my guest." It was hard to stay nervous when you were looking at a naked woman. As she passed him, he reached out and let his hand stroke the curve of her buttocks.

"I think yours is cuter," she called in a deadpan voice as she shut the bathroom door.

Okay. Let's get it over with, Piper. He squatted and began undoing the wire just as Audrey came out of the bathroom. She knelt beside him.

"Why are your tapes in here when you have that entertainment center in there?" she whispered.

"When the movers brought the furniture in, they left my dresser facing the wall, so I stuffed my clothes in the entertainment center."

"At least you turned the dresser around."

He smiled thinly. Carmen had waited a week, then done it herself. "I just want to take a quick peek in here." Swallowing hard, he opened the cabinet, very aware of Audrey's chin behind his shoulder.

"There's a secret passage in there?" she asked.

"Yeah. They're built so that they stay closed." He shined the light inside, saw nothing unusual.

"Where's the door?"

"You have to hold the latch to open it."

"So let's see."

What the hell. He pushed the lever, and the door slid open, revealing velvet blackness.

"Rick, I swear that's one of the sounds I heard earlier."

"The door opening?" Shocked, he looked at her.

She nodded. "But it's such a soft sound, I doubt that you could hear it from the bedroom."

She nodded. "It was very quiet in there. I really think that's what I heard."

"But . . ." He hesitated.

She crawled forward. "Can I see?" She took the light from his hand. He backed up and waited nervously as she slipped her head and torso into the cabinet.

Rick leaned back, enjoying the view until he realized that she was going to find the knife. He'd left it there in the first place because it seemed dirty and horrible and he didn't want to touch it. God, he wished he'd thrown it out. He waited for her to say something about it.

Instead, she eased her way out of the cabinet and handed him the light. "I don't think I'd want to go crawling around in there. Yuck." She stood up. "Do you think Cody came in and explored while we were out?"

"I locked the door."

"That's right. Could he have come through the tunnel?"

"I blocked the passage in his room, and he doesn't know about any others," he replied as he took the light and quickly examined the interior of the passage.

The knife was gone.

Trembling, he pulled out of the cabinet. "Excuse me," he said, rummaging in a packing box on the dressing room floor. He pulled out an old tie, looped it through the handles several times, then knotted it three times.

"That'll do the trick," Audrey said.

He nodded. "I'll be right back," he said, pulling on his robe. "I'm just going to go down the hall and check on Cody." He tried to sound casual, but inside, he was shaken.

Cody was fast asleep, without a trace of grime on his face. *Maybe Carmen's right about the ghost,* he thought, returning to Audrey.

Wearing his shirt, she waited for him in the doorway.

"That looks better on you than me," he told her. They went back inside, and he noticed that she locked the door behind them.

"How's Cody?" she asked, removing the shirt, then climbing back onto the bed.

"Fast asleep. Angelic." He threw the robe across a chair and joined her. "Maybe I undid it without thinking. Sometimes I don't think my brain works quite right."

She took his hand and traced a circle on his palm. "You want to talk about it?"

He nodded. "I was putting off what we did tonight until I did tell you about it, but you said you didn't care if I was a raving maniac, you still wanted my body . . ."

She looked him in the eye. "I wasn't kidding, Piper."

He hesitated. "I lied about something."

"Your cousin in Scotland?" she asked wryly.

He stared at her in amazement. "Did Dakota tell?"

"Dakota hasn't told me anything. You told me about the greenjacks, you acted antsy outside, and you started talking about your cousin in Scotland, wondering if he was crazy because he claimed to see them. You wanted information." She kissed his lips quickly. "Even if I hadn't caught on then, I would have later, when you refused to talk about it again."

"Oh." He couldn't look at her. "If you already knew, then I guess you really meant it about making love to a madman."

"Christ, you're hard on yourself." She shook her head. "Listen, Rick, I did a lot of research, and it's not at all out of the realm of possibility that you really are seeing something."

Hopefully he looked up. "Really?"

"Really." She smiled at him. "I've delivered lectures before, but never naked."

He chuckled in spite of himself. Audrey certainly had a knack for saying the right thing to relax him. "Believe me, I'll hear every word and never take my eyes off you."

"Better not." She cleared her throat. "There are several possibilities, Rick. You might have an extra set of cones that give you an ability to see colors that other people can't."

"But the jacks are green."

"Because your brain has to put it in a context you can understand. I don't really think that's what's going on, though. Are they only visible at night?"

"Yes. My cat saw them, too."

"Really?"

Quickly he explained. "Does that knock out your theories?"

"No. It makes sense. Let me tell you another one."

"Shoot."

"Well, there's synchronous retinal firing, but I've been looking at your eyes all evening and I think that's out."

"Huh?"

"Jiggling of the eyes—it occasionally happens, and I thought it could possibly put your perception in synch with the greenjacks' frequency. But you don't jiggle."

"Thank God. So, Doc, what *do* you think it is?"

"I think it's one of a couple things, and, Rick, they can't be proven, because the only way to know for sure is to dissect the eye."

"Charming."

She smiled. "You see them at night—and Quint sees them, too, so what do you have in common with a cat?"

"I once coughed up a hairball."

She stifled a laugh. "Be serious. Cats see very well in the dark. You might have extremely good low spatial frequency perception. It would let you tell the difference between shadows and substance. Like a cat." She paused. "Normally humans only have good high-contrast, high spatial frequency—we can see the black letters on the white eye chart, but the same black letters on a dark gray chart would be very difficult. But I don't think that's it either. I think it's more likely to be pigment migration of your rods and cones."

"That sounds disgusting."

"It's not." She laughed. "It's common to fish, amphibians, and birds."

"Primitive creatures," Rick observed dryly.

"Well, yes, basically. How far back do the stories about greenjacks go in your family?"

"As far back as the family. Grandfather once talked about a Piper in the Crusades who had the sight, but I don't know . . ."

Audrey shrugged. "Let's say a thousand years, then. And that means it goes further back. It has to."

"He said we weren't the only ones, that you only had to look for places all over the world that are overgrown by vegetation, and you'd find a bloodline that carried the gene."

"It all fits, Rick," Audrey said, not bothering to hide her excitement. "Okay, now, listen. You have normal vision in normal light conditions, but at twilight and after dark, pigment migration would come into play. Your cones would retract and the rods move forward.

"Normally cones are useless for night vision, but in pigment migration, you've got retro-directional movement of the cones, which changes their normally angular orientation, thereby enhancing the Stiles-Crawford Effect and making them more sensitive than normal."

"Stiles what?" he asked.

"The Stiles-Crawford Effect says that cones are directionally sensitive to light that hits them head-on, but that their sensitivity falls off rapidly as the light hits them obliquely—like when you look through a paper towel tube. Rods aren't affected—they respond to any light at all. Follow me?"

"Sort of. You're saying that if I had this pigment thing, then it might make sense that I could see things other people can't."

"Yes. And it could very well be inherited, as well as apply to other creatures who see well at night—like cats. It means your eyes work differently—if I'm correct, then you have more visual abilities than most people—and your average man on the street wouldn't—couldn't—comprehend it, and would label you either a charlatan or a madman."

Rick nodded. "So it's a sixth sense? Every time I've ever seen a psychic on television, I always think that person's just out for the money or totally nuts."

"Exactly." She gave him a crooked smile, and made a gentle *tsk-tsk* noise. "Of all people, Rick, you should be willing to believe that at least some of the psychics are on the level." She paused. "But you don't even believe *you're* on the level, do you?"

"No."

"You need to exorcise your brother, Piper. He's still controlling your mind."

"Yeah, I guess." He took her hand and kissed it. "I think you believe me more than I believe myself."

"I think you're right."

"There're just a couple flies in the theory. Things I didn't tell you," he confessed.

"Tell me."

"First, I *hear* them too. In my head. I'm no expert, but I think that makes me schizophrenic."

"Rick, some psychics see things, others hear or feel them, and some do all three, so why not see *and* hear greenjacks?"

Rick thought she sounded slightly less confident now, but decided he had to go the distance. "I've also seen Big Jack."

"Big Jack . . . the one they build out of plant life on Halloween, right? The Green Man?"

He nodded and quickly told her his memories of the night he and Robin fought the monster in the tree. "But," he added, "maybe I never saw it at all. I think maybe I invented all that because I felt like Robin's falling was my fault."

Silently she studied him. "Who have you told this to?"

"Nobody, really. Carmen knows—she always protected me when I was little—but I don't think she believes it much." He shook his head. "She's trying to talk me into letting her take Cody away overnight on Halloween. I think she's more worried about what I might do to him than anything else. Frankly, I don't blame her." He paused, then added, "Of course, she thinks this house is haunted by Robin, so I guess her opinion doesn't mean too much."

"Who's to say that it isn't?" Audrey pushed her hair from her face. "Do you believe in ghosts?"

"Of course not. Do you?"

"I don't *dis*believe any more than I believe. But, Rick, have you been talking to a therapist, or what?"

"No. Only Dakota."

"Of course," she added with a nod. "Has he been giving you advice? Like suggesting that your guilt made you invent that story about Robin in the tree?"

"How'd you know?"

"I know Duane. He loves pop psychology. The therapists he sees are the kind that write the books that are supposed to change your life in thirty days. Not that that's bad for Duane—it's done him a lot of good. But don't let him tell you how *you* think—he'll try to sell you on what works for him."

"I don't know what works for me."

She studied him. "I don't know either, but I'd guess that giving yourself the benefit of the doubt until you have proof one way or the other might be a good way to start."

"So do you want to come over Halloween night and see if we can spot Big Jack together?" His hands were trembling. "If I see him and you don't, we'll know I'm nuts, once and for all."

"And if we both see him, we'll know you're not." Audrey put her hand on his chest and gently pushed him back against the pillows before leaning down and kissing him lingeringly on the lips. Her nipples hardened as her breasts brushed against his chest. "You're going to have to get a lot crazier than this to get rid of me, Piper." She kissed his lips again, then his neck.

She meant what she said, he knew that, but he would not, *could* not, let her ruin her life for him. She pulled one of his nipples into her mouth, biting gently, then moved to the other. As she trailed her tongue down his belly, he prayed that she would see Big Jack too. Then, a moment later, he gave up worrying about anything at all.

37

October 16

"Man, Rick, there's some disgusting stuff in this pond." Hector Zapata took off his baseball cap and pushed his fingers through his black hair. "No wonder the pump's been clogging so much, even with that two-inch hose."

"At least there aren't any mosquitoes." Rick squinted at the emptying pond. The sludgy water continued to gurgle into the wide, formerly white hosing, making obscene farting and belching sounds. The smell was so bad on this unseasonably warm day that he wished he had a handkerchief to put over his face.

"No mosquitoes. I don't think anything's lived in there since Howard took to pissing in it." Hector's laugh reeked of disgust. "He dumped other stuff in it too. Antifreeze, that's probably what killed the fish. He bragged about that. Did it to piss off your brother."

"Robin loved those fish," Rick said. They were the only living things he could remember his twin having any fondness for. He knew that Howard urinated in the pool, he'd seen it time after time over the years, but he didn't know about the antifreeze. A chill passed through him despite the warm sunlight. "How many years ago did the fish die?"

Hector put his hat back on. "It was the same year that the carnival came through for the last time. You remember?"

"I remember." A heavy, hard lump suddenly formed in his stomach. That summer was the last time he saw Delia Minuet, the last time he saw Robin.

July 5, 1981

It was Fourth of July weekend, and Rick was sixteen years old. He'd spent all his free time at the Masello Brothers Carnival and Sideshow riding the rides, eating corn dogs and cotton candy, talking to Delia whenever she had a break, and avoiding his brother, who loved the carnival as much as he did, but for very different reasons.

Robin loved to show off, to shock and to steal attention, and racing through the fairgrounds on his hands was a good way to do it. His arms were extremely powerful, and he could execute all sorts of stunts, from his all-time favorite handstand running to using his arms like frog's legs to leap three feet up and six across at a time.

John and Vince, the all-powerful Masello brothers, adored the ground Robin walked on and even seemed pleased when he'd break into regular performers' shows, swinging his little body up a rope or leaping into the middle of the clown show's fire engine act. From the first time he did this—the year following their parents' death—Delia told Rick that the performers didn't like it one little bit, but they couldn't do much about it since the Masellos were so taken by him.

Robin systematically charmed people who mattered, and wasted no time on those who had no power. Watching people fall for his act was frustrating. The sole thing that gave Rick pleasure where his twin was concerned was his lack of success with any of the animals. They hated him, one and all. Where the Ewebean poodles, who also hated him, just whined and pranced nervously around Jade's legs, the circus animals' response to his presence spoke abundantly of their feelings toward him. The elephant trumpeted, and the big cats put their ears back and growled when he approached.

The organ grinder's monkey had strangled itself in its attempt to get away from him.

The animals sensed the truth about Robin Piper.

So did many of the performers, most notably the denizens of the ten-in-one show. These people had certain things in common: physical abnormalities, a strong dislike for the bleeding heart liberals who were trying to take away their livelihood, a camaraderie deeper than most people ever experienced, and the ability to see through the veneer of false personality. They listened to their instincts, and if one didn't sense something himself, he invariably trusted the word of those who did.

That's why Rick was so at home among them; they accepted him from the first time Delia introduced him to her extended family, just as they uniformly shunned his brother. As far as they were concerned, the Masello brothers were the handicapped ones because they were blinded by their own greed, but they accepted this fact as part of life.

Though he only saw her a few days a year, Delia had remained Rick's best friend since that very first summer. He could talk to Carmen, though he rarely did, but Delia was the only person his own age with whom he could share his secrets. He could tell her anything, and she never made fun of him. She had always accepted his stories at face value.

This year he'd looked forward to seeing Delia as much as ever, and when the carnival had arrived three days ago and they met again, things were slightly different between them. She'd looked him up and down and whistled. "You turned into a man this year. Look how tall you are."

"Five seven." He didn't tell her he felt like a shrimp.

The next day she made an observation in her fast-talking, no-bullshit way. "There's a cut on your cheek. Do you have to shave now?"

Finally, today, she'd asked, "Do you have a girlfriend?"

He'd never told her about the cheerleader two years before or about the minor flirtations he'd experienced since. "No girlfriends."

"Come on, Ricky, you must have at least one. You're too cute not to."

He blushed. "My brother has enough for both of us."

Delia made a face. "Stupid girls. They don't see anything but that fake charm. So I bet he screws everything that moves, right? Probably those poodles even have to watch out."

He grinned. Delia knew all about Jade's sexual proclivities, as well as her dogs. "Probably. So do you want to take a walk?"

"You're way too tall," she told him. "We can't talk and walk anymore."

She didn't know she'd hurt his feelings, and he wasn't about to tell her.

Tonight was the last night the carnival was in town, and he wanted to spend all the time he could with her. They needed to find a place where they could sit and talk for hours, and suddenly inspiration hit. "Jade and Howard will be at the carnival tonight, then they'll go to the Dew Drop Inn and not get home before two-thirty in the morning. Want to come over and watch TV?"

Her eyes lit up: Television was a rare luxury for Delia. "Yes! What time?"

"Six?"

"I'll be there. Will *he?*"

She meant Robin. "I hope not. He's hardly ever home on the weekends."

That night Rick and Delia sprawled on the couch and feasted on Swanson TV dinners, Dr. Peppers, and Oreos as they talked and watched TV. By nine P.M. they were holding hands. Delia, despite her abnormal bone structure, was very attractive with thick brown hair that waved halfway down her back and eyes the same color, as deep and rich as liquid chocolate.

At nine-thirty, he kissed her. She climbed into his lap and returned the kiss, putting her arms around his neck, holding him close. And at that moment Rick fell in love for the first time in his life.

They didn't hear Robin come in a few minutes later, didn't know he sat in the shadows and watched them as they whispered and caressed and kissed. They didn't know he was there until he spoke.

"Well, icky Ricky, here you are getting ready to fuck the dwarf. And all this time I thought you were queer."

"Eat shit, Robin," Delia said, boredom in her voice.

"I'm more your size, Delia," Robin said, leering as he slap-slapped his way across the room. Balancing on one hand, he helped himself to an Oreo and pulled it apart. He licked the frosting out, never taking his eyes off Delia. "I bet you'd like me to lick you like I'm licking this cookie, huh, dwarf?"

Rage built in Rick like pressure in a volcano. "Robin—"

"You don't want to fuck him," Robin continued smoothly. "What I lack in legs, I make up for here." He grabbed himself and squeezed, grinning obscenely.

Rick's ears rang as he stood up, dizzy in the fury he felt. "Shut up or I'll—"

"You'll what?" his twin interrupted. "Go whining to Carmen? Lock yourself in your room and cry? What? Huh, icky Ricky? Tell me, I *really* want to know."

He took a step toward his brother. "Oh, my, aren't you a brave dicky Ricky when you've got a dwarf cunt to impress."

Rick said nothing. He extended his arms, intent on his brother's throat, knowing he was going to strangle him with his bare hands.

"Rick, no!" he heard Delia call from behind him.

Robin stayed where he was, moving up and down almost imperceptibly, doing the spider. "Don't worry, dwarfie, he doesn't have the balls!"

His cackle abruptly ceased as Rick's hands encircled his neck and lifted him off the ground. He squeezed harder and harder, feeling a smile spread across his face as a sound like the ocean's echo in a seashell filled his head. In the distance, he heard Delia's high-pitched screams.

"Fuck you," he whispered as he watched Robin's face turn the color of pickled beets. "Fuck you."

Robin's huge arms flailed wildly, ineffectually.

Suddenly Rick realized that he was only supposed to scare his brother, to teach him to leave him and Delia alone. He shouldn't be trying to kill him.

But he wanted to. He *really* wanted to.

He loosened his grip on Robin's neck the tiniest fraction, heard his brother take a strangled, gasping breath. "Don't you ever fuck with Delia again," Rick whispered.

"What about you?" Robin's voice was a hoarse cracking sound. "Can I fuck with you?"

"Rick! Watch out!"

The sudden pain in his groin made him scream and lose his hold on his twin.

Robin continued to squeeze Rick's testicles even after he'd fallen to the ground. Rick, screaming, kicked and flailed at him, but he wouldn't let go. Instead, he twisted them, and even Rick's heavy Levi's provided little protection from Robin's grip. He kicked and punched, but it did no good. Robin laughed and began hopping on one hand, trying to pull him across the room. Rick was jerked a few feet, his brother's marionette, and was ready to give up consciousness to give up and die.

"No!" Delia's scream cut through his agony and suddenly she was there, pushing between them, trying to pry Robin's fingers loose.

Rick moaned. She was making it worse.

"No!" she screamed again, then opened her strong-jawed mouth as wide as she could and sunk her teeth into Robin's forearm.

He let go. Rick doubled up, holding himself, groaning and sobbing, wanting to die. He knew he was vomiting only because he could see it; the sensation was lost entirely to the pain in his groin.

Vaguely, he saw Robin flailing at Delia with his free arm, trying to hit her. Doggedly she kept her teeth sunk into his other arm.

Rick reached toward Delia, wanting to help her, then blackness came and took away the pain.

"Ricky! Ricky!" Slowly he awoke, and the pain began again, less sharp, a horrible aching agony beneath freezing cold. Carmen sat in a chair beside the couch where he lay. She was patting his face with a cold, damp cloth.

"God," he moaned, reaching for his groin, shocked to find his pants were gone. An ice pack sat on his jockey shorts. The cold, he thought, staring at Carmen in shock.

"Hector checked you," she said bluntly. "There was blood. We thought maybe you had to go to the hospital. If the swelling's not down, we'll take you tomorrow. She handed him two aspirin and a glass of water and waited silently while he took the pills.

His hand shook as he handed the glass back to her. "Where's Delia?" he managed.

She looked surprised. "Hector and I got home at ten-thirty. We came in to make sure everything was okay and found you on the floor. No one else was here. What happened, Ricky?"

He tried to sit up so he could see the clock, but he was too sore. "What time is it?"

"Just past eleven. Ricky, tell me what happened."

"Delia was here. We were watching television. Robin came in and . . ."

"And what?" she prompted.

"He said things. About Delia."

"Dirty things?"

Rick nodded. "I got mad. I tried to kill him."

"Madre de Dios."

"I was choking him, I was going to do it, then all of a sudden I realized what I was doing. I started to let go, and that's when he got me."

"I think he did a lot more damage to you than you did to him."

Carefully Rick pulled himself upright. God, it hurt. He set the ice bag on the coffee table. "We have to find Delia."

"Hector already checked the house, but no one was here except you. He's out checking the grounds. We thought maybe you had a run-in with your brother, but Hector thought he should look around and make sure we didn't have any prowlers. Let me help you."

She took his arm as he stood. He felt trembly and light-headed, and oh Lord, did his balls hurt.

"Ricky?"

"I'm okay. Delia was fighting with him when I passed out, Carmen. I'm worried about her."

"Okay. You sit and I'll look again."

"No. I'm going with you."

She looked at him skeptically. "If you insist. You want me to go up and get you a pair of sweatpants?"

He smiled thinly. "Please."

He leaned against the wall until she came 'back. As he gingerly pulled on the pants, he avoided looking at the bloodstains on his shorts.

"I found this, too," Carmen said, handing him a sealed envelope with his name on it. He didn't recognize the hand-writing.

He opened it and saw that the note was written on school paper. He scanned the letter quickly, then reread it, not wanting to believe what he saw.

"Dear Rick," it said, "I thought you were a nice person, but if you were, you wouldn't have tried to kill your own brother. Don't come to the carnival. I never want to see you again. Delia."

Stunned, not knowing what else to do, he handed it to Carmen. After she read it she asked, "Ricky, do you know her handwriting?"

"No. I don't think I've ever seen it. Why?"

"I'm thinking this might be your brother's idea of a joke."

Rick looked up hopefully. "Should I go to the carnival and talk to her?"

"I don't think you're in any shape to do that. Where's the carnival going next?"

"The high desert. They're stopping for a few days in Victorville, then they're going to Nevada."

"Tomorrow night you try to call up there. If you can't get through, Hector will drive you, okay?"

"Maybe I could call tonight . . ." he began. Fear rose in his gut. "Or maybe I should wait. I was really weird tonight, Carmen. I . . . I think I went nuts for a few minutes. She probably doesn't want to see me."

"Call, Ricky. Just see if she's there so you can stop worrying about her. I don't believe that letter."

He was about to say he didn't either when there was a knock on the front door. Carmen opened it.

"Robin," she said coldly.

"Hi, baby brother."

Rick's heart skipped a beat.

Robin padded directly up to him. "I walked your girlfriend back to the carnival. She doesn't like you anymore, icky Ricky. She thinks you're a meanie." He feigned a grab toward Rick, who gasped and backed up.

Robin laughed. "Gotcha good, didn't I, little brother? Self-defense. Hope I didn't crack your nuts. Hope you can still make babies."

"Robin!" Carmen said angrily.

"It was self-defense," he said smoothly.

"Did you write this?" Rick asked, brandishing the note.

Robin looked mildly surprised. "No. What is it?"

"You know what it is," Carmen said.

Robin pushed the sleeve up on his shirt and displayed a perfect set of red tooth marks. "She told me she was sorry she did this. She said she got so scared when you tried to kill me that she didn't really know what she was doing."

"Did you write this?" Carmen asked again.

He peered at her. "Nope. She said she was going up to Ricky's room to leave him a nice, private note. I never read it." He slap-slapped to the bookcase and felt for the lever.

A moment later, the case turned, revealing the dark, narrow stairwell. Robin turned and looked directly at Rick.

"You'll be happy to know that I'm running away with the circus, icky Ricky. Just gonna get my things."

"You can't just leave," Carmen began.

"Oh, now, be honest, Carmen. You don't want me here any more than he does. I'm sixteen, I'm leaving. The Masellos made me an offer I can't refuse. My own trailer, star billing, lots of bucks. I'm going." His grin was horrifying. "Nobody's going to miss me but Jade. And she's going to miss me something awful. Dicky Ricky, maybe if your nuts heal up, you can give her what she wants. She's old, but she's got nice tits." He made a face. "And you gotta admit, it's better than fucking a dwarf."

Carmen advanced on him, saying things in Spanish that Rick was happy he didn't understand. Rick himself was too sore and tired to summon up anything but cold disgust. Laughing, his twin disappeared into the stairwell, the bookcase swinging closed behind him.

For fifteen minutes Rick tried to get through to Delia on the phone, but no one answered—the phone was in the office trailer, and no one was there this late at night.

Hector returned, and a moment later, Robin came back. The three watched in silence as Robin, a bulging knapsack strapped to his broad back, hummed to himself and crossed to the front door. "Give my love to Jade, Ricky," he said, opening the door. "Give it to her *good*."

Rick didn't answer.

No one did.

The door shut.

"Good riddance," Carmen hissed.

July 6, 1981

After midnight, Rick lay in his bed in his locked room, not quite awake, not quite asleep, always in pain. Sometime during the night, he heard Jade and Howard come home.

Drunk and foulmouthed, they argued all the way to their room, their voices fading only after they slammed the door.

A long time later a pair of sonic booms rattled his windows. Soon sirens broke the silence of the night. He thought and dreamed continuously about Delia, worrying, wondering, so unsure of himself that it was yet another physical pain. As dawn approached, he made up his mind to see her before the carnival left for Victorville. He got up.

The swelling wasn't so bad now, but peeing was an exercise in torture. It took him twenty minutes to get dressed, but finally, dressed in sweats and zoris, because he found he couldn't bend over to put on shoes and socks, he slowly made his way down the stairs.

Dawn had arrived. He glanced at his bike by the back door. That was out of the question. He dreaded walking. The Zapatas weren't up yet, so he couldn't ask Hector for a ride.

But Jade and Howard would sleep at least till noon. They had hangovers every time they went to the Dew Drop. He took the car keys from the hook by the back door and went out to the driveway and let himself into their Bulgemobile, a monstrous Impala they'd bought a year ago. Since they'd moved into the Piper house, they'd gone through a series of Bulgemobiles, trading them in every other year for something new to slowly destroy.

This one, parked at a crazy angle, was already missing one headlight and part of a bumper. He slipped the keys into the ignition, and the car started after a couple coughs and a sputter.

He turned it around and slowly pulled out the driveway and onto the street. He'd only driven the driver's ed cars before this monstrosity, but all things considered, he thought he did all right.

He drove down through the circular maze of streets that made up his neighborhood. The air, warm already, was layered with a fine mist. There were no other cars out at five in the morning, and the huge pine trees lining the narrow road loomed ominously, watching and waiting.

Finally he made it down the hill and continued on toward

the fairgrounds. A light turned red at the school corner, and he sat there and waited for no traffic, his stomach nervous, his heart beating too fast. The light changed and he glanced up and saw the low pall of smoke over the fairgrounds.

Numb, not allowing his imagination to run wild—*probably the corn dog stand, an oil fire, that's all*—he drove down the street and pulled to a stop across the street from the entrance.

He got out of the car and started across the street.

He saw nothing unusual at first, except for two police cars and a single fire engine at the inside edge of the vast field that served as the fairground parking lot. There was a faint smell of smoke in the air.

Ducking under the rope that closed the lot, he started across the field. He could see the ticket booths just beyond the police cars and then the square little carnival buildings that should have been dismantled by now. *Maybe they're just a little slow this morning.* Maybe they'd started tearing down from the other side of the carnival, near the trailers where everyone lived.

He couldn't see those from here.

Ignoring the pain, he began to run, then, ducking another set of ropes, he entered the carnival grounds, the smoke acrid and cloying in his nostrils. None of the buildings had been torn down yet, as far as he could see.

"Son?"

He looked at the yellow-coated fireman who called him. "What happened? Where is everyone?"

"Do you have friends here?"

"Yes! Where are they?" Panicked, he shot forward, but the fireman reached his arm out and caught Rick's elbow. "What's your name, son?"

"Rick."

"Rick, do you have relatives here?"

He hesitated. "Robin!" he blurted. "Robin Piper, he's my brother. He's here. I want to go to the trailers, I have a lot of friends here—"

"Hey, Ed," the fireman called over his shoulder.

"Yeah?" called a young cop with dirt smudged on his face.

"Stay here, Rick," the fireman said, and went to talk to the cop. A moment later, the cop came up to him.

"I want to go to the trailers," Rick said.

"There's been a fire." The cop wasn't much older than him, Rick realized. He looked scared, his blue eyes sort of glazed. "There was an explosion. It's bad. There are a lot of fatalities."

"How many?"

"We don't know yet."

"I want to see if Delia's all right."

The cop eyed him. "I thought you were looking for your brother."

"Yes, he's here, but so's Delia and her family. And Clarisse and Omar and—"

The policeman's skin looked too white under the ashes smudged on his cheek. "Rick, most everyone was in their living quarters when the explosion hit. It was very sudden and the fire was so fierce and hot—"

"I thought I heard sonic booms. Was that it?"

The cop nodded. "There's not much left. They had the trailers well away from the carnival. The grounds are so big and all . . ." The young cop looked around him, and Rick thought the guy was trying not to cry.

"What are you saying?"

"I'm saying the carnival wasn't blown up, the living quarters were, and you don't want to see. So far, there are no survivors. A lot of bodies." He shook his head. "They didn't stand a chance. Is your family . . ."

"We live on Via Matanza."

The cop looked relieved. "Maybe you'd better go tell them. We don't even know if we can identify the remains." He pulled out a notebook. "Give me your name and number. We'll be in touch."

Rick did. "I need to see. Just for a moment."

The policeman studied him. "Okay, but not close up. We've got professionals losing their cookies over this."

Rick could tell this man wasn't exaggerating by the sick look in his eyes. "Okay."

They walked together around the rows of buildings until the trailers came into view. There was nothing but charred, blackened ruins dotted with yellow bags. More police cars, fire engines, and a bunch of ambulances sat nearby. As he watched, Rick saw another cop with a handkerchief tied over his mouth and gloves on his hands pick up something long and jointed and put it in a sack.

It was an arm.

"Go on home now," the cop said gently.

38

Rick leaned on a shovel and listened to the pump gurgle. A week after the explosion, they'd held Robin's funeral, and Jade had sobbed histrionically, the poodle in her lap whining along with her. Howard and the Zapatas were there, and some kids from school showed up, but that was all. When they laid the tiny coffin containing a few charred bones in the ground, only Jade cried.

Rick had been glad that his brother was dead, but the loss of Delia hurt him terribly. It still hurt, as did the knowledge that he could never know if Delia really hated him, or if Robin had made it all up. He was sixteen years old and he hated Santo Verde more than ever. He had already started planning to graduate high school a year early and go to UNLV, where he would be surrounded by nothing but sand for four years. There was nothing left in Santo Verde for him. Nothing at all.

The papers, he recalled, had said that police had reason to believe the explosion had been set intentionally, but the perpetrators were never caught.

Rick watched Hector readjust the pump. The only other thing that happened before he left home was Howard's death on Halloween night. Officially it was a heart attack, and the coroner said cirrhosis of the liver would have got him if his heart hadn't.

Evidently he'd been sitting out on the porch as usual,

nursing his Jack Daniels and smoking his Tiparillo, when he decided to take a walk, probably to pee in the pond.

That night, for a reason attributed only to drunkenness, Howard had missed the pond by twenty yards and wandered into the deep front grounds. Hector found him there the next morning, his eyes wide open, his mouth in a rictus of a scream. A cop commented that he looked like he'd been scared to death. The cop wondered about all the grass stains on the clothes and skin, and the leaves in his mouth, and the coroner said he must have thrashed around in the foliage before he died.

What the coroner said was true, Rick had known as he stood there staring coolly at his dead uncle. It was truer than he'd ever know. Uncle Howard had had a little run-in with Big Jack himself.

"Rick?"

Hector's voice startled him out of his reverie. "Yeah?"

"I think we're ready for the dirty work. We can't siphon any more out."

Oh, joy, Rick thought, looking at the greenish black mounds of glop and garbage at the bottom of the pool.

"I'm going to get a couple masks out of the toolshed," Hector announced, pulling off his rubber gloves.

"I guess I should have hired this job out," Rick said.

"It's bad, but we can do it." Hector's lip curled as he studied the muck. "We don't want to get that stuff on us. I'm gonna get some thicker gloves for us, and I think there are a couple pairs of hip boots hanging in the garage. Your grandfather left them here."

"Thanks," Rick called as the other man trudged away. Hector was right—they couldn't climb into that mire unprotected. If they did, they'd both end up on antibiotics from staph infections.

Hector returned a few moments later with the masks, gloves, and dusty but intact waders. They put them on, took garbage sacks and shovels, and climbed down the steps at the shallow end of the pool.

Rick picked his way into the deepest part of the pool,

where the muck reached almost to his knees, and, resigned
to his task, began shoveling.

The sludge was mainly liquid compost, probably years-
old leaves and grass, and dissolved fish and frogs, though
he occasionally found tree limbs, dishes, liquor bottles, and
beer cans. There were two oil filters and what might have
once been a cowboy hat, all in one corner of the pool. Glancing behind him at Don Quixote, glinting in the midday sun,
he wondered what the knight would have pretended this
slimy enemy to be.

He moved to the other side of the deep end and began
working once more. A few minutes later, his shovel ran into
something solid. He pulled back and tried again, and again
met resistance. *It's big, whatever it is.* The goop sucked
against the shovel, not wanting to give up its prize, but finally he pulled it partway out before it slipped off the shovel
and disappeared again.

"Damn." Rick leaned the shovel against the wall and bent
over, digging his gloved hands into the mess. He pulled the
object out and held it up, trying to see what it was under
the dripping goo.

"It's a bone," Hector said, slogging over.

"My God." Hector was right. It was too big to be an
animal bone, but it was odd-looking, too. Hector took the
bone and set it on the cement edging the pool. Rick dug in
again, this time pulling out an oddly shaped rib cage.

"Mother of God," Hector breathed. "It's human."

He didn't offer to take the ribs, so Rick set them aside
himself, then grimly he went back to work, pulling more
bones from the mire. Finally he extracted the skull, and
moaned, his suspicions confirmed by the uniquely ridged
brow. "Dear God," he moaned. "It's Delia."

"I'll get Carmen," Hector said.

Numbly Rick nodded and climbed from the pool. He set
the skull next to the other bones that dried in the sun, and
took the time to study the stunted leg bones. "My God,
Delia." Tears ran down his face.

They weren't so much for Delia—he was long used to

the idea of her death—but for himself. Now he knew that his brother was behind the note, behind the death. They were tears of relief.

39

Later that afternoon, Carmen, Hector, and Rick buried Delia's bones beneath a willow tree in the front yard. Hector planted a white rose bush on top of the grave to mark it, and Rick stood by the grave between the couple and said a little prayer to a god he didn't know.

The Zapatas were gone now, leaving him to sit beside Delia's grave. He was thankful for that and for Carmen, who had instantly stopped his knee-jerk intention to inform the police, by pointing out that both Delia and her murderer were officially dead and had been for many years. There was no point in stirring things up.

"Oh, Delia," he whispered. "I wish I could avenge you. I wish I'd known." His voice broke and he let himself sob out his grief.

At last he got to his feet and walked the overgrown path back to the pond, where he stood by Don Quixote and watched Hector working. They'd gotten a lot done before he'd found the bones, far more than he'd realized—the job was near completion.

Staring into the emptying pool, at its slimy green sides, considering the secret that it had held, he had a sudden thought:

Paulie.

Paulie had started to laugh. It was an unholy sound.

"Dear God," Rick whispered, "Oh dear God, no." He grabbed the metal muzzle of the horse to keep from falling.

"Rick?" Hector turned and looked at him. "You okay?"

"I—I—"

"It's bad about Delia," Hector said gently. "And you've been out in the sun too long already. I can finish up here, no problem. Why don't you go to the cottage? Carmen's got a fresh pitcher of lemonade made up."

"Thanks," Rick managed. "I'll do that."

It took all his willpower to make it to the cottage and knock on the door. Carmen opened it a moment later, took one look at him, and insisted he sit in Hector's easy chair while she fetched the lemonade.

Quint poked his head out of the Zapatas' bedroom, then eeled into the room, flirting and rubbing against the furniture as he made his way across the room. He leapt into Rick's lap an instant before Carmen brought in a huge tumbler full of lemonade and ice.

"Thanks." He sipped the juice. "Carmen, about Paulie."

"You remembered," she said. "I can tell by the look in your eyes.

"I killed him."

"Yes, you did," she replied somberly. "You were still holding him under the water when I came out and found you. He was beyond saving."

"I murdered him," Rick whispered.

"How did you know the greenjacks got him? How did you know?"

"His laugh. He was sort of half sitting up when I came back to him after Big Jack came apart at midnight. I squatted down and asked him if he was all right. He started laughing.

"He'd changed, like Robin. He sounded like a demon—it was horrible to hear. And then he said, 'We're gonna getcha, icky Ricky.' He laughed some more, and I remember just staring at him. The greenjacks were everywhere, taunting me, singing their rhymes." Rick rubbed his temples. "Even in the dark, his eyes looked wrong, and then I remembered what Robin—the greenjack that was Robin—said. He said, 'Remember Thomas,' and right then I understood what he meant."

Even as he said the words, he knew they sounded insane, but it was too late now to take them back. "In Grandfather's story about Thomas, he always said that when his parents brought Thomas in, unconscious, his father waited with a sword, ready to run him through if a greenjack had taken his body. That always seemed really horrible, but important, that a father would kill his own son." He paused. "But really his son would have been already dead. He would have been kicked out of his own body and forced to live with the jacks until his stolen body was killed. So really, if Thomas's father had had to kill his body, it would have been the ultimate act of love.

"That's what I thought about while I held him under the water. While I murdered him."

Carmen said nothing for a long time. "Ricky, do you still believe that he was taken by the jacks?"

Rick thought of Audrey telling him to give himself the benefit of the doubt until he had proof. *Do I really believe he'd changed?* Finally he looked Carmen in the eye. "Yes, I still believe he was possessed by a jack. Just as my brother was," he added.

"If that's true, Ricky, then you're no murderer. You committed an act of mercy."

"What do you think, Carmen? Do you believe me?"

"Frankly, Ricky, I don't know. I've never known. Your brother, he changed, that's for sure. But maybe he just went bad. That happens."

"Yes, it does." He took a long swallow of lemonade, but barely felt it go down. "Our secret," he said softly. "The secret we will carry with us to our graves."

"We still will, Ricky. We still will."

He studied her, remembering how she'd coached him on what they would tell the police, and how she'd had him run in the house and call the ambulance while she made a show of resuscitating the lifeless little body. That was their secret.

"You've known that all these years," he said wonderingly.

"Two days after it happened, you forgot the truth. You believed the story we made up, Ricky. Years later, I thought maybe you never came home because you *had* remembered."

"No. Not until now. Carmen, why did you cover up for me?"

"Whether he turned into a greenjack or not, you believed he did. That was the important thing."

"That's more than any person should ever have to do for another."

"I didn't have to, Ricky. I wanted to. When you love someone, that's how it is."

He thought again of Audrey and realized the truth in Carmen's words. "I told Audrey," he said.

Carmen raised her eyebrows.

"She says there are some good scientific reasons why a person could see something like a greenjack."

"Good."

"I told her about Big Jack, too."

"What did she say?"

"She said she's going to stay with me on Halloween and we're going to watch for him together. Carmen, I know it sounds crazy, but at least I'll finally know."

"It's not crazy," Carmen said, smiling gently. "It's brave."

40

October 28

"You sure you don't mind, Dad?"

"As long as Leanne's parents are there somewhere, I think it's a great idea, Shel." He started to swivel his chair back to the computer, then stopped. "No drinking, right?"

Shelly laughed, still shocked that her dad had immediately given her permission to go to an all-night coed Halloween party. "Her parents will be there, and they don't drink or smoke at all." She gave him a crooked smile. "You met them at back-to-school night. I don't think they even have sex."

His expression turned stern. "I hope you're not intending—"

"No, Dad. That was a joke."

"I hope so." His features softened. "They do look like they probably grew Leanne in a test tube." He paused. "You're not going to repeat that, are you?"

"No, Daddy." Was he kidding? She loved it when he talked to her like an equal instead of his little girl. He'd been doing it more and more since they'd moved here, and she loved it. In Vegas he was always asking questions and calling people to see where she was, and now she knew he trusted her a lot more. Of course, he had more reason to; she knew that, too. "Mr. and Mrs. Larson may look like turnips, but they're very nice."

"Is it a costume party?" he asked.

"Uh-huh. I'm going to be a French maid." She couldn't resist tweaking him again. He was so predictable.

"No French maids, dear heart. Promoting a sexist im—"

Oh no, she'd pushed the lecture button. "Daa-dd! I was joking. I'm going as a Supreme Court judge, okay? A Democrat."

He stared at her. "Shel, it's late, I'm tired."

"Okay. I'm going to be a gypsy fortune-teller. I'm going to ask Carmen to help me. Okay?"

"Okay." He smiled faintly. "I'm sorry, kiddo. I just want to finish this last paragraph and get some sleep."

She leaned over and kissed him on the forehead. "I'm sorry I teased. What are you going to do for Halloween? Are you and Audrey going to a party?"

Dad didn't say much about Audrey, but Shelly knew they were getting hot and heavy and was pretty sure they were sleeping together. She was glad: Her dad was much easier to get along with now.

"No parties. We thought we'd take Cody trick-or-treating, then just stay in and watch horror movies."

"That's a good idea. Get scary ones so Audrey will hang on to you!"

"Shelly . . ."

"Sorry." She meant it this time. He really did look tired tonight with those dark smudges under his eyes. "I think Audrey's great, Dad."

It was his turn to stare. "You do?"

"A bunch of us were talking about our parents dating, and some of the kids hate it, like Jenny Morton. Her mom is seeing Bill Manderson's dad, and she's *so* embarrassed. She says her mom never pays any attention to her."

"But you approve of Audrey?"

"Heck, yes. She's Dakota's sister, and he's one of the best guys in the world. He's kind of one of my best friends." She called him every week and told him about school and work.

Dakota also gave great advice: not quite so prudish as a parent, but more like what she thought an older brother might dispense.

"Dakota's a good guy," her dad agreed.

"I know." She really did like Audrey a lot, but there was another reason she wanted them together, one she'd realized on back-to-school night, when Audrey had come along. Her girlfriends didn't try to throw themselves at her dad if he had a woman with him, which was a big relief. Back in Vegas, especially when he had the TV show, she never knew if her girlfriends liked her or just wanted to try to catch his eye.

"Bedtime, Shel," he said.

"When will the pool be ready?" she asked. At dinner the day after he and Hector drained the koi pond, Dad had told her how it used to be a swimming pool back in the thirties. "It's ready as of today," he said, smiling at her. "But do we really want to fill it this time of year?"

"Yes!" She turned puppy-dog eyes on him. "We can heat it, can't we?"

"Sure. Why not?" He smiled. "Don Quixote can be the lifeguard."

He'd said that about a million times too. "What is it with you and Don Quixote, Dad?"

He considered, crossing his arms and tipping back in the chair. Finally he said, "We both tilt at windmills."

Well, *that* made a whole lot of sense. She decided she'd better read the book sometime. "Good night, Daddy." She kissed his forehead once more. "Thank you."

"Night, Shel." He turned back to his computer as she shut the door behind her.

In her room she dressed for bed, did a quick page of English homework, then climbed into bed and read a Stephen King novel until she was sleepy. Between work and school, that never took too long.

She awoke disoriented, knowing it was the middle of the night, and certain that someone was in her room with her. Flicking on the bedside lamp, she looked around the room but saw nothing unusual, and after a few minutes, she turned off the light and lay back in the big bed, still listening, still hearing absolutely nothing. *I must've been dreaming.*

After a few minutes, she closed her eyes. It was silly to worry, because she always locked her bedroom door—at least since those dead poodles had shown up in her room—and only her dad had the extra key.

Right after he finished the sculpture, he'd also gone through the house and nailed a bunch of secret passages shut. She was sorry he'd done it since she'd never had a chance to check them out. Her room had been sealed since her dad was a kid, so he didn't make her drag all her stuff out of her closet. He did all the others, though, telling her how his brother used to use the tunnels to spy on people, but that now they were infested with vermin, maybe even some raccoons and opossums.

She drifted off again and began to have pleasant dreams about Ryan Levine, SVHS's star quarterback and the object of her considerable interest. "Don't open your eyes, Shelly," he whispered, kissing her neck, stroking her bare arms. "Don't open your eyes." She sighed as his fingers slipped under her shirt.

"Ryan," she whispered in her sleep.

Ryan kissed her lips, and she drew his plump lower lip into her mouth, sucking on it as his hands roved lower. He began to pull her panties down her legs.

She raised her buttocks to help him, and as she did, her sleep lightened a little and she passed into a semiconsciousness that allowed her to realize that she was having a very dirty dream. *Safe sex,* she thought, giving herself back to the dream, letting it become a half-waking fantasy as she imagined that Ryan was pushing her legs apart and climbing on top of her. Keeping her eyes closed, she relaxed her legs, her awareness centered on the demanding ache in her crotch. Pushing against him, she felt his erection against her pubis, felt it nudge inward, slowly, gently, deliciously. He would take his time, she told herself, he would take hours if necessary, before he finally and painlessly relieved her of her virginity.

Suddenly there was tremendous pain between her legs. She opened her mouth to scream, but before any sound could escape, a wad of cloth was thrust roughly into her mouth. Choking, she tried vainly to spit it out. Hands pinioned her shoulders, and his penis was like a knife, holding her hips to the bed. She flailed her legs, but that only let him nudge deeper into her. She pulled her legs tightly together, but couldn't push him out. Unmoving, he used his body to hold her prisoner.

This is no dream!

In the dim glow of the night-light, she turned her gaze to her attacker's face.

And recognized it.

Her father's face, twisted and cruel, his eyes boring blackly into hers. He smiled broadly.

Blackness swirled into her ears and eyes. She was going to faint. *No!* She forced herself to stay conscious because if she lost it, her legs would relax and he'd start moving again.

Dazed, disbelieving, she struggled to free her arms.

"Let's be a good little girl," he said in her father's voice. He lowered his face, her father's face, toward her, and stuck his tongue out, played the tip over her lips, teasing them around the gag.

Shelly's mind went coolly calculating. She knew what to do. She moaned. Moaned again.

"If I take the gag out of your mouth, will you be a good girl and not make a sound?" His breath smelled hot and sweet, like candy.

She nodded, and forced herself to moan again as he lowered his mouth to hers and extracted the cloth. He pulled back, eyes glittering, a pair of her panties hanging from his teeth.

Controlling the urge to vomit, she remained silent and hoped her face hadn't betrayed her repulsion.

He dropped the panties and put his mouth back on hers.

This isn't Daddy! It can't be!

His tongue slipped between her lips and thrust against her clenched teeth.

Fighting revulsion, she slowly let her mouth open. Immediately his tongue thrust into it, moving everywhere, along her gums, under her tongue, exploring the soft palate, as if he were tasting her, not kissing her. He tasted of Tootsie Rolls. She forced another moan and slowly drew her tongue to the back of her mouth. He didn't notice. He was moving again, rocking, trying to work his penis in further.

He extended his tongue into a long, narrow dart and thrust it against the inside of her left cheek. She bit down with all her force and held. He groaned.

Suddenly his face snapped back and his hands left her shoulders. Instantly she shoved him off, jabbing at his eyes with her fingers, trying to slam her palm up against his nose.

He hit her on the side of her face. She saw stars and fell back, numb and dumb, expecting him to climb back on and finish his rape before she could regain control.

But he didn't. He said nothing, just made angry little noises that got farther and farther away. Finally there were no sounds. She reached over and flipped on the bedside lamp.

"God," she whispered, starting to tremble uncontrollably. "Oh God." She reached up and touched her face where he'd hit it, felt a knot rising already. She touched her mouth and felt stickiness everywhere. Blood. *Oh, God.*

Then she realized there was something in her mouth. Horrified, sick to her stomach, she spit it out.

A small piece of pink flesh landed on her bare abdomen. The tip of his tongue. The blood belonged to *him*.

Keep your shit together, Shelly! Not letting herself think, not considering anything but the necessity of getting out of there, she slipped on her robe and tiptoed down the hall to the bathroom. In a few minutes she'd cleaned herself up, relieved to find that, not only hadn't he finished his act, but there was no blood. He hadn't even gotten all the way in. Quietly she returned to her room and packed a bag.

As the sun came up, she pulled out of the driveway and

headed for the one place she could be sure she was safe: Dakota O'Keefe's. She didn't think about her father as she drove, nor did she wipe away the hot, silent tears leaking from her eyes.

41

"Damn!" Inside Dakota O'Keefe's apartment, the phone began to ring, and Dakota, still two doors away, broke into a trot. "Damn!" he cried again as one of his black stiletto heels caught in an old cigarette burn in the hall carpeting. He regained his balance and raced to the door, digging frantically through his purse for the keys and swearing steadily now because he'd counted six rings, and that meant Lil had left the machine off. Again. At last he found the key, stuck it in the dead bolt, found out she hadn't bothered locking it, and, thoroughly pissed, tried the knob. The door swung open. *Magil would forget her own tits if they weren't attached!*

By the time he tackled the receiver, it was halfway through the tenth ring. Though it was unlikely the call would come at seven in the morning, he had his fingers crossed for a plum part in a new show. If he lost it because of a missed call, he'd string Lil up alive. By those firmly attached tits.

"Hello?" He tried not to pant.

"Dakota, thank God."

"Piper?" he asked, disappointed and pleased at the same time. "Is that you? You sound like shit."

"Is Shelly there?"

"Shelly? Why would Shelly be here?"

There was a pause. "Because she's not *here,* Dakota."

"She ran away?"

"I don't know, I think so, but it doesn't make sense. She seemed happy with the move and she was happy last night and now she's gone, and God, Dakota, there's blood on her sheets—"

"Calm down, Piper," Dakota interrupted. "You're talking like a machine gun. Get a grip."

"Yeah, yeah—"

"How much blood?"

"A little."

"Is her car gone?"

"Yes."

"Then she probably wasn't taken by force. Is that what you thought?"

"Y— No. I don't know. She told me she was happy we'd moved, and last night she came to see me. She wanted to go to a party and I said yes and she kissed me good night and now she's gone and it doesn't make sense—"

"Take a deep breath, Ricky. Where's the blood?"

Rick's voice shook. "On her pillow and wiped on the sheet. It wasn't much, but it's still blood and she's gone—"

"A nosebleed, maybe?"

"Maybe."

"Piper, she's hardly ever home, right?"

"But she never gets up early on the weekend."

"Does she tell you every time she goes somewhere?"

"No, but—"

"Calm down. Have you called her friends?"

"Yes. No one's seen her."

"And you probably made a lot of enemies waking them all up, right, Piper?"

No reply.

"Does she have a boyfriend?"

"What are you saying?"

"Lust makes people do strange things, Piper."

"She wouldn't—"

"Maybe, maybe not, but I think you'd better calm down

and give her a chance to come home. It's probably nothing, Piper. Why are you so nervous? You're acting weird, Rick. What gives?"

Piper didn't answer for a long time, and when he finally spoke, there was a different kind of waver in his voice. "The past dies hard, Dakota."

"That's very poetic," he said with brusqueness he didn't feel. "But what the hell does it mean?"

"It means you're right." Rick's voice sounded normal now. "It's probably nothing. I was so tired last night that I didn't hear half of what she said. It's probably something like cheerleading practice. But if it's a boy, once I get her home safely, I'll skin her alive."

"Okay, good," Dakota said, relieved that Piper's voice sounded nearly normal. "Now, how long has she been missing?"

"I, ah, I don't know exactly. She went to bed last night around eleven. That's the last time I saw her."

"So it's been about eight hours. How long ago did you find out she was gone?"

"An hour."

"If I hear from her, I'll call you. But I think she'll show up, safe and sound. Call me the minute she does, but let the phone ring a long time. I'm just going to bed, and Lil's not here." He paused. "How's my sister?"

"Wonderful."

"Good. Give her a call. She'll calm you down."

"I will. Thanks, Dakota."

"No problem." He paused. "Rick? Don't go having a nervous breakdown."

"I'll be fine."

Dakota hung up the phone, and as he got ready for bed, he wondered if Rick Piper wasn't already in the middle of a breakdown.

Two hours later, someone started banging on the door. Dakota tried to ignore it, but the idiot wouldn't go away.

Finally, ready to curse out a Mormon missionary or a magazine salesman, Dakota dragged himself to the door and opened it. "What the hell—" he began, then stopped, shocked to see Shelly Piper. There was a bruised red swelling on the side of her face, and she had a suitcase in her hand.

"What happened?" he cried as he pulled her into the apartment. "Give me the bag, sit down. Did someone hit you?"

She looked up at him, her lip starting to tremble.

"Daddy," she said.

"What?"

"He hit me. He, he tried . . ." She fell into Dakota's arms and cried for at least half an hour before she told him what had happened.

Dakota couldn't believe what he was hearing. He'd known Rick Piper for nearly five years, and he'd always seemed sweet and slightly sad, too intense for his own good, a worrywart, but a hell of a good father. Cody adored the ground he walked on, and even at her worst, Shelly couldn't find anything very awful to say about him. And now this. Dakota studied Shelly's face. She was telling him the truth as she saw it; of that, he was certain. Something had happened, but what?

He had a gift for seeing beyond the packaging into the product. Audrey's husband, for instance; he'd had him pegged from day one. Beneath the Armani suits, twinkly eyes and all, he knew the man was rotten. He'd sensed this about other people, men and women both, and he'd never been wrong. But though there was something undeniably unusual about Piper, something he couldn't quite pinpoint, he sensed none of the corruptness he'd detected in those other people, and he couldn't believe that Rick was capable of what his daughter alleged. But why would she lie?

"Shelly, honey, are you sure it was your dad? Was it dark?"

"The night-light was on."

"So it was almost dark?"

"Kind of. But it looked like him, and sounded like him. He looked crazy."

Don't have a nervous breakdown. That's what he'd said to Rick two hours ago. "Shelly, has your dad been acting funny lately?"

She shook her head. "No. We've been getting along great, and he and Audrey are dating a lot. She's nice." For a moment her voice was normal, then reality—or unreality—set in again. "I mean, he wasn't acting weird or anything." She touched her face, tears threatening.

"Shel, I think we have to solve this now."

"I don't want to go back. I don't want to see him."

"We have to. Tell you what. We'll relax today, then head for L.A. first thing in the morning. If I drive your car and drop you off at a friend's, whatever you want, will that be okay? Then I'll go see your dad. If he's responsible for the attack on you, he needs help."

That undefinable thing about Piper, was it mental illness? O'Keefe wondered after Shelly went into the other room to nap. Certainly some of the things he'd spilled about his childhood—those jack-off things he said he could still see, the sex-crazed aunt, finding his parents murdered . . . Dakota shook his head . . . and that evil twin, for Christ's sake—any one of those things could make for a little instability. Or a lot. *You quiet types, we just never know what you're up to*. How many times had he teased Piper with that line?

For a brief instant it occurred to Dakota that perhaps Rick Piper didn't have a twin brother, that Rick's brother was an alternate personality . . . "No," he said aloud. Who was he going to believe? A man who'd become his best friend or the guy's teenage daughter, who wasn't above manipulation to get what she wanted? He knew that from experience.

Neither, he decided. Shelly wasn't faking, and Rick was stable until proven otherwise. Dakota would do nothing until he saw him in person, not even tell Audrey. The thought of his sister made his heart ache a little: More for her sake than any other reason, he hoped Rick was in the clear. Audrey was falling for him hard, she'd confided, and he wanted her to be happy. For a moment he considered warning her, but decided against it: She'd told him she'd be out of town until tomorrow, attending a small convention. She'd be safe, if there was anything to be safe from.

Clearing his throat, he picked up the phone and called in a couple favors, which resulted in a long overdue week's vacation. Next, he swallowed his nervousness and dialed Piper's number.

Rick answered on the second ring.

"She's here," Dakota said lightly, determined not to show his hand.

"Thank God." The immense relief in Piper's voice gave him hope. "Dakota, do you know why she ran away?"

"All I know is that she's here," Dakota said slowly. "Something frightened her last night."

"Frightened her. What?"

"I don't know," he lied, "but she's not crazy about coming home. She doesn't want to be in the house. I told her I'd drive her back and drop her at a friend's house."

"Which one?"

"I don't know yet. Listen, I'll see what else I can get out of her on the ride." He paused. "She has a bruise on her cheek. It's pretty nasty." He waited for the reaction.

"She's hurt? My God, how? Maybe you should take her to the doctor. Let me give you the insurance number."

If he hurt her, Dakota wondered, *would he want her to be seen by a physician?*

"It's not that bad. Just a bruise," he said. "Rick, maybe you should check around the house, make sure all your windows and doors are bolted."

"Why? Did she—"

"She won't talk," he lied again. "But I get the impression someone broke into her room."

"It wouldn't be the first time," Rick said with sudden firmness.

"It wouldn't?"

"Jade put her stuffed poodles in Shelly's room one night, scared the hell out of her."

Shelly had told Dakota that story, and now it made him suspect that the old bat was somehow involved in things. Shelly disliked Jade, but evidently the old lady absolutely despised the girl. *She's jealous of her youth.* Dakota thought. "Maybe it *is* Jade's doing," he said. "Anyway, I've been wanting to visit you, Piper, and I've got a week's vacation, so I'll see you tomorrow." He hesitated. "I'll be there for Halloween. Do you have a costume or would you like me to bring you one? You'd make a gorgeous Betty Boop."

"I'll pass on the costume, O'Keefe; I'm not much on Halloween." A thrum of tension belied the resignation in his voice. "Just bring me my daughter. Please."

42

October 30

Dakota O'Keefe was fine until he dropped Shelly off at Leanne Larson's house in San Antonio Heights, but as he drove into Rick's neighborhood, he began to sweat and wish he'd remembered his bottle of Di-Gels. Shelly hadn't said much on the ride in, except to reiterate that she couldn't believe what happened. It had been a frustrating conversation because, although she saw some merit in blaming Jade, she rightly pointed out that her attacker was a man.

Almost immediately after dropping her off, he got lost on the curvy streets and screeched to a halt at the curb. After consulting the map, he took off again. *Slow,* he told himself, *slow down.* The trip from Vegas to Santo Verde had been accomplished in just under three and a half hours, a new record for him and, he sincerely hoped, for Shelly's Bug. They'd stopped just once, at the rest stop east of Madelyn, and that had been a disaster because he was so accustomed to wearing drag that he'd walked into the ladies' room wigless and makeupless, dressed in tight jeans and a boxy bomber jacket that hid his bosom. Without the accoutrements of femininity, his strong chin and broad shoulders—not to mention the proud bulge of his one-eyed trouser weasel—betrayed his sexual roots all too easily.

A woman in a tacky plaid jumpsuit had stared at him,

then frantically whispered something through the crack between the door and frame of the nearest stall. Thinking fast, Dakota unzipped his jacket, putting his thirty-eights on display, and groaned, "My bra is killing me." After that, he was left to pee in peace.

Leak taken, he'd paused long enough in front of the metal mirror to fluff his brown hair into a less masculine style and apply a trace of lipstick and eyeliner. Back in the car, he took time to consult the map, trying to memorize the off-ramps and intersections he'd need to find, because he wasn't too sure Shelly's directions were good and he didn't want to talk to Piper again until they came face-to-face.

He didn't really want to talk to him at all before he had a chance to figure out what—if anything—was really going on between Piper and his daughter. *Either Shelly's on drugs or Rick's lost it,* he told himself. He didn't want to believe either theory.

"Damn!" Again he pulled over and dragged out the map. Santo fucking Verde was made up of a series of illogical, curvy streets that made no sense whatsoever. *Too rich for its own good,* he thought, trying to figure out where he was. Via Matanza, where Piper lived, was a twisted little road at the north edge of town, close to the mountains, a stone's throw from the cemetery. Problem was, it was one of a zillion curvy little streets not far from the mountains and the cemetery. The goddamned map looked more like an English hedge maze than a street directory.

Okay, he told himself as he tossed the unfolded map carelessly over his shoulder, *this is it. I'm going to find it this time.* He shifted gears and started out, turning left instead of right and taking a corkscrew street as opposed to the countercorkscrew.

He passed gnarled pepper trees lining Via Sangre—all *these fucking Spanish names,* he thought, annoyed that he didn't know the meaning. *Via* meant go or way or something. Something like road. *Sangre* sounded like some kind of wine, and he wondered if Via Sangre meant "Go Wine. He could get behind that about now. But he doubted that meaning: By the looks of things, Santo Verde had a proverbial broom up its proverbial ass. Dogs wouldn't dare shit in Santo Verde, and the town must employ half the gardeners in the state. It had to; he'd never seen a place so overflowing with well-coiffed trees and bushes and grass and flowers. Even this time of year.

Maybe it's Spanish for Wino Road, he told himself as he began to believe he'd taken yet another wrong turn. There were several unofficial Wino Roads in Vegas. "Eureka, baby!" he cried as he approached the bazillionth street sign and read it. "I have found it!"

Via Matanza, at long last. He burned a little rubber rounding the corner, then cruised slowly, watching for Piper's house. The address was 667. Neighbor of the Beast. Before, that seemed funny; now it didn't. *God, Piper, did you really do what Shelly said?* No, Rick would never do such a thing, a thing so bad that Dakota couldn't name it, not even in the privacy of his own head. *If he's ill, he might be able to do it,* his subconscious reminded him.

If he was having a nervous breakdown, if he imagined his brother, or hated his parents? *He found their bodies; he could've killed them . . . Would you question him at all if he weren't dating your sister?*

No, he told himself, *probably not.* But he didn't know if that was true or not, all he knew was that he had been compelled to drive to Santo Verde to find out and that his very lack of instinct about Piper worried him immensely.

There it was, 667, painted black on white on the stone curb in front of the most unusual—and only run-down—yard on the block. You could barely see the house for the trees and bushes. Everything else on the street looked like photos from *Better Homes & Gardens* or *Architectural Digest* with their huge, perfect lawns and landscaping. Freeform topiaries, he noticed, seemed to be the in thing in Santo Verde.

But 667 was a mongrel, and a shaggy one at that. In another neighborhood it might have been presentable, but not here in Beamerland, where all good Republicans go to live and everyone wears Dockers and Izods to play golf on Sundays.

He could see that attempts were being made to fix the place up—the lawn was freshly cut, though not nearly short enough, and only half the trees were pruned. As he drove up the long, long driveway toward the house, he noticed something reflecting sunlight between the trees, and a moment later realized it was Rick's metal statue.

At last the house came into full view, and he realized that its being hidden from the street was probably a major blessing. As Rick had said, it needed paint. It also needed a remodel. The place looked like an eccentricity Edward Gorey would draw. *A lunatic must have built it,* Dakota thought, then remembered that Piper had said as much about his ancestor or grandfather or whichever Piper had built it. Said he was as nutty as a nougat bar. He wondered again if Rick had inherited that trait.

"Hmmph." Impatiently he downshifted, grinding the gears as he pulled close to the other cars, Piper's Celica and an older Ford pickup. He almost clipped the Celica when be pulled in next to it, even though the driveway in front of the garage was wide enough to hold six or seven cars parked close together. "Shitty driver, O'Keefe," he muttered. "Shitty."

A minute later he was contemplating the ugly door on the ugly house. As he knocked on it, he thought it looked like the entry to Quasimodo's closet. A dog barked. He knocked again. More barks. And knocked once more. Yippy little barks, closer now. *Poodles from hell,* he remembered as he started pounding. "Come on, Piper, put your dick away and answer the door!"

As he heard his own words, a chill ran down his spine. "Piper!" he called, angry both at himself and his friend. "Piper, open up!"

Within, the floor creaked beneath footsteps so slow, they hurt. Then a wicked-witch voice called out, "Who's there?"

"A friend of Rick's," he replied.

After a long moment of silence, the voice asked sharply, "What do you want?" The poodle yelped a sharp coda.

"To see Rick," he answered, totally pissed. Then he added, more diplomatically, "You must be his aunt Jade. He's told me *so* much about you. He adores you, dear, and I can't wait to meet you."

That did the trick. He could hear chains being removed, then a bolt slid and the big thumb latch clicked up and down. The door opened an inch or two, and an anxious pink dog nose poked out below. Above, a wicked-witch eye to match the voice peered at him. Then it asked, "What the fuck are you?"

"I'm a Vegas show girl, Jade, dear. Ricky's best friend." The door opened wider, barely. Two eyes. The old broad— not as old as he'd expected—was a tall one with puffy skin and full lips held pursed and coated under too much coral lipstick. She might've been a looker, way back when. Still could be if she did something with herself. Nice cheekbones.

"You one of Richard's girlfriends?" she asked suspiciously.

He loved that. "Wish I was," he told her. "But he just thinks of me as a . . . sibling . . ." He let his voice trail off wistfully.

Jade snorted. "What d'you want?"

Old bitch, he thought. He could imagine her skulking through the house with a meat cleaver in hand, but he smiled sweetly. "I'm here to see Rick."

"Why?"

With effort, he held his tongue. "Is he here?"

She harrumphed. "He's in the workshop."

"Could you direct me, dear?"

"Back of the garage. Crazy good-for-nothing boy, he is." She looked down at her dog, and her voice changed to a warm, cracking ooze. "He's a bad boy saying bad things about my wittle lovedottie. Calls him names."

Suddenly the poodle slipped out the door, barked once, then attached itself to Dakota's leg and began humping with a vengeance.

"Shit!" Dakota tried to shake the dog off. "Get off me, you perverted little shit!"

"Don't you talk to my wittle—"

"Get your wittle fucker off me!" he cried, kicking harder. The dog flew off, sailing straight back until it thudded against Jade's leg. Righting itself, it growled at Dakota. Dakota curled his lip and growled right back.

"How dare you!"

Before Dakota could form the perfect response, Jade Ewebean slammed the door in his face.

Clearing his throat, straightening his posture, and regaining his dignity, Dakota turned and walked back to the driveway and up to the garage. He followed the narrow sidewalk around it and suddenly realized that the building behind it, shadowed in trees, was enormous. He continued up the side. "Rick? Where are you? Piper?" he called, not too loudly. From within, he could hear metal on metal, hammering, a high screeching, more hammering. "Piper?" He came to a set of huge closed double doors, the size of garage doors, then saw a normal one, just beyond. The knob turned freely in his grasp. "Piper?" he called again, beginning to push the door open.

The hammering ceased. "Dakota?" Soft, surprised. Then, hopeful, "Dakota? Is that you?"

Heartened, O'Keefe shoved the door the rest of the way. "Piper! My Lord! What in the world are you doing in here?"

Rick stood on a stepladder in front of a large metal *thing*. He wore a welder's mask over his face and hair, tight Levi's, and no shirt. His compact body was looking good, pale skin sheened with sweat, pecs and biceps carved with the weight of the acetelyne torch he held. It was phallic as hell.

"You oughta pose for *Playgirl,* Piper. You look good enough to eat."

"Get a new line, O'Keefe." Rick pushed back the mask, set the torch aside, and climbed off the ladder. "Is Shelly with you? Did she tell you anything else?"

"Piper . . ." he began, then stopped, riveted by the look on Rick's face. He saw the pain and didn't know what to say, saw the pain and knew the answer, and for a moment, was so ashamed of himself for ever doubting Piper's honor or motives that he couldn't look him in the eye. *But if he's crazy,* he reminded himself roughly, *he could be guilty . . . If he's crazy, he could be his own evil twin.*

"Shelly's okay," he said. "She's fine."

Rick took the helmet off and hung it on a hook above a long workbench. "Well, where is she?" he asked eagerly. "Did you drop her off or is she in your car?" He headed toward the door.

Dakota put his hand out and stopped Rick before he could pass. "She's fine, but she's not here."

"When I get my hands on her, I'm going to . . . to hug her, then I'm going to strangle her, then I'm going to ground her until she's thirty . . ."

"I left her at her girlfriend's house. She'll be perfectly safe there. She's just fine. Now, Piper, calm down and tell me about this." He gestured at the metal thing. "What is it?"

"Can't you tell?"

Piper sounded disappointed, and Dakota, suddenly realizing that maybe this was something more than a heap of scrap metal, really looked at it for the first time. "My God, Piper," he blurted. "It's art, isn't it!"

He circled it. "It's a tepee. No? A pyramid?"

"I guess it does look like a pyramid at this point," Rick said. "It's going to be a windmill for Don Quixote. I was climbing the walls waiting for you to show up. I couldn't just sit still and I couldn't concentrate on the column. So here I am."

"It's *so* bizarre," Dakota said, pointing at the pyramid. "Where'd you learn to do this?"

"My dad built cars. He let me play with the scraps."

"I saw Quixote as I pulled up. He's wonderful. I think you should do a whole series of horses and riders. You should sculpt Wilbur and Mr. Ed next. 'Willlbur,' he whinnied, 'what're you doin' back there, Willlbur? Carol's gonna be jealous!' " He saw by the look on Piper's face that he wasn't improving his frame of mind. "Well, I love your Quixote," he blithered. "Most people have pink flamingos, or little dwarves."

Rick just stared at him, the ghost of a smile etched in his eyes, tilting the corners of his mouth. Dakota had an obscene thought and the good sense to keep it to himself. "We need to talk about Shelly."

"I'm listening."

"No. We need to sit and talk. There's some weird shit going on, and we need to figure out where it's coming from"

"You want to go in the house or something?"

"No, Jade hates me. But her poodle loves me. It tried to fuck me, but it didn't have a condom, so I kicked it." He smiled coyly. "I was thinking we might go to a drinking establishment, but I guess you can't leave Cody with the wicked witch in there?"

"Lord, no! He's with Carmen. They're working on his Halloween costume." He didn't look very happy about that, then his expression changed. "Jesus, Dakota. I wouldn't leave a juvenile delinquent with Jade!"

"Not that I blame you, but you *really* don't like her, do you?"

"No, I *really* don't. She's as bad as I remembered. Worse maybe. Come on. There's an overpriced English pub oozing atmosphere over on Via Pecado. Your sister likes it."

"Sounds great. Stupid street name, though."

"I guess you're not a Southwest native."

"Manhattan, hon."

Rick nodded sagely. "Come on. I'll get cleaned up and let Carmen know we're leaving."

While Rick showered, Dakota had a short, gleeful reunion with Cody, during which he promised to bunk in with him, and met Carmen, whom he adored instantly, primarily because she told him he was gorgeous, and he knew sincerity when he heard it. She gave him a nickel tour of the house, and his only disappointment was that Jade's dead poodles were not on display. The good news was that Jade was nowhere to be seen.

Within a half hour, he and Rick were in Briarwood Tavern, sipping from chill mugs of British ale in a dark corner of an authentically sawdusted room while a couple guys who looked like redneck college grads—if there was such a thing—threw darts badly, at a board just close enough for discomfort.

Vapor curled up from Rick's mug. "What about my daughter? Is she all right? Why won't she come home?"

"She's fine. Now, slow down. This is weird, okay?"

"What's weird?" Piper asked sharply. "You keep saying 'weird.' Has something happened?"

"No. Yes. I don't know."

"Jesus Christ, would you explain already?"

"If you'll shut up for a minute, I will," Dakota said testily. "She says . . . she says she's afraid of you, Piper."

Rick sputtered, sending beer drops spraying. "Afraid of *me?* For God's sake, why?"

"Look, I don't know why or how, but she thinks . . . well, she thinks . . ."

"Just spit it out, for Christ's sake!"

The dart boys looked, and Dakota smiled at them. "Keep your voice down, Piper. If you don't, I won't tell you."

"Okay, okay."

"Promise?"

"Yeah, yeah, I promise. What the hell is going on?"

"That's what I want to know," Dakota said, his voice low and intense. "She says—this is really hard, Rick. She was so upset."

"Go on," Piper said grimly.

Dakota nodded. "Okay. Don't get all excited when I tell you."

Piper nodded impatiently.

"Don't have a shit hemorrhage—"

"Tell me," he growled.

Dakota swallowed. "Shelly believes you attacked her."

"What?"

"Be quiet. She says you tried to rape her."

"Rape her?"

"Shhhh! Shut the hell up."

Piper lowered his voice a tad. "Rape her? My own daughter says *I* tried to rape her?"

"She says she woke up sometime during the night and found you on top of her and that when she fought you, you socked her in the head."

"Enough." Rick slammed his mug down, and beer sloshed across the table. "I've heard enough."

The dart boys gave them another glance, then one shrugged and said something, no doubt derogatory.

"Look, Piper. I know you're upset, but we have to figure out what's wrong, what *really* happened to her."

"Yeah. Oh, Lord, Dakota." He ran his fingers through his hair, the expression on his face so boyish and confounded that Dakota had to resist the urge to take his hand. "She was happy. She told me she liked it here, and then all of a sudden she splits and says—Oh Lord. I'd never, *never*— "

"I know, Ricky. And she does, too, deep inside, but something scared the shit out of her." He paused. "You're white as the driven, Piper."

"My brother's voice," Piper said slowly. "Sometimes I hear old memories. I just heard one. My brother's voice, singing, 'Lay, lay, roll in the hay.' He sang that about Evangeline. That was Jade and Howard's daughter, Evangeline. He claimed they did it in the hay a lot. Old dirty hay that had been in the garage for years."

My brother's voice, Dakota thought. Considering that they had the same voice, the remark seemed odd. "Who did it in the hay?"

"Robin and Evangeline. He liked to screw her. He liked to screw Aunt Jade too. And he talked in rhymes. 'Jade got made, I made Jade. Evangeline lying, lying for me. Wheee,' " he said dryly. "Evangeline was a hard one for him to rhyme. But not to screw." He downed his ale. "He— my brother, my twin—he would have raped his own daughter, just as surely as he raped his aunt and cousin."

"That may be, but you're not your brother."

"I hope not."

"Don't go getting esoteric on me, Piper." Dakota paused. "It doesn't sound like he actually raped them, does it?"

"No. I doubt it. I think he seduced them. He was sort of a Svengali type. All charm."

"Or maybe it was just the freak angle?"

"What?"

"You know. Amputee lust, do it with dwarves, like Snow White. Necrophilia with Sleeping Beauty. Swamp Thing and his lady love. Freaks are very popular," he added. "You wouldn't believe the offers I get. There are a lot of fucked-up people out there."

"You ought to know," Piper added dryly.

"At least *I* admit it," he said, motioning the bartender for another round.

Rick stared at him. "What are you implying?"

"You know exactly what I mean. You're fucked up as hell. You gotta get over this brother thing; you're letting him run your life even though he's been dead for years. You're apologizing for what he did. And I think you're letting Jade run you into the ground."

"No, I'm not."

"The fact that she's in that house speaks volumes. It's your house. I think she's probably behind your problem with Shelly. Get her out of your house, Piper."

"I'm thinking about it. Did Shelly say something about her?"

"Not much. She said you act funny around the old douche-bag, something like that. She was so busy being freaked out over the other thing that I didn't hear much else."

The fresh ale arrived. "Thanks, hon," Dakota said to the barman, who looked O'Keefe up and down, trying to figure out just what he was talking to. He was cute, and Dakota wished he had his blond wig and makeup on. "Look, Piper," he said after the man walked away. "Think. What could have happened to Shelly? A nightmare wouldn't hit her."

"I don't know. I really don't. I went through the house and didn't find anything unlocked or broken. Jade's the only answer, but still, that's not really good enough."

"Jade," Dakota repeated. "It must be."

"I don't think so," Rick said, a hint of finality in his voice. "It's too farfetched. God, this whole thing gives me the creeps." He drank more beer. "You know, two weeks ago I even went through the house and nailed all the hidden passages closed. Shelly keeps her door locked, so I just don't see how—"

"Secret passages?"

Rick nodded. "Robin used to use them to travel all over the house."

"I should've known that mausoleum has secret passages."

"Of course. And Robin loved them. He showed up all over the place. Including on top of me."

Dakota raised his eyebrows. "To frighten, not rape. He put a pillow over my face and tried to smother me on a number of occasions. There's a mark in the wall in Cody's room where he came after me with a knife."

"My God, Piper! You told me he was disgusting, but you didn't say he was murderous." Behind the look of concern he'd plastered on his face, the possibilities horrified him. "Why didn't your parents stop him?"

"Because they didn't know. Robin convinced me that they'd send me to the funny farm if I told. I moved into Carmen's old room when she got married. She gave me a key to the door lock and showed me that she'd nailed the passage to her room closed. That's Shelly's room now."

Carmen, Dakota realized, could verify some of this, if necessary. He smiled at Rick. "You're getting drunk. Let's order some fish and chips."

"Good idea."

"Now, tell me all about your brother."

Two hours passed, dinner was eaten, more ale drunk, and Dakota got further into Piper's mysterious mind than ever before. That was part of the reason he liked the guy so well—you couldn't read him. Piper sat there all suave and handsome and charming in spite of the tenseness he couldn't hide. Piper, Dakota decided, was glib, a good daddy, probably a good lover, sincere as hell, and contained not a drop of snake oil. But there was something else there, hiding just below the surface, that forever eluded Dakota, a secret of some sort. He suspected now that it had to do with the abuse he'd suffered at the hands of his brother. Piper had told him about everything from finding Jade's poodle in his shower to the details of Delia's death and the guilt he felt over it. He'd talked about his wife, Laura, for the first time. She'd been run down by a drunk while on her way to meet Rick for lunch, and he obviously felt responsibility for her death too.

He confessed then that he was falling in love with Audrey and that he was afraid he'd hurt her, too. Dakota, warmly drunk, felt one moment of anxiety before tears sprang to his eyes. He wished he knew how to take Rick Piper's pain away, how to make him understand that Laura's and Delia's deaths weren't his fault.

"Dakota?" Rick said. "Are you crying?"

Dakota wiped a tear from his cheek. "Indulging in romance, Piper. It must be lonely in there."

"Huh?"

"In you."

"No."

"Oh, shut up and listen." He reached across the table and patted Rick's hand before he could draw it away. "You need love, Piper. Don't be afraid."

"I'm flattered, but I'm not into—"

"No, you moron, not me. My sister. She's nuts about you. You are *so* fucked up, Piper. You're so afraid." Even as he said it, he wondered if he meant it. Everything Rick had told him tonight could mean he was a dangerous lunatic who only *thought* he was the victim. He could be throwing his sister to a maniac. Still, Dakota's intuition told him that, no matter how farfetched Piper's stories were, the man was okay, and when push came to shove, Dakota always listened to his intuition.

43

Back at the house, Audrey, just back from her convention, joined them for the evening. Rick insisted on telling her the details about Shelly, and for that, Dakota was glad. He watched his sister carefully, but she showed no signs of mistrusting Rick, only support and puzzlement.

Around eleven, Jade's almost nightly moaning and groaning started up, and to Dakota's disappointment, Rick wouldn't stay for the show, but took them out on the front porch to talk. Rick kept looking out toward the oak tree, trying hard to hide his nervousness.

"I wouldn't have believed it if I hadn't heard it myself," Dakota said. "Maybe she really does have something to do with Shelly's scare, Piper. She's a nympho. A psycho nympho. Hey," he added suddenly, "when you shut off all those secret passages, did you do the ones in her rooms too?"

"No, I didn't, but I guess I should. I'll get Carmen to take her somewhere, and do it." He frowned. "But even if she did have something to do with it, how'd she manage to look like me?"

"I don't know, I just think she might be involved. She's jealous as hell of Shelly, isn't she? She picks on her."

"She picks on everyone."

"Rick," Audrey said. "Duane—I mean Dakota—has a point." She glanced toward the old oak. "Look at those leaves blow. At this rate, the trees will be bare in no time."

"Naked trees," Dakota purred. "How totally kinky. Piper, are there any jack-offs there?"

"Yes," he said slowly. "Lots of them."

"I wish I could see them," Dakota said softly.

Rick looked at him in amazement. "You really mean that, don't you?"

"Yes" He sniffed. "I feel deprived."

"Me, too," Audrey said. Rick shook his head. "I can't believe what I'm hearing."

"Where's Quint?" Dakota suddenly asked. "You said he can see them, too?"

Rick nodded. "Come on inside."

Jade's orgasms were over, thank God. They were hilarious on one hand, Dakota had decided, but horrifying on the other.

"I'll be right back." Rick left them in the living room and headed up the stairs. When he returned a few minutes later, he held his cat—wearing a leash and collar—in his arms. "Quint's been staying at Carmen's since the poodle incident, but she and Hector were going out tonight, so I brought him back early and locked him in my room."

He carried the cat to the covered picture window. "Quint can see them," he explained. Gently but firmly, he gripped the loose skin at the cat's neck with one hand and trapped his body against him, holding the back legs loosely with the other. The cat faced the stairwell.

Rick smiled grimly. "He doesn't like them at all. Open the drapes, please, Audrey."

She did.

"Now, watch the cat," Rick ordered, turning the feline to face the window.

Quint's eyes grew huge, then his ears went flat back and the fur ridged up on his back. Dakota shivered; the cat was scared shitless. A low growl started in its throat, rose to a shriek, and suddenly the animal exploded in Rick's arms, kicking and hissing and biting. One front leg shot free, and claws raked across Rick's cheek. He let go of the cat, and it flopped on the floor in its panic, righted itself, and raced up the stairs, dragging its leash as it disappeared in the direction of Rick's room.

Rick gingerly patted his cheek. "A lot of good the leash did. Do you believe me now?"

"That was incredible," Audrey said.

"Jesus Christ," Dakota breathed. "I've got goose bumps on my balls."

"Please answer my question," Rick said, even more softly.

"I believe you, Piper."

The color had drained from Audrey's face. "Me too. Rick? Your cheek's bleeding—"

"It's okay," he interrupted. "Excuse me. I have to take care of the cat. I'll be right back." He turned and went up the stairs.

Dakota looked at Audrey. "I don't know what the fuck is going on here."

"Me either. You want to come back to my place tonight? You can have the couch."

"No. I promised Cody I'd bunk with him. Besides, I want to keep an eye on things. Until we have an explanation, you know."

Her eyes were sad. "He didn't do what Shelly says he did. He's not capable of it. He's the most gentle man in the world."

"He said he almost killed his brother once."

"Almost. He also said he realized what he was doing and stopped."

"Audrey, be careful. I don't want to think he did it, and my instincts don't believe it, but I'm afraid that could be because he's not stable . . ."

She opened her mouth, but he shushed her.

"I think that if he is responsible, he isn't *responsible,* you know what I mean?"

She shook her head no.

"If he did do it, I don't think he knows he did it. Maybe he's got a split personality or something. All that brother stuff."

Audrey looked stricken. "I don't believe it."

"Then let's find proof."

Audrey nodded. "If you're wondering if Robin existed, I can tell you that he did. Rick showed me some photos taken before their parents died. And Carmen talked about him too. He was horrible. He died in a fire. Carmen has the newspaper clipping. I saw it."

"Christ, I'm glad to hear that. Audrey, I *don't* think he did anything. I'm just playing devil's advocate."

"I know, Duane. You're good at that."

"Besides, you're my sister. What kind of brother would I be if I didn't worry about you?"

Audrey stood on her tiptoes and kissed his cheek. "I know, and I appreciate you very much."

"Boy, was that cat pissed," Rick said as he came back into the room. "Supremely pissed." He had washed the claw marks, and they stood out blatantly against his pale skin. "But I think he's okay now."

"Good. We won't put him through that again." Audrey glanced out the window. "I'm exhausted. I'm going home to bed. Will you fellas see me out?"

They walked her to her car and watched until she was out on the street. Dakota shivered, watching the leaves in the grass. "You know, Piper, it's scary knowing those jack-offs are there and not being able to see them."

"In this case, what you can't see won't hurt you," Rick said dryly. "Believe me, if I could trade you eyes, I would."

"Let's go in."

"Yeah." They went inside, and Rick locked the door, then pulled the drapes closed. "Tomorrow night is the dangerous night, Dakota. Halloween."

"Shelly's going to a party?"

"The overnight," Rick said. "I hope to hell we know what happened before then, but either way, she won't be here."

"What about Cody?"

"Audrey and I were planning on taking Cody trick-or-treating, very early. Do you want to come?"

"Yes." He grinned. "I brought a costume. I love dressing up for Halloween."

"You just love dressing up."

Dakota gave him a shit-eating grin. "Do you have any lines on parties?"

"No. We're coming back before full dark and staying in, where it's safe." He hesitated. "We're planning on watching for Big Jack." He hesitated, obviously trying to make light of something that was deadly serious to him. "If we both see him, we'll know I'm not a raving lunatic."

"It's Big Jack night. If I stick around, do I get to see him, too?"

"I hope so. I'd like you both to see him. That would make me feel . . . less weird." Yawning, he checked his watch. "Let's get some sleep."

A few minutes later, Dakota entered the upstairs bathroom to brush his teeth, then stripped to shorts and T-shirt before quietly letting himself into Cody's room. The boy was fast asleep on the race-car bed by the window. Dakota eased his six-foot-four-inch frame onto the old twin bed near the door. His legs hung over the end, and he knew this wasn't going to be much fun.

He lay quietly on the bed, unable to sleep, his brain going a hundred miles an hour, asking himself questions he had no answers for. As he was about to give up and go take a sleeping pill, he heard a scratching noise emanating from somewhere near the closets. "Cody, Cody!" whispered a voice.

Across the room, the boy sat up.

"Cody!" the voice whispered again.

"Hi, Bob," the little boy said.

"Cody, Cody, let's hit the roady!"

The boy giggled, then shoved his hand over his mouth, looking toward Dakota, who studiously feigned sleep. Quietly, Cody got out of bed and approached the closet. As he opened the door and stepped in, Dakota could hear him giggling. There was a funny sliding sound and the giggling grew faint, then disappeared altogether.

Rising, Dakota turned on the overhead light and crossed to the closet as quietly as he could.

He looked inside.

Cody wasn't there.

A half dozen nails, some slightly bent, were scattered on the floor. He saw empty nail holes around a two-and-a-half-foot square on the wall.

"Shit." With a whole new load of goose bumps rising on his balls, Dakota went to tell Rick.

44

"Piper! Open up!"

Dakota's voice cut through Rick's nightmare, and the pounding on his bedroom door brought him bolt upright. "Hang on," he grunted, extracting Quint's claws from his forearm.

"Piper!"

"Shut up, you're scaring the cat!" The feline suddenly raced painfully across his bare chest and thumped to the floor, heading for the safety of the headboard.

"Hurry up!" Dakota's voice was lower, but he rattled the hell out of the doorknob.

Rick's feet hit the floor, and a moment later, he unlocked the door. Dakota pushed his way inside,

"Christ, O'Keefe," Rick said, shutting the door.

"What is it with you and locks?" Dakota said. "Listen. You know how you can see those greenjacks?"

"Yes."

"Well, I just heard Bob the Invisible Friend."

"What?"

"You heard me. He called Cody's name, Cody answered him, then walked into the closet."

"What?" Rick listened to Dakota's words, hardly able to comprehend what he was hearing. "Cody!" He started for the door, but Dakota grabbed his arm.

"Rick, wait. Cody's not there."

"The passages are blocked; he *has* to be there!"

"Calm down and listen to me. The nails have been driven out from the inside."

"That's impossible!" He tried vainly to pull free of Dakota.

"It must be Jade, Rick," Dakota said. He was breathing fast now, catching Rick's fear. "It has to be Jade. You're here and . . ."

"And what?" Rick asked, his head beginning to throb.

Dakota stared hard at him. "And you're here."

"You mean you thought that *I* might be Bob? That I tried to assault my own daughter?" Furious, he yanked free of O'Keefe and glared at him. "I thought you were supposed to be my friend! You son of a bitch!"

"Rick, you're my best friend and I believe you, but you've been under a lot of stress and, shit, if you were in my place, you'd have to make sure, too."

Stonily Rick nodded. "Well, then, is there anything else I can do to prove to you that I'm not skulking around scaring my children at night? Do you want me to write it in blood?"

"Don't be sarcastic, Piper. You'll just have to apologize to me later, after you've had time to think."

Rick didn't know whether he wanted to cry or commit murder. "You won't tell me where Shelly is because you're not sure I'm not guilty. That's it, isn't it?"

Dakota drew himself to his full towering height and crossed his arms. "We don't have time for bullshit. Yes, Rick, that's right. I don't think you're guilty, but I can't take a chance on Shelly's safety. You'd do the same."

"You fucking bastard." Rick felt his body tense, imagined his hands around O'Keefe's throat. "You fucking—"

"Piper, listen. What if somebody assaulted Cody while I was watching him for you? Wouldn't you be worried about leaving him with me even though you didn't really think I did it? My sexuality is a little strange. Wouldn't you think that maybe, just maybe, I'd branched out into pederasty? You'd worry, wouldn't you? Even though I'm your closest friend, you'd worry."

Fury gave way to grudging understanding, and Rick nodded. 'You've made your point. I have no right to be angry with you for looking out for my kids. I'm sorry." He felt beaten. "God knows, with the stories I've told you about my childhood, you must think I'm completely nuts."

"No. To be blunt, it's a possibility—as you yourself say—but I don't think so. Frankly, I happen to believe you, Piper."

"Thanks. But what do we do now?" Rick asked dully.

"Check passages?"

"This place is a honeycomb. We'd never find him from the inside. Also, you'd never fit, and I'd be a tight squeeze in most of them."

"So let's see if any other ones are missing nails. Where's the one in this room?"

He picked up his flashlight and handed it to Dakota. "In here." He led O'Keefe into the dressing room and pointed. "Look in that cabinet."

Dakota opened the doors, then got down on his hands and knees, shining the light inside. He gasped, pulling back so quickly that he hit the back of his head. He stood up, his eyes boring into Rick's with an intensity he'd never seen before. "We have problems, my friend," he said, his voice shaking.

"The nails are gone?" he asked, thinking, *and proof of my innocence.*

"For a start. Take a look."

Dumbly Rick took the light and squatted. "Dear God," he heard himself say. "Oh, dear God."

Within the cabinet, among the nails, was the filleting knife and Jade's poodle, which lay in a pool of its own blood. Its mouth was taped shut and the hind legs were dismembered and lying several inches from the rest of its body.

"Dear God." Blindly Rick stood and rushed into the bathroom, where he hugged the toilet bowl, violently ill.

Dakota said nothing until Rick had brushed his teeth and splashed his face with water. Then, firmly, he placed his hand on Rick's shoulder. "The dog's body is still warm," he said, his voice cool and businesslike. "We'd better find Cody."

"Yes." Rick walked past Dakota and picked up the phone.

"Who are you calling?"

"Carmen. She'll help."

Dakota nodded. "I'm going to get my shoes. Back in a flash."

45

Carmen stood with Dakota, Hector, and Ricky in Cody's room and stared into the passage within the closet. They'd called his name for fifteen minutes, but there was no reply, and now there was talk of going inside the walls to look for him. Only Rick and Hector were small enough to fit into the passage, and Carmen did not want either of them to go in, though Hector appeared more than willing.

"No," she told him. "It's not good to go in there. Something bad will happen."

"All the more reason to go after him," Hector insisted.

"Cody could be anywhere," she said. "Those passages run all over the house. If we found him, it would be by sheer luck."

Ricky, who looked pale and ill, nodded. "I should go. I've been in them before." Nervously he ran his fingers through his tousled hair. "God, who else is in there?"

"It's a spirit," Carmen said.

"I'll bet it's a kid," Dakota cut in quickly. "Maybe a friend from school? An older kid. You know, people, he knew exactly what he was doing—he's obviously been in there before—and whoever it was didn't know I heard him, so there's no reason to think that he won't come back out sooner or later."

"Dakota has a point," Hector said.

"Yes," Rick agreed. "Except tomorrow's Halloween."

"Here's what we're going to do," Carmen said abruptly. "Hector, you go clean up the mess in Ricky's room—"

"Should we leave it for the police?" Dakota asked.

"We don't need police," she said with finality. "After that, Hector, please take the cat and put him back at our house. Make sure you cover his eyes outside so he doesn't see those jacks. Then come back here."

Hector nodded silently, leaving her to eye Ricky and Dakota. "Did either of you check on Jade?" she asked.

They shook their heads.

She pulled a key from her pocket. "Let's go." She bustled toward the stairs, Dakota and Ricky following. "If he's not with her, we'll keep looking until we find him."

Instead of knocking on Jade's door, she inserted the key in the lock and turned it silently. The door opened on the shadowed room. Putting her finger to her lips to signal silence, she led them into Jade's living room, crossing herself as she always did when she saw the murky forms of the stuffed dogs. They seemed to watch her as she moved through the room. She paused to whisper to Ricky. "You know where the openings are?"

He nodded.

"Check them. Check for dust." Without being told, Dakota remained with his friend. That pleased Carmen, because Ricky looked too close to panic to be left alone, and she feared he might fall apart completely. She watched him tiptoe toward a coat closet that contained an opening, then let herself into Jade's bedroom. The old woman snored in her bed, blissfully unaware that her poodle had been killed. The one that died a couple months ago was perched on the night table, fresh from the taxidermist, eternally licking its privates. Carmen crossed herself again, then checked Jade's closet.

Nothing blocked the opening. Jade continued to snore as Carmen pushed the latch. The panel slid open silently, letting cool, stale air waft over her face and making the hairs on her arms and neck stand on end. Involuntarily she shivered, then put one hand inside the opening and wiped it across the floor before letting it shut.

Quietly she left the bedroom, then waited for Ricky to finish up. Afterward, she led them out of Jade's quarters, locking the door behind them.

In the living room light, she examined her fingers. No dust. "Ricky? Was there dust?"

"In the one in the closet," he said, wiping his fingers on his sweatpants. "But not in the one by the back stairs."

They heard the back door open, and a moment later, Hector came in. "Everything's taken care of."

"Quint's at your place?" Rick asked.

"Yes. Boy, that cat didn't like it outside." He held up his arm, displaying scratch marks. "He's okay now." He looked at Dakota. "Shelly wants to talk to you," he said.

"Shelly's here?" Ricky interrupted hopefully.

"No. She's on the phone." He turned back to Dakota. "She only wants to talk to you. I told her to call over here, but she wouldn't do it. The front door's not locked; you can go on over."

Dakota touched Ricky on the shoulder. "I'll be right back. Don't worry."

Carmen watched Ricky as Dakota left, and her heart ached for him, he looked so stricken. "Hector," she ordered. "You check the rest of the passage openings down here. If they're open, call Cody." She turned to Ricky. "You and I will check the upstairs. Come on." She grabbed his hand and began to lead him toward the staircase. "We'll find him right away.

She hoped she spoke the truth.

46

Numbly following Carmen into Shelly's room, Rick felt as if he were drowning. He couldn't seem to think anymore, couldn't comprehend what was going on around him. Vaguely humiliated, knowing that she was treating him like a child, coddling him, leading him, he didn't have the strength to take over the search for his son, let alone protest, though he knew he should.

At least he hadn't told Carmen the reason Shelly had run away. Then he'd get the same pitying and nervous questioning glances from her that Dakota had given him since he'd arrived. Rick didn't think he could stand that.

They'll think you're crazy and send you away.

"Shut up," he whispered.

"What?" Carmen looked at him.

"Nothing. Nothing."

"I remember the day I nailed this one shut," she said, her hand on the closet doorknob. "I heard noises in here one night. It scared me so much, I stuck a chair under the knob. The next morning, I looked inside and found one of my dresses was on the floor. It was damp." She shook her head. "I didn't know what was on it, I just threw it away. Then I got a hammer and drove twenty-four nails into the panel. I counted every one."

She glanced at him as she opened the closet door. "Ricky?"

He froze. "Yes?"

"Why did Shelly run away?"

He didn't want to answer, but her expression demanded it. "She says someone attacked her." That was enough truth for now.

"Do you believe her, Ricky?"

"Yes." *I didn't, I couldn't have.*

"So do I. Look." She stepped aside so that he could see inside the closet. Even without a flashlight, he could tell that the panel below Shelly's dresses and shirts had been tampered with. One corner was splintered, the nail next to it bent and only halfway removed. More nails littered the floor. A spray of dark spots that might be blood stained the floor. "I cleaned this room a week ago," she told him. "This wasn't like this then." She bent down and called, "Cody? You in there? Cody?"

"Piper!" Dakota's voice, not Cody's, jolted Rick. He spun toward the door.

"Up here!" Rick yelled.

Immediately he heard O'Keefe's heavy footfalls come up the stairs two at a time. *Seconds are passing,* he thought as he heard him running up the hall, *and they feel like hours.*

Dakota finally appeared in Shelly's doorway, windblown and breathless. He rested against the doorframe, leaning his head back, and took a deep breath. He exhaled noisily.

"What is it?" Rick demanded, impatient with O'Keefe's dramatics. "What did Shelly say?"

"Piper," he said, coming into the room. "Stick your tongue out."

"What?"

"Stick it out. Now."

"No."

In two broad steps Dakota reached him. "Why not? What are you hiding?" He glared down at him.

"I'm not hiding anything," Rick avowed angrily.

"Then stick out your tongue!"

"Why?"

Dakota reached out and grabbed the front of his T-shirt,

twisted it in his fingers, drawing Rick closer, pulling him up onto his toes until they were nose to nose. Dakota's words were precise and clipped. "I'll tell you after. Do it."

Rick glanced at Carmen for help, but she was watching him almost as closely as Dakota. He moved his gaze back to Dakota and, unable to read the expression in his friend's eyes, slowly stuck his tongue out. Dakota studied it carefully. After a long moment, his fingers slowly let go of Rick's T-shirt. "Okay," he said softly. "I'm sorry."

Rick almost bit it as Dakota grabbed him in a fierce bear hug, pulling him off the ground again in his enthusiasm. Rick flailed, his breath cut off by O'Keefe's huge breasts.

Dakota let go. "Sorry. Oh, shit, Piper, when I saw that dead dog in your room and that knife and all those loose nails, I started to think—"

"You thought I was crazy," Rick said softly.

"Forgive me?"

"Why did my tongue change your mind?"

"Shelly. She remembered something. She bit the attacker's tongue." He grimaced. "She said she spit out a piece of it. It's probably on the bed somewhere." So saying, he crossed to the bed and pulled the sheet straight, examined it, then did the same to the yellow blanket. "Aha," he said, pointing at something. "Look at that!"

Rick approached, Carmen following. He leaned over and saw a tiny red lump, no thicker than a dime.

"That's supposed to be a tongue?" Carmen asked doubtfully.

"The tip," Dakota said impatiently. "The tip."

Rick gingerly poked it with his finger. He couldn't tell what the hell it was, but in spite of that, he felt a smile creep across his lips. They knew he wasn't crazy. *You were wrong, Robin, you bastard, you were wrong.*

"It's all dried up," Dakota was saying. "She took a nice healthy hunk off the guy." He looked at Rick. "I'll bet we're dealing with some sort of psycho high school kid with a crush on Shelly."

If you tell, they'll think you're crazy.

No they won't, he told his brother's voice, *you lied.*

"Piper?"

Blinking, he looked at Dakota. "What?"

"I asked you a question."

"Ask me again."

"Has Shelly been getting any weird phone calls?"

"She has her own line." Rick tilted his head toward the phone on her dresser. "I don't know."

Dakota crossed to the phone and picked up the receiver. He turned his other hand, revealing a phone-number on his palm written in blue ink. He punched it in.

"Shelly?" he said a moment later. "It's okay." He paused, listening. "Yes, he's fine. Listen, do you have any weird guys asking you for dates or anything?" He listened again. "Any obscene phone calls?" He listened, then nodded. "Okay. Hang on." He extended the phone to Rick. "Your daughter wants to talk to you."

Rick's hand trembled as he took the phone. "Shelly."

"Daddy, I'm sorry," she cried.

"It's okay," he said, feeling strength flow back into him. "It's okay, honey."

"I didn't mean to, I mean I didn't really think you'd . . . That man just looked like you, he really did. I'm sorry, I'm so sorry."

"You did the right thing by going to Dakota. I'm just glad you're *safe.*" Sudden fear rushed back into him at those words. "Shel, what do you know about Bob?"

"Cody's pretend friend?" She was silent a moment. "Nothing, really," she said finally. "Why?"

"He's real. He's probably your attacker." Quickly he told her the details.

"Daddy, he looked just like you!"

It can't be—"Shel, are you at Leanne's?"

"Yes. Do you want me to come home?"

"No, kiddo, I want you to stay right where you are. In the morning you can come and get your costume for the party."

"Well, okay," she said doubtfully.

"Thanks, Shel."

"Dad, have you called the police?"

"Not yet, but if we don't find him soon, we will. I'll call you as soon as he turns up."

"I love you, Dad."

"I love you, too. Good night."

He hung up, surreptitiously wiping his eyes before turning to Carmen and Dakota. "Maybe we should call the police."

"Daddy!" Cody's voice carried up the stairwell. Then Hector called out, "I found him!" Rick looked at Dakota, then at Carmen, who was busy shoving a chair under the closed closet doorknob. Without a word, he raced downstairs. Hector and Cody stood in the living room.

"Hector, where was he?" he asked, scooping the smiling child into his arms.

"In the workshop." Hector shook his head. "I went out there to get some wood screws. You didn't need to nail those panels; the levers lock from the outside. Nobody can break through except with a drill if you do that."

Now he tells me. "Cody, what were you doing in the workshop?"

"Bob took me there."

He glanced back as Dakota and Carmen joined them. "How? Did you go outside?"

The little boy shook his head. "Uh-uh. We went in a tunnel."

God, Rick thought, *we're living in an ant farm.* He hadn't even known there was a tunnel to the workshop. *It must go underground,* he thought. "You know the rats in the icky car in the workshop, Daddy?"

"Yes?"

Cody giggled. "It wasn't rats. It was Bob. He was watchin' you."

Rick's stomach knotted itself up, and he took the boy to the couch, set him on it, and knelt in front of him. "Cody? I have to ask you some questions, and I want you to answer the best you can, okay?"

"Okay, Daddy."

"What do you and Bob do at night?"

Cody hesitated, looking at his feet.

"You can tell me, Cody. I won't get mad, I promise."

"He just shows me all the secret places in the house."

"Is that all? Really?"

"Sometimes we sneak food and stuff." Cody finally met Rick's eyes. "I'm sorry."

"It's okay, son. What else do you do?"

"We go outside and play. Daddy?"

"What?"

"Promise you won't get mad?"

"I promise."

"Sometimes Bob likes to spy on people."

"On who?"

"Well, he said he watched Shelly get undressed. He wanted me to watch, too, but I wouldn't."

His stomach filled with lead. "I'm glad you wouldn't look." He glanced at Dakota, saw the loathing on his face. "Cody, is that all?"

"No." The child looked away again.

"What else?"

He didn't answer.

"Did he spy on me, too?"

"Uh-huh," he said, not looking up.

"It's all right. Just say it."

"He likes to watch when you and Audrey have sleepovers."

Rick was careful not to look at Dakota. "Do you know Bob's whole name, Cody?"

"Uh-huh. But he told me I couldn't tell or he'd hurt you." He met Rick's eyes. "I don't want him to hurt you, Daddy."

"Are you afraid of him?" *It can't be,* he thought. *It's impossible.*

"I wasn't at first. But sometimes now. I don't think he likes you, Daddy."

A pervert was living in his house, corrupting his son, attacking his daughter. Watching everything they did, hearing everything they said. Anger gave Rick strength. He'd kill the son of a bitch, whoever he was. Whatever he was.

"He wanted me to tell you something, Daddy."

"What?" Rick could barely keep from shaking the boy to get his words out faster. "What does he want you to tell me?"

"Well, it's not nice. He called you a name."

"It's okay to tell me, Cody."

"You won't be mad?"

"No. I promise."

"Okay. He said, 'Happy Halloween, icky Ricky.' "

"Holy shit," he heard Dakota say somewhere behind him. Carmen crossed herself.

He couldn't believe it. He wouldn't. *It's some kind of trick.* Outside of the Zapatas and Jade, no one but the O'Keefes knew about that name. He swallowed. "Cody," he said in a strangled voice. "Does Bob have legs?"

"How'd you know? Do you know Bob?"

"Maybe."

"He walks on his hands, Daddy. He does neat tricks and he looks like you, except he's little."

Stunned, Rick stared at his son.

"Madre de Dios," Carmen whispered. "It's his ghost. I knew it."

"Tell me Bob's real name, Cody," Rick said numbly.

Cody shook his head. "He'll hurt you if I do."

"He won't know."

"Yes he will!" Cody spat the words, his fear obvious. "He's listening right now. He always listens. He knows everything you say, Daddy. He says you're crazy, Daddy!"

"Your father's not crazy," Carmen said firmly. She sat next to the child. "But Bob is."

Dakota squatted next to Rick. "Bob's a turkey, Cody," he said, the strain in his voice belying the lightness of his tone. "Gobble, gobble, gobble."

Cody almost laughed, then caught himself. "You shouldn't make fun of Bob. He gets mad."

"Well, where is he right now?" Dakota asked.

Cody shrugged. "I dunno. In the bookcase, probably. That's where he likes to listen from."

Rick glanced back, saw Hector doing something to the lever. "Well, if he's in there, he can't get out anymore."

"Yeah," Dakota added, then raised his voice "Hey, Bob, you're a turkey! Gobble, gobble!"

"Shhh!" Cody was scared now, really scared. "Don't make him mad! He'll hurt you."

"Like he hurt Jade's dog?" Rick asked.

"Uh-huh."

"Cody," Rick said. "Tell me his name, son.

Cody shook his head.

"Then I'm going to guess his name. You tell me when I'm right. Okay?"

Cody thought it over, then nodded once.

"Is his name Robin?"

Cody nodded and began to cry.

Carmen scooped him into her arms. "I'm taking him back to our house and putting him to bed. Dakota, did you lock the door after you used the phone?"

"Uh, I don't know."

She nodded brusquely. "Hector, come on. We've gotta make sure nobody's in our house." She looked at Rick and Dakota. "You two better come along. It's not safe here, not with the *espíritu* loose in the walls."

"It's not a ghost, Carmen. It tried to rape my daughter. It gave her a black eye."

"Ghosts can do that, Ricky." She stared hard at him. "Your brother's dead. He's buried up there in the cemetery. It's his ghost."

"It must be someone who looks like Robin," Dakota said, looking at Rick.

"Who has no legs?" Rick asked grimly. "Who walks on his hands and calls himself Robin, and me icky Ricky? That's too much coincidence for me."

"Robin's dead," Carmen insisted.

"Maybe my brother is," Rick said slowly. "But his body isn't. Take Cody, Carmen. We'll be along soon."

He waited until he heard the back door close, then turned to Dakota. "Are you up for a little visit to Santo Verde Cemetery?"

Dakota regarded him doubtfully. "What for?"

"To see what's in my brother's grave."

"Grave robbing?"

"No. Just looking."

"Jesus X. Christ, Piper. That's crazy."

He flinched at the dreaded word, then composed himself. "No, it's not. I have to know if he's really dead."

"You didn't see him at the funeral?"

"O'Keefe, I told you, he burned in a fire. It was closed casket."

"If he burned, how can you tell if it's him?"

"The bones," he said impatiently.

"I was afraid you'd say that. Look, Piper, can't this wait until morning? We could inquire at the office and—"

"And what? See if we can get a court order to check the grave?" Rick shook his head. "No way. His message was 'Happy Halloween.' Something's going to happen tomorrow. He has plans, and I have to make sure I know what I'm dealing with. We're going to the cemetery. Now."

"Look, Piper. There's an intruder in this house. No matter who he is, he's breaking the law. Let's call the cops."

"What are they going to do? Check every passage in the house? They'd be no match for someone who knows their way around there. They can't do squat."

"Well, we could go sleep at Carmen's, then, first thing in the morning, call the exterminator and have your house tented."

Rick smiled, momentarily tickled by the notion. "That's not a bad idea."

"Good, then it's settled."

"No, Dakota, it's not settled. Just think how bad that body would smell once it started rotting."

Dakota made a face. "You could move back to Vegas."

Rick studied his friend. Even an hour ago, he might have agreed to it, might have jumped at the thought, but there was something so foul and intrusive in the things Cody had told him, combined with the sudden knowledge that he had told and been judged sane, that he couldn't entertain the idea.

"I'm going out to the toolshed for a shovel. I'm going to the cemetery and I'm going to see what's buried in Robin's grave. You can come with me or not. Either way, I'm going."

Dakota gave him a sick grin. "You were easier to get along with when you weren't so macho, Piper."

"Are you coming or not?"

"What are friends for?" he said, and followed Rick to the shed.

Five minutes later, they walked from the house to Rick's car. The greenjacks were going wild, but Rick ignored them.

Five minutes of driving through swirling fog brought them to the cemetery. They'd parked on the lightless street behind it, then hoisted themselves over the wall. It proved easier than expected, especially since the moon had gone down now, and at two in the morning, no one was around to catch them.

Rick had never been here at night. Whereas he found the place soothing and serene in the daytime, the presence of the jacks—not nearly as many as at home, but enough to make him anxious—and the shadowy angles and orbs and crosses poking through the mist made him nervous. He had a second thought, and refused it: He'd finally found some courage, and he was damned if he was going to let go of it now.

They soon found the Piper plots. Rick glanced up at the statue of the piper. "How they hanging, Thomas?" he whispered, then, without allowing himself to think, he began to dig. Soon Dakota fell in alongside. The soil was surprisingly soft, blessedly soft, and before three-thirty, Rick's shovel thunked against wood.

At quarter to four, he sat in the grave on top of the bottom half of the coffin and brushed the dirt off the upper portion. Dakota peered down at him from above, his face a pale moon against the darkness. Rick felt for latches, found one, and worked it until it came undone in his hand. Still the casket wouldn't open. "Hand me the crowbar."

Silently Dakota passed it down.

He worked it along the edge. Suddenly it gave, letting stale air, smelling faintly of charcoal and nothing else, drift into his nostrils. "Turn on the flashlight," he told Dakota. A moment later, a shaky beam of light illuminated the coffin from above.

"Here goes." He pulled the lid up.

At first, the blackened bones contained within told him little. The explosion that had caused the carnival fire had been of tremendous force, and it was obvious that these bones had been close to the center of it. They were unidentifiable: part of a skull, a couple longer bones that might have been arms, and most of a rib cage and the spinal column, whose end he couldn't see. "Give me the light."

Dakota handed it down. Rick held his breath and bent over, shining the light under the lower half of the coffin. He peered below, his face uncomfortably close to the charred skeleton.

He saw an intact pelvis. One hip cavity was empty, but the other contained a ball joint. Following it down, he saw that the leg bone itself extended into the darkness of the casket, out of sight.

"Well?" Dakota hissed.

"Hip bone's connected to the thigh bone," Rick said. "This isn't Robin. They probably just put bones into caskets at random."

"So he's alive?"

"Probably. At least we have no proof that he's dead."

"It's no ghost, Carmen," Rick said an hour later. "He's almost certainly alive."

It was five-thirty in the morning, and he sat at Carmen's

kitchen table, dressed in Hector's robe. He'd already showered the graveyard dirt from his body, and now Dakota was in the bathroom doing the same.

"Madre Dios," she said. "He's in the house, and Jade, she knows, doesn't she? All these years, she's known." She glared. *"Puta."*

"We don't know he's been here the whole time. Chances are he hasn't been."

"Oh, I think he has. I always thought the ghost was there. How could I be so stupid?"

"We went to the funeral, Carmen, we thought he was dead. A ghost makes more sense." It felt good to do the comforting for a change.

She shook her head. "I was stupid. I saw things. I always thought Jade ate like a horse. Food disappeared in the night, but I thought it was her."

Dakota came out of the bathroom dressed in one of Carmen's flannel nightgowns. It ended just above his knees.

"So what are you two talking about?"

"We're wondering if Robin's been living in the house ever since his alleged death," Rick said sourly. A little voice in the back of his mind congratulated him on continuing to keep his door locked after his brother's "death."

Dakota leaned forward. "So do you think that every time old Jade moans and groans, it's because your brother's sticking it to her?"

Carmen stood up. "I'm going back to bed."

Rick watched her go. "She doesn't like dirty talk."

Dakota ignored him. "So do you think he is?"

"Yes. Let's get some sleep." He gestured at the sofa bed Carmen had made up for them.

"My dreams come true," Dakota said, batting his eyelashes.

"Try anything and I'll tell your sister on you."

After they lay down on the lumpy mattress, Rick stared at the ceiling a long time, wishing sleep would come.

"Piper?"

"Hmm?"

"What are you thinking?"

"I'm thinking about my brother. After he changed, Robin became obsessed with leaving his mark on everything. He'd get into other people's clothes, my mother's makeup, the food. Remember, I told you he peed in the lemonade? He'd take my schoolbooks and jerk off on them—I caught him in the act once. After we were twelve or so, he masturbated on anything that moved. And laughed about it. He didn't care if I saw. He used everyone's toothbrushes. I kept mine locked in my room."

"What a fucker."

"Yes," Rick agreed. "His greatest pleasure came from the violation of other people's privacy."

"A rapist in every sense of the word."

"That's right." Memories flooded him, leaving a bitter taste in his mouth. "And now he's doing it again. To my son, my daughter, and to me. I'm going to stop him, Dakota, or die trying. I'm not running anymore. I'm going to take back what's mine."

47

October 31

"I feel like Roddy McDowell standing outside Hell House," Dakota O'Keefe said.

"I know what you mean." Rick raised his hand to shield his eyes from the noontime sun, bright and clear on this chill autumn day. "I don't think anything will happen for a few hours. Not until dark."

"I still think you should tent the place." Dakota smirked. "Exterminate the pests."

"I wish it was that easy." Rick shoved his hands in the pockets of his sweatpants. "Winter's coming."

Dakota nodded, hugging himself. Like Rick, he'd had to put his grave-robbing clothes back on—a pair of shorts, running shoes with no socks, and a sweatshirt, all filthy. "I'm freezing my nuts off. Hey, is the pool water warm yet?" He glanced across the lawn at the sparkling blue water. "That would help."

"No. We only finished filling it yesterday. It'll take days before it's warm enough. Listen, I have jackets upstairs. One's a humongous fleece job. It'll fit you." As he spoke, the cold wind cut through Rick's T-shirt, making him shiver.

"Well, we have to go in, right?"

"Right. It's okay, Carmen's already been inside."

"Then why don't we ask *her* to get the jackets?"

Rick rolled his eyes. "Are you chicken?" he asked, terribly pleased to be the one delivering the words instead of receiving them.

"I'm a hell of a lot more cold than I am scared, Piper." Dakota gave him a wobbly smile. "Let's go for it. Hell, let's get crazy and get an entire change of clothes."

"Good idea." As he unlocked the front door, Rick felt his nerves giving underneath his newfound bravado. *You can't back out now,* he told himself, *not after you called O'Keefe chicken.*

Nothing looked out of place as they moved through the living room. Beyond Jade's closed door, he could hear Maury Povich's voice blaring.

"Hector hasn't finished locking the openings up, has he?" Dakota asked when they reached the kitchen.

"I doubt it." Rick opened the refrigerator and withdrew a carton of milk. He stared at it a moment, then took it to the sink and poured it out.

"Piper? What the hell are you doing?"

"If my brother's really here, you don't want to drink this." Returning to the fridge, he took out a couple apples, examined them, then washed them thoroughly, just in case. He tossed one to Dakota. "Hector's been out in the yard all morning. I don't think he wants to be alone in here any more than we do. And I don't blame him."

"Piper, why don't we just call the cops?"

Rick sighed. "I told you, if someone doesn't want to be found in this house, they won't be found." As true as that was, there was more to it than that, but Rick kept it to himself because he knew O'Keefe would do his best to talk him out of it.

For a long hour at dawn, Rick had lain on the lumpy sofa bed pretending to be asleep while he thought about what he'd told Dakota: that he was going to take back what belonged to him.

When he'd said it, he'd been talking about more than his children, more than his house: He had also been talking about his self-respect. The time had come for him to battle the real monster and leave the windmills behind.

Rick had never stood up for himself, had never ceased to question his own worth. He'd known for years that his lack of fight stemmed from the insecurities that Robin had so carefully instilled in him so long ago, and even now, part of him screamed that if he took a stand, he'd be wrong and everyone would find out how totally inadequate he was.

All his life he had taken the path of least resistance, compromising, making nice, turning the other cheek. His powers of calm persuasion were so considerable that even back in elementary school he could use words to avoid showdowns with school bullies. As an adult, he used them to charm bosses and co-workers, even policemen who wanted to give him speeding tickets. His charm had never failed except where his brother was concerned, but there it had failed miserably, leaving him floundering and helpless to fight back. But now that all had to change.

Returning to Santo Verde and facing the past had been the first step in taking control of his own life. Getting through the last two days without cracking had been the next step. Then, last night, when Dakota and Audrey said they believed he saw the greenjacks and he realized they meant it, the first tingle of real confidence passed through him.

If he called the police now, perhaps they could do something: set a trap, stake out the house, he didn't know what. But chances were, as he told Dakota, they would fail. And if they didn't—if they caught Robin—Rick would again escape the confrontation he had avoided all his life, the final confrontation.

He knew that this was something he had to do on his own, and this morning he began to figure a way to get Carmen to leave for the night. All his life she had been his crutch, and he knew that her presence here tonight might well bring out his old weaknesses. He couldn't take that chance. Instinctively he knew that if he met the confrontation head-on, faced it on his own, with nothing to rely upon but himself, and if he succeeded in overcoming it, he would have control of his own destiny for the first time in his life and would no longer be a prisoner of his own cowardice. He'd been handed a second chance.

And that was something he couldn't explain to Dakota, who lived for confrontations and drama. He would never comprehend how important it was for Rick to fight this battle alone.

"I'm going upstairs," he told Dakota, who had sat down in a kitchen chair. "Do you want your suitcase? It might be a good idea to take some things over to Carmen's for the night." He put his hand on the back stairs rail.

Dakota tossed his apple core in the trash can. "I'll come with you."

The atmosphere in the second-floor hallway seemed as murky as the light filtering in through the windows of the few rooms with open doors. Rick pushed the door to Cody's room wide without allowing himself to indulge the goose bumps rising on his arms.

The closet door stood wide open. Rick saw the closed panel, with the holes where the nails had been, but he ignored it, taking Cody's jacket and the Halloween costume Carmen had helped him make from the hangers. He laid the clothes on his son's bed, then closed the door, using Cody's wooden desk chair to secure the knob.

Across the room, Dakota had hurriedly changed into jeans and a clean shirt, and was now gathering his things and stuffing them in his suitcase. Rick opened Cody's drawers, took underwear, socks, pants, a shirt, and a sweater out, then took the boy's backpack and folded the items and placed them inside it. The costume went on top. A red cape and shorts and blue leotard with a big red *S* sewn on. Rick approved, half wishing he had one just like it.

"Ready?" he asked Dakota.

"Ready."

He went to Shelly's room and repeated the process, then looked around, curious to see if anything had been disturbed. Nothing had. The chair still blocked the closet door, the bed with the spray of bloodstains and the minuscule piece of dried flesh hadn't been touched.

Maybe he's gone, Rick thought. *Maybe it never happened.* His confidence declined the tiniest bit. "Let's get my stuff," he said, heading out the door. Dakota followed quickly.

It was the same here. He extracted the coat for Dakota and another for himself and threw them on the bed. Barely glancing at the closet cabinet in the dressing room, he swiftly changed into fresh clothes, jeans, and a flannel shirt. "Almost done," he called to Dakota, who stood peering out the window onto the orchard below.

A moment later, he'd gathered his toiletries and a brown cable-knit sweater.

Dakota looked at him. "Can we go now?"

"One more stop. I want my laptop. Come on."

The study door was closed, and as he opened it, Rick was surprised to see that the little computer was open and turned on. He had left it plugged in to recharge, he remembered, but as he stared at the starburst screen-saver pattern on the screen, he was fairly sure he hadn't forgotten to turn it off yesterday—or was it the day before? He never forgot. *But the last couple days haven't exactly been normal. You could've forgotten.*

"What's wrong?" Dakota asked from behind.

"Nothing," Rick replied, handing his belongings to O'Keefe. Slowly he walked across the room to the desk. "I just don't remember leaving this on."

If Dakota hadn't been waiting for him, he would have pulled the desk chair out and sat down to check the contents of his article files. As it was, he leaned across the massive desk chair and touched one key, just so that he could make sure everything looked okay on the screen.

The screen bloomed in the dim light, but the desktop didn't appear. Only two white words broke the sea of blue:

ICKY RICKY

He touched my computer. He's probably read my files. "You little fucker. You son of a bitch." He nearly laughed as he realized his outrage had restored his confidence.

"Shit, Piper," Dakota breathed behind him. "Let's get the hell out of here."

"I'm surprised he figured out how to get into the system." Rick leaned farther over the back of the chair and pushed the page down button. Nothing else was on the screen, just the file's end mark. "He's probably never had access to a computer."

"He's here alone with Jade most of the time. He has access to television, magazines, all of that. He could figure it out."

Rick nodded as he scrolled up the screen. "Shit. He *did* get into my files." The words had been written below last week's column. "The little shit." He turned to face O'Keefe. "Maybe he learned how to use this by watching me. He liked to sit in the dressing room and watch our parents make love. He'd be two feet from them, and they didn't know. He could go anywhere, and nobody ever heard him or saw him. Unless he wanted them to. He'd just watch, with this horrible grin plastered across his face." Involuntarily he shivered. "Let me unplug this and we'll leave." *For now,* he added silently.

Rick shut down the computer and pulled the jack from the back. He needed the power pack, too, which was a pain because he had to climb under the desk and reach up behind it to get to the electrical outlet and unplug it. "Shit," he said again, and pulled the chair away from the desk. "This will take a couple minutes."

He could see Dakota's foot tapping impatiently as he got down on his hands and knees. The massive desk was as deep as it was wide, and as he crawled beneath, his body blocked the light. Wishing he'd remembered the flashlight, he began to feel along the cord, intending to follow it to the outlet.

"What the hell?" he muttered as his fingers hit something cold and hard. Feeling along the floor, he realized it was a curved metal object and that the cord lifted off the floor to feed into it. What the hell was it?

"What's taking you so long?" Dakota asked nervously.

"There's something funny down here."

"Swell, just swell. For Christ's sake, be careful, Piper!" Dakota ordered. "He was fucking with your computer. You might get electrocuted or something! You've got the adapter, just get the fuck out of there! You can get another cord at the store."

"You're right." He grasped the cord just where it fed into the metal, thinking that if he couldn't pull it out of the wall socket from here, he'd do exactly what Dakota said. He yanked the cord.

Metal crashed against metal, so close that the wind of its passing blew into his face. He heard himself scream, felt his skull crash painlessly against the underside of the desk as he scrabbled, frantic to get out of the dark hole. Dakota was yelling something behind him, then suddenly his ankles were grabbed out from under him. He flopped onto his belly as O'Keefe dragged him out from under the desk.

"Rick! Are you okay?" Dakota cried.

"Yeah." He still held the cord, and now he saw the metal object he pulled along with it. "Holy Christ!"

It was a bear trap. A big rusty bear trap.

"My God," Dakota whispered as he saw the trap. *"Now* we call the cops."

Rick sat up, rubbing the back of his head as pain started to set in. "No," he said, pulling the trap forward.

"Why the fuck not?" Dakota demanded.

"It belonged to Conlin Piper." The excuse came easily since it held some truth. "It's an heirloom, and I'm not going to let the police take it as evidence. According to family history, he was fond of hunting bear in Holcomb Valley." He pointed to an area of bare wall to the left. "When I was little, there was a bearskin hanging right there. Supposedly it was Conlin's catch, but personally, I think he bought it."

"Piper, why in hell are you talking about frigging bearskins?" Dakota exploded suddenly. "You were almost killed just now, and you're acting like nothing happened!"

He didn't know why he was so calm, so instead of answering, Rick found the catch on the trap and released it, opening the jaws just enough to allow him to pull the cord free. "This thing could use a squirt of WD-40," he told Dakota, letting the jaws close again. The teeth had a quarter-inch gap between them, and he realized that if he'd put his arm in it, as had been intended, it wouldn't have been severed—quite. An unexpected giggle escaped his lips, heralding an impending case of hysterics. He pinched the back of his hand, twisting the skin between his thumb and forefinger until tears sprang to his eyes and the laughter receded.

"Rick?"

"I'm fine," he said. "It looks like the cord is, too." He looked at Dakota. "Sorry. It was a little unsettling having that thing crash down in my face. I'm lucky I still have my nose." He stood up and wrapped the cord around the adapter, then slipped it and the laptop into his computer case and put the strap over his shoulder. "Let's go."

Dakota pointed at the trap. "Are you going to leave *that* here? God knows where you'll find it next."

"Good point." He reached down and retrieved the trap. "This thing weighs a ton. I wonder how he moved it."

They descended the main staircase only to find Jade sitting in his suede recliner, petting one of her stuffed dogs. *Great. This is all I need.* "Aunt Jade?" he said stiffly.

"Stinkums is dead," she announced as she stroked the poodle, a mangy yellowish one with a faded green ribbon around its neck. It was posed so that it appeared to be sleeping, with its nose tucked beneath its tail. "He's dead, isn't he, Luvems?" She scratched Luvems behind its ear, and a clump of fur came off. "Luvems," Jade intoned, sitting up straight, "was a champion!"

"I'm sorry about—" *I can't say "Stinkums"* "—your dog," Rick finished lamely.

"He's so jealous," she said dreamily.

Rick traded glances with Dakota. "Who's jealous, Aunt Jade?"

"Why, my darling little Robin, of course. He's such a good boy. Except when he's jealous."

Jade often spoke of his brother as if he were still living, and Rick had never taken it seriously. How stupid he'd been. "Where's Robin now, Aunt Jade?"

She looked at him sharply. "Why, he's dead, Richard. You know that. He's dead and buried." She laughed, a sound like nails raking a blackboard. She stared pointedly at the bear trap. "That's a dangerous toy, Richard. Don't hurt yourself."

"What do you know about this?" Rick demanded.

"What should I know?"

"How it got under my desk. Do you know that?"

She giggled and scratched her dog's ears. "He's so jealous. And it makes me mad when something happens to my little lovedotties, but he says it means I'm his. His alone, and no one else can have me." She blushed, the cackling giggle growing m intensity.

Dakota tugged his elbow, tilting his head toward the door. Rick nodded and followed him outside.

"She knew about that trap, Piper."

Rick looked at Dakota. "I agree."

"She's psycho." O'Keefe paused. "So's your brother. Anyone who would make love to that dried-up old snatch-cracker would have to be mad."

"I agree." Suddenly the consumer spot on the morning news sounded attractive. "Tomorrow I'll find a place to send her and her lovedotties."

They walked toward Carmen's. "Why not today?"

Rick glanced at his watch. "Well, it's two o'clock already, for one thing. Let her have one more midnight fling." He smiled grimly. "For old times' sake."

48

Dakota was more worried about Rick now that he had acquired the determined, set look to his face and shoulders than he'd even been when the guy had been scared half to death and worried that he was losing his marbles.

Now, as Dakota sat in Carmen's bedroom applying his Marilyn makeup, he didn't know what Piper was up to. Less than an hour ago, Rick had assured him that he had no intention of doing anything, like going back into the house tonight, but Dakota wasn't sure he believed him.

After leaving their things at Carmen's, Rick had insisted on going into the workshop and pushing the old Rambler out of its spot in the corner. The two back side windows were broken out, and there were candy wrappers, apple cores, and white Styrofoam meat trays with bits of dried-up meat still clinging under the edges of the cellophane hidden beneath a blanket in the back of the car. The interior smelled like rotting garbage, dirty skin, and worst of all, an X-rated peep show booth. It was foul.

After that, they explored the area where the car had been stored. There were no openings in the floor, but before long, they found a well-hidden passage built into the paneled wall. Piper hadn't even known it existed. To Dakota's surprise, Piper made no attempt to block it, just stared at it with that new and disturbingly resolute set to his jaw.

Back at the Zapatas', Rick set about convincing Carmen

that she and Hector should go away for the night. Dakota could hear parts of the conversation, low, intense discussion that worried him, but when he opened his mouth to say that in his opinion the Zapatas should go nowhere tonight of all nights, Carmen and Rick stared at him as if he were something from another planet. Then Carmen had squeezed Piper's hand and said solemnly that what had to be, had to be.

Next they talked about removing Cody for the night, but the boy came home from school in the middle of that and insisted he wanted to stay home, and Piper, surprisingly, sided with him. When Carmen objected, he pointed out that three adults would be with him at all times. A few minutes later, he had Cody put on his Superman costume, then took him along with him to see Shelly and deliver her costume for the sleep-over party at the Larsons' tonight.

An hour later, they returned, the visit with Shelly, Piper said, having gone very well.

Makeup complete, Dakota pinned his blond wig on, then slipped off his robe in favor of panty hose, high heels, and one of his retired performance white chiffon dresses.

"Voilà," he said, striking a pursed-lip pose in the mirror. "Marilyn is reborn."

He swept into the living room. "Trick or treat, big boy!"

Cody looked up from the television and laughed with delight. Rick, who sat on the couch silently brooding, smiled thinly.

"Well, is that a Tootsie Roll in your pocket or are you just happy to see me, Piper?"

"Dakota," he said wearily, and glanced at his son.

"Sorry. Where are Carmen and Hector?"

"In their bedroom."

Dakota raised his eyebrows suggestively, but Rick just looked bored.

"They're getting ready to leave for her sister's place in Madelyn."

"Piper, this makes no sense." Dakota asked. "Why do you want them to leave? What's your plan?"

"No plan," Rick said nonchalantly. "It works well for everyone. Since we don't want to stay in the big house, we'll have plenty of room here. Carmen doesn't mind at all, and she really wanted to go visit her sister anyway. After we go trick-or-treating, the four of us can come back here, lock ourselves in, and watch movies till dawn. We'll have our own little Halloween party, right, Cody?"

"Right!" the boy said enthusiastically. "You know what? After we saw Shelly, we rented movies and everything. We got *Blazing Saddles* and *Young Frankenstein* and . . . what else, Daddy?"

"Love at First Bite. And *Frankenhooker* for later."

"Well, they're almost horror movies," Dakota said.

"Close enough." Rick's gaze drifted to the clock. "It's almost five. I hope Audrey gets here soon."

Dakota planted himself close to Rick and waited until Cody was lost in cartoons. "Piper," he said softly. "Why do you want your son here?"

"If Big Jack exists, I want him to see it. So he knows that it's a real danger."

The Zapatas came out of their bedroom carrying overnight bags, and the look on Hector's face when he saw Marilyn instantly put Dakota in a better mood. Grabbing his long white scarf, he strutted forth and sang a few breathy bars of "Let Me Entertain You." Carmen laughed and applauded. Hector, grinning and blushing, backed into the wall as Dakota descended upon him, flipping his scarf behind Hector's head and pulling the compact little man forward. He jumped back just before his nose made contact with Dakota's breasts, and O'Keefe let him go, purring, "A hard man is good to find." Hector blushed, smiling uncertainly.

"Ricky?" Carmen asked as Dakota strolled up. "You sure this is okay?"

"I'm sure," he said firmly. "We'll take good care of the place, I promise."

"I brought some extra sheets and towels over from the main house," she said. "They're on the bed."

"Thanks."

A knock on the door made Dakota glance around.

"Audrey's here!" Cody sang, and ran to the door. She stepped inside, wearing jeans and a chambray shirt with a red bandanna in her pocket. On her head she wore a pair of springy antennae topped with blue glittery Styrofoam balls that bounced every time she moved.

"That's not much of a costume, sister dear," Dakota admonished.

"It's a hell of a lot better than Rick's," she countered.

"He's a poop."

"I can see that."

Costumeless Rick remained on the couch, smiling impassively.

"Well, sis, what are you?"

"Hillbilly space alien."

"Lock all the windows tonight, Ricky," Carmen said as she crossed the room, Hector on her tail. "Lock *all* of them. And the doors."

"Don't worry, I will."

"You all be back here before full dark, and don't leave the house until morning," Carmen continued, her voice filled with grave innuendo. "It's Halloween, you know."

"We'll be good," Dakota promised, eyeing Piper. "I'll see to that."

Rick stood as the Zapatas left, crossed to Audrey, and self-consciously pecked her on the cheek. She countered with a solid kiss on his lips.

"So," Rick said. "Let's go trick-or-treating."

"Be ready in a sec. Gotta powder my antennae." Audrey disappeared into the bathroom.

Cody was still staring at the TV, so Dakota pulled Rick aside.

"What are you up to, Piper?"

"What do you mean?"

"You're planning something."

Rick shrugged. "Yeah, right. I plan to make popcorn and watch movies."

"Let me put it another way. Where do you plan to sleep tomorrow night?"

"In my house."

"Why will it be safe tomorrow night?"

"I hope to have Jade moved out by then."

"Besides that. What about . . . the other problem?"

Rick stared at him. "Pest control," he said simply, and turned to Cody. "Let's go, Superboy!"

49

Watching Cody and Dakota, who would never grow up, trick-or-treat while he and Audrey held hands and waited on the sidewalk had been fun, but Rick had been so anxious to get back to the house that he could barely concentrate long enough to make coherent conversation. He told Audrey that it was because he was nervous about seeing Big Jack, and she accepted that, but her brother kept watching him. He knew there was more going on than Rick would admit to, and now Rick worried that O'Keefe would be a problem later. All afternoon O'Keefe had asked him what his plans were, which was actually sort of funny because he truly didn't have any plans. All he knew was that tonight he would confront Robin.

Rick announced that the trick-or-treating was done at six forty-five, and Cody and Dakota, who had collected more candy than Rick had ever seen, both protested, but only mildly. They returned to the car and headed for the house.

The last light of day died as they pulled up the driveway. His stomach in a knot, Rick killed the engine and got out, scooping Cody into his arms.

As they passed the oak, the jacks were as thick and active as Rick had ever seen them, but there was no sign of Big Jack, and he felt so little fear that even the talismanic phrase *I'm Thomas* was unnecessary. Even when they combined and rose right in front of him, he steadfastly ignored them, walking unflinchingly through their greenish forms, feeling the chill wind that went with them and not caring.

He stopped at the front porch and handed Cody to Dakota. "Wait just a second. I promised Carmen I'd look in on Jade."

"Piper—"

Rick ran up the steps. "I'll leave the door open and I'll be right back."

"I'm going with you," Audrey said, trotting after him.

That was fine. He entered the living room and began to cross to Jade's door, intending to do as Carmen asked, just knock politely and tell her good night.

"Fuck me," Jade moaned from within her rooms.

Behind him, Audrey made a strangled sound. Rick turned and grimaced at her, then whispered, "Let's go."

"That was fast," Dakota said as Rick locked the front door.

"She's having her last fling."

"Last fling?" Audrey asked.

"Piper's going to find her a rest home tomorrow," Dakota explained as they quickly walked up the side of the house and around to the Zapata cottage. "Hopefully one well stocked with dirty old men."

The interior of the cottage was warm and cozy, and while Cody spread his booty on the floor and Dakota checked the locks on the house's two entry doors and the latches on all the windows, Rick and Audrey started making popcorn in the microwave.

"We're as tight as bugs in rugs," O'Keefe announced, entering the kitchen. "What have we got to drink?"

"Pepsi or Dos Equis," Rick said.

Dakota opened the fridge, took a beer for himself and a plastic bottle of orange juice for Cody. "What do you two want?"

"Beer," Audrey said absently.

"Pepsi," Rick said, ignoring Dakota's look of surprise. He took a bag of popcorn from the oven, stuck another one in. "Did you want to change clothes, O'Keefe?"

"Piper, dear, I *like* dressing this way." He grinned. "It makes me feel sexy."

"Sorry. I forgot. Watch out for the cat," he added, forcing a grin, trying to act normal. "His claws will shred your frock."

By eight o'clock, halfway into *Young Frankenstein,* Cody had passed out on the floor, the victim of excitement and too much chocolate. While Audrey put him to bed on the little couch in the tiny second bedroom where Carmen kept her sewing machine, Rick stood and sauntered into the kitchen.

"Get me another beer, will you, Piper?" Dakota called.

"I have something better," Rick called back, eyeing the bottle of Sauza Gold on top of the refrigerator.

"Well, bring whatever's better, but bring a beer, too."

"Sure," Rick said. He took the bottle down. A few shooters would make Dakota stop worrying and watching.

Icky Ricky, icky Ricky, come out and play.

He shivered. This was the first time he'd really heard the greenjacks' song all evening. *You heard the voices because you let your guard down.*

"Boo!" Audrey cried, poking his ribs from behind.

He jumped, almost dropping the bottle.

"Oh, Rick, I'm sorry. I didn't mean to scare you!"

"It's okay," he said shakily. "You're allowed on Halloween."

"What are you going to do with that?" she asked, pointing at the bottle.

"Well," he said, opening the fridge and rummaging in the fruit bin until he found a lime, "have you ever had a shooter?"

She made a face. "Yes. Yucko. Is there any margarita mix?"

"Try that cabinet."

Maybe Audrey's was the better idea. After all, he didn't want to get the O'Keefes too plastered to take care of Cody, just relaxed enough not to miss him when he slipped out the back door.

"Eureka," she said, pulling out a green bottle of mix. She set it down. "Glasses?"

"Over there."

He waited until she'd set them beside the mix, then shooed her out of the room. "I'm the host," he said, a tub of margarita salt in his hand. "I'll do the mixing."

"Rick, let me help you—"

"No." He kissed her nose, then led her into the living room, instructing her to sit on the couch by the lovely Marilyn, who demanded his beer.

Rick just smiled. "Forget beer," he told him. "I'm making margaritas. It's better for that girlish figure."

Dakota batted his eyelashes. "I didn't know you cared."

"Slut," giggled Audrey, poking him in the ribs.

Rick left them to their teasing and returned to the kitchen, where he mixed three large drinks, two with double shots of tequila, one with no alcohol.

By nine they were running *Frankenhooker,* and Rick had just delivered a third drink to Dakota. Audrey had stopped at two, saying she'd fall asleep if she had any more, but long, tall Dakota seemed to be a bottomless pit.

"You don't seem very drunk, Piper," he commented as Rick sat down next to Audrey, who was giggling at the movie.

Rick didn't feel capable of anything more than a stupid grin, so he gave Dakota that and said, "I'm just tired." He sipped his drink and grinned again. "I'm a little sleepy."

"This is supposed to be a party," Dakota said, his voice slurring slightly. "Don't go pooping out on me. You either, Audrey."

They sat there for twenty minutes, Dakota engrossed in the movie, Audrey half-asleep. Quietly Rick stood, intending to slip away.

"Where the hell do you think you're going?" Dakota demanded.

Inspiration hit. "I'm going to lie down for a few minutes. I'm really tired, but a nap ought to be enough to keep me up for the rest of the night." His smile, he hoped, was winsome. "Would you do me a favor and wake me up in half an hour?" Judging by Dakota's heavy eyelids, he wouldn't be awake that long himself.

Dakota looked doubtful. "Well, okay. But only a half hour." He glanced at his dozing sister. "You two aren't much fun."

"Sorry," Rick said, heading toward the back of the little house. "I'll be more fun after a nap."

Dakota didn't answer, his attention already back on the TV screen. Rick slipped into the bathroom, and when he came out again, Dakota didn't notice him. He slipped into the room Cody was sleeping in and opened the unobtrusive second door, which led into the kitchen on the far side of the refrigerator.

Picking up the six-inch knife he'd used to cut the lime, he slipped it in his jacket pocket, then let himself out the kitchen door.

In the bedroom, Cody awoke to the closet door creeping open. The sight of his friend scared him at first, but when Bob smiled, the little boy felt much better.

50

Standing on Carmen's side porch in the chill windy night, Rick Piper stared at the back of his house. No lights were on, even though he'd purposely left several burning. Possibly Jade had doused the downstairs lights, but he doubted that she was responsible for the upper floor.

Adrenaline coursing through him, he scanned the yard. The orange trees loomed close around him, and he knew that here, even if Big Jack was standing right beside him, he wouldn't know it. Quickly he walked down the path that led out of the orchard, and as he crossed the small lawn, he could vaguely hear the jacks' taunting calls, though he saw only three or four at the edges of the trees. They were in front, he knew, and many of them were probably busy with Big Jack at the moment.

As he reached the back door and inserted the key in the lock, the wind howled and whistled through the citrus trees behind him. *Big Jack?* he wondered as he fumbled with the lock. "Come on, come on, come on." The whistling sounds grew nearer, then he heard the crunching of footsteps approaching—the familiar sound of Big Jack's tread, like someone walking in a pile of autumn leaves.

Terrified, he jiggled the knob. Nothing happened, and he twisted it harder. "Come on, goddammit!"

Suddenly the lock gave and he swiftly entered the house, pulling the door closed behind him. He didn't bother locking it—greenjacks couldn't leave their natural habitat without donning a human body. Leaves and bark wouldn't do the trick.

Swallowing, he forced himself to turn and look out the window. Something moved among the liquid amber trees, just a flicker at the edge of his vision. *It's nothing,* he told himself, moving deeper into the house.

He didn't want to turn on the lights, and he realized that, as usual, he'd forgotten to bring a flashlight. Trying to move silently, trying not to knock against anything in the dark, he moved through the dining room and into the living room.

Now what? Without a clue, he sat down on the couch so that his back was against the wall and he could see all the corners of the room. He waited a moment, then rose and crossed to the picture window. He drew the drapes wide open. *Might as well see everything you're waiting for.*

The front lawn was a madhouse of activity, and he had to force the jacks' intrusive voices out of his mind, to refuse to acknowledge their attempts to frighten him with their oozing, shifting shapes. He flipped them the bird.

"That's not nice, icky Ricky."

The voice drifted down from the top of the stairs, nearly stopping his heart.

He turned and peered up into the darkness. "Robin?" he called softly.

His brother's laugh was a harsh, ugly sound. "You think you've changed, little brother, but you haven't. You're still a chicken, icky Ricky."

"And you're not my brother." He approached the stairs and stood in the safety of shadows.

"You tell people that, they'll think you're crazy."

"Better get a new line, jack-off. That one doesn't work anymore."

"Oh ho, ho boy, and I thought baby brother was still a scaredy-cat, but he's grown some balls." Robin cackled to himself. "Or maybe he's just really, *really* crazy. Is that it, icky Ricky? Are you crazy?"

The old taunts still worked. Rick's confidence slipped a

notch. *Don't listen to him. This is how he gets you. He's
pushing your buttons to get what he wants.*

"Baby brother, are you still there?"

"Go to hell."

Robin only laughed. "You *must* be crazy if your own little
girl thinks you tried to fuck her. Have you ever seen your
daughter naked, icky Ricky? She's got nice tits and a tight
little cunt that—"

"I'm going to kill you, you bastard!" Ricky's cry rico-
cheted up the stairwell as he stepped onto the bottom riser.

Robin laughed. "You should give your girl a whirl, baby
brother. She's hot, she's hot, and she'll beg you for more!"

He's trying to lure you upstairs. In spite of his overwhelming fury, Rick forced himself to remain where he was.
"I'm going to kill you tonight," he said, his voice shaking
with unleashed anger. "You can count on it."

"Oh boy, icky Ricky really does have balls." Peals of
maniacal laughter floated down. "Your daughter's snatch
smells good, did you know that, icky Ricky?"

I will not react, I will not react, I will not react. But his
other foot moved onto the steps of its own accord.

"I watched you fuck your girlfriend. Remember when we
watched good old Mom and Dad fuck, dicky Ricky? Remember that?"

Rick didn't reply. Slowly he continued up the stairs, keeping to the shadowy edges, his hand gripping the hilt of the
knife.

"Hey, I read your stories, icky Ricky. I guess you think
you're a big hotshot, don'tcha, pricky Ricky? Did you like
the surprise I left for you under the desk?" He paused. "Jade
helped me move it. She's all the snatch I got these days,
baby brother. I think you'd better start sharing your daughter
and your girlfriend." He cackled evilly. "It's the brotherly
thing to do. You with all that nooky, and all I have is that
dried-up old douche-bag. I did it to her in your water bed
tonight, icky Ricky. It was fun." He cleared his throat. "Your
cock's almost as big as mine, little brother, but you need
some lessons. I can show you how to *really* fuck your girl-

friend. How about I show you how to fuck your daughter, too?"

"No!" He couldn't stand it any longer, and suddenly he was tearing blindly up the staircase, the knife out, intent on murder.

Something sharp and cold sliced across his shinbone as he reached the landing. It withdrew, then came again, and this time he could feel the chill of it inside the meat of his calf. The coldness pulled free, and Rick whirled in the dark, stabbing the knife in front of him.

Metal hit metal, the knife deflecting Robin's next thrust, and Rick backed up, feeling for the light switch on the wall. His brother laughed again, then something whizzed through the air, grazing his midriff and clattering to the floor somewhere beyond.

"I'm gonna go play outside, icky Ricky. Why don't you come and play with me?"

slap-slap slap-slap slap-slap

The sound of hand-slaps descending the stairs chilled him. His fingers finally found the light switch, flipped it on.

He stepped forward, nearly tripping over his left leg, grabbing the railing for balance. Looking down, he saw that his brother was gone. The front door hung open. "Jesus," he whispered as the pain hit him. Clutching his leg, he dropped to the floor.

"Sweet Jesus," he breathed. The side of his leg was sheathed in blood. He couldn't see the wounds, but blood was pumping out of him rapidly, and he had to stop it now. Using the railing for leverage, he pulled himself up and started for his bedroom. Then, a moment later, his foot hit something. He looked down.

The sword Audrey had given him lay on the floor, the blade coated with his own blood.

Grimly he grabbed it by the hilt and took it with him. His brother had managed to climb all the way to the shelf in the dressing room, seven feet off the ground, to get to it. *So what else is new?*

Safely inside the bedroom, Rick turned on the light and

locked the door behind him, then limped through the dressing room, pausing only to slide the sword through the cabinet doors to ensure that his brother couldn't get in. Entering the bathroom, he flipped the toilet lid down and sat heavily, dizzy from shock and, perhaps, blood loss.

He pulled open the vanity, found the scissors, cut his pant leg off at the knee, then began to pull the material, but it was stuck in his flesh. Gritting his teeth, he pulled it free.

Both wounds were in his lower leg. The saber had run clean through the fleshy part of his calf, and it hurt like hell. The other was near his knee. The blade had glanced off his shinbone, and his stomach turned as he saw the white bone under the meat. *Dakota will be pleased. I'll consent to stitches this time.*

Resolutely he pulled a clean towel from the cabinet and began wrapping the leg. As he worked, he purposefully set about building his anger, thinking about the things Robin had said about his daughter, so that by the time he grabbed a roll of adhesive tape and began wrapping it tightly around the towel, his outrage outweighed his pain. "You little fucker," he whispered, limping into the dressing room. He pulled the sword free. "You're dead, you're dead, you're dead."

Using the sword as a cane, he entered the bedroom and eyed the phone on the side of the bed. Maybe he should call Dakota or Audrey and let them call the police.

He reached for the phone and stopped as he realized his expensive bedspread was soaking wet. *What the hell?* He grabbed the edge of the comforter and pulled it back, revealing sodden bunched blankets. He pulled those away, too.

"Dear God," he whispered.

Jade was in the mattress. Not on it, in it, floating in the water and air baffles, her sightless eyes staring at him through a thin covering of water.

I did it to her in your water bed.

He saw the X-shaped slit in the mattress and knew that Robin must have lured her up here onto the bed, then killed her and sliced the mattress open with the sword. The plastic liner and high sides had kept any water from escaping.

He picked up the phone, heard no dial tone, then saw that the cord had been cut. "Shit."

The lights went out.

Ordering himself to remain calm, he felt for the nightstand, opened the drawer, and grabbed the flashlight. He switched it on, and found that there were only minutes of dim glow left before the batteries failed altogether. Leaning on the sword, holding the light, he hobbled toward the staircase.

"Daddy! Are you okay? Bob said you were hurt."

The sound of Cody's voice turned Rick's gut to ice. *Don't panic.* He halted and shined the light down the long hallway. His son stood partially visible in the open doorway of his room. "Cody!"

"Daddy! Bob said I had to come!"

"Come here, Cody! Run! Now!"

"Daddy!" the child cried, then Robin's laugh boomed down the corridor as a huge arm thrust Cody farther out into the hallway. Robin's head appeared in the doorway, his silhouette only slightly shorter than Cody's.

"Come and get him, icky Ricky!" Cackling, he yanked the boy back into the room. "Catch him if you can!"

Robin's going for the oak tree! Swearing, he tried to run. He had to get there before Robin opened the window. "Christ." His leg twisted painfully and he fell. Biting back a scream, he pulled himself up and continued on, dragging his leg behind him. It seemed to take forever.

Cody screamed. Robin laughed.

"I'll kill you, you son of a bitch," Rick yelled as he stumbled toward the room. Angrily he shook tears of pain from his eyes.

He made the doorway, only to see that, across the room, the window was already open. "Cody?"

"We're out here, icky Ricky. We're having a little monkey climb."

Robin rested his short body in the thick crotch of the tree, Cody trapped in his bulging arms.

"Cody!" Rick staggered forward.

"Daddy!"

"Come and get him, icky Ricky!" Robin taunted. "Come out and play!"

Rick made it to the window and pulled himself onto the ledge, memories of that other night so long ago flooding his mind. That night Robin had given up his life to save Rick's.

Tonight Rick had to save his son. "Hold on, Cody. I'm coming."

"Balls, balls, icky Ricky has balls." Robin turned to Cody. "Your daddy was a coward, did you know that? Oh yes, we all thought he was crazy. Crazy, crazy, crazy! He had no balls, no balls at all. But now he does. He thinks he does! Look at him coming out here with his sword, just to save little old you."

Rick edged into the tree, leaving the flashlight behind. The full moon cast plenty of light, and for the first time, he saw his twin's face.

It was like looking in a distorted mirror at a carnival. It was him, but not him, a twisted ugly vision of himself, paper white from living in the tunnels, and warped with anger and hatred. He remembered his grandfather saying that when greenjacks can't communicate with their own kind, their frustration and loneliness overwhelm them and turn them from mischievous, selfish creatures to twisted, evil things. *He's insane, not me.* A tiny thread of pity twisted through him, and was gone.

"You going to stick me with that sword, icky Ricky?" Robin sang as Rick edged closer. "If you do, I'll drop your little baby boy right on the ground, head first, and his head will break open and all his brains will goosh out."

Cody began to cry.

"Let him go," Rick said softly. "He can't see them."

"I know that, you asshole."

"You want *my* body."

"Of course I do, and if I let your baby boy go, you're just going to hand it over, right?"

"No. Let him go and I'll fight you for it."

Robin regarded him, then looked down as a windy whistling sound began below. Foliage crunched.

"He's here, icky Ricky, he's here."

A skeletal hand appeared on the branch where Robin sat. A second appeared.

Rick stood paralyzed, his pain forgotten.

Big Jack's face appeared, just as he remembered it, brown and green, with huge, leering, fathomless black pits for eyes, and vines growing out from between the bark-chip teeth.

It opened its mouth, and he heard the whistling sound again, like wind hissing. In its neck the jugular vine pulsed with life; in the torso, obscenely green growth glistened and throbbed among the white net of tiny roots.

One long leg bent, and it placed its twig-and-stick foot on the limb next to Robin. An instant later, it pulled itself up.

To Rick's horror, Robin handed Cody to Big Jack.

"Save him, save him, icky Ricky!" Robin screeched before descending the tree, swinging down like a monkey.

Rick stepped forward, raising the sword. Big Jack hissed, sibilant, snakelike, and Cody cried, squirming in its grasp.

"Cody," Rick called softly. "Cody, you can hurt it. It's just leaves, son. Pull the leaves, hard."

The boy did nothing for a moment, then suddenly yanked on one vine, then another. With a cry, he plunged both hands into the heart of the thing and began yanking with all his might.

Rick sliced the sword through the air but hit nothing, but Big Jack was fending off Cody's attack and didn't appear to notice. Rick sent the blade whickering through the air again, and this time it struck the heavy branch that made the monster's thighbone.

It cracked. Big Jack wavered.

"Cody, grab the tree!" Rick ordered as he struck again.

"Piper!" Dimly he heard Dakota calling him from somewhere below. "Piper! Where the hell are you?"

The thigh snapped and Big Jack fell, taking Cody with him. The boy's thin scream cut through Rick like a knife.

They seemed to fall forever. Out of the corner of his eye, he saw Dakota, still in drag, and Audrey, running across the lawn.

Big Jack caught a limb halfway down and held on. Cody clung to its torso. "Climb down," Rick called. "Climb down its leg and you can jump from there. Go to Dakota."

"Piper! Cody!" Dakota called.

"Here!" Rick screamed as loud as he could. "The oak tree!"

Cody had slithered almost the entire length of Big Jack's body when Dakota appeared below. He reached up and snatched the child into his arms, then Audrey took Cody from him and retreated, moving toward the house.

Dakota remained where he was, staring upward. "Shit, Piper," he cried. "That's the damned Big Jack, isn't it?"

"Yeah," Rick called. "And it's pissed." He paused. "Dakota, be careful."

Dakota yanked on the remaining leg, once, twice, then the creature fell. Almost instantly it was upright, balancing on one foot. "Piper, its other leg's growing back!" Dakota backed away. "What the hell do I do now?"

"Run! Lock yourselves in the cottage! Now!"

"Piper!"

"Get my son and your sister in that cottage! *Now!*"

Before Dakota could move, Big Jack lurched forward, its arms out. It grabbed at O'Keefe, snagging the hem of his chiffon skirt.

"You fucker!" Dakota cried. He brought his high-heeled foot up and kicked it, but Big Jack caught his ankle, and then Dakota was down on his ass, the Green Man all over him.

"Duane!" Audrey cried from the walk near the house. She stepped forward, Cody in her arms.

"No!" Rick yelled. "Get Cody inside!"

She looked up, her face stricken.

"Go! He'll be okay."

Audrey didn't move, forward or backward, and directly below, he could see flashes of Dakota's white dress as he grappled with Big Jack. The thing was probably trying to strangle him. *I have to do something now!*

Painfully he climbed back into the house, then hobbled down the hall to the back stairs. There had to be a way to stop the thing. The sword would do it, if he could get there in time.

By the time he made the bottom of the stairs, his leg felt numb. He limped out the kitchen door and moved toward the workshop, expecting every moment to run into Robin, every second to hear Cody scream.

Then he saw the garage. "Don't be locked," he whispered as he went around to the big door to check. It wasn't even latched, thank God, and he quickly pulled the door up. Even before it thunked against its springs, he was inside the dark building, frantically trying to see where he was going.

In a glint of moonlight, he found it. Hector's riding lawn mower.

Its engine started on the second try, and he rode it out, past his car, toward the front lawn, the smell of fresh-cut grass clear in his nostrils.

As he rounded the bend, he saw Audrey and Cody still standing in the glow of the front porch light. Dakota was on his feet, but still struggling with Big Jack.

"O'Keefe," Rick yelled, "get your ass out of there!" Revving the engine, he punched the gas, and the mower trundled forward. Audrey saw him and set Cody down by the steps, then ran to Dakota and grabbed at the white material floating around him. Suddenly Rick saw the cloth give, then Dakota was loose. Audrey yanked him toward the front steps, scooped up Cody, then pointed. Dakota looked, and Rick could see his grin even from here.

"Gotcha now, Jack," he said as he aimed the machine at the creature. It turned and looked at him, then, with the combined roar of a dozen greenjacks, moved toward him.

"You're a stupid Big Jack, aren't you!"

The mower hit the monster in a shower of twigs and leaves, and the sound of a thousand snakes hissing rent the air as Rick watched the little jacks leaping from the mangled body. He backed up and ran over it again.

O'Keefe ran up as Rick took the engine down to an idling purr. "What the hell do you think you're doing out here by yourself?"

"Don't talk, O'Keefe. Get them in the cottage. Make sure it's empty, then lock yourselves in, and don't come out until I tell you."

"What? And leave you out here?"

Audrey, carrying Cody, approached. "What's going on?"

"All of you, get in that cottage now!"

"You're hurt," she said.

"I'm fine. Get inside."

"And just leave you out here?" she cried.

"I know what I'm doing."

"Where's Robin?" Dakota asked.

"We're having a meeting just as soon as you three get out of here."

"Piper, there's no way in hell that I'm going to leave you out here by yourself," O'Keefe declared.

Rick stared at him. "Yes, you are. This doesn't concern you."

Audrey kept her eyes on Rick as she handed Cody to her brother. "Duane, he has to do this by himself."

"What? Audrey, don't tell me you're buying that macho shit."

"Macho shit has nothing to do with it," Rick said grimly.

"No—"

"Duane, do you think I want him out here by himself any more than you do?" Audrey demanded. "Do you?"

Dakota shrugged.

"I don't. But he has to!"

"Okay." He punched Rick's arm. "Win one for the gipper," he said, "whatever that is."

"Thanks." Quickly he kissed Cody, then Audrey, and

watched as they disappeared around the corner of the house.
A moment later, the pool lights came on, illuminating the
blue water, highlighting Don Quixote as he sat on his horse,
holding his lance.

Another figure sat just behind the knight.

"Robin," Rick whispered, turning the machine and riding
toward the pool.

Robin waved at him as he parked the mower across the
pool from the statue.

"Icky Ricky, didja come out to play?" Robin called.

As Rick turned off the motor and dismounted, Robin
climbed down the statue, calling, "Icky Ricky's an artist,
too, whoop-de-do."

He showed off, turning upside down and walking toward
Rick in a handstand, his hands slap-slapping against the
white pavement. Rick stood there, leaning on the sword,
waiting. The church bells struck midnight.

Robin halted three feet from him. "A fight for possession
of your body? Wasn't that your offer?"

"It doesn't count now. That was if you handed over my
son. You didn't. Now I just get to kill you."

"You don't have the guts."

"Try me."

Robin's face twisted into a malignant smile. "Remember
the last time you tried to kill me? You didn't have the nerve
then, either." He put his callused hand out, palm upward,
and slowly closed the fingers with a hard, twisting motion.
"I'm surprised you could father children after I got through
with you."

"You murdered Delia."

His grin was malicious. "You pissed me off, trying to
strangle me like that. It's all your fault."

Rick hesitated, caught by the words. *It's not your fault,*
he told himself sternly. *Don't listen to him.*

"Of course, I screwed her brains out before I killed her,"
his twin taunted.

Don't take the bait. Rick held his ground. "You killed
Mom and Dad because they were going to send you away."

Robin nodded. "All your fault, Ricky."

"And you set the explosion at the carnival to stage your own death."

"You catch on quick, icky Ricky."

His leg throbbed, and a lead weight filled his stomach. "Do you even know how many people you killed that night?"

Robin laughed. "Nope. Who cares?"

Rick lifted the sword from the ground and stepped toward his twin. His leg almost twisted out from under him, but he managed to keep his balance. "This is for my parents and Delia and for all the carnival people you killed." He aimed the saber. "This is for my children. And this is for *me*."

"You can't kill me," Robin said, undaunted. "They'll put you in jail."

"No. You're already dead. If you hadn't killed Jade, I'd just kill you for good and bury you out in the yard among your friends. But you committed murder and left mountains of evidence, so I'll just kill you in self-defense and tell the police all about it. No problem."

For the first time, Robin showed concern. His gaze traveled toward the left side of the house. Rick knew what he was thinking. "They won't call the police until I tell them to. It's just you and me."

On the grass at the edge of the cement, several jacks appeared to be watching. One, dimmer than the rest, waited unmoving.

"Robin," Rick said softly.

"Robin?" his twin mimicked immediately. "I told you you couldn't kill me, you sentimental asshole."

Ricky . . . The voice strained with effort to be heard. *Help me.*

Rick nodded at the quiet little jack, then turned his attention back to Robin. "My brother's here. He's here and he's watching. He's waiting for you to die so that he can go free."

Robin had been resting on his hands, doing the spider as he spoke. Suddenly, before Rick could react, his twin bent his elbows into a crouch, swung his body back, and propelled himself at his legs. The sword flew out of Rick's hands and clattered to the cement and his leg exploded with pain as he fell backwards into the cold pool water, Robin attached. He tried to kick his way to the surface, but Robin held his legs together, a lead weight pulling him down, deeper and deeper.

Fresh blood seeped redly into the clean water.

The world moved in slow motion. His lungs burned. *He's going to hold me under until I pass out, then he'll drag me out and move in.* Robin would kill the old body and assume his identity. *What am I going to do?* Black spots filled Rick's vision. He was almost out of time.

Frantically he reached down and grabbed Robin's hair, yanking his head up. His twin glared at him, and started to climb up Rick's body.

No! Rick pushed his free hand through the water and smashed it against Robin's nose, but the fluid resistance was too strong. His twin's hands dug into his thighs, crawling toward his groin, and Rick let go of his brother's hair and immediately shoved one thumb into each eye as deeply as he could.

One second. Two. Robin's hands let go of Rick's legs and flew to his wrists, trying to yank them free. Rick kicked frantically toward the surface.

His head broke water and he gulped fresh, cold air. It gave him the strength to hang on to Robin, to keep his thumbs pressed against his eyes. He winced as his twin bit into his wrist, once, then again, but he managed to keep his head above water, and Robin's below.

"Rick!"

Dimly he heard Dakota's cry. "Go!" he screamed. "Leave!" He had to concentrate on what he was doing or Robin's powerful arms would pull him free.

Long seconds passed, and finally his brother's hands loosened, then fell away. Rick grabbed one limp arm and swam to the edge of the pool. Wearily he climbed out. He turned and pulled Robin's body from the water and laid it on the cement near the grass.

The dim greenjack hovered next to it. Rick glanced

around, saw Dakota watching from the front porch. Relieved, he said, "He's dead."

Ricky!

"Trick or treat, little brother!" Robin sat up, the flesh around his eyes looking puffy and bruised. "Fooled you, didn't I?" He lunged.

Rick rolled backwards out of the way, felt the sword under his arm and grabbed its hilt. He brought it around and held it out as Robin flew at him.

Robin's eyes grew huge as he saw the sword, but it was too late. He couldn't stop, and the saber drove straight into his chest.

Screaming, he fell back on the grass, and the sword pinned him to the ground below. Rick knelt beside him and saw that it had run him through just below the heart.

Robin breathed rapidly, his eyes open and furious as the little greenjack approached. "I hate you," he snarled.

Then, for a brief second, the face went blank, and at the same time the little jack flared with bright color and its face vaguely resembled Robin's.

Icky Ricky icky Ricky icky Ricky icky Ricky.

The words faded as the ousted jack sped away toward the oak.

"Ricky."

"Robin."

His brother's face looked like his own now, open and youthful. "Robin? It's you, isn't it?"

"It's me." Robin coughed. Rick gently lifted his brother's head, letting it rest on his uninjured leg. He wiped flecks of blood from Robin's mouth and pushed the dark, wet hair from his eyes. He looked at the sword piercing the body, back at Robin.

"Leave it," his brother said.

"Okay." Rick looked toward the house. Dakota was gone, thank God.

"Every night I came out and watched you, wishing I could talk to you. But I couldn't." Robin coughed a little more blood. "I wasn't strong enough. Sometimes you heard me, though, didn't you?"

"I did."

"I thought you did. I thought I heard you answer." He reached up one trembling hand and felt the contours of Rick's face. A corner of his mouth crooked up. "We're good-looking, aren't we?"

Rick smiled. "Yes, we are. Robin, were you happy with the jacks?"

Almost imperceptibly he shook his head. "It was fun running and moving, but there was nothing else. I wasn't one of them. Their senses are different. There's no taste or smell. You can't touch anything." As he spoke he took Rick's hand. "I should have listened to you, Ricky. I shouldn't have teased you. I should have believed you."

"We were kids, Robin. Just kids."

"Yeah." Robin's voice broke. "Just kids."

"Yeah," Rick repeated, cradling his twin closer. His tears splashed down on his brother's cheek.

Robin reached up and touched a tear with his finger. "It's hot. I can feel it." He started to cry, until coughing stopped the tears. "Oh, Ricky, I missed you."

"I missed you, brother."

Robin's breath hitched a little and the color began to drain from his face. Rick took his hand again and held it against his own beating heart, barely able to see his brother, his eyes were so full. "Thank you for saving my life that night in the oak tree."

"You're welcome," Robin said softly. For an instant his eyes drifted, then he seemed to force them to focus on Rick. "Thank you for saving *my* life tonight."

Rick wiped a bubble of blood from Robin's pale lips. "I'm a little late."

"Better late than never." Robin gave him a small smile and coughed up more blood.

Rick wiped it away. "I'm sorry."

"No, don't be. Wow, this is weird." Robin seemed to be looking at something beyond Rick.

Rick glanced behind him, saw nothing. "What?"

"I can see some pretty light. I hear Mom and Dad. Do you?"

"No, I don't. Robin?"

Robin pulled his gaze back to his brother.

"People you love are coming for you. They come in the light. The light's good."

Robin coughed. "I believe you this time." He smiled slightly. "For once, I can see something you can't. Ricky, thank you. I guess we can talk more later."

"In another place," Rick said gently. "Or time."

Robin said something Rick couldn't understand. His respiration had slowed to a faint hitch that came at longer intervals.

Suddenly Robin squeezed his hand. "Ricky, I love you. I've always loved you." His hand went limp and his gaze drifted to the beyond.

"And I love you." Rick bent and kissed Robin's forehead. "Never forget," he whispered as his brother sighed and set free his final breath. "I love you."

He closed his brother's eyes and held him, and after a time, he didn't know how long, he carefully eased Robin's head down against the grass. Then, wiping his eyes, he rose and took the pool net from its holder to use as a staff.

He limped around the pool, then paused to look back across it at his brother's still form, then up at Don Quixote, who stared heroically into the night. Rick saluted him, before turning to make his way painfully across the lawn and into the backyard.

Limping up the little walkway to Carmen's cottage, he saw the warm yellow light glowing in the windows. He rapped on the door, and Audrey opened it immediately, kissing him frantically as she and Dakota put their arms around him and helped him inside, exclaiming, loving, accepting him. Berating him, too, he realized happily. Cody, asleep on the couch, woke and tried to climb into his wet lap, but Dakota gently pulled him away, telling him later, there would be plenty of time later.

"You can call the cavalry now, O'Keefe," Rick said. He suddenly felt so tired that he could barely keep his eyes open.

"Cavalry hell," Dakota said as Audrey wrapped a fresh dry towel around his leg. "I'm just calling the cleanup crew." He looked Rick up and down as Audrey draped a blanket around his shoulders. "Piper, dear, *you* are the cavalry."

Dear Readers:

I hope you've enjoyed BAD THINGS. I had a lot of fun writing it. The greenjacks (and Big Jack) are a type of element that ties into the lore of the Green Man. He is an archetypical nature god dating to the earliest humans. The most famous variation is Pan, and it was his horns and cloven hooves that the European invaders assigned to Satan. As usual, the god of the old became the devil of the new.

Sometimes called Jack O' the Green, the nature deity was banished by church of Rome missionaries sent to the British Isles by Pope Gregory the Great in 600 A.D. Pagan artists forced to adorn the churches quickly began sculpting many of their nature deities (primarily the Green Man) into the ornamentation of these buildings. That way the people could secretly worship their own gods.

My next novel is an unusual ghost story. Psychologist Will Banning is haunted by a just-out-of-reach memory from his childhood. Trying to uncover this forbidden secret dominates his thoughts until his attention is diverted by life-long friend (and should-be lover) Maggie Maewood, who tells him about the strange behavior of animals in her veterinary clinic. Will, having already noticed strange avian behavior, is fascinated.

Then people begin acting strangely too. His office is filled with patients, old and new, exhibiting sudden signs of schizophrenia, seeing ghosts, hearing voices. After one patient tells him something that, on the surface, seems outrageous but has a ring of truth, Will delves deeper and deeper, unconcerned with the danger of asking too many questions.

As always, I look forward to hearing from my readers. You can visit my Web site at www.tamarathorne.com.

Best,
Tamara

ABOUT THE AUTHOR

Tamara Thorne lives with her family in California. She is the author of five horror novels published by Pinnacle Books: HAUNTED, MOONFALL, ETERNITY, CANDLE BAY, and BAD THINGS. Her newest horror novel will be published in November 2002. Tamara loves hearing from readers; you may write to her c/o Pinnacle Books or e-mail her at tamara@vividnet.com. Please include a self-addressed, stamped envelope if you wish to receive a response.